'She spotted the car park
standing beside it. As she w
ment across the street caugh
side door of a Volkswagen v
ing the door of a white Fiat. She saw the guns in their hands and as the first shots rang out, she came to a stunned halt. The man had turned, reaching under his jacket, and then Creasy reached her, an arm coming around her waist, sweeping her off her feet into a shop doorway. She found herself on the pavement under his heavy body. More shots, and she screamed as glass shattered above them. She saw the gun in Creasy's hand, held low down by his side. Sounds — the slamming of the van door and the squeal of tyres and a racing engine and finally silence.'

A. J. Quinnell is the pseudonym of the author of ten novels including ***Man on Fire*** which was made twice into Hollywood Films — most recently directed by Tony Scott for Twentieth Century Fox in 2004, starring Denzel Washington, Christopher Walken and Dakota Fanning. The book sold more than eight million copies in paperback and was translated around the world.

Full list of titles:

Man on Fire

The Mahdi

Snap Shot

Blood Ties

Siege of Silence

In the Name of the Father

The Perfect Kill

The Blue Ring

Message from Hell

Black Horn

MAN ON FIRE

'Fast, lethal . . . and highly suspenseful'
Chicago Tribune

'Imaginative . . . appealing . . . satisfying!'
New York Times

MAN ON FIRE

MAN ON FIRE

A. J. QUINNELL

First published in Great Britain by Macmillan London Limited in 1980

Published by 48

ISBN-13: 9781908426642

Give me, God, what you still have, Give me what no one asks for; I do not ask for wealth

Nor for success, nor even health — People ask you so often, God, for all that That you cannot have any left.

Give me, God, what you still have; Give me what people refuse to accept from you.

I want insecurity and disquietude, I want turmoil and brawl,

And if you should give them to me, my God, Once and for all

Let me be sure to have them always, For I will not always have the courage To ask you for them.

— ZIRHNHELD
The Paras' Prayer

CONTENTS

PROLOGUE

Winter in Milan. Expensive cars lined a suburban avenue. In the large building, set back behind the trees, a bell rang faintly, and minutes later children, wrapped up against the wind, spilled down the steps and scattered to the warmth of waiting cars.

Pepino Macchetti, eight years old, head pulled down into his raincoat collar, hurried to the corner where his father's driver always parked the blue Mercedes. The driver watched his approach in the mirror and leaned behind to open the door. Pepino dived gratefully into the leathered warmth, the door clunked shut, and the car pulled away. The boy struggled out of his raincoat and the car had reached the next corner before he looked up to discover that the driver was not Angelo. As a query formed on his lips, the Mercedes pulled in again to the curb, the door opened, and a heavyset man got in beside the boy. The driver waited patiently for a gap in the homebound traffic and then pulled smoothly away. It was only January, but Pepino Macchetti was already the third kidnap victim in Italy that year.

The weather in the Corsican port of Bastia was unseasonably warm, prompting one bar owner to put chairs and a table out on the cobbled pavement. A solitary man sat drinking whisky and watching the docks where the ferry to Livorno made ready for sea.

He had been there for two hours, frequently beckoning inside for a refill, until the owner had brought out the bottle and a large plate of black olives.

A small boy sat on the curb across the road, watching intently as the man steadily washed down the olives with the whisky.

It was quiet, out of the tourist season, and the stranger was the only thing to occupy the boy's attention. The man aroused his curiosity. He had a stillness, an air of isolation. His eyes didn't follow the movement of the sparse traffic; they just looked out across the road to the docks and the waiting ferry. Occasionally he glanced at the boy, eyes without interest set into a square face. There was a vertical scar over one eye and another on his chin. But it was the eyes that held the boy's attention. Set deep and wide, and heavy-lidded. Narrowed as if to avoid cigarette smoke even though he was not smoking.

The boy had heard him order the whisky in fluent French, but he guessed that the man was not French. His clothes, dark blue corduroy trousers and denim jacket over a black polo neck sweater, looked expensive but much used, as did the leather suitcase which lay at his feet. The boy had much experience in assessing strangers and particularly their financial worth. This one confused him.

The man glanced at his watch and poured the last of the whisky. He drank it in one swallow, picked up his suitcase and walked across the street.

The boy sat still on the curb watching him approach. The body was like the face — square, and only when the man was close did the boy realize that he was also very tall — well over six feet. The walk was curious against the man's bulk, light, and with the outsides of the feet making first contact with the ground.

He glanced down as he passed, and the boy turned and noted that, in spite of the whisky, he walked naturally and steadily. The boy jumped up and ran across the street to scoop up the half dozen olives left on the plate.

Half an hour later he watched the ferry warp out from the dock. There were few passengers, and he saw the stranger standing alone at the stern rail. The ferry gathered speed, and on an impulse the boy waved. It was too far to see the stranger's eyes, but he felt them on him, then he saw the hand lift off the rail and gesture briefly in acknowledgment.

It was warmer still in Palermo, and in the walled villa set in the foothills behind the city the windows and shutters were open, letting the mild, southerly breeze flow into the first floor study. A business meeting was in progress: three men, one sitting behind a large polished desk, the other two facing him. The breeze helped to disperse cigar smoke. They had already discussed routine matters. The man behind the desk had listened as the other two reported on a range of enterprises spanning the country from the Alpine north to the southern tip of Sicily. Occasionally he had interrupted briefly to have a point enlarged or clarified, but mostly he had just listened. Then he issued a series of concise instructions and the other two had nodded in unison. No notes were taken.

Having disposed of routine matters, they discussed the situation in southern Calabria. Some years earlier the government had decided to build a steel complex in that poverty-stricken area. The man behind the desk had collaborated with them unofficially. Thousands of acres had been purchased from a large variety of landowners. Such dealings involved long and laborious negotiations, and in the meantime the composition of the government had changed. Ministers had come and gone and the Communist party was questioning the feasibility of the whole project. The man behind the desk was irritated. Businessmen everywhere had legitimate grievances against vacillating governments. But still, large amounts of money were involved. There should have been better control.

The two men finished their briefing and waited as their boss considered his decision.

He sat on a flat cushion on a high-backed chair, for he was a small man, barely five feet tall. Although he was over sixty, his face remained smooth, slightly plump, matching his hands, which lay motionless on the desk. He was dressed in a dark blue three-piece suit, beautifully cut, disguising his slight corpulence. His lips, thick for the face, pursed slightly in thought. He was, in appearance, sleekly small.

He reached his decision. "We shall withdraw. I foresee more problems. Don Mommo will have to take all responsibility."

The two men nodded. The meeting over, they rose and moved to the drinks cabinet. The small man poured three glasses of Chivas Regal.

"*Salut*," said the small man.

"*Salut*, Don Cantarella," said the two in unison.

BOOK ONE

CHAPTER ONE

She looked out through the French windows and across the lake. The lights of the Hotel Villa D'Este on the far bank shimmered on the smooth water.

She was a woman of classic Neapolitan beauty. But petulance showed in the mouth. Wide and full lipped, it dominated her face, which was set in a series of curves. High cheekbones, large, slanted eyes, and a cleft chin balancing exactly a rounded forehead. Heavy ebony hair hung straight and ended in one inward curve to her shoulders. The curves continued down through a slim neck to a body narrow-waisted, long-legged, and full and high in the breast.

She wore a simple, straight dress tied at the waist and cut square across the shoulders. Its richness came from the texture of knitted silk and dark printed pattern in shades of blue. Her skin had a depth, like velvet under glass.

Her beauty controlled her mind. From an early age it had allowed her to tread different paths from most women. It was a weapon, and a vehicle in which to travel through life. An armoured vehicle, protecting her from discomfort and indignity. She had a good mind and in a body even slightly less beautiful it would have been free to expand and develop and see beyond the circle of light which her beauty illuminated. But when the vehicle moved, the shadows were pushed back and she could not see them.

Such women have to be self-centred. Eyes watch them, ears listen. If the character is strong enough to survive until the beauty fades, it may emerge independently; but such transitions are rare. The fading beauty is usually accompanied by a grievance that nature should take away what it had earlier bestowed.

The door opened behind her and she turned as the girl came into the room. They could only be mother and daughter, the child an embryonic cameo of the woman, but still leggy and skittish. The face pale and animated, as yet unaware, open in its innocence. There was no sign of petulance, although her mouth was tight and her eyes angry.

"I hate her, Mama! I hate her!"

"Why?"

"I did the algebra. I did the best I could, but she is never satisfied, that one. Now she says I have to do algebra again tomorrow for a whole hour."

The woman embraced the child. "Pinta, you have to try harder or else when you go back to school you will be behind the others."

The child looked up eagerly. "When, Mama? When do I return to school? I hate having a governess."

The woman released her and turned to look again across the lake.

"Soon, Pinta. Your father gets back tonight, and I shall talk to him about it. Be patient, *Cara*, it won't be much longer."

She turned and smiled.

"'But even at school you will have to learn algebra."

"I don't mind," laughed the girl. "At school the teachers have to ask lots of girls questions, but with a governess I get everything myself. It's no fun, Mama. Try to make it soon, please!"

She reached up and hugged her mother.

"It will be soon," came the reply. "I promise."

———

Ettore Balletto drove from Milan to Como with mixed feelings. After a week away he missed Rika and Pinta, but the homecoming was going to be stormy. Decisions had to be taken and Rika wouldn't like them, and for her dislike and acceptance were incompatible. He drove the big Lancia quickly through the evening traffic, with only automatic attention to the road.

In thirteen years of marriage he had learned not to underestimate the difficulty. He thought about those years and asked himself whether he regretted them; but the question had no answer. While he was married to her he was an addict. Never off the drug and so unable to question its effect.

He didn't see himself as a weak man, and neither did his friends. It was a simple situation. He had a beautiful, wilful and self-centred wife. He knew she was not going to change, so he could either accept her or leave her. He had long ago discovered that the decision was clear-cut. Acceptance was possible, leaving her was not. There could be no cold turkey withdrawal, no methadone treatment.

In the early marriage it had been physical more than mental. A tactile sating, a conscious abandonment. Now it was the knowledge of possession that held him. The intense pride of ownership and the counterpoint — the mirror to reflect envy and even respect from men who did not possess her. He was a willing and complacent addict.

The Lancia turned right as the road forked at the lake, and his thoughts turned to Pinta. He loved his daughter. The emotion was definite but narrow. In the spectrum of his feelings the strong colours were absorbed by Rika. He didn't see the girl as a separate entity but as an appendage of her mother. A child might split a father's emotions, even compete for them, but for Ettore, Pinta was a daughter loved in the shade.

The three sat at dinner, Ettore and Rika facing each other across the wide mahogany table with Pinta between them. The maid served. It was a stylized, formal setting and lacked family warmth. This was because meals for Rika were something of a ceremony and on this occasion a tenseness anticipated a confrontation.

Rika had greeted her husband affectionately, mixed him a large martini and listened with decent interest about his trip to Rome. But while Pinta was out of the room, she had told him that the girl was unhappy and something must be done.

He had nodded emphatically and said, 'We'll discuss it after dinner, when she's gone to bed. I've made up my mind about it."

So she knew an argument was inevitable and sat through dinner preparing her tactical dispositions. Pinta sensed the atmosphere and the cause of it and kept silent. As soon as dinner finished she jumped up, kissed her parents, and excused herself.

"All that algebra gave me a headache," she said pointedly. "I'm going to bed."

She left a silence, finally broken by Rika.

"She doesn't like the governess."

Ettore shrugged.

"I don't blame her. Besides, she's lonely without her school friends."

He got up and walked to the bar and poured a cognac and stood sipping it slowly while the maid cleared away the dishes. When she had closed the door behind her, he said, "Rika, we must discuss things and discuss them rationally. First, Pinta has to go back to school, and secondly, you must cut down on your extravagances."

She smiled at him without mirth.

"My extravagances?"

"You know what I mean. When you want something you don't ever consider its cost." He gestured at a painting on the wall.

"While I was away last month you bought that — nine million lire."

"But it's a Klee," she answered, "and a bargain. Don't you like it?"

He shook his head irritably.

"That's not the point. We just cannot afford it. You know that business is not good. In fact, it's very bad. What with the government in such a mess and the competition from the Far East, we'll show a big loss this year, and I'm heavily in debt to the banks."

"How heavily?"

He shrugged expressively. "Four hundred million lire."

She shrugged in turn.

"As my father used to say, 'A man's worth can be judged by what he has or what he owes. Only the amount matters,"

His anger erupted.

"Your father lived in a different world. And if he hadn't died in bed with those two underage *putas*, he would have lived to be the most sordid bankrupt this country ever saw."

She smiled mockingly.

"Ah, Papa, he had such a sense of timing and such style. Something you seem to lack even with your impeccable breeding."

He brought himself under control.

"You have to face reality, Rika. You cannot go on spending money without thought. Unless I reach agreement with the banks in the next month or so, I could face great embarrassment."

She sat still for a while thinking, and then asked, "What are you doing about it?"

He answered her carefully — anxious that she should understand.

"There are two sides to the problem. First, we are losing our monopoly on knitted silk. The Chinese in Hong Kong have already perfected the techniques and they buy their yarn from across the border twenty percent cheaper than I can. So by the end of the year we shall have lost the market for plain silk fabrics. We have to compete by widening the range of both fabrics and patterns. We have to rely on selling fashion and style and leave the low end of the market to them."

She had been listening intently and now interjected, "So what's stopping you?"

"Machines," he answered. "Our knitting machines are twenty years old. Very slow, and good only for basic fabrics. We need to equip with new Morats and Lebocés, and they cost thirty million lire each."

"And the bank won't help?" she asked.

He turned back to the bar and poured more cognac before answering.

"That brings us to the second problem. The mill is already heavily mortgaged, together with this house, and the apartment in Rome. So I need a new loan to purchase the machinery and it has to be guaranteed from outside. That's what I'm working on."

"Have you talked to Vico?"

He held down his irritation.

"Of course I've talked to Vico. We meet again for lunch next week to discuss it. *Cara*, all I'm asking is that you keep these problems in mind. Don't spend without thinking."

"I should change my whole lifestyle," she asked, "because you can't compete with a few little Chinese?" Her smile was back, but not mocking any more. "Ettore, bring me a cognac, please."

He poured the drink, and walked over and stood behind her, and reached over to put the glass on the table. She remained absolutely still, and his hand left the glass and came to the back of her neck, under her hair. She raised her own hand and covered his and squeezed his fingers and moved her head back until it rested against his shirt and rolled it slowly back and forth, her hair brushing against him. She stood, and turned, and kissed his eyes and his mouth, and said softly,

"*Caro*, don't worry. I'm sure Vico will think of something."

In bed she kissed his eyes again and took him into her and soothed his body, and, for a while, his mind.

Later, he lay back propped up against the pillow in the old ornate four-poster. She had left the bed, naked, to go downstairs to fetch more cognac and cigarettes. He reflected that only after lovemaking did she spoil him so. She always led him when they made love. She directed and guided, but remained female — like a perfect dancer leading a well-coordinated partner. Afterward he felt not drained but weakened. A violin overplayed, its strings slack.

She came into the bedroom holding a balloon glass of cognac in one hand and cigarettes in the other. She gave him the glass and stood beside the bed lighting two cigarettes — long-stemmed, like a rose with all thorns intact, smelling pungent from the love-making. It took an effort to bring his mind back to reality.

"Pinta," he said flatly. "She must go back to school. It's no good for her with a governess. She's eleven already, and falling behind."

She got back into bed, handing him a lit cigarette.

"I agree," she said, to his surprise. "I was talking to Gina about it only yesterday. You know, they are sending Aldo and Marielle to Switzerland. It's a very good school — just outside Geneva, and they teach in Italian. There are many Italian children there."

He sat up straighter.

"But Rika, that makes no sense. She will be even more unhappy away from home, and you know what that school will cost. Vico is a successful lawyer, and makes a fortune, much of it outside the country. Besides, they spend a lot of time in Geneva. It's almost a second home."

Rika rearranged the pillows behind her back, and settled down to what she knew was going to be a difficult argument.

"Ettore, I have worked it out. We sell the apartment in Rome, prices are very good right now, and Rome has become boring lately anyway. Then we use the money to buy an apartment in Geneva. It's only a thirty-minute flight from Milan, and it takes you that long just to get here by car."

He sighed, but she carried on.

"Besides, I get very bored here in winter, and you are away so much, or staying over in Milan. I could spend a lot of time in Geneva and be with Pinta at weekends and you could fly over at weekends as well."

She ended on a rising note of utter reasonableness.

Ettore said impatiently, "*Cara*, the apartment in Rome is mortgaged, as I told you. If I sell it, all the money goes to the bank. They will not relend it to me, especially to buy property outside the country. Also, Geneva is the most expensive city in the world. Property prices there are double those in Rome. Even if I could do as you wish, all we could afford would be a very small place that you, of all people, could never bring yourself to stay in. Even for a weekend."

There was a long cold silence while Rika digested this. Finally she lay down in the bed and pulled the sheet up to her chin and said, "Well, you'll have to think of something. My child's safety is at stake. I will not allow Pinta to be at risk. Look what happened to the Macchetti child. He was taken right outside his school." Her voice rose. "Right outside — in broad daylight. In Milan! Have you no thought for your daughter? You have to find a way."

He spoke patiently.

"Rika, we have been through this before. The Macchettis are one of the richest families in Milan. Nobody is going to kidnap Pinta. God knows we are not rich — and so do the people who plan such things."

His tone was bitter. He knew that his problems were becoming known in financial circles in the city.

She was not deterred.

"How could they know? We live as well as the Macchettis, or better. They are a mean family who hide their money. Look where it got them."

He persevered.

"You don't understand, Rika, it is not amateurs who arrange these kidnappings. It's very big business, carried out by professionals. They have their sources of information and they don't waste time taking children whose fathers are virtually bankrupt."

"Then what about the Venucci child?"

She had a point. Eight-year-old Valerio Venucci had been kidnapped six months before. The Venuccis were in the construction business and had come on bad times. The boy was held for two months while the kidnappers reduced their demands from one billion lire to two hundred million, which the family finally scraped together.

"That was different," he said. "It was done by outsiders. Frenchmen from Marseilles. They didn't know enough about the Venucci family, and they were stupid. They were caught two weeks after they got the money."

"Maybe," she conceded, "but young Venucci lost a finger and has been a mental case ever since. Is that what you want for Pinta? Is that all you care?"

It was hard to argue against such a line and he felt his temper rising again.

He turned to look at her. The sheet had slipped to her waist, and even lying on her back her breasts retained their shape, high and firm.

She saw him looking and rolled onto her side away from him.

"Anyway," she stated emphatically, "I will not allow my daughter to go back to school in Milan unless she has protection."

"What are you talking about?" he demanded. "What protection?"

"A bodyguard."

"A what?" He pulled her over to face him.

"A bodyguard." Her face was set and determined. "Someone to be with her, and protect her — maybe against Frenchmen," she added sarcastically.

He threw his arm up. The discussion was going all wrong.

"Rika, you are being illogical! A bodyguard will cost a fortune, and what better way to attract attention? There are thousands of children going to school in Italy whose parents are richer than we are, and they don't have bodyguards."

"I don't care," she said flatly. "They are not my children. Do you only care about what it costs? You put a price on Pinta's safety?"

He tried to get his thoughts together, find a line of argument that would convince her. There was something here that he didn't understand.

He spoke quietly and reasonably.

"Rika, we discussed the financial situation earlier. Things are very bad. How will I afford what is, after all, another silly extravagance?"

She glared at him.

"Pinta's wellbeing is not an extravagance, not a painting on the wall or a dinner party or a new dress. Besides, the Arredos and the Carolines — even the Turellas — have hired bodyguards for their children"

It was out in the open now. Not a simple concern for Pinta's safety, but an important social adjustment. She couldn't live with the idea that they should be thought unable or unwilling to match her social rivals. He wondered how many other Italian industrialists had been brought to their knees by the same incredible conceits that afflicted their society.

She remained glaring at him and he knew that the limits of communication had been reached.

"We'll talk about it later."

She immediately relaxed.

"*Caro*, I know you worry about the money. But it will be alright and I'm only thinking about Pinta."

He nodded. His eyes closed.

"Will you talk to Vico?" she went on. "He knows about these things, he gives advice to many people."

He opened his eyes and asked sharply, "Have you mentioned this to him?"

"No, *caro*, but at lunch yesterday, Gina told me that Vico was advising the Arredos. He has such good connections. They are our best friends, Ettore, and you always tell me he is such a good lawyer."

Ettore thought about it. Maybe there was a way out. If Vico were to tell her what a crazy idea it was, perhaps she would listen.

He reached out and turned off the light. She snuggled up against him, her back to him, warm bottom easing close.

"You will talk to Vico, *Caro*?"

"Yes. I'll talk to Vico."

She snuggled still closer, happy in her victory and pleased with her cunning. She had side-tracked him with her talk of Geneva and slipped under his defences. Who would want to live among all those cold Swiss?

She turned over and reached a hand down but Ettore was asleep, above and below the waist.

CHAPTER TWO

Guido Arrellio moved quietly onto the terrace of the Pensione Splendide. In the dawn light he could just discern the bulk of the man sitting in the chair. The sun had risen behind the hills but here, facing the bay, it would be a few minutes before the light developed enough to see the man clearly. He wanted to see him clearly.

Pietro had called him at his mother's house in Positano just after midnight to tell him that a stranger had arrived. A man called Creasy.

Guido watched as the man's features became defined. Five years, he thought, and there's been a change. A year earlier someone passing through, he forgot who, had told him that Creasy was going downhill and was drinking. The light now showed the empty bottle.

He sat slumped in the chair, his body slack, somnolent, but he was not asleep. The eyes, heavy-lidded in the square face, looked down the hill as the light turned the terraced houses into clear shapes. Then the face turned and Guido stepped out from the shadows.

"*Ça va*, Creasy."

"*Ça va*, Guido."

Creasy pulled himself up and stretched out his arms and the two men embraced and laid cheek to cheek and held each other for a long moment.

"Coffee," said Guido, and Creasy nodded, but before letting him go held the smaller, younger man at arm's length and studied his face. Then he dropped his hands and sat down.

Guido went to the kitchen, deeply troubled. Creasy really had let himself go and that indicated things were very wrong, for he was a man who had always kept himself well, always cared for his body and his appearance. They had last met just after Julia's death.

The memory added to Guido's troubled mood. But then Creasy had been well, looking hardly older than when they had first met. As the coffee warmed, Guido calculated: twenty-three years, it would be, and Creasy had always seemed ageless — fixed at a young forty. He calculated again. Creasy would be nearing fifty now and looked it, and more. What had happened in those five years?

The last time, Creasy had stayed two weeks, silent as usual, but his quiet presence had given Guido strength when he needed it, putting a link back into a broken chain.

The sun was over the circling hills as he came back onto the terrace, and Naples was waking up, the noise of traffic dull but distinct. A warship lay at anchor in the bay and, beyond it, a large liner showed its stern. Guido put the tray on the table and poured the coffee and the two men sat quietly, drinking and looking at the view.

Creasy broke the silence.

"Did I interrupt anything?"

Guido smiled wryly.

"My mother, having one of her mysterious and periodic illnesses."

"You should have stayed with her."

Guido shook his head.

"Elio will arrive this morning from Milan. She gets these bouts when she feels we're neglecting her. It's not so bad for me, only forty minutes' drive, but it's a hell of a nuisance for Elio."

"How is he?"

"Good. They made him a partner last year, and he had another baby, a son."

They sat in silence again for several minutes. An easy silence, only possible between good and long friends who don't need talk to hold the link. The liner was almost over the horizon before Guido spoke.

"You're tired. Come on — I'll find you a bed"

Creasy roused himself.

"What about you? You haven't slept all night."

"I'll nap after lunch. How long can you stay?"

Creasy shrugged. "I have no plans, Guido. Nothing on. I just wanted to see you, how you were."

Guido nodded. "That's good. It's been too long. Have you been working?"

"Not for six months. I've just come from Corsica."

They had been walking to the door, but, hearing this, Guido stopped and looked a question.

Creasy shrugged again.

"Don't ask me why. I didn't even see anyone. I just happened to be in Marseilles and on an impulse jumped on the ferry."

Guido smiled. "You did something on an impulse?"

The smile was returned, tired and wan. "We'll talk about it tonight. Where's that bed?"

Guido sat at the kitchen table, waiting for Pietro to get back from the market. The pensione had only six rooms, but it was busy, and at lunch and dinner they had a good local trade. Julia had started that, quickly building a reputation for simple, well-cooked food. Her Maltese style rabbit stew had become well-known in the district and she had soon mastered the local dishes. After her death Guido had carried on and found to his surprise that he too had a touch. The clientele had stayed, first, perhaps, out of sympathy, but later because of the merits of the food.

Guido wondered what had happened to Creasy. He had never been easy to understand, but Guido knew him better than anyone. He doubted it could have been a woman. In all the years there had never been a woman to affect Creasy in more than a passing way. Even twenty years before, when Creasy had taken up with a French nurse in Algeria. Guido thought that she had been special, but after three months she had moved on.

"It's like trying to open a door with the wrong key," she had remarked to Guido. "It goes into the lock but it won't turn."

Guido had repeated the remark to Creasy, who had just said, "Maybe the lock's rusty."

Guido also doubted that Creasy had been involved in any event which had traumatically marred him. After a lifetime of events that would leave few men unmarked, Creasy had always been just Creasy.

He lay sleeping now in Guido's own room. After ten minutes Guido had looked in on him. He had lain on his side, the sheet at his waist in the heated room, and Guido had examined him covertly. The body was slack with a faded tan and all the scars were old scars. The back laced with faint pale weals which curved round to each side of the stomach. The small puncture marks under the left ribs. The backs of the hands mottled with the marks of old burns. He knew that underneath the sheet one leg had a badly stitched scar above the knee, stretching almost to the groin, The face had not escaped, a thin scar going vertically from the right eyebrow to the hairline and another, smaller, on the left side of the jaw.

They were all familiar to Guido and he knew their histories. There was nothing new. The body of the sleeping man had been much abused, but that abuse had never before been self-inflicted.

Pietro interrupted his thoughts, coming into the kitchen with two baskets under his arms. He stopped in surprise at seeing Guido.

"I expected you later in the day," he said, putting the baskets on the table.

"An old friend," said Guido, standing up and peering into the baskets.

Pietro started to unload the fruit and vegetables for Guido's inspection.

"Some friend, to bring you from your mother's sick bed so quickly."

"Some friend," agreed Guido. "He's sleeping now."

Pietro was curious. He had worked for Guido for four years, ever since Guido had caught him stealing the hubcaps off his car. He got a severe beating and some questions. Then, learning that he had no home, Guido had taken him back to the pensione and given him a meal and a cot under the stairs.

He hadn't known then, and didn't know now, that Guido had seen himself at the same age.

Guido always treated the boy much as he had on the first day — gruffly, always abrupt, and without the least sign of affection. Pietro, in return, retained his original cheeky, disrespectful attitude. Both knew the affection that existed, but it never showed. It was a very un-Italian relationship. Over the years, Pietro had developed into a practical right arm for Guido and, with the help of two aged waiters who came in to serve lunch and dinner, they ran the small pensione between them.

In spite of living with him for so long, Pietro knew little of his past. Guido's mother came to the pensione on rare occasions and was garrulous and had talked about Guido's brother and his family in Milan, and about Julia, who had died five years before. But she was strangely silent about Guido's own past. Pietro knew that he spoke perfect French and passable English and Arabic, and assumed he had travelled widely. He never asked questions. Guido's reticence had rubbed off on him.

So the new arrival puzzled him. When the bell had rung just before midnight he had assumed that Guido had returned early. The big man standing under the light had appeared menacing at first.

"Is Guido in?" he had asked. Pietro had noticed the Neapolitan accent.

He had shaken his head.

"When is he coming back?"

Pietro had shrugged. The man had not seemed surprised by this lack of cooperation.

"I'll wait," he said and brushed past the boy and walked up the stairs and out onto the terrace.

Pietro considered for a few moments and then followed him. He felt he should get angry, demand an explanation, but the feeling of menace was gone. The man was sitting in one of the cane chairs that were scattered about. He was looking down at the lights of the city. His manner and demeanour reminded the boy of Guido.

He asked if the man wanted anything.

"Scotch," had come the reply. "A bottle if you have it."

He had brought the bottle and a glass, and then after some more thought had just asked the man his name.

"Creasy," he answered. "And you?"

"Pietro. I help Guido here."

The man had poured the Scotch, taken a sip, and looked hard at the boy.

"Go to bed. I won't steal anything."

So Pietro had gone downstairs and despite the late hour phoned Guido at his mother's. Guido had said, "Alright, go to bed. I'll be back sometime tomorrow."

They were preparing lunch when Guido surprised the boy by suddenly remarking: "He's American."

"Who?"

Guido pointed at the ceiling. "My friend. Creasy."

"But he speaks perfect Italian — Like a Neapolitan."

Guido nodded. "I taught him."

Pietro's surprise continued as Guido went on to talk at length.

"We were in the Legion together, and afterward — until eight years ago, when I married."

"The Legion?"

"The Foreign Legion," Guido said. "The French one."

The boy became excited. For him, as for most people, the words conjured up all the wrong images: sand dunes, remote forts, unrequited love.

"I joined in 1955 in Marseilles." Guido smiled at the keen interest on the boy's face. "I was in for six years." He stopped chopping at the vegetables and his normally impassive face softened slightly at the memory.

"It wasn't like you think. It never is. They were good years — the best."

It was the arrival of Creasy and the boy's obvious curiosity that triggered Guido's memory and took him back to 1945. Eleven years old. A father dead in North Africa. A six-year-old brother, always hungry, and his own hunger. A mother whose faith and fatalism were such that her only answer to catastrophe was to pray, harder and longer, in the church at Positano.

Guido had no such faith. He had walked the fifty kilometres to Naples. He knew the Americans were there and so food was there.

He became one of the army of scroungers, and discovered a gift for it. He had a keen intelligence, and what he couldn't beg, he stole. He quickly established himself, with a corner of a cellar to sleep in, among half a dozen other urchins, and he learned the ways of the Americans, their weaknesses and generosities.

He learned which restaurants they ate in and which bars they drank in, and the brothels and the women they sated themselves in. He learned the best time to beg: when drink had fuelled their generosity; and the best time to steal: when sex and desire diverted their attention. He learned every bend and corner of the narrow, cobbled streets, and he survived. Once a week he walked the coast road back to Positano, carrying chocolate and money and tins of meat. Elio no longer went hungry and his mother prayed and lit candles in the church, her faith justified, her prayers answered.

Hunger and necessity are poor teachers of morality. A society that cannot provide the basics of life does not get its laws obeyed. Guido never went back to live in Positano. Naples was his school, his breadbasket, and the horizon of his future. First he just survived, living like a rodent on the refuse of the city; after the mere fact of survival, his intelligence took him on. By the time he was fifteen he led a dozen others like him, organized into a gang that stole anything that couldn't be bolted or cemented down. Childhood simply passed him by. He knew nothing of children's games, of childlike emotions. "Right" was first survival and then possession. "Wrong" was weakness and getting caught. He learned early that boldness was the key to leadership. Others watched and waited, and when they recognized boldness, they followed.

The Americans liberated the city and they liberated crime. Under the Fascists, first Italian and then German, the criminals had lean pickings. Without the protection of fair, democratic, and therefore pliable justice, they lost their power. Even the biggest and most highly organized criminals had been shot or thrown into jail, and many innocents as well. The Americans released the innocents, and the criminals with them. Justice and crime returned to Italy hand in hand.

By the early 1950's the organization had clicked back into place. Prostitutes, many of them coerced by hunger, were brought under control. The bosses assigned districts, designated pimps, and took their percentages. The wartime damage was repaired. Marshall Aid funded the reconstruction, and the bosses took their cut. Restaurants and shops and taxis and landlords began making profits again and the bosses protected them against criminals and were naturally paid for the service.

Guido fitted neatly into this pattern. With his well-organized gang of adolescents he operated as an instrument in the reborn structure. He was recognized and rewarded as a coming young man. His particular asset was his violence — calculated, but seemingly mindless in execution. He had learned the lesson early that unexpected pain is the quickest way to get someone's attention. He used to tell his followers:

"Always retaliate first."

He was assigned an area behind the docks and his main job was to emphasize to the local small businessmen that protection was necessary. Having provided the proof, he then provided the protection. So he had prospered, and as an additional reward was allowed to operate on the docks themselves. He and his gang practised larceny on a grand scale. As supplies and equipment for the post-war reconstruction poured through the docks, a gratifying amount was diverted and usually resold to its original consignees. With accumulated profits, he bought the building that housed the present pensione.

It had been the house of a moderately wealthy merchant and was spacious and well-built, with a fine large terrace overlooking the bay. The merchant had died, and his two sons had been Fascists, and in the confused situation at the end of the war, they too had died. The house passed to a nephew who had also been a Fascist — but not confused. He decided to go to America, and with the money he got for the house was able to arrange the necessary papers.

Guido bought the place in his mother's name, since he was still a minor. Then he partitioned the large rooms and turned it into a brothel for the exclusive use of American officers. It did well and was known familiarly as the Splendide. Guido's mother, unknowingly but happily, banked the profits and lit candles in the church.

By 1954 Guido had put himself in a position to move up within the structure and foresaw a long and rising career ahead of him. But as the bosses above him prospered, so they argued, and finally they fought. The structure, nationwide, had not yet become as solidified and disciplined as in pre-Fascist days. The old bosses from the south had not yet been able to impose their authority. They had just begun to do so in Rome and in the industrial north, but they had left Naples until last. It was traditionally the least tractable city in Italy, and its criminals were no exception.

Two factions struggled for power in Naples. Guido had had to choose, and so made the first mistake of his budding career. He aligned himself with a boss called Vagnino, and this was perhaps natural, as Vagnino's strength lay in prostitution and the docks. But Vagnino was old, and had spent too long in prison, and lacked the will. Consequently, the war went badly for Guido and his gang. Being low in the scale of things, they were in the forefront of the battle. Within a month, half his gang were dead or had deserted, and Guido himself was in the hospital, his back and buttocks pitted with lead from the blast of a shotgun. He was lucky — he could have been facing the other way.

While he lay on his stomach, his mentor Vagnino, tired and careless, ate dinner in the wrong restaurant and was shot to death before he finished the *fritto misto*.

At this point, the police made a belated show of their authority. Newspapers and politicians demanded action. Deals were struck between the victors, led by one Floriano Conti, and the public prosecutor.

Evidence was provided and an assorted dozen low echelon operators were tried and sent to prison. Guido was among them. Sitting stiff and sore in the caged box in the courtroom, he heard the judge sentence him to two years in prison. He was eighteen years old.

Prison had been a terrible shock. Not the hardships or the indignity — his upbringing had prepared him for that. He discovered that he suffered from mild but positive claustrophobia, which manifested itself in acute depression. The Italian penal system of the time took no cognizance of such problems and he suffered badly.

For two months after his release he stayed in Positano. Not in his mother's home, but on the hills above the town, sleeping in the open, high above the cliffs and with the space of the ocean in front of him and the hills ranging far behind. He slowly readjusted and he resolved never to allow it to happen again. The experience had not reformed him, but in the future getting caught was not an option. Out there in the open, he also thought about his future. The Splendide brothel in Naples had been closed down by the police; the building was unoccupied and producing no income. In the past two years, Conti had tightened his grip on the city and cemented working alliances with influential officials, both in the police and the local government. Guido knew that to put the Splendide back into business he would need Conti's tacit approval, so his first act on arriving in Naples was to seek a meeting.

Conti was still a young man, in his middle thirties, and he was of the new breed of bosses. Having established his territory by violence, he now adopted the posture of the practical businessman. He realized that to take full advantage of his power it was necessary to come to arrangements with other nationwide bosses. Cooperation was the theme, and when emissaries had arrived from Palermo he had agreed to a series of meetings to establish spheres of influence and a pecking order of power.

These meetings during 1953 — 54 were curiously similar to the election of a Pope — held in great secrecy, and the result announced by something less than a puff of smoke. A great deal of jockeying for position went on. The hard traditionalists from Calabria did not want the more sophisticated bosses from Milan and Turin to have too much power. Similarly, those in the centre from Rome and Naples wanted more of a say than had been normal before the war. Everybody accepted that there had to be order and structure and that someone had to be an arbitrator — which, in effect, meant the man of most influence.

The bosses of the north wouldn't accept the Calabrians and vice versa. Moretti in Rome was considered too weak and Conti himself too young.

As usual under such circumstances, a compromise was reached. The meetings had been instigated and organized from Palermo. The boss there was Cantarella. Small, dapper, and a diplomat. He was quietly determined to re-establish Palermo as the fountainhead and he had read the signs properly. The compromise installed him as interim arbitrator. None of those present fully appreciated his cunning and political genius and were not to realize that over the next twenty years those gifts would sustain and strengthen his position. The scene was set for a long period of relative peace — and great profit for all concerned.

Guido had been surprised and gratified by the warmth of Conti's greeting and also impressed by the business-like appearance of the offices. The savagery of two years ago truly was a thing of the past. Bygones were bygones, Conti assured him. Things were different now. Certainly he should reopen the Splendide. They would cooperate. Financial arrangements would be made.

Guido had left the office feeling confident. His confidence was misplaced. Conti had not forgiven. Guido and his gang had been the most lethal arm of the opposition and Conti would not allow him to re-establish himself.

But one of the first edicts from Palermo had been that internal fratricide was to be kept to a minimum. Conti did not yet feel strong enough to defy the new arbitrator. He had an obvious solution. Let Guido reopen his brothel, and at an appropriate time Conti would withdraw his protection. The police would do his job for him and his connections in the judiciary would ensure that Guido was put away for a long time. It was a modern, progressive solution.

Guido did not explain all this to Pietro. He started his story at the point when he received a tipoff that his protection had been lifted and that the police were coming for him. He never knew who it was who called him that night, but obviously Conti had his own enemies. It had been a terrible moment. He realized that Conti had not forgiven and he reviewed his options. They were bleak: He could hide, but not for long. Either the police or Conti's people would eventually find him. He could fight, but he couldn't win. Finally, he could leave the country. He never considered trusting himself to the courts. Prison was not an option.

He had written a letter to his mother, giving her the name of an honest lawyer in Naples and instructing her to have that lawyer rent out the property and ensure that the proceeds were used for her support and Elio's continued education. He finished by telling her that he would be away, perhaps for a long time. Then he went down to the docks where he still had friends who could hide him, if only for a few days.

His mother received the letter the next day and went to the church and prayed. The same night Guido was smuggled aboard an old freighter and two nights later was smuggled off in Marseilles. He was twenty years old, with little money and no prospects. The next day he signed on with the Legion and within a week was in Algeria at the training camp at Sidi-bel-Abbès.

"Were you frightened?" asked Pietro. "Did you know what to expect?"

Guido shook his head and smiled briefly at the memory.

"I had heard the usual stories and I thought it would be terrible, but I had no choice. I didn't have papers. I couldn't speak anything but Italian, and I had very little money. Besides, I figured after a year or two I could desert and come back to Naples."

It hadn't been like the stories at all. Certainly it was tough, especially the first weeks; and the discipline was implacable. But he was tough himself, and the training interested him and developed latent talents. The discipline he accepted, for again he had no choice. Punishment for disobeying orders was either a spell in the punishment battalion, which was hell on earth, or, for minor offences, the stockade, in which his case would have been worse. He was careful, therefore, to obey all orders, and was a model recruit, which would have surprised a lot of people in Naples.

He too had surprises. The first was the food — varied and excellent, with good wine from the Legion's own vineyards. His mistaken concept of the Legion as an old-fashioned romantic desert army was quickly dispelled. It was highly modern, with the most up-to-date equipment and techniques. Its officers were the cream of the French army and its non-commissioned officers, promoted from the ranks, were veterans of Europe's armies and had been battle-hardened all over the world. There was a large German contingent, whose collective memory went back only to 1945. East Europeans, who didn't want to or couldn't go back behind the Iron Curtain. Spaniards, who might have been debris from the Civil War. A few Dutchmen and Scandinavians, and several Belgians, some of whom were probably French, as French citizens were not accepted in the Legion except as officers. There were very few Englishmen, and only one American.

The Legion was reconstituting itself after the shambles of Vietnam and Dien Bien Phu. Several thousand Legionnaires had been captured at that battle and over fifteen hundred killed. By its nature and composition, it was a corps invariably used as a last resort. Its history was a history of lost, last, futile battles. For a government losing an empire with poor grace, it was gratifyingly expendable.

Such an army under such a sentence could be excused for a lack of purpose or morale, but to Guido this was another surprise, for the Legion generated its own purpose. It fed off its lack of nationalism to create its own entity. A Legionnaire was a mental orphan — the Legion itself the orphanage. Guido discovered that it was the only army in the world that never retired its soldiers. When too old to fight, a Legionnaire could, if he wished, stay on in the Legion home, or work in its vineyards or its handicraft centre. He was never forced to go out into a world he had rejected.

The French people took pride in the Legion. They believed it fought for France, thought of itself as French. This was a misconception. It fought for itself. That it was an instrument of French Government policy was incidental. Even the French officers found their loyalties pulled more to the Legion than to their country.

The training lasted for six months. During that time Guido's short, thickset body filled out. The hard work and the good food brought him to a peak of fitness. He found himself taking pride in this, for like many young men he had never realized his physical capabilities. The Legion had a traditional pride in being able to outmarch any other army on earth, and within a month Guido had completed his first twenty-mile route march, carrying fifty pounds of equipment. He took pride also in his handling of weapons, especially the light machine gun. Its power and mobility pleased him and he found an affinity with it. This was noted by the instructors.

It was a period of mental adjustment. He had always been taciturn and self-contained, and this aspect of his character deepened. He didn't make friends among the other recruits. He was the only Italian among his intake, and as he struggled to learn French he felt out of place. Early on he had been tested as to whether he could be pushed around. His reaction had been savage and uncompromising. A big Dutchman, mean and hard, had needled him a point too far. Guido got his retaliation in first and the Dutchman took a painful beating. He had not broken discipline. The training NCOs allowed this kind of thing to happen. They wanted to know who could take it.

After that, Guido had been left alone, and the instructors guessed that the Italian might develop into a good Legionnaire. After training, he volunteered for the elite First Paratroop Regiment based at Zéralda, twenty miles west of Algiers. The Algerian war was building into a major confrontation, and naturally the Legion was at the forefront. The 1st R.E.P. was to be the most successful and feared unit in the French army. Guido was assigned to "B" Company. The company sergeant had just returned to active service after nine months at a Viet Minh prisoner-of-war camp. He had been captured at Dien Bien Phu. He was the American, Creasy.

It had been several months before the two men recognized the empathy between them. There was a gap at first — Guido, an untried Legionnaire and Creasy, a decorated veteran of Vietnam and a top sergeant. But there were similarities of character: both taciturn and introspective, shunning normal contact, and intensely private, in an environment where privacy was hard to find.

The first time that Creasy talked to him, apart from issuing orders, was after an action near a town called Palestro. A patrol of French conscripts had been ambushed by the Front Liberation Nationale and many killed. The Legion went after them, and it was the 1st R.E.P. that caught up. "B" Company was dropped to cut off the escape route, and Guido saw action for the first time. He was confused by the noise and movement, but quickly settled down and used his light machine gun to good effect. The FLN unit was wiped out.

That night the company camped in the hills above Palestro, and as Guido ate his field rations Creasy came over and sat beside him and talked a little. It was only the gesture of a company sergeant letting one of his new men know that he had done well in his first action, but Guido had felt good with the contact. He already had a deep respect for Creasy, but this was universal in the Legion. He was known as the complete Legionnaire, an expert with all weapons, and a natural tactician, Guido knew that he had fought for six years in Vietnam and before that had been in the U.S. Marines, for how long nobody knew. His favourite weapons were the grenade and the submachine gun, and he always seemed to carry more grenades and spare magazines than anyone else.

Shortly after Palestro, the company had again been dropped behind a retreating FLN unit. This time the FLN had got away, and again at the evening meal Creasy had brought his rations over to sit with Guido. They talked about small arms and their effectiveness. Guido always carried a pistol and four spare clips. Creasy told him that it was a waste of weight. A pistol was useful only if it had to be concealed. In combat, concealment was unnecessary. The submachine gun, on the other hand, was the perfect weapon for close combat. Creasy told him to forget the pistol and carry more spare magazines for his SMG.

Guido was a willing pupil. Having decided he liked the life, he was determined to succeed, and in Creasy he recognized the perfect teacher. He had been told of the remark made by the legendary Colonel Bigeard after watching Creasy retake a position at Dien Bien Phu: "The most effective soldier I have ever seen."

So Guido took the advice to heart and modelled himself on his sergeant, and by the time the battle of Algiers started in January '57 he had made his mark and had been promoted to Legionnaire first class. A year later he too was an NCO and the friendship between the two men had grown into a recognizable pact. It had been a slow process, for both had long emotional antennae and these probed carefully. They were at first unaware of the process. Few words were exchanged, and these related almost entirely to military subjects, but as Guido's knowledge increased, the conversations became less teacher-to-pupil dialogues and more discussions between equals. Both noticed also that the silences between them were never oppressive or strained, and it was this that brought the surprising realization to each that he had found a friend.

At that time Colonel Dufour commanded the regiment and as the pace of the war quickened he recognized both the ability of the two men and their friendship. The 1st R.E.P. was constantly in action, and Creasy and Guido were put together with their units whenever possible. They made a formidable partnership and became well-known throughout the Legion,

When it became obvious that de Gaulle was planning a political settlement of the war, the white settlers, the *pieds noirs*, reacted in fury. They set up barricades in Algiers and defied the army. Many of the professional soldiers were in sympathy, particularly the tough "para" units, who had borne the brunt of the battle.

The gendarmes were ordered to clear the barricades, and two para units, one of which was the Legion's 1st R.E.P., were ordered up in support. Both units dragged their feet and the gendarmes lost many dead and wounded in the operation. Colonel Dufour was relieved of his command, but instead of being replaced by a politically reliable officer, the high command put Elie Denoix de St. Marc in temporary charge. St. Marc was the epitome of a Legion officer. Tough and idealistic, and uncompromisingly brave, he was worshipped by his men and could have led them anywhere. He chose to lead them into the "generals' rebellion" of 1961 against de Gaulle, and the 1st R.E.P. became the cornerstone of the generals' plans. They expected the rest of the Legion to follow suit, but they had miscalculated, and only the 1st R.E.P. under St. Marc was active against the government, even arresting Gambiez, the Army Commander-in-chief.

The rebellion failed, and on the 27th of April, 1961, the twelve-hundred Legionnaires of the 1st R.E.P. dynamited their barracks and fired off all their ammunition into the air. The *pieds noirs* lined the route and wept as the paras drove out of Zéralda, singing Edith Piaf's "*Je ne regrette rien.*"

The regiment was disgraced and disbanded. It had lost three hundred men in the war for France, but de Gaulle was in a vengeful mood. Rank and file were absorbed into other units of the Legion. The officers fled to join the O.A.S., the underground extremist army, or surrendered to stand trial for mutiny. The senior NCOs were discharged — Creasy and Guido among them.

They had done only what they had been taught to do — obey their officers.

"They kicked you out?" asked Pietro incredulously. "Even though you had only followed orders?"

Guido shrugged. "It was a time of great political passion. At one point we expected to parachute onto Paris itself and arrest de Gaulle. The French people as a whole were horrified, and with good reason. At that time, the Legion's strength was over thirty thousand men, and nothing could have stopped us if the Legion had acted as a whole."

He worked silently for a while and then continued.

"It was the first time that the French realized what a threat the Legion could be to France itself. That's why, even today, the bulk of the Legion is based in Corsica and other locations outside mainland France."

"So what did you do?" asked the boy.

"Creasy and I stuck together. The only training we had was military. I was still wanted by the police here and Creasy had nowhere to go. So we looked for a war and found one in Katanga."

"Katanga?"

Guido smiled. "I keep forgetting how young you are. Katanga was a province of the Belgian Congo. It's called Shaba now. When the Belgians pulled out in '61, Katanga tried to break away. They're a different tribe, and they had most of the mineral wealth. A lot of mercenaries went to fight in Katanga."

They had joined a French ex-para colonel called Trinquier. He knew them from Algeria and was delighted to recruit such experienced men. So they became mercenaries, which wasn't much change really, except that they missed the Legion. This joint feeling of loss brought them even closer together and their friendship developed into a bond rare between two people of the same sex. Their fighting skills soon became a byword among the other mercenaries. They were so mentally tuned that they moved and fought as a single entity without apparent communication. They were particularly adept at "laundering buildings" — clearing the enemy in an urban situation. They had their own techniques, giving each other cover and moving from room to room or building to building in a rhythm so precise that other mercenaries would stand and watch in admiration. They brought the use of grenade and submachine gun to a fine art.

With the failure of the Katanga secession they joined other mercenaries in the Yemen under Denard, but moved back to the Congo as soon as Tshombe returned from exile. Denard ran the French 6th Commando, and Guido and Creasy fought throughout the messy, convoluted war until Mobuto triumphed. Then, together with hundreds of other mercenaries, they retreated to Bukavu. They ended up in internment in Rwanda under the auspices of the Red Cross. They had to give up their weapons, and for Guido the next five months were a torment. Although they had plenty of room to move about, the fact of restriction brought on his claustrophobia. To keep his mind occupied, Creasy taught him English and had Guido teach him Italian. Guido found the English hard going, but Creasy proved to have a good ear for languages and quickly mastered Italian. They began speaking the language more and more together until, about a year later, they switched to it completely from French.

After five months in Kigali they were repatriated out to Paris. Two weeks in the bars and brothels of Pigalle wiped out the bad memories, and they started to look for work. Mercenaries were not very welcome in black Africa, and anyway they thought a change of location might be stimulating. Apart from his months in the P.O.W. camp, Creasy had liked Indochina, and when they received a tentative approach from a certain Major Harry Owens, U.S. Army (retired), they listened with interest.

The Americans were by now deeply involved in Vietnam and finding the going surprisingly tough. It was becoming apparent that sheer weight of manpower and ordnance might not be enough.

The Central Intelligence Agency naturally had definite ideas on how to win the war and with a huge budget was busily recruiting and training a series of private armies, both in South Vietnam and neighbouring Laos. They needed instructors for Laos, and ex-sergeants of the Legion made excellent instructors. Creasy's experience in French Vietnam was an added bonus.

So they found themselves in Laos, nominally working as loading supervisors for the CIA front company, "Air America." This was a charter firm which was supposed to ferry freight around Southeast Asia. In fact, it supplied equipment and food and much else to the CIA's private armies.

Creasy and Guido spent eighteen months training Meo tribesmen on the Plain of Jars.

As things got worse for the Americans, the CIA responded by setting up "intrusion units." These were mercenary groups that intruded into North Vietnam and Cambodia to harass the Vietcong supply lines. Creasy and Guido were "promoted" to such a unit, designated on the CIA computer at Langley Field, Virginia, as P.U.X.U.S.P.40. This meant "penetration unit non-American personnel containing 40 men." The computer considered it to be expendable.

By late 1971, P.U.X.U.S.P.40 had been expended to the tune of thirty of its original members. Creasy and Guido decided to take a long, or perhaps permanent, break. They had done twelve covert missions and picked up several wounds apiece. They had also accumulated a great deal of money — the computer had been generous.

In the meantime, Guido had learned that the Naples police could be persuaded not to look for him if he returned, and that Conti, having prospered, had moved his base to Rome, leaving Naples to a viceroy who had no great memory of events during 1953.

The two mercenaries decided to take a trip to Europe so that Guido could visit his family and check out his property. Then they would take a look around and see what offered itself.

Guido had found his building in Naples in a state of good repair. It was rented out to the Church as a dormitory for unwed mothers — a quaint link with its past. They stayed in Positano with his mother. Elio was in his last term at Rome University, studying economics. Guido's mother, aging now, gave thanks in the church for her son's safe return and lit a dozen candles. Such generosity, she knew, would have its reward.

"And that was the end of my mercenary days," Guido said to the engrossed boy.

"The end? You just stopped?"

"We went to Malta," answered Guido shortly, "and I got married and came back here,"

Pietro knew that, for the time being, he would learn nothing more. They worked on in silence. In half an hour the first lunch customers would arrive.

CHAPTER THREE

Ettore and his lawyer had lunch at Granelli's. They sat in the semi privacy of an alcove table and ate *prosciutto* with melon, followed by *vitello tonnato*, accompanied by a bottle of vintage Barolo. Slightly too heavy for the veal, but Vico liked it, so that's what they drank.

They discussed Ettore's financial problems. Vico was smoothly reassuring. Matters could be arranged. He would personally talk to the bank managers. Ettore must not be pessimistic.

Ettore felt at a disadvantage. He always did with his lawyer. Vico Mansutti was urbane, handsome, immaculately dressed, and cynical. He wore a silk worsted suit with a faint pinstripe, tailored, Ettore knew, by Huntsman's of Savile Row. His shirt was Swiss cotton voile, his tie Como silk and his shoes Gucci. There was nothing synthetic about Vico — at least on the outside. He wore his hair fashionably long, and a black moustache balanced his lean, tanned face. As they talked his eyes noted every movement in the restaurant, and he would occasionally acknowledge a greeting with a flash of even, white teeth. At thirty-six, two years younger than Ettore, he was acknowledged as the cleverest, best-connected lawyer in Milan.

So his words calmed Ettore but did nothing to dispel his feelings of inferiority.

A waiter drifted by and poured more Barolo, and Ettore moved on to his next problem — Rika. He explained about her obsession over Pinta's safety and, because Vico was a friend, explained about the social factors. Vico listened with an amused expression on his face.

"Ettore," he said, smiling at his friend's doleful look, "I envy you profoundly. The problems you think you have are tiny problems, and the advantages you ignore are real and enormous."

"Tell me," said Ettore. "I seem to have misplaced them."

Vico put down his fork and held up his left hand with fingers spread. "Number one," he said, putting his right forefinger onto his left thumb. "Your reputation is such that, even owing the banks so much, they will continue to support you until conditions improve."

"You mean my family's reputation," interjected Ettore, "particularly my father's."

Vico shrugged. For him it was the same thing. He moved onto the next finger.

"Number two — your house on Lake Como, which you bought eight years ago for eighty million lire, is today worth two hundred fifty million and still appreciating."

"And mortgaged to the bank for two hundred million," said Ettore.

Again the shrug; the finger moved on.

"Number three, you have a daughter whose charm and beauty is only matched" — the finger moved again — "by number four — your wife, Rika. Yet you sit there looking as though your pupick dropped off."

He signalled the waiter, ordered coffee, and turned back to Ettore.

"You must get things into perspective. You have this little problem because you indulge Rika too much. That's entirely natural. Any man on earth, married to Rika, would do the same — I would."

He paused to drink some wine and then continued.

"The mistake you made, if I may say so, was allowing Rika to take Pinta out of school after the Carmelita kidnapping."

"Now wait!" Ettore protested. "I knew nothing about it. I was in New York. When I got back she had already hired the governess. It was a fait accompli."

Vico smiled. "Yes, well, of course Rika is impulsive, but at the time she made quite a drama of it. Now to send Pinta back to school under the same conditions would be to admit she was wrong." He raised an eyebrow. "When was the last time Rika admitted that she was wrong?"

Ettore smiled ruefully at the rhetorical question.

"So," continued Vico, "you must, as the Chinese say, allow Rika to save face."

"And how," asked Ettore, "do I accomplish that?"

Vico shrugged. "Hire a bodyguard."

Ettore became irritated.

"Vico. You are supposed to have a trained logical mind. We've just spent half an hour discussing my financial position — or lack of it. One of the reasons for this lunch was to ask you, as my friend and lawyer, and as Rika's friend, to explain to her the realities of the situation."

Vico reached forward and patted Ettore's hand.

"My talking to Rika will not save her face and that's the immediate problem. Besides when I suggested you hire a bodyguard, I didn't specify what type of bodyguard."

They were interrupted by the waiter with the coffee.

"What do you mean?" Ettore asked when they were alone again. Vico leaned forward, speaking more quietly now.

"Ettore, there are many sides and angles to this kidnap business. You know that it's highly organized and nearly always carried out under the auspices of organized crime. It has become a huge business — eighteen billion lire last year. The big boys control it."

Ettore nodded. "The Mafia."

Vico winced. "Such a melodramatic word. It conjures up a bunch of Sicilian peasants stealing olive oil."

He caught the waiter's eye again, and ordered two cognacs, then took a leather case from an inside pocket and extracted two cigars. A small gold guillotine appeared from his fob pocket and the cigars were meticulously beheaded. He passed one over to Ettore, and the waiter returned with the cognacs and a light. Vico favoured him with a smile, puffed contentedly, and resumed his lecture.

"Most families who feel threatened either send their children abroad, usually to Switzerland, or arrange very elaborate protection — specially guarded schools, bulletproof cars — and, of course, highly competent bodyguards."

"Expensive bodyguards," Ettore said.

Vico agreed. "About thirty million lire a year. All told."

Ettore raised his eyes expressively, but the lawyer went on unperturbed.

"Such bodyguards are supplied through specialized agencies. The best are even international, with branches in several cities, including Milan and Rome. There is, however, a shortage brought about by all the terrorism going on in Europe — Red Brigades, Red Army, Basque Nationalists, and so on. So really good bodyguards are hard to find, and the price is rising accordingly."

"I understand," interrupted Ettore, "and it doesn't solve my problem. Just the opposite."

Vico held up a hand. "Be patient, my friend. There is another aspect to this business. As an additional and purely financial consideration, many wealthy families take out insurance against having to pay ransoms. The government does not allow Italian insurance companies to write that kind of policy. They believe, quite reasonably, that it might encourage kidnapping. However, insurance companies abroad are not so restricted. In fact, Lloyd's of London leads the world in this type of coverage. Last year they collected over one hundred million pounds in premiums. Two of their underwriting partnerships specialize. One even has a subsidiary that will negotiate with the kidnappers. It's all very civilized and British. There are two conditions. One, that the premiums must be paid outside of Italy, and the other, that the insured must never disclose that he is insured. The reason is obvious."

Ettore was slightly bored. "It's very interesting, Vico, but what's it got to do with my problem?"

Vico pointed his cigar at him. "Is your factory insured?"

"Of course it is, and the beneficiary is the bank."

"Right," said Vico, "But when you negotiated the premium, the rate depended on the amount of security you provided — correct?" Ettore nodded, and Vico continued.

"Of course they insist on burglar alarms and so on, but if you provide a security service — watchmen, even guard dogs, the premium rate is much reduced. Well, the same thing applies to kidnap premiums, and because the rate is so high, and the amounts very large, any saving is a major factor."

He warmed to his subject.

"Consider a typical case. An industrialist takes out kidnap insurance for one billion lire. The rate could be as high as five percent, or fifty million. If, on the other hand, he hires a fulltime bodyguard, the premium could be reduced to three percent or thirty million lire. So he saves twenty million."

Ettore shook his head. "But you just told me that a bodyguard costs thirty million lire a year. Where's the saving?"

Vico smiled. 'There are such people as 'premium bodyguards.' They wouldn't do much to foil a kidnapping, but they do allow a lower premium rate, and they are cheap. About seven million lire a year."

"But Vico," said Ettore, "I don't want to insure against a kidnapping that isn't going to happen."

But he suddenly got the drift, and Vico laughed at his change of expression.

"Now you understand! You hire one of these cheap premium bodyguards for a few months and then fire him for incompetence or something. In the meantime, Pinta is back at school and Rika's face is saved."

Ettore sat quietly thinking a few minutes and then asked, "Where can I locate such a man?"

Vico smiled contentedly. "First you pay for this excellent lunch and then we go around to my office where I have the name of an agency right here in Milan."

Ettore had known that somehow he would end up paying the bill.

Guido turned off the Naples coast road and drove up a narrow dirt track. It led to an olive grove on the lower slopes of Mount Vesuvius. Just below the grove the hill crowned off, and the track ended on a grassy slope overlooking Naples and the sweep of the great bay. He turned off the ignition and the silence was complete. It was late evening and the sun, blood red, was edging onto the horizon.

He had been again to see his mother, and the presence of her two sons had healed her. It would be at least another month before the symptoms reappeared. Guido had talked to Elio about Creasy's arrival three days before, and Elio had offered a possible temporary solution. Guido needed to think it out.

The truth was that Creasy couldn't find the reason anymore to go on living. He had reached the point where he was unable to generate even slight enthusiasm for a new morning.

The night after his arrival, he had talked to Guido in his usual reticent and disjointed way. Sentences related only by the silences in between. Long pauses to think out and frame the next words. Guido had said nothing. Just sat and nursed a drink and let his friend drag out his thoughts. The whole convoluted monologue was summed up at the end when Creasy said:

"I just get the feeling that I've lived enough or too much — a lot happened — I'm a soldier, nothing else ever — never wanted anything else — known anything else — but I'm sick of it. Have been for the last five years or so."

He had become embarrassed then. Expressing such feelings, even to his only friend, had been painful and out of character. Guido had stretched out a hand and touched his shoulder in a gesture of understanding.

For Guido did understand, completely. He had gone through the same thing after Julia's death. It had been two years before he could adjust to a life without her. But the difference between them was fundamental. He had known a love and a happiness which had sharply defined his outlook on life. Its clarity was partly a result of its unexpectedness. He had fought and killed, drunk and whored his way around the world with hardly a passing thought about the effect he had on others. He had long assumed that the deep feelings of love, or compassion, or jealousy, or possession, were not inside him. His only feeling for any human being was for Creasy and, vaguely, his mother and brother.

His conversion had been dramatic. After a week with his mother, the two mercenaries had gone to Malta to look up a contact from their Congo days. The contact had been recruiting for a sheikdom in the Persian Gulf, but they hadn't liked the terms or the prospects. They decided to stay on a few days and look around. They ended up on the sister island of Gozo in a small hotel in a fishing village. It had been warm and relaxing and the people friendly.

Julia had worked at the hotel as receptionist, Guido had a way with girls, even shy, very religious, and highly protected girls, and within a few days she had agreed to meet him for a drink after work. She was slight and beautiful, and very direct in speech and manner. She repulsed his early advances, telling him she was a good girl and a virgin. Guido was intrigued. He had never known a virgin. Creasy looked on at the pursuit with benign amusement and agreed readily to stay on in Gozo while Guido talked and charmed and persuaded.

The conquest took three weeks, and it was not how Guido had imagined. They had gone, late at night, to swim at Ramla Bay and afterward sat on the dull red sands and talked for a long time. She had told him of her life, simple and unexceptional, her family farmers for generations. He found himself talking also about his life and it was difficult to convey because she kept asking "why" and he couldn't answer. The sun was coming up before they stopped talking and he had forgotten his original purpose. Then she told him that her parents would be very upset. In Gozo for a girl to stay out all night was the paramount crime.

"But we haven't done anything," protested Guido and saw her enigmatic look and realized that perhaps he was not the pursuer.

They had made love, and she had truly been a virgin and Guido had hesitated but she pulled him into her, cried out, and pulled him against her still harder. Guido would never forget those moments and all the women he had known were suddenly not women.

In the growing light he saw the blood on her thighs, the only blood he had ever seen caused by love. He watched her wipe it from her and look up at him and smile, shy but proud, and he knew that his life had changed.

They had walked together up over the hill, through Nadur to her parents' farm. Her father, already in the fields, watched them, still and silent, as they approached.

"This is Guido," she had said. "We are going to be married."

Her father had nodded and gone back to work. He knew his daughter. A night away from home meant a son-in-law.

They were married in the Church of St. Peter and St. Paul in Nadur. A young priest officiated. He was big and strong and reminded Guido a little of Creasy. He didn't look like a priest and his manner was abrupt and gruff, but the people of Nadur liked him. He worked hard and was practical. Farmers appreciate that. Gozitans give everyone nicknames and this priest they called "the Cowboy."

Guido had been concerned over how Creasy would react to this marriage. They had been friends for over fifteen years and had hardly ever been separated. But Creasy had been pleased and not really surprised. He had realized the girl loved Guido and had seen the strength in her and was happy for his friend.

He was best man at the wedding, silent and as gruff as "the Cowboy," and afterward at the wedding feast had drunk a lot of the strong Gozo wine and felt in himself a great deal of Guido's joy. It was happiness by proxy, but for all that a good emotion.

Julia had instinctively understood the friendship and didn't resent it. She looked upon Creasy as an integral part of Guido. When they left to go to Naples, Creasy had taken them to the airport, and when he bent down to kiss her cheek she had put her arms around him and held onto him for a long moment, and when she drew away he saw the tears in her eyes,

"Our home is your home," she said simply.

He nodded, his face strangely set, and said, "If he snores at night, just whistle — it shuts him up."

She had smiled and turned away unable to say any more. In the plane she had asked Guido what Creasy would do and he had answered that he would go and find a war somewhere.

So Guido returned to Naples with a wife and bought back the lease on his property and turned it into the Pensione Splendide. His mother's cup had run over and the church in Positano was bright with candles.

Creasy had visited them in Naples several times, coming or going to a war. He never wrote or phoned, just arrived. He always brought a present for Julia. Something distinctive. Once it had been a batik painting from Indonesia, rich and detailed, another time a string of natural aquamarine pearls from Japan. They were presents not bought on the spur of the moment, but thought about and distinct. She knew this and it gave her more pleasure than their beauty or obvious value.

He usually stayed only a few days, relaxed and comfortable, and then one evening would announce he was leaving and in the morning would be gone. But on the last occasion he had stayed more than a month. He was never idle, busying himself with small repairs around the building. He liked working with his hands.

When the last customers had left after dinner, the three of them would sit around the big kitchen table, watch television or read or just talk. Julia used to smile at the conversation of the two men, their mental rapport so acute that whole sentences would be reduced to one or two words. Guido might start it off with a question about a past acquaintance.

"Miller?"

"Angola."

"Still bitching?"

"As ever."

"But sharp?"

"A needle."

"The Uzi?"

"Wedded to it."

Much of the conversation would be incomprehensible to her, especially when they talked of weapons. After the first couple of visits, Guido would be restless for a few days following Creasy's departure, but she said nothing. And by the last visit he was settled and adjusted and happy. On that last visit when Creasy announced he was leaving in the morning she had told him flatly that he was welcome to stay with them and make his home. Guido had said nothing; he didn't need to. Creasy had smiled at her, one of his rare smiles, and said, "One day I might do that and fix all your wiring and paint the place once a month." They knew he meant it. He would come and just never announce that he was leaving, and it would be good and right.

But Julia had gone shopping one day and the local football team had won and the supporters were driving in convoy through the city, horns blowing and flags flying, and one of the cars with eight drunks aboard had lost control and smeared her against a wall.

Creasy had arrived a week later, tired from a long journey. Guido had forgotten to ask how he knew. He stayed a couple of weeks and his presence brought Guido through.

Now Guido sat in his car and watched the twilight over the bay. The sun had gone, leaving only refracted light. He tried to imagine his life if he had never known Julia and he could picture it and so could understand Creasy now.

He needed to do something different, if only for a while. Something to occupy his time and his mind. Something to halt the slide.

Creasy had gone to Rhodesia and tried to fit in. He had trained young white recruits and led them in the bush. But it was a different world, and he couldn't identify. He didn't try to differentiate between right and wrong on the war. He sympathized with the whites. They were not bad people. Time had just caught up. They lived in the wrong century. They had come as pioneers, opening up a new country, and they looked on themselves as akin to the early American settlers. But times had changed. They couldn't wipe out the blacks as the American Indians had been wiped out, or the Australian aboriginals. Most of the whites wouldn't have wanted to and the few that did found that some of the blacks had land mines, grenades, rocket launchers, and Kalashnikovs. It was a different world. The terrible thing was the futility. It stared Creasy in the face. The others couldn't see it, but he had a lifetime to recognize it. Dien Bien Phu to Algeria to Katanga, back to Vietnam and into endless circles of futility. The war in Rhodesia brought his whole past into focus. Futile battles fighting for people who talked of patriotism, final stands, and never say die — but death to the last man. He looked into his future and saw the exact same sequence. If not in Rhodesia, then somewhere else. Futile: it was an epitaph on his past and an adjective for his tomorrow.

He had lost interest. He started drinking heavily and let his body slacken and become lethargic. Finally they took him off operations and made him just an adviser. They would have kicked him out, but they remembered his earlier days and were grateful. It wasn't long before he realized the charity, and his pride picked him up and took him away. He went to Brussels, where he had known a woman, but she had moved on and so he took the train to Marseilles and on an impulse caught the ferry to Corsica. The main contingent of the Legion was based in Corsica and an instinct led him there. Many years had passed since the 1st R.E.P. had mutinied. The Legion itself had forgiven. There was a home there. Maybe the orphan could return to the orphanage.

He had arrived in Calvi in the afternoon and sat in the square and had a drink. The barracks lay up the hill and as he tried to decide whether to go up or not he heard the sound of singing. It was the Legion marching hymn, "*Le Boudin*," and then they came around the corner with the distinctive slow march — eighty-five paces a minute. It was a unit of recruits, smart in their new uniforms, showing off their drill for the first time. He looked at the faces, young and scrubbed, and he felt a thousand years old.

When they had passed and the last sounds had died away, he finished his drink and walked to the station. The next day he was in Bastia, sitting by the docks drinking again and waiting for the ferry to Livorno. He would go and see Guido. Maybe they would get together again. Maybe it wouldn't be futile.

He had watched the few passengers go aboard and crossed the road to join them, passing the boy. As the ferry pulled out, he stood at the stern and saw the boy wave at him. He waved back. Goodbye, Corsica. Goodbye, boy.

"A bodyguard," said Guido.

Creasy looked at him blankly.

They sat in the kitchen and Guido explained about Elio's suggestion.

His brother had prospered. After a good education he had qualified as an accountant, all paid for by Guido. He had joined a firm of auditors in Milan and had done well. He had explained to Guido that one of his clients was a security agency that supplied bodyguards to industrialists. There was a great demand and a shortage of trained men. The pay was excellent. Guido had demurred. Creasy was totally unfit and virtually an alcoholic. It would be taking a job under false pretences, and Creasy wouldn't do it. Then Elio had explained about "premium bodyguards" and Guido had become interested. "But the pay is lousy," Elio had remarked. That didn't matter, thought Guido. He knew that Creasy had plenty of money. He had earned a great deal over the years and spent little.

So he made the suggestion to Creasy and Creasy looked blank.

"A bodyguard," repeated Guido.

"You're crazy," replied Creasy. "In my state I couldn't guard a corpse."

Guido told him about "premium" bodyguards, but Creasy was unconvinced.

"People would hire a complete has-been — a drunk?"

Guido shrugged.

"It's just a device to keep premium costs down,"

"But a drunk?"

Guido sighed.

"Obviously you would have to keep the drinking under control. Drink at night. You do here, and you don't look so bad during the day."

"And what happens if there's a kidnap attempt?"

"You do your best. You're not paid to perform miracles."

Creasy thought about it but remained sceptical. He had always worked with military people of one kind or another. He raised a further objection.

"A bodyguard has to be close to someone all the time. I'm not good at that — you know it."

Guido smiled.

"So you'll be a silent type bodyguard. Some people might appreciate that."

Creasy thought up other problems, but Guido pressured him gently. Elio had invited him to stay in Milan for a few days.

"Why not go up anyway, and look around?"

Finally Creasy agreed to see what kind of job was available. Then he went to bed, shaking his head and muttering incredulously, "Goddamn bodyguard!"

Guido fetched paper and a pen and wrote a letter to Elio. He knew that the agency would require information on Creasy's qualifications and that Creasy would be reluctant to provide anything but the barest details. He wrote for a long time, first sketching Creasy's career in the Legion and later in the various wars in Africa, the Middle East and Asia. Then he listed familiarity with different weapons. It was a long list. Finally he mentioned Creasy's decorations. Italians are impressed by medals.

He sealed the letter and left it on the table with a note asking Pietro to post it first thing in the morning. He went to bed feeling more encouraged than at any time since his friend's arrival.

CHAPTER FOUR

"Did they provide you with the gun?"

"Yes."

"Show me, please."

Creasy took his right hand off the steering wheel, reached under his jacket, and passed it over.

Ettore held it gingerly. He had never before held a pistol, and he was fascinated.

"What is it?"

"Beretta 84"

"Have you used this type before?"

"Yes, it's a good pistol."

"Is it loaded?"

Creasy took his eyes off the road and glanced at the Italian.

"It's loaded," he said dryly.

Ettore handed the weapon back and they drove on towards Como.

He had asked the American to drive the Lancia so that he could judge his capability. He was relieved that Creasy drove easily and smoothly.

It had been less simple finding a bodyguard than Vico had suggested. At least, a bodyguard to suit Rika's requirements.

She had been delighted with the result of his lunch with Vico and had immediately started making plans. She decided that the bodyguard would have a large room at the top of the house. She and Pinta busied themselves putting in extra furniture; a small table and a large easy chair, and several casual rugs. The room already had a big brass bedstead, a chest of drawers, and a wardrobe. He would eat with Maria, the housekeeper, and Bruno, the gardener, in the kitchen.

She drew up a list of his duties. Driving Pinta to school and picking her up in the afternoon were the most important. In between, he could chauffeur Rika herself to shopping and lunch engagements.

Naturally he would have to be presentable and of a polite and respectful disposition. She had also urged Ettore to hurry as the new school term started soon, and she wanted to join Ettore on his coming trip to Paris.

All this created problems. The first two applicants had been patently unacceptable, little more than street toughs whom Rika wouldn't have let through the door. The third had been an obvious homosexual, and Ettore had a thing against homosexuals. He had phoned the agency and complained about the quality of the applicants, but they had answered that bodyguards were scarce. They also implied, politely, that you got what you paid for. Nevertheless, they rang up the next day to arrange for an appointment for a fourth applicant — an American.

Ettore had not been encouraged. A foreigner was something unexpected, especially an American. He anticipated a gum chewing, crew-cut gangster.

So he was pleasantly surprised when Creasy had been shown into his office. He looked hard enough, with the scars on his square face and the menacing eyes, but he was dressed smartly in a dark blue suit and beige shirt. He stood at the door holding a large Manila envelope sealed with red wax, looking at Ettore without expression.

Ettore gestured and Creasy moved forward and took a seat in front of the desk. Then he handed over the envelope.

"The agency told me to give you this."

His Italian was almost perfect, with a slight Neapolitan accent.

Ettore took the envelope and asked, "Would you like coffee?" He was encouraged. He had not offered coffee to the others.

Creasy shook his head and Ettore broke the seal, pulled out the file, and began to read. It was a report on Creasy's qualifications and history provided by the agency from Guido's information.

Ettore read in silence and when he had finished he looked at the man in front of him for a long time. Creasy gazed back impassively.

"What's the catch?"

"I drink," came the flat reply.

Ettore digested this for a moment and glanced again at the file, then asked, "In what way does it affect you?"

Creasy's eyes narrowed in thought and Ettore sensed that he would get the absolute truth.

"As it relates to this kind of job, it affects my coordination and reaction time. My ability to shoot fast and accurately is impaired. If I was a rich man, convinced that I or my family were going to be attacked, I wouldn't employ a man in my condition."

Ettore asked, "Do you get so drunk that you are incapable or a nuisance?"

Creasy shook his head.

"You wouldn't notice anything. I only drink at night. In the morning I might feel bad but I look alright."

Ettore studied the papers again. As long as Rika didn't know about the drinking, there should be no problem.

"The pay is not good."

Creasy shrugged. "If top professionals try to kidnap your daughter, the service will be on a par with the pay."

"And what if amateurs try it?"

"If they're truly amateurs, I'd probably frighten them off, or even kill them — is it likely?"

Ettore shook his head.

"I doubt it. Frankly, it's my wife who is mostly concerned. She's overreacting about all the recent kidnappings. Incidentally, part of your duties will involve transporting her about. She has her own car." He glanced down at the file again — at the lists of wars and battles and weapons.

"You would have to become a little domesticated."

"That's alright," said Creasy, "but I'm not good at social chit-chat. I'll do my job, best I can, that's all."

Ettore smiled for the first time.

"That's fine. Can you start immediately?" A thought struck him. "Do you have a gun?"

Creasy nodded. "The agency provides one. You will have to give them a letter. They will arrange the police permit. It will be on your bill." He stood up. "I can start anytime."

They had walked to the door, Ettore saying, "I go up to Como tomorrow evening for the weekend. Please be here at six with your things. No one is to know about your drinking problem, and that includes my wife."

The two men had shaken hands. Ettore said, "I can't be sure how long the job will last. It depends on circumstances, but my contract with the agency will be for a three-month trial period. After that we can both review the situation. After all, you might not like the job."

When they entered the lounge, Rika was by the French windows. She wore a plain black dress. Her face was a white oval in a framework of ebony hair.

Ettore made the introductions and she asked, "Would you like a drink?"

"Thank you — Scotch and a little water."

She crossed to the bar and the two men moved to the French windows and looked out over the lake. Creasy could sense Ettore's unease and wondered at it. Rika brought over the whisky and a martini for her husband.

"I didn't catch the name exactly," she said.

"Creasy."

"You are not Italian?"

"American."

She looked at Ettore with a slight frown.

"But his Italian is excellent," he said hastily.

She was disconcerted.

"You have done much of this work before?"

Creasy shook his head. "Never."

Her frown deepened and again Ettore quickly interjected, "Mr. Creasy has a lot of experience in related work. A great deal of experience."

Creasy studied the woman with interest. He had needed time to get over the first impact of her beauty. He was indifferent to her reaction on hearing he was an American, but he was curious about her relationship with her husband.

Ettore had appeared positive and self-assured, but his weakness was now apparent. The woman, either through her beauty or personality or both, dominated him. Her confusion showed. Naturally she'd had a preconceived idea of the kind of man Ettore would hire. He would obviously be Italian, polite and deferential, young and athletic, and experienced in the work.

The man in front of her was first of all an American and, like many Italian socialites, she tended to look down on Americans. Also, although he was big, he wasn't young, and he didn't look very athletic.

She noted his clothes, casual and expensive: beige slacks, a fawn, knitted, polo neck shirt, and a dark brown jacket. She saw that the hand holding the glass had mottled scars on the back and that the tip of the little finger was missing. Then she looked up at his face and realized how tall he was. She took in the scars on his forehead and jaw, and the heavy-lidded eyes, indifferent as they gazed back at her. And she realized the effect he had — he frightened her. It was a shock. Men just didn't frighten her. She had never before felt fright at the sight of a man.

Ettore broke the silence.

"Where is Pinta, darling?"

Her mind snapped back. "Upstairs. She'll be down in a moment."

Ettore could see that her irritation had gone, but it was replaced by a look of confusion.

She smiled slightly and said to Creasy, "She's excited about having a bodyguard."

"I'm the first?" asked Creasy.

"Yes. You speak Italian like a Neapolitan."

"I was taught by a Neapolitan."

"Have you lived there?"

"No, only visited."

Creasy heard the door open and turned.

The girl was dressed in a white T-shirt and jeans. She stood at the door and looked at Creasy with interest.

Her mother said, "*Cara*, this is Mr. Creasy."

She walked across the room and very formally held out her hand. As he shook it, she smiled tentatively.

The top of her head came level with his chest. Her small hand was lost in his.

"Why don't you show Mr. Creasy to his room?" Rika said. "Perhaps he'd like to unpack."

Creasy finished his drink and the girl led him out solemnly.

As the door closed Ettore waited for the explosion. But Rika sipped her drink reflectively.

"He's very well qualified," said Ettore, "and really, it's hard to find good people in this line."

She didn't say anything and he went on persuasively.

"Of course it's a pity he's American. But as you heard, his Italian is excellent."

"Has he worked in Italy before?" she asked.

"No." He opened his briefcase and gave her the agency report. "That's his background."

She sat down and opened the file, and Ettore went to the bar and made himself another martini.

She read the report in silence, then closed it and put it on the coffee table.

Ettore nursed his drink and kept quiet. She was deep in thought. Then she said, "He frightens me."

"Frightens you?" He was astonished.

She smiled.

"I think it's nice he's American. It's different."

"But why does he frighten you?"

She thought about it and shook her head. "I don't know." She looked down at the file. "Perhaps the answer is in there. You realize that you've brought a killer into the house. God knows how many people he's killed. All over the world."

Ettore started to protest, but she smiled again and said:

"He dresses well — like a European."

Ettore was relieved but puzzled. Evidently Creasy was acceptable.

She got up and kissed him on the cheek.

"Thank you, darling. I feel better now."

She said it as if she were thanking him for a present — a piece of jewellery or even a bunch of roses.

After dinner, Creasy cleaned the gun. He worked automatically, his fingers moving from long practice, while his mind ranged over the events of the evening and the people. In the past, whenever he had started a new job, he had always catalogued the people around him and their possible effect on him and on the job itself. Now, even though the work was totally different, habit made him follow the same procedure.

Ettore, he decided, was preoccupied. Probably with business matters. When he told Elio who his new employer was to be, Elio had recognized the name. Balletto Mills was one of the largest producers of knitted silk fabric in Italy and therefore in the world. Ettore had inherited the business from his father, who had been very respected in Milan's business community. Ettore himself was considered a good businessman but, like many other Italian textile producers, was facing fierce competition from the Far East. He was also known for the beauty of his wife.

Creasy's thoughts moved to Rika. Quite dispassionately, he considered her effect on him. She had qualities in her looks that he particularly admired in women: a lack of obvious decoration, an uncluttered look, very little makeup. Her hair hung naturally; her fingernails were long and unpainted. She needed no aids, but he had also noted the lack of perfume. She was, he decided, completely female in herself. Her personality was linked to her looks, an extension of them.

Physically, she had attracted him with a jolt. It was a factor that had a bearing on the situation. He had watched her reaction to him carefully. The initial hostility and irritation, fading into curiosity. In his experience she was the type of woman who would respond to his past, be intrigued by its violence. She liked to dominate and find out the limits domination could take, first mentally and then perhaps physically. He would treat her with great caution.

He finished cleaning the gun and took a small can of oil and lubricated the trigger mechanism and the magazine release catch. He thought about Maria and Bruno. During dinner in the big, comfortable kitchen they had not been talkative and he had not encouraged them to be. His natural reticence had been obvious and he expected that after a while, once they got used to his presence, they would fall back to whatever their pattern of conversation had been before his arrival.

Maria, he guessed, was in her middle thirties, stout and cheerful and obviously curious about him. Bruno would be in his sixties, a small man with a brown, pointed face and a placid disposition.

The food had been good, and homey. *Gnocchi verdi* followed by chicken marinated in oil and lemon juice. Although of late his appetite had not been good, Creasy was very fond of Italian food and knew a lot about it. He recognized the Florentine style of cooking and had asked Maria if she was from Tuscany.

She had been pleased at the question, recognizing its source. Yes, she had originally been from Tuscany but had come to Milan five years before to seek work. He had asked Bruno to show him around the grounds in the morning so he could fix the layout in his mind, and then had excused himself and come up to his room.

He emptied the gun's magazine of the short, 9 mm bullets and tested the spring and those of the two spares. Then he opened a box of shells and filled all three. That done he picked up the new shoulder holster, and, with a cloth, started working oil into the leather, softening it still further.

Pinta — she would be the main problem. He was not good with children in general and he guessed this one would be no exception. He had no practice at it. Children had been no part of his life, except as an object of pity. In all the wars he had ever fought, children had suffered the most. Confused, often separated from their parents, nearly always hungry. He remembered them in the

Congo, swollen bellied, eyes uncomprehending. And in Vietnam, looking like dolls, and all too often caught in the middle. Bombed and mined and shot. He had been told that there were over a million orphans in South Vietnam and, at times, he felt he had seen them all. He had grown a shell so he could ignore their suffering. Either you did that or you lost your mind. He had done it early. He saw them, but the message from the eyes to the brain got diverted.

Of all the brutalizing effects of war, the numbing of compassion was the most acute. But now he was to be put into close proximity with a child for the first time. Certainly not a child hungry, or hurt, or homeless, but for all that a problem to him.

When Pinta had shown him up to his room, she had stayed behind and chatted while he unpacked. Obviously his arrival was a big event in her life. An only child, she was too often bored. It was natural that she should look on Creasy as more than a mere protective presence.

Her first questions had been about America. He explained that he hadn't lived there for years, but that hadn't diminished her enthusiasm. She asked him what part he had come from and he answered, the South — Tennessee.

He finished oiling the holster and slipped in the Beretta. Then he walked over to the bed and hung the harness over the knob on the brass bedstead. The butt rested close to the pillow. Back at the table he opened a road map of the area between Milan and Como, his mind now occupied with the technicalities of the job. Although he had never worked as a bodyguard, he viewed it in simple, military terms. He was to protect an "asset." A potential enemy might attempt to capture it. He considered the tactics, and a lifetime of experience made him view the situation from the opposition's point of view. They could attempt to capture his "asset" at its base, i.e., the house; or outside the base, either at another often used location or on route to it, i.e., the school or on the road.

In the morning he would check the grounds from a security standpoint and later, it had been decided, Pinta would show him where the school was, and he would have a chance to examine their security arrangements. He decided that if an attempt was made it would most likely occur on the road; therefore it was important to vary the daily route on a random basis. He traced the road network on the map and made notes in the margin.

This done, he went to the wardrobe and lifted down his suitcase. Inside were several bottles of Scotch wrapped in newspaper. He opened one of them and fetched a glass and poured his first drink. Then he thought about the main problem again — the girl. The important thing, he decided, was to get the relationship established on the right basis at the beginning. The right basis would be functional and nothing more. He was not a paid companion but a protector, and she must be made to understand that, even if he had to be blunt and unkind to do it. Her parents would also have to understand it. He would make it very plain and if they couldn't accept it, they would have to find someone else.

He hadn't thought about this aspect before taking the job, but meeting the child had brought it very much to mind. He could feel her enthusiasm and expectation, and it made him uneasy. She would have to be stopped short.

He drank steadily until the bottle was empty and then went to bed; a big, battered, introspective man, unsure about his new job.

But Guido had been right. His mind was occupied.

Below, in the main bedroom, Rika and Ettore made love. She was very demanding, her breath coming in short gasps, her fingers digging deep into his shoulders. She always paced herself with him, raising the tempo in tiers until she brought him to the top, knowingly and surely.

But tonight she was concerned only for herself, taking her pleasure in mental isolation. He tried to match her but felt her building to a climax, shuddering into her orgasm. He had not matched her and was left behind and felt her subside beneath him. He wasn't concerned. He knew that later she would rouse him again and play him like an instrument, using her magnificent body and mouth until all his passion was sated. She prided herself on her skill with him, enjoyed the control over his body. She never teased him sexually, but was imaginative and varied, and revelled in her skill.

Her breathing evened out and she ran a hand from his neck down his back and sighed contentedly. He could expect endearments and soft kisses, and later she would roll him onto his back and repay him slowly and artfully, smiling down at him, as in a conspiracy.

"She likes him."

He came out of his reverie.

"Who?"

"Creasy — Pinta likes him."

He shook his head.

"She likes the idea of no more governess. She'd like him if he was Count Dracula."

"No," she said. "When I put her to bed she told me he was like a bear. 'Creasy Bear,' she calls him."

Ettore laughed.

"She thinks all bears are like the toy one she cuddles at night. But bears can be dangerous."

"Why would he want to be a bodyguard?" she mused. "It's a tame job after the kind of life he's been used to."

They were getting onto dangerous ground.

"He's probably tired of it," he said. "Besides, he's no spring chicken."

"Forty-nine," she commented, remembering the file. "And no family, no children. Does he have a home anywhere?"

"I don't know, I doubt it. That kind of man doesn't put down roots."

He wondered at the cause of Creasy's drinking. Perhaps that was part of it. A lifetime of fighting and adventure and then getting too old for it, and not knowing what to do.

Rika's thoughts were paralleling his.

"There's a flaw somewhere there," she said.

"A flaw?"

"Yes. There's something about him. As though he's been very ill recently. He's very self-assured, but there's something not quite right. Maybe it was a woman."

He smiled. 'That's a typical woman's guess."

But then she shook her head.

"No, I don't think it's a woman. Something else. Something missing. A part of his personality is missing. He interests me, this Creasy — at least he's not boring."

Ettore was content. It would never occur to him that she would be interested in Creasy in any sexual way. He had long ago closed his mind to such thoughts. But he knew how she liked to analyse people. Slot them into neat categories. She would try to do this with Creasy. She wanted him numbered, tagged, and tidy, within her view of the world. He thought that might prove difficult with the man upstairs. He was outside her world. Right outside it. The influences and emotions that guided her were alien to the American. Still, Ettore was content. She had accepted the man, Pinta was going back to school on Monday, and he could concentrate on sorting out his business problems. Then he remembered something curious.

"You said he frightens you."

"Yes. But perhaps 'frightens' is the wrong word. In a way, he's menacing. A bit like an animal that's been domesticated, but you're never quite sure. Do you remember that Alsatian the Arredos had? After five years, it suddenly turned on him and bit him."

"He's not a dog, Rika!"

"It's just an example. He seems to be brooding. Smouldering. It's only an attitude, I'm not worried. It's interesting, really. I'd like to know more about him — his past — I mean how he feels about things."

She yawned and slipped lower in the bed. Her words had reminded Ettore how little he did know about Creasy. Perhaps he should have dug deeper. Still, he presumed the agency would have been satisfied. They must have checked for a criminal record, at least. Anyway, it was done now.

Rika moved against him slightly, and her breathing deepened. She was asleep.

It wasn't until the morning that he remembered she had left him unsatisfied.

CHAPTER FIVE

Pinta sat quietly in the front seat beside Creasy. He told her that he needed to concentrate on the route. She was a little mystified because they were on the main Como-Milan road and that was easy enough to follow. But Creasy wanted to look out for potential danger spots. Places where he would have to slow for a sharp bend and which were away from buildings. He simply transposed a military ambush situation for a kidnap attempt and his trained eye picked out and noted the likely places.

After half an hour Pinta pointed out the turnoff, and a few minutes later they pulled up in front of the school gates. She jumped out and pulled a metal handle set in the wall. Creasy remained in the car, taking note of the high, spike topped walls and the lack of cover in front of the heavy gates.

A shutter opened at eye level and Pinta held a conversation into it and the gates were opened slowly by an old watchman. She beckoned and walked through and Creasy followed in the car. Inside was a big, rambling, ivy clad building set in spacious grounds. Creasy parked in the courtyard and followed Pinta as she pointed out the features, a playing field and running track to the left of the building and a small copse on the right, well back from the circling wall. They walked around to the front, with Creasy concluding that the school itself was reasonably secure.

An elderly grey-haired woman appeared from the entrance and Pinta ran over and kissed her on both cheeks and brought her over to Creasy.

"This is Signora Deluca, the headmistress."

She turned to the woman and said with a note of pride, 'This is Creasy, my bodyguard."

"Mr. Creasy," admonished the woman.

"No, Signora, he told me just to call him Creasy."

They shook hands and she invited them in for coffee.

She had a small apartment on the top floor, comfortably over furnished, every flat surface supporting framed photographs. She noticed Creasy looking at them.

"My children," she laughed. "Hundreds of them, grown up now. But for an old schoolteacher, they are always children."

It was all very strange to Creasy. He had never thought of schools as being warm, happy places. His own brief experience had been the opposite. He had an inkling now of why Pinta was so anxious to return.

A maid brought in a silver tray with the coffee and, as she poured, the headmistress chatted to Pinta about the school. Then, feeling perhaps that she was neglecting Creasy, she turned to him.

"Have you been long in this kind of work, Mr. Creasy?"

"No," he answered. "I've only just started, but I've done similar things."

The woman sighed. "It's a terrible business. I have had two of my children kidnapped. Not from here, of course, and neither of them was hurt, but it's an awful experience, and they take a long time to get over it."

She put her hand on the girl's knee.

"You must look after our Pinta. We are so pleased she is coming back to school."

"Not as pleased as I am," laughed the girl, and went on to relate the terrors of her governess.

After a few more minutes, Creasy caught Pinta's eye and they rose to go.

"You are not Italian?" the woman asked as she walked them back to the car.

"He's American," piped up Pinta, "from Tennessee."

The woman smiled at Pinta's enthusiasm.

"Then I compliment you on your Italian, Mr. Creasy. Did you learn it in Naples?"

"From a Neapolitan."

She nodded in satisfaction.

"I can detect the accent." She pointed to a door at the back of the building. "That's the kitchen. We try to get the girls away on time but if you have to wait, the maid will give you coffee." She smiled ruefully. "Quite a lot of the girls have bodyguards."

Creasy thanked her and Pinta kissed her cheek and they left.

He decided to take a different route home. The girl was curious, but he told her that he wanted to try another way and drove on, concentrating again on the road and its surroundings.

Pinta kept quiet for a while, but the visit to the school and seeing Signora Deluca had excited her. She kept glancing at the big silent man next to her and finally asked: "Did you like school, Creasy?"

"No."

"Not at all?"

"No."

His short answers should have discouraged her but didn't.

"But why not?"

"It wasn't a school like yours and there was no one like Signora Deluca."

They drove on in silence while she thought about that, and then she asked, "So you were unhappy?"

He sighed in irritation and said, "Being happy is a state of mind. I never thought about it."

The girl sensed his mood but was not old enough or aware enough to respond to it. Since his arrival had coincided with and had even been the cause of her happy feelings, she wanted to share them. But his mood confused her. She didn't know that he was always taciturn and withdrawn. But she did want to get to know him. She looked at his hands on the steering wheel with their disfiguring scars, and she reached out and touched one of them.

"What happened to your hands?"

He jerked away and said sharply, "Don't touch me when I'm driving!"

Then he seemed to reach a decision. "And don't ask questions all the time. I'm not here to make small talk. You don't want to know about me. I'm here to protect you — that's all."

His voice was hard, cracking at her, and she withdrew, hurt, to her side of the car.

Creasy glanced at her. She sat staring ahead at the road, her mouth in a straight line. Her chin quivered.

"And don't start crying," he said in exasperation. He took a hand off the wheel and gestured. For some reason he was genuinely angry.

"It's all kinds of a world out there. All kinds. Not just the simple kind of being happy or not so happy. Bad things can happen. You'll find out when you're no longer a child."

"I'm not a child!" she flared back. "I know bad things can happen. I had a friend who was kidnapped and his finger was cut off. I had to stay at home for months, never going out, and now I have you with me all the time with your silences and sour looks — and I'm not crying."

But there were tears in her eyes, even though they glared at him angrily.

He pulled the car onto the side of the road and stopped. Only the sound of her sniffling disturbed the silence while he thought.

"Listen," he said finally. "It's just the way I am. I don't get on with kids. I don't like lots of questions. You have to understand that or ask your father to find someone else. OK?"

Her sobbing ceased and she sat still, staring straight ahead. Abruptly she opened the door and got out and then into the back seat.

"You can take me home now — Mr. Creasy."

She emphasized the "Mr."

He glanced back at her. She wouldn't look at him. Just sat, straight-backed and angry.

He drove on, his feelings ambivalent. He didn't want to hurt her, but he wasn't hired to be a nursemaid. It had to be done. Anyway, it could well be over. Her parents ought to realize she needed a friend — a companion. He was the last person fitted for that role.

On Sunday, after dinner, Creasy was reading when the tap came on the door. He wasn't feeling good. The night before he had drunk more than usual. Apart from his meals, he had stayed in his room. He had been expecting Rika or Ettore to come up.

It was Rika.

"I wanted to make sure you have everything you need," she said, standing at the door.

He put the book down.

"I have everything."

Her eyes swept the room.

"Is the food alright? Maria tells me you have hardly eaten all day."

"The food is good. Very good. I've just been off colour. I'm alright now."

She came farther into the room.

"Do you mind if I talk to you for a moment?"

He indicated the chair and moved over and sat on the bed.

He admired the way she moved as she crossed the room and sat down. Like a dancer — controlled and smooth and flowing. She crossed one leg over the other. He noted with surprise that she wore stockings with seams. He hadn't seen that for years. They looked right on her.

"How are you getting along with Pinta?" she asked.

He replied bluntly.

"We'll get along fine when she understands that I'm not a new toy."

She smiled.

"It's only natural that she's excited — having a bodyguard and going back to school. She's been bored — you must be patient with her, Creasy."

"I'm paid to protect her, not amuse her."

She inclined her head in acknowledgment and asked, "Did you argue? She wouldn't tell me, but last night she was very quiet and seemed disappointed."

He got up and walked to the window and looked out with his back to her.

"Look," he said. "Maybe this isn't going to work. I didn't think much about it before, but I'm not the type to be a social companion. Maybe you'd better ask your husband to find someone else — someone younger."

He turned to look at her. She was shaking her head.

"No, you're right. You were hired to protect her. Nothing more. I'm confident you'll do that."

She was looking at the bed. The gun had attracted her attention. It hung in its holster from the bedstead.

"I didn't realize you had a gun." She smiled. "I know — that's a silly thing to say, but it makes the whole thing so serious."

He said nothing and she went on.

"I suppose I thought you would be a karate expert or something." Then she remembered the report. "Unarmed combat, is that right? Weren't you an instructor?"

"Yes," he said. "But armed combat is more effective. Anyway, the gun is a deterrent. I don't expect to use it."

She considered that,

"But you will if you have to, if Pinta is in danger?"

"Naturally."

Now he could sense her interest and guessed what was coming.

"You must have killed a lot of people."

He shrugged, and she looked at him speculatively.

"I can't imagine it. I mean in a war and from a distance, yes. But close up, face to face, it must be horrible."

"You get used to it. And getting used to it is not great preparation for being a nursemaid for a child."

She laughed. "I suppose not. But we didn't hire a nanny." She abruptly changed the subject. "We have a spare radio downstairs. I'll give it to Maria for you. Do you like music?"

He nodded slowly, wondering at her change of direction.

"Some."

"What kind?"

"Country and Western, that kind of thing."

She stood up and said, "Ah yes, Tennessee — Pinta told me. Well, it plays cassettes, but we don't have any Country and Western."

She walked to the door, turned, and said, "But I'm sure you can find some in Milan. We are going there tomorrow. I'm having lunch with friends."

She looked at him reflectively, then said, "It would have been better if we had had more children. She's quite lonely, but . . ."

She shrugged and opened the door and left.

He went back to the chair and took up the book, but she had distracted him. He couldn't pick up the thread. So he went to the wardrobe and pulled down his suitcase and took out a bottle.

It would be good to have some music. The Country and Western was about the only trace left of his youth. Tomorrow he would look around in Milan and see what the record shops had. Probably only new stuff, but he knew Johnny Cash was popular in Italy, and he had heard Dr. Hook on the radio and liked him, and Linda Ronstadt. He had heard her "Blue Bayou." It had become a favourite. He poured a drink and picked up the book again, but it was no good. The woman was on his mind.

"I'll be finished at about two-thirty." She pointed to a side street next to the restaurant. "You can park up there."

Creasy nodded and said, "If the police move me on I'll circle the block. Just wait on the corner."

She got out of the car and walked across the street. Creasy's eyes followed. She wore a slim, straight skirt, something that few Italian women over thirty can do or should do. Her figure was just the right side of voluptuous and her height made it perfect. She disappeared inside and he pulled out into the traffic and glanced at his watch. Two hours to kill.

He considered it his first real day on the job. They had left the house just before eight, mother and daughter sitting in the back. Rika told him she had left the cassette radio with Maria. Pinta studiously ignored him.

A uniformed security guard stood outside the school gates. He had peered into the car and Rika introduced Creasy. The guard had studied his face, memorizing it, the gates were slightly ajar and Pinta was about to get out when Creasy's voice stopped her. "Stay where you are."

He got out and walked past the guard and looked inside the gates. Satisfied, he went and opened the back door of the car and nodded at the girl. She kissed her mother and then jumped out and walked past Creasy without a glance. The security guard gave Creasy a hard look and stood and watched as they drove off.

"You're careful," Rika had commented.

"Habit," came the reply.

"I talked to Pinta. Explained that she wasn't to bother you, just let you get on with your job."

"She seems to have got the message," he said.

"Yes, but I didn't mention our talk last night. I just told her that you weren't used to children. I don't want her to end up hating you."

He drove to the railway station and browsed through the bookstall there, picking up several paperbacks. Then he walked over to the telephone office and put a call through to Guido.

Yes, he'd started, he told him, and no, he wasn't sure how he'd like it, but he'd give it a chance. Anyway, the food was good. Then he called Elio and thanked him for his hospitality. In a couple of weeks, he would like Elio and Felicia to have dinner with him on his day off.

He had felt welcome during the few days he had spent in their house. Felicia was a tall, attractive woman from Rome. She had met Elio at the university. They were happy and their house was relaxed. She had treated Creasy like a prodigal uncle and teased him gently — he liked her.

He wandered around the station. He liked stations — the movement and noise and people going places. He also liked trains. It was a good way to travel. You saw things go by and felt you were going somewhere. Long journeys on good trains gave him pleasure. You could get up and look around and have a meal.

He saw a shop selling cassettes and browsed through it and found a couple of Johnny Cash and one by Dr. Hook. He couldn't find anything by Linda Ronstadt, but when he was paying the girl he inquired and she dug around in the back and found one. It had "Blue Bayou" on it and so far the day was moving along alright.

At 2:30 he was waiting in the street by the restaurant, At 2:45 a policeman came by and motioned him on. He beckoned the policeman over and showed him his bodyguard's licence.

"Does it pay well?" asked the policeman.

"Not bad. But a lot of sitting around on your ass."

"Better than flattening your feet on the streets."

A rapport was established and the policeman moved on to harass less fortunate citizens.

Just after three o'clock Rika appeared with a man and a woman. They were in a relaxed mood. Creasy got out of the car and was introduced.

'This is Vico and Gina Mansutti — Creasy."

They were a handsome couple. He might have thought her beautiful but she was shaded in Rika's light. The man was tanned, impeccably dressed and neat. Fastidious, thought Creasy. The kind of man who would only masturbate into a clean handkerchief.

They studied him with interest and the man said, "I understand you were in the Foreign Legion at one time."

Creasy nodded.

"And captured in Vietnam."

He nodded again.

"It must have been unpleasant,"

Another nod, and Gina giggled and whispered to Rika, "Does he talk?"

"Of course," said Rika sharply. She turned to the man and kissed his cheek.

"Vico, thank you for a lovely lunch. I promise not to let Gina spend too much." The two women got into the car. Creasy nodded at Vico again and drove off. Vico remained standing at the curb watching as the car negotiated the traffic. Creasy saw him in the rear-view mirror. He seemed preoccupied.

For the next hour and a half Creasy drove from shop to shop, opening and closing the trunk for a variety of parcels. Then he reminded Rika that he had to pick Pinta up at five. She looked at her watch in surprise. "It's so late? — Never mind, you go on. I'll phone Ettore to pick us up."

At the school there were several cars in the courtyard and girls were already coming out to them. Creasy sat and waited.

Finally Pinta came around the side of the building with two other girls. They stood and talked for a while, glancing frequently in his direction. Then they split up, the two girls going over to a blue Mercedes and Pinta going back around the side of the building. The Mercedes left. Twenty minutes later Pinta reappeared, carrying some books held together with a strap. Creasy got out and opened the back door. As she passed him, she held out the books. He took them, holding them by the strap.

"Your mother's returning with your father," he said.

She inclined her head, and he closed the door.

They drove home in silence.

That night Maria made *stracciatella* from the broth of Friday's chicken, followed by *saltimbocca*. They ate in silence. The food was delicious. Then, with the coffee, Creasy picked up a paperback and started to read. He remembered something.

"You have a talent, Maria — the food was excellent."

Maria beamed with pleasure and Creasy went back to his book. Maria and Bruno started discussing the Pope. They accepted Creasy and his silence. The kitchen was relaxed.

Later, up in his room, Creasy put a cassette into the player and listened to Dr. Hook sing about love and yesterdays. He took down a bottle and poured a drink. He didn't really hear the words, but the tone and the music crept in under the shell.

He reviewed the day. Day one as a bodyguard. Not too bad. At least he had established a working attitude. Everyone knew what he was, and what he was not. It was a start.

One floor below Pinta lay in bed awake. Next to her, with its head on the pillow, lay a very old brown teddy bear with button eyes and a lot of patches holding in the stuffing. Her window was open and she could hear the faint music. After a while it stopped and a different tape started. A woman sang. Pinta didn't know the song, but when it finished there was a pause and the same song came again. She started to drift into sleep. The music was plaintive, haunting. It was "Blue Bayou."

CHAPTER SIX

With Creasy installed, Rika felt free to travel with Ettore again. One of the unforeseen results of her hastily withdrawing Pinta from school was that she too had been confined to the house. It wouldn't have done to keep her daughter home for safety and then leave her with only the servants.

Most of Ettore's trips lasted a week or ten days and involved visits to the major European cities and occasionally to New York and Toronto. She enjoyed these excursions and was a help to Ettore. He was usually selling and with her looks and charm she was an asset.

He had forgotten to discuss with Creasy the question of time off. Obviously, while he and Rika were away, Creasy would have to stay with the girl. He left Rika to break the news and she was relieved at Creasy's easy acceptance. Time off was not something he had really thought about. Occasionally, he told her, he might want to go out to dinner, but he could do that while they were at home. She realized that having a bodyguard without roots or family had distinct advantages, and she left for Paris with her mind at rest.

Ettore was going to negotiate the purchase of new Lebocé knitting machines. The total cost would be over four hundred million lire, and unless the French could be persuaded to give very generous credit terms, it would be a nonstarter. Still, he was a persuasive negotiator and, with Rika along to add charm to the social occasions, he was optimistic.

The absence of her parents meant that Pinta took her meals in the kitchen. Creasy was relieved that they had developed what to him was a sensible and satisfactory relationship — she ignored him. She wasn't rude and had dropped her attitude of hurt indignation — she simply treated him as a necessary but uninteresting fixture.

So at meals she would talk only to Bruno and Maria, being serious and respectful to the old man and lightly teasing the woman, especially about some supposed suitor in Como. Creasy could see that they were very fond of the girl and enjoyed having her eat with them.

But it was a pose. Like her mother, she was a natural actress. Her attitude to Creasy was assumed.

Children are tenacious. She wanted to be friends. The obstacles made her even more determined. She had nodded dutifully when her mother instructed her not to bother Creasy, and then she had considered long and carefully and finally arrived at her strategy. She was an intelligent girl and warm-hearted and her character, unlike her mother's, was composed of two main elements. On the one hand, her parents' lifestyle and her lack of brothers or sisters had matured her beyond her eleven years. She was used to the company of adults and was an accurate observer of their behaviour. On the other hand, she had a keen and stimulating curiosity and was constantly delighted with new discoveries. She was moving into life expectantly and with a wonderfully open mind. Disappointments and setbacks would not cloud her optimism. She was like a small puppy, all energetic curiosity, jumping back a pace when confronted with something strange, but then inching forward again, nose twitching.

So, she had jumped back when Creasy had rounded on her in the car, and now she was edging forward, but cleverly, and from an angle slightly outside his vision.

She judged him right. Any frontal attack would be instantly recognized and repulsed.

She would just wait and watch for any weakness in his defence. She was sure it was there. Nobody could be as disinterested in life and the world as he appeared. So she waited, and chatted lightly to Maria and Bruno, and seemingly ignored him.

Over the days, Creasy's state of mind solidified into tolerance of his current position. Without consciously thinking about it, he was holding himself in abeyance, his brain slipping into neutral. No decisions were necessary, no plans, no emotional issues. The job itself was undemanding, and the conditions comfortable. He didn't consider how long he could go on. For the moment he was reasonably content and felt that he had stopped, or at least slowed on a path that had confused and upset him. He had no external responsibilities, no ties, and no demands on him. He could take each day as it came, not expectantly, but not with total resignation.

His drinking had eased slightly. It was still a malign factor, dulling him and sapping the strength in his body; but occasionally now, in the mornings, there would be some Scotch left in the bottle. It was no longer desperate drinking but more an overdone habit. Still, he knew that if he wanted to arrest his physical decline before it was too late he would have to cut back sharply. It was something to think about— but not strenuously.

The routine settled in. Creasy would drive Pinta to school in the mornings and pick her up at five o'clock. In between he had free time. Occasionally he would go into Milan and buy a few books or cassettes, but usually he went back to the house. There he would help Bruno on the large grounds. He liked using his hands, building things. Guido had once joked that it was a guilt complex from spending most of his life blowing things up or knocking them down.

In the Legion there had been opportunity for both destruction and construction, for the Legion had a history of civil engineering, particularly road building. In the early days in Algeria they had, like the Romans, built roads to help pacify the country. They had carried on this tradition in other parts of Africa and in Vietnam. Legionnaires were trained for this work, and Creasy enjoyed it.

Bruno was hard put to keep the large grounds tidy. He had concentrated on the front garden and lawn, which extended down to the roadway. At the back of the house the ground rose steeply up a pine covered, rock-strewn hill. This part was largely overgrown. A wooden fence surrounded the property but was in a state of bad disrepair. Bruno had asked for funds and a casual labourer to help fix it, and Ettore had promised to do something about it but never had. Creasy worked on this fence. He went into Como and bought some timber, spending his own money. He would tell Ettore that it was a security need, although even the repaired fence wouldn't keep out a determined intruder.

He spent several hours a day on this job, but it was going to take a good few weeks to finish it. Meanwhile it occupied his spare time, and he managed to sweat out some of the whisky even though it was barely spring and still cold.

In the evenings they would have an early dinner and afterward Creasy would stay on in the kitchen for an hour or two, either reading or watching television, listening with half an ear to the conversation of the others.

It was at such a time, a couple of days before her parents returned, that Pinta first spotted her opening. If there was nothing good on television, she would read the day's newspaper and magazines.

Her lively curiosity meant that Maria and Bruno were often asked questions.

Neither of them was well read or had travelled and their answers were limited. Creasy heard these conversations only as a background murmur but on this particular evening the name 'Vietnam" caught his attention.

Pinta had been reading about the mass exodus of refugees from the south — the boat people. She asked Bruno why so many were fleeing their own country. He shrugged and talked vaguely of Communism.

Creasy's interest was stirred and for the first time he found himself drawn into the conversation. The girl listened with interest as he explained that the majority of the boat people were ethnic Chinese and had always lived as a separate community. They were not liked by the Vietnamese, who traditionally distrusted them. With the ending of the war, a united Vietnam decided to get rid of them. As a community the Chinese were wealthy and could afford to pay the middlemen, usually Hong Kong Chinese, to smuggle them out by boat. It didn't take much smuggling since the authorities turned a blind eye and even actively encouraged the departures. So it wasn't so much the effects of Communism that caused the problem but deep-seated racial differences.

Pinta astutely drew a comparison with the migration of labour in Europe from poor countries to rich. She had read recently about the bad feelings Italian workers were facing in Switzerland and Germany.

It was deftly done, and a follow-up question had Creasy explaining about the effects of minority Chinese communities in Malaysia and Indonesia, where they controlled most of the economy and again created resentment. He told her that over one hundred thousand Chinese had been slaughtered in Indonesia after the failure of a Communist coup.

She wanted to know how the Chinese got there in the first place, and he told her of the great labour importing by the early colonial powers. The Chinese made good workers for the plantations, clearing jungle and building roads. The local populations were less inclined to work as hard. There were many examples, he told her: the Asians in East Africa who had been imported to build the railroads and who had stayed on to take over almost all the retailing and distributing networks, and the Tamils in Sri Lanka, imported from southern India to work the tea plantations. There were examples all over the world, and usually they created a rift that led to hatred and bloodshed in later years.

Abruptly he stopped talking and picked up his book. It had been an uncharacteristic monologue. She didn't press him or say another word to him. Instead she started to talk to Maria. A few minutes later Creasy stood up, said a gruff good night, and went up to his room.

As the door closed behind him, Pinta smiled inwardly.

"The first step, Creasy bear," she said to herself.

The next day on the way to school, and on the way back, Pinta didn't say a word, and after dinner that night she watched television. Creasy didn't exist. He was relieved. The night before, up in his room, he'd felt disturbed, a feeling he always got when he'd done something out of character. But if he had realized the girl's strategy, he would have been even more disturbed, although forced to admire it from a military point of view: Reconnoitre the target carefully. Note points of weakness. Make a diversionary attack to draw fire and then quietly slip in the back way and effect a capture. Pinta would have made an excellent guerrilla leader.

Creasy took Elio and Felicia to dinner at Zagone's in Milan. Maria had recommended it. She had worked there as a waitress when she had first come north; the owner was from Florence and she vouched for the food, although — she explained apologetically — it was expensive. For Felicia it was an occasion. Having two young children kept her at home in the evenings, but tonight a trusted neighbour was babysitting and she was determined to enjoy herself.

Maria had phoned for a reservation, and she had obviously been a good waitress and popular, because the owner gave them personal attention and a good table. He told Creasy that Maria was being modest in telling him that she had been a mere waitress. She had helped in the kitchen as well, and was a fine cook. The Ballettos often ate there and that was how they came to hire her. He joked with Creasy that, after Maria's cooking, the meal would be an anti-climax.

It wasn't. First they had a light pasta — *penne alia carrettiera*, followed by lamb braised with wine, peas and rosemary. They were a relaxed trio. It was Creasy's first night out since starting the job, and Felicia's obvious enjoyment was infectious.

Elio was surprised at Creasy's mood. It was a distinct change from that of a month before. He wasn't loquacious or smiling from ear to ear, that wouldn't have been Creasy, but he took Felicia's good-natured teasing easily and even cracked a couple of dry jokes. Felicia wanted to know all about the Balletto household and particularly Rika, who was well known as a socialite and hostess. Was she really as beautiful as her reputation had it? Creasy affirmed it. By any standards, she was beautiful, and naturally so.

"Are you attracted by her?" Felicia asked with a disarming smile.

Creasy nodded without hesitation. Any man would be. It was just a fact of life. He pointed to her plate where the lamb was fast disappearing. "Just as the taste buds are attracted to fine food, or a special wine."

"What about the girl? Is she like her mother?"

Creasy considered carefully, and the other two could see that the question interested him.

He decided that, as to her looks, she would turn out equally beautiful. It was already beginning to show. He thought her character might be different. She was more of an extrovert. She's curious, he told them, curious about everything. But who knew? With her full blossoming she might change. Great beauty often brought inhibitions.

Creasy found himself thinking about the girl. Since the night he had explained about the boat people, she had asked him one or two other questions in a direct and open way, obviously keen to widen her knowledge. Just the day before, driving to school, she had asked from the back seat about "human rights." It had become a big issue in the papers, with President Carter expounding on the subject and other statesmen jumping into the act.

He had answered that it meant freedom of the individual and the right of all to the basics of life within a community.

Again she had probed with well put questions until he had amplified that oversimplification, and they had arrived at the school with him talking about left and right-wing regimes and the meaning of democracy.

He had expected her to take up the subject on the way home, but she had remained silent.

His thoughts were interrupted by a man approaching their table. It was Vico Mansutti, who had come in with two other men.

"It's Mr. Creasy, is it not?"

Creasy introduced him to Elio and Felicia and watched him turn on the charm, white teeth gleaming beneath the wide black moustache.

"You have excellent taste," he said to Creasy. 'This is one of the best restaurants in Milan. How was your meal?"

They all agreed that it had been excellent, and with a final flash of teeth at Felicia he rejoined his companions.

A few minutes later Zagone came over to offer them a liqueur, compliments of Mr. Mansutti.

"He's charming," said Felicia, after ordering a cognac. Creasy looked at Elio and a gesture of the shoulders, very Italian and expressive, told him that they agreed about Mansutti.

"A shark," said Elio. "But a clever one. He's building a big reputation. His contacts with government and business are solid. It's also rumoured he has connections with the Mafia." He made a wry face. "But that's not unusual. These days it's hard to find the dividing lines between crime and government and business. Incidentally, there's talk that he's having an affair with your boss's wife."

Creasy was surprised. Not that Rika might be having an affair, but that she would have picked a man like Mansutti. Elio's next words offered an explanation.

"He's apparently helping Balletto arrange bank guarantees to reequip his plant. There's talk of Mansutti's personal guarantee being involved. He's very rich and it seems that Balletto Mills have a cash flow problem."

It could be the reason, Creasy thought. He couldn't see much standing in Rika's way if her lifestyle was threatened. Elio's words raised another question.

"If Balletto's tight for cash, it's unlikely that his daughter is a potential kidnap victim," Creasy said.

Elio agreed and thought it might be a social thing. "A lot of Rika's friends would have bodyguards."

"You mean I'm a social asset?" asked Creasy dryly, and Felicia laughed at the idea. But Creasy remembered his short interview with Ettore and the whole thing made sense. Ettore was keeping his wife's image burnished at a cheap price. It also explained why he was reluctant to spend money improving the security of the house. He had been pleased to find on his return from Paris that Creasy was repairing the fence and had cheerfully reimbursed him the small amount that had been spent for timber. However, when Creasy had suggested a modern chain-link fence and other measures, he had been decidedly unenthusiastic.

"Does your firm audit his books?" Creasy asked.

Elio shook his head. "No, but we hear things."

Felicia snorted. "Hear things! Accountants are the biggest gossips in the world. Worse than a bunch of housewives." She smiled at her husband. “It’s a little Mafia all its own, but they use pocket calculators instead of pistols.”

Elio nodded benignly in agreement and said to Creasy, “Perhaps she’s right. I suppose we do exchange information more freely than we should, but it’s for our own protection. Italian businessmen are very secretive, especially with the tax laws we have. An accountant’s ammunition is information — so we tend to scratch each other’s backs. Besides, it makes up for the boredom of looking at columns of figures all day.”

Zagone appeared and offered them more liqueurs, this time with his compliments, and by the time they left Felicia was slightly drunk and walked between the two men, an arm linked with each.

They paused at Mansutti’s table, and the three men stood up and exchanged introductions and pleasantries. One of Vico’s guests was an Englishman — dressed like a banker, very British in pinstripes and waistcoat. Vico made a point of telling him that Creasy was the bodyguard of the Balletto girl. “Very experienced,” he said, smiling.

Creasy felt irritation. He was a private man and didn’t like to be discussed by strangers.

Outside the restaurant Felicia kissed him on both cheeks and thanked him and made him promise that he would come to the house for a Sunday lunch in the near future.

“Yes, he’s much more relaxed,” Elio said on the phone. “I was surprised. He seems to be settling in. He even told a joke or two.”

Guido also was surprised. He hadn’t expected it to go quite that well. It was a relief. Creasy had been much on his mind,

“Does he get on with the girl?”

“He says she’s got an inquisitive nature,” Elio answered. “I suppose he tolerates her — otherwise it wouldn’t work.”

Guido said, "I can't see him tolerating her if she pesters him with questions all the time."

"Well, obviously she doesn't," Elio said thoughtfully, "but he did say she was curious about everything."

Guido thanked him for calling and for helping with Creasy, and was assured it was no problem. Elio hero-worshipped his elder brother and would do anything for him.

Guido hung up, a little mystified. An inquisitive child with a relaxed Creasy was a definite contradiction.

Perhaps Creasy was getting old. Mellowing, even. Or maybe the whisky was addling his brain. Anyway, so far, so good.

Pinta had reached an impasse. She was conscious that to move on to the next step in obtaining Creasy's friendship she needed a device. It was not enough to keep drawing him out with questions on subjects that interested him. It was not really a dialogue. She wanted to learn more about him personally — about his own life. They had reached the point when almost every day she could get him to talk — about politics or places or people. But he always remained remote himself, and she was wary of asking him personal questions.

She had quizzed her mother about his past and had learned the simple facts of his career. Rika had been reluctant at first because of the association with violence, but Pinta was adept at handling either of her parents and she extracted the information easily. Besides, Rika was proud of their bodyguard. She would tell Ettore that none of their friends had anyone who could compare. After all, Creasy had the Croix de Guerre, and many campaign medals and lots of scars and was an ex-paratrooper. Undoubtedly, Creasy was a feather in her social cap, and she was not shy about telling her friends of his past.

As a result of this, Vico brought up the subject when he next lunched with Ettore.

"How did you get him so cheap?"

"He drinks. He's an alcoholic."

Vico nodded in understanding.

"He hides it well."

"That's true, he drinks only at night, but he told me himself it affects him badly. Meanwhile, he can drive a car alright, and from outside appearances he looks competent enough." He smiled complacently and said, "It was a good investment. He's also a handyman. He likes fixing things."

He told Vico about the fence repairing and other odd jobs Creasy did about the grounds and house.

Vico grinned.

"You would have to pay a carpenter more than you pay him. And Rika is happy. I saw her in Granelli's the other day and she joined me for a cocktail afterward. She's much happier now."

"Yes," agreed Ettore, "and it shows in other ways. She spends less. With her, being unhappy leads to a lot of extravagance — I suppose to compensate. She still comes into Milan to shop quite a lot but she doesn't buy too much."

Vico nodded wisely.

"Probably spends more time window-shopping."

The two men went on to discuss business matters, Vico doing most of the talking.

So Pinta knew about Creasy's past and tried to get him to talk about it.

She had taken to dropping into the kitchen after dinner even when her parents were home, and one evening she asked about the Foreign Legion. There had been an article in the newspaper about the Legion being sent to Shaba Province in Zaire.

He told her about the Legion, how it was formed and some of its history. She decided to press a little.

"Weren't you in the Legion once?"

He looked at her sharply.

"How did you know?"

She answered innocently. "I heard my mother telling a friend on the phone, just after you arrived."

Bruno looked up from the television.

"I was in the Army once — in the war. I was captured by Montgomery in North Africa."

It was said with a touch of pride, as if Montgomery had effected the capture personally. Creasy nodded briefly and went back to his newspaper.

Bruno said, "If you were in the Legion, that makes us both old soldiers."

Creasy looked up at him and a trace of a smile touched his lips.

"Yes — both old soldiers." Then he stood up and went to his room.

Later, lying in bed, Pinta decided that a direct approach to resurrect old memories was not going to work. She could hear the music coming faintly from his room and she knew that before long she would recognize the song he always played. She knew what it was now. One afternoon while he was working on the fence she had slipped into his room and looked at the tape in the cassette player. It was always the last one he played at night. Linda Ronstadt's "Blue Bayou."

The breakthrough, when it came, was an accident, literally. Her parents were in London for a week and she was in the kitchen when Bruno came in and announced that a nightingale had nested in a bush behind the house. There were two chicks in the nest. It was barely light but she begged him to show her. The nest was high up the steep slope and, as she scrambled eagerly up, she stepped on a stone, turned her ankle and fell heavily against an outcrop of rock. Creasy was off to the left, just packing up his tools, when he heard her cry out.

She lay on her back, holding on to her side, her face twisted in pain. Bruno had scrambled down and was cushioning her head.

Creasy felt her ankle, his thick fingers surprisingly gentle. It was swelling, but he judged it was just a sprain. Then he took her hand from her side and pulled up her T-shirt. There was an abrasion just below the ribs. He carefully put his fingers on the ribs and probed very gently. She winced.

"Does it hurt badly?" he asked.

"Not so bad. It hurts more lower down."

She pointed with her chin. "I hit the rocks there." Her voice quivered as she tried not to cry.

"I think you've just bruised yourself," he said. "At least you haven't damaged your ribs."

Maria arrived, puffing up the hill in a state of high anxiety. Creasy stopped her fussing and calmed her down. He decided to take Pinta into Como for an X ray just to be sure. Maria was to stay in the house in case her parents called. He told Bruno to stay with her, as the old man's agitation would not help calm the girl. Then, being careful not to put pressure on her side, he picked her up and carried her down to the car.

Later Maria was to remember how gentle he had been, how reassuring. He could not be such a man, she thought, not as uncaring as he seemed. But in fact Creasy's attitude had been an automatic one. In his life he had frequently dealt with wounded people, often terribly wounded. The first criterion was to calm them and reassure them.

The X-rays confirmed that nothing was broken, and the doctor bound up the ankle and gave her some pills for the pain. He agreed with Creasy that she probably had some internal bruising under her ribs, but nothing serious.

Back at the house he reassured Maria and Bruno, carried the girl up to her bedroom, and left while Maria put her to bed. Then he put a call through to the Savoy Hotel in London just in case Rika or Ettore phoned while he was out of the house. Maria would certainly overdramatize.

Rika answered and he told her of Pinta's fall. No, she needn't rush back. It was only a sprain and a bruise. The child could probably go to school in the morning as usual. Yes, he could give her their love. He hung up, and then went upstairs to see that the girl was comfortable.

She was sitting propped up against two pillows. Beside her was a stuffed brown bear, very battered. He sat at the foot of the bed.

"You feel alright?"

She nodded shyly.

He looked at the bear.

"Do you always sleep with that?"

She nodded again.

"What do you call him?"

"He has no name," she replied.

Her hair was jet black against the pillow, her face very pale. The huge eyes looked at him solemnly. There was a long silence, and then he abruptly stood up. "The pills will make you sleepy. If you wake up with any pain in the night, take two more."

He reached the door and turned.

"I spoke to your mother on the phone. They send their love."

"Thank you. Good night, Creasy."

"Good night, Pinta," he said gruffly.

The pills made her feel drowsy. She switched off the light and hugged the bear and was soon asleep. She had lied to him. It did have a name.

In London, when Ettore returned to the hotel Rika told him of the phone call. He was in a rush to get ready for dinner with his agent and she stood at the bathroom door while he showered.

"You don't want to go back?" he asked. "There's a night flight to Milan."

She shook her head. "Creasy said she's alright."

His hand groped for the shampoo and she moved to give him the bottle.

"It's nice, isn't it," she said.

"What's nice?" he asked, lathering his hair.

"Having a man like that in the house while we're away. Maria would have panicked and I would have felt obliged to hurry back. And tonight's dinner is important, no?"

He turned up his face to the wide stream of water pouring down from the huge, old-fashioned shower head. It was one of the reasons he liked the Savoy. Their bathrooms were bigger than most hotels' bedrooms, and the fittings matched the size.

"Yes," he agreed, stepping out and enveloping himself in a huge white heated towel. "Very important. Roy Haynes is excited about the new range, and if he decides to promote it we could have a very good season here." He moved to the basin and started to shave, draped in the towel like a Roman senator. She moved behind him and rubbed the towel against his back and shoulders.

"Promote it how?"

"In the press and at shows. They do it very well. But it costs a lot and he has to have confidence. I will press at dinner tonight." He looked at her face in the mirror and she smiled at him.

"Leave the pressing to me. I'll be very subtle."

He smiled back and continued shaving. Yes, Creasy was a good investment.

They ate in Parkes, in Beauchamp Place. Ettore refused to eat Italian food in London. Not that there was a lack of good Italian restaurants, but, when he travelled, he liked to vary his diet.

Also, Parkes with its fresh flowers on the huge plates was a favourite of Rika's.

Roy Haynes was another favourite, the kind of Englishman she liked. Big and bluff and well-travelled. It was no hardship turning her full powers of persuasion on him. He sat, eating and smiling, fully aware of her motives. He had already decided to give Balletto's line a big promotion and tomorrow he would give Ettore a large order, almost twice the value of last season's. In the meantime he kept his counsel and let the lovely woman opposite flatter and charm him. After dinner he would take them to one of London's elegant gambling clubs, and before they left for their hotel he would be won over and give them the good news.

For Rika, such evenings were what life was all about. She felt useful and appreciated.

In the early hours of the next morning, lying in bed between the crisp, starched, linen sheets, she looked back on a well spent day, shopping at Harrod's in the morning and on Bond Street in the afternoon. Her hair done at Sassoon's, followed by tea and ridiculously thin cucumber sandwiches at the hotel. Then Creasy's phone call of reassurance, the delicious dinner and good company, and the gambling afterward. Even that had gone well, her favourite roulette numbers, 17 and 20, favouring her in turn. Finally Roy Haynes saying good night and, as an afterthought, mentioning to Ettore that at tomorrow afternoon's meeting he would be greatly increasing his order and would fully promote the new line.

She stretched languorously. Yes, a day and a night well spent, the only slight cloud being that Ettore had drunk a little too much, and had not been up to the lovemaking that had just ended. Never mind. Before he got up in the morning, that would be remedied. At the thought of the morning, her mind clicked awake. With Creasy's phone call and everything else, she had forgotten. She turned and shook Ettore, who was almost asleep.

"*Caro* — I forgot. A man called you about an appointment tomorrow. He said eleven a.m. in his office." She snuggled up against him. "What's it about?"

"Just a financial matter," he answered sleepily. "He's a friend of Vico's."

"Is it important?"

He mumbled something inaudible and moments later was asleep.

Pinta hobbled down the front steps to the car and Creasy opened the back door. She hesitated and said, "I think I'll sit in the front. There's more room for my foot."

As they drove out the gates, he asked, "Did you sleep alright?"

"Yes. Those pills did make me sleepy. I only woke up once, when I turned over."

"Does the ankle hurt? Can you put your weight on it?"

"It's not bad," she answered. "Will it take long before it's better? — School sports day is in five weeks and I want to run in the hundred metres."

"There should be time," he said. "Don't favour it too much. Put as much weight on it as you can. In a week or two, you won't notice it."

When they reached the main Milan road he asked, "Are you fast?"

She nodded. "But I'm no good at starts. By the time I catch up, it's too late."

"You should practice more."

She nodded. "I will."

Creasy didn't know much about the technique of sprint starts, but he knew all about coordination and reaction time. He knew that he could teach her, but then he caught himself. Enough was enough.

"Well, just walk on that foot as much as you can. Even if it hurts a bit."

They lapsed into silence.

The girl's attitude had changed. It was no longer just a game — trying to get Creasy's friendship. She desperately wanted it. There was an accumulated effect. With her natural curiosity and awareness, she had caught tiny glimpses of the man inside. She wanted to see more and to give something. She had never seen him smile. Always stern — always remote. She believed that, if he opened up, something wonderful would appear. It was no longer just curiosity. She felt a link with him, tenuous but definite. She desperately wanted to build on that link.

In fact, the impetus had already shifted. It was Creasy now who would let it happen. Not consciously, but not fighting it. He too felt the link. It disturbed him, because he couldn't understand it. The idea of him with an eleven-year-old girl as a friend was about as likely as a rabbit getting on with a fox. He couldn't accept it, so tried not to think about it. But he couldn't banish her from his mind and found himself not wanting to.

That afternoon, driving home, she asked him about the discovery of America. They had been learning about it in school and she was fascinated that an Italian had discovered it first.

"Not necessarily," he told her. "Some people believe that the Vikings came first, or even an Irish monk."

This started a discussion about explorers and he told her of Marco Polo and his journeys to China. She knew a little but was avidly interested to learn more, and this prompted Creasy to do something totally out of character. A couple of days later he brought a package down to dinner and passed it to her across the kitchen table. It was a book describing Marco Polo's journeys.

"I noticed it in a shop in Milan," he said.

In fact he had searched an hour before finding it.

"For me? It's a present?" Her eyes were shining in excitement.

"Well, it's for you." He was uncomfortable, and it showed. "You seemed interested. He's Italy's most famous explorer — you should know about him."

'Thank you, Creasy," she said softly. She guessed she had broken through.

But it was not until the following Sunday that she knew for certain.

"He brought her to lunch."

"He did what?"

"Brought her to lunch. At the house — today. They just left."

Guido held the phone away from his ear and looked at Pietro across the kitchen and slowly shook his head.

"What is it?" asked the boy, smiling at his boss's startled expression.

Guido ignored him and said into the phone, "Just like that — just turned up."

Elio laughed at the other end.

"No, he was supposed to come anyway, but he rang up this morning and said that her parents had been delayed getting back from London, so he had to cancel. Felicia suggested he bring her along and he said OK. Felicia almost passed out!"

"What's she like?" asked Guido.

There was a long pause while Elio considered.

"She's full of life," he said. "A beautiful child, polite and intelligent, and she worships that big, ugly friend of yours."

"And him — how does he react?"

There was another pause, and then Elio said, "It's very strange. He's sort of stern and gruff with her. He doesn't show much — you know what he's like — but it's more than just toleration. Of course, Felicia, being a woman, thinks that he sees her as the child he never had."

"He talks to her?" Guido asked, full of curiosity.

Elio laughed. "Certainly, he explains things, she's full of questions about everything. She sees him as a sort of oracle. Wait a minute, here's Felicia, she's been putting the kids to bed."

Felicia talked to Guido for a long time.

Creasy had changed, she told him. He was definitely fond of the child. Bemused, perhaps, and not really understanding, but she thought he liked it. Anyway, the girl was adorable. With anyone else it would be natural. They were surprised only because it was Creasy.

Guido agreed. It was totally unexpected. After all the years they had been together, he found it hard to believe that a child could break through that crust. There had never been an indication. But later, after ringing off, Guido thought about it some more. Perhaps Creasy had finally lowered his guard.

Guido was happy for his friend. He wondered where it would lead. Whether the mellowing would continue.

CHAPTER SEVEN

"Creasy — what's a concubine?"

He took his eyes off the road and glanced at her, no longer surprised by the content of her questions.

"A sort of wife."

She was astonished. "A sort of wife! But the Emperor of China had over one thousand. How can that be?"

He found that it was not a delicate subject. In spite of her youth, she was mentally mature. The book he had given her on Marco Polo had prompted several similar questions. She did not giggle and act girlish when he explained that many cultures were not monogamous. He told her of the religions of Islam and the Mormons, and was quietly amused that her sympathies lay with the man.

"It must be difficult, having a lot of wives," she said thoughtfully. Perhaps she was thinking of her mother. One of Rika was as much as any man could comfortably handle. The thought of her multiplied a thousandfold staggered the mind.

Creasy always answered her questions fully and spoke as he would to an adult. He didn't have the artifice to talk down to her. He often found her responses provocative. It was his first exposure to a fresh and unconditioned mind. He found himself viewing controversial issues through her eyes, and it was stimulating.

She didn't like to watch political broadcasts on television because the politicians talked too much and didn't smile naturally. Religion was good, but the priests were always right and enjoyed it too much. She loved school, but was only good at the subjects when she liked the teachers. She was fond of Maria and Bruno, but they exasperated her because they weren't interested in things.

In short, the whole world was a vast, unexplored, and fascinating territory. She had the perception to understand that she was placing her foot on the first step of discovery. Creasy became her guide. Her mother lived in her own limited world and her father treated her very much as a child, and this was reflected in his manner and conversation.

So Creasy was a revelation and she quickly realized the importance of not just listening to him but of commenting on what he had to say. So she always responded, and after a while a dialogue developed that scanned two opposite backgrounds and several generations.

The watershed had been the Sunday lunch with Elio and Felicia. She knew that Creasy had opened the door, and she passed gratefully through.

It was acceptance, and she had been happy but careful, responding slowly at first to Elio and Felicia and constantly looking to Creasy for a lead. But he had been relaxed and unconcerned, not like a parent, but like someone who had brought a friend to meet friends. So she too had relaxed and played with the children and helped Felicia in the kitchen and joined her in teasing the men. It had been a wonderful day, and since then she had been easy with Creasy, understanding him and opening him up with a delicate mental crowbar. He even started answering questions about himself. She first asked about Guido. The two men had talked of him over lunch. She learned of their friendship and the years they had been together. She noticed that when Creasy talked of Guido, the hard lines of his face softened. She decided she would like to know him.

For Creasy, it was a catharsis. He found talking to Pinta easy. Maybe it was her lack of knowledge and experience. Maybe her uncluttered mind. But he talked and felt better for it. Even the bad things, the pain of war, the brutalizing. She had led the way, consciously, as if it were a test. Driving home from that lunch, she had reached out and touched one of his hands.

"Creasy, what happened to your hands?"

He hadn't jerked away as before but glanced down at the mottled scars, and his mind went back to 1954 and the end at Dien Bien Phu. Surrender, humiliation, and then three weeks of forced marching to a P.O.W. camp. Every day dragging one foot after the other. Little food and much death. When a man fell and couldn't get up, the guards shot him. Many fell, but Creasy stayed up and survived and carried a young wounded officer on his back. After survival, interrogation. The suave, Sorbonne educated, Viet Minh captain sitting small and immaculate across the wooden table from the huge, gaunt Legionnaire. The questions, the many questions, and the shake of his head to denote refusal to answer. The Vietnamese captain chain-smoking and always the Gauloise cigarettes being stubbed out on the backs of Creasy's strapped down hands.

"A man once asked me questions. He smoked a lot. There was no ashtray."

She understood immediately and was long silent. Tears filled her eyes.

He glanced at her.

"Bad things happen in the world. I told you that, once."

She smiled through the tears.

"Good things happen, too."

After that she was free with personal questions, but she learned only sparsely of his youth. His parents, poor and crushed by the Depression. A small holding in Tennessee — barely enough to eat. Joining the Marines at the earliest possible age. Korea — the recognizing of a talent for fighting. Striking an officer who had been stupid and let good men die — disgrace, and nowhere to go back to. So then the Legion and all that followed.

Apart from Guido, this eleven-year-old child learned more about Creasy than anyone on earth.

Rika was radiant. Spring had arrived and lightened her life. Creasy was definitely a factor. She talked to her friends about her "gem." Told them how fond he was of Pinta. The big shambling bear with the puppy gambolling along behind. She didn't recognize the profound change in him. To her, he was still silent and remote and mysterious. Pinta had tamed him, she said to Ettore, and he had nodded in acquiescence. He didn't see Creasy as more than an adjunct to his life. Useful in that Pinta and, more importantly, Rika were happy; but still just an employee — poorly paid, and with a secret drinking problem.

But the drink had ceased to be a big problem. Now, most nights, Creasy would consume less than half a bottle. The need to blot out the mind was eased. He had never been an alcoholic in the clinical sense. It was not an addiction, and although its accumulated effect still conditioned him and slowed him, his mind had sharpened again. Also, he was mentally preparing to get his body back into shape. It had started with Pinta and the forthcoming sports meeting. As soon as her ankle healed, Creasy knocked up a pair of starting blocks and set them into the front lawn. Then, with Pinta in a blue and white track suit, they worked on her starts. Creasy told her about reaction time. "Your ears hear the bang of the starting gun and pass the message to your brain; then your brain sends out a message to the nerves in your legs and arms. This message says GO. The secret is to cut down the time needed for sending those messages."

He taught her how to concentrate on the sound itself. Not to consciously listen for it or anticipate it. When the bang came, her reaction must be automatic.

He simulated the starting gun by clapping his hands, and after an afternoon's practice she was coming up out of the blocks like a startled deer. Every day, he told her — every day we practise for an hour, and on the big day, you will win.

That night he lay in bed listening to Johnny Cash and thinking about the girl. She was so alive, so quick, her body tuned and fit. It made him think of himself. He decided that after the three months, when he was confirmed in the job, he would locate a gym in Como or Milan and spend a couple of evenings a week getting fit. If he left it too much longer, it would be too late. He recognized what the girl had done to him. A vacuum was filled. In a way he had changed his course. She had a life in front of her. He would watch her develop. Play a part in her moving mind. There were no deaths, no destruction, no mutilation — it was not futile.

Johnny Cash finished and he reached out and changed the tape.

Linda Ronstadt sang "Blue Bayou"; and downstairs Pinta smiled as she heard the music.

Rika came out of the hairdresser's and looked around for the car. It was a dull, overcast day and the Milan traffic was heavy. She spotted the car parked about thirty metres away, Creasy standing beside it. As she walked toward him, a flurry of movement across the street caught her eye: two men jumping from the side door of a Volkswagen van. They ran toward a man unlocking the door of a white Fiat. She saw the guns in their hands and as the first shots rang out, she came to a stunned halt. The man had turned, reaching under his jacket, and then Creasy reached her, an arm coming around her waist, sweeping her off her feet into a shop doorway.

She found herself on the pavement under his heavy body. More shots, and she screamed as glass shattered above them. She saw the gun in Creasy's hand, held low down by his side. Sounds — the slamming of the van door and the squeal of tires and a racing engine and finally silence.

"Wait here, don't move." His voice was calm, flat, and positive. The weight eased off her as he stood up, carefully backing away so that glass didn't fall on her. She lay still, watching, as he walked back to the car. His gun had disappeared. He stood by the car looking across the street. Her eyes followed. A man lay across the bonnet of the Fiat — red blood on the white metal. Instinctively she knew he was dead. He lay that way. Creasy opened the back door of the car and walked back to her. He put down a hand and helped her up. She was unsteady, but he put an arm round her and walked her slowly to the car. People were moving again. A woman was sobbing in shock. A siren sounded, wailing closer. He put her into the back seat.

"Stay in there. It will take some time. The police will put up roadblocks and ask questions all around."

She was shivering slightly, her face very white against her black hair. He reached forward and put the back of his hand against her cheek. It was cold. He cupped her chin and raised her face, looking into her eyes. They were dull — glazed.

"Are you alright? Rika, look at me!"

Her eyes focused, and she nodded slowly. A police car had arrived, its rhythmic light flashing, its siren dying. Excited voices, and more sirens homing in. She nodded again, her mind functioning.

"Stay here," he said. "I'll talk to the police. We'll leave as soon as possible." He looked at her closely, then, satisfied, closed the door and walked across the street.

It had been a Red Brigade killing, the victim a prosecuting attorney. Not an unusual event in Milan. Creasy showed the police his bodyguard's licence and told them what he had seen, which was not much. He gave them a description of the two gunmen that could have fitted a hundred thousand youths in the city. Also the number plate of the Volkswagen, which was certainly stolen.

Half an hour later he drove out of the suburbs toward Como with a silent Rika in the back seat. They were halfway home when she suddenly burst out:

"Animals! Shooting people down in the street — Animals!"

The shoulders in front of her shrugged.

"You had the gun in your hand," she said. "I saw it. Why didn't you shoot them?"

"Nothing to do with me — or you," he answered shortly. "Besides, apart from the driver, there was another one in the front of the van. He had a sawed off shotgun. If I'd started shooting at his friends, he would have blasted us. As it was, we were lucky. The victim got off one shot. It passed only a couple of feet over us."

That silenced her for ten minutes. He watched her in the rear-view mirror. Her private world had been invaded. Violence had leapt off the television screen and slapped her in the face. He saw her visibly compose herself, relate again to her own world. She leaned forward and picked a tiny shard of glass from his hair.

"You were so fast, Creasy. I never saw you coming — thank God you were there."

He pulled in through the gates and up to the front door.

"I need a brandy," she said, stepping out. "A big one. Come on in."

"Pinta," he said, staying at the wheel.

"Pinta?"

"It's quarter to five."

"Oh, of course. That thing made me forget. Go ahead. I'll see you later."

She stood at the foot of the steps and watched as he reversed the car and drove off. Then she went in and poured the large brandy. Shock wore off, and she re-enacted the scene in her mind. The sudden sharp movement — the sounds — breaking glass and the weight of Creasy lying over her. His stillness. The copper taste of fear in her mouth. Creasy so sure — so calm. Later she would phone Ettore in Rome and tell him about it. And then some of their friends. It was an event — the bodyguard justified. He had been so unaffected — looking at the dead man without expression or emotion. He had seen it all so often. She remembered his hand against her face, cupping her chin. The scarred hand — Pinta had told her how. The heavy eyes studying her — steadying her. She poured another brandy and sipped it slowly. She would not call Ettore tonight. The morning would be soon enough.

He had not been fast — far from it. At least not by his standards. He lay in bed thinking about it. He didn't play a cassette and he wasn't drinking. Part of his mind was waiting, part analysing. He decided that if Rika had been the target, she would now be dead. A time ago he could have picked off the man with the shotgun and the two on foot before they had gone five paces. They were novices. Determined amateurs. The victim had got off a shot; a wild one, but the terrorists had been lucky. They should have done the job with the shotgun and never left the van. Both barrels from ten metres would have been totally positive — amateurs.

But still he had been slow. His reactions dull.

Rika would have been dead.

It decided him. All his life he had considered his body as a weapon. Cared for it as he cared for his other weapons. Nursed it back from injury. Exercised all the parts and kept it responsive to his brain. Now it would be difficult. Unlike a gun, he couldn't take a cleaning rag to it, burnish it up, lubricate the moving parts. The whole thing had to be rebuilt, and slowly. It would be a long and painful process. He didn't look unfit — was barely overweight. Only Guido, who had known him in earlier days, could discern it — the slackness and the lack of muscle tone. A fine machine rusted and neglected. It would take months. Carefully at first, ten minutes of circuit training in his room every morning, stepping up the tempo. Then sessions in a gym, using weights and bars. It would come back. It was not too late. He had caught it just in time.

It was after midnight when the soft tap came on the door. The waiting had ended. She wore a nightdress, white and long, and she carried, cradled in her hand, a large goblet of cognac. Silk rustled as she crossed the room. The cognac was proffered and he took it with a touch of fingers. She sat on the bed and watched as he sipped. The sheet came to his waist and she studied his face and upper body, then reached out and traced a finger down the scar on his shoulder. She picked up his free hand and placed it against her cheek, pressing against it, moving her head gently, ebony hair swaying. He put the glass on the bedside table and moved his hand behind her neck pulling her towards him. The kiss was long — searching.

She stood and the white silk slipped to the floor. She showed herself to him, standing just out of reach. Not evocative, not posing, just showing. This is my body, look at it; I'm going to give it to you. A gift — a gift that only I can give.

The single, shaded light fell on her softly. Long and full and curved. Perfect proportion from the bell of hair to points of colour at eyes and wide, full mouth. Soft shadow in the cleft chin, curved strong neck. His eyes passed down, unhurried, appreciating. More shadows under high breasts, nipples erect, a young girl's waist, and then the sweep out. Shadowed triangle above long symmetry of leg.

She stood absolutely still, her eyes never leaving his face as he took her in.

He understood at that moment. Understood how any man could be captured and drugged by such beauty. It saturated the mind.

He looked up again into her eyes and she moved back to him. Still standing — but close. He ran a hand slowly down from her waist to the soft flesh behind her knee. Her skin trembled slightly at the contact.

She moved again, sitting on the bed, pulling away the sheet. Her turn to look. Again she traced a scar with her finger — from his knee almost to the groin; and then the black hair swung down and her mouth and tongue followed the finger and moved higher. It was sudden. His breath forced out as moist warmth took him in.

A hand came up over his chest to his face and mouth. Long fingers felt his lips and probed between them.

He felt the cool air as she lifted her head and slid up beside him. Her mouth joined her fingers, her tongue moved alongside them. She raised her head now and looked into his eyes, hair falling to the pillow, darkening her face, and his. She positioned herself and lowered, never shifting her gaze. Moist warmth again, like her mouth: but different. So slowly — first contact; just joining, pausing; and then the warmth moving down and clamping tight, and the soft belly against his and her release of breath, and pleasure, and breasts moving on his chest, and rippling tremors.

For a while he was passive — receptive. Then his arms came around her, one over her shoulders, holding her tight, the other lower, to her undulating bottom, resting lightly — shaping the curve, steadying the rhythm. Then he twisted, holding her close and pulling her under him.

Now she closed her eyes. Senses lost. She had wanted to control. To lead. But that had gone. She felt his mouth on her face, on her closed eyes and then her lips. A quickening of movement and breathing. His grip tightened. Instinct told her he was near. She wanted it to be together and thrust up to him. She would be late. She felt the spasms in him. Her back arched, and she opened her eyes and above her, inches away, saw the dull blue grip of the pistol jutting from its oiled holster and she came to the top suddenly, shuddering against him and together.

They lay for a long time — no words. Just feeling. Mostly his hands over her. Feeling and moulding like a blind man seeing with his fingers. Occasionally he kissed her face, tracing its contours with his lips.

She rose at first light, picking the silk nightdress up from the floor. She looked down at his sleeping face and shivered slightly and slipped on the nightdress. She would not come again. In the night she had felt like a child, giving away her will, all her emotions. It frightened her.

And she knew he wouldn't call her. Would not need to. Since she had entered the room, they had not spoken a word.

"Why don't we use your gun?"

"Because it's not that kind of gun."

They were driving to Como. Creasy had decided that more realism was needed in her training. Clapping his hands was no substitute for the real thing. They would try to find a sports shop that stocked starting pistols or, failing that, a toy shop that had cap guns.

"But it makes a bang, doesn't it," she persisted.

"Yes," he said. "And it also fires a bullet."

"But you could aim into the air."

"Pinta, what goes up must come down, and a bullet dropping from over a mile could be dangerous."

She saw the logic in that and turned her attention to the local newspaper. She was looking for an advertisement for a sports shop. Instead she came across the horoscopes.

"What's your sign, Creasy?"

He looked puzzled.

"Your stars. When is your birthday?"

"April fifteenth."

"April fifteenth! But that's in a few days!" She calculated. "On Sunday!"

He shrugged, uninterested, but she was at an age when birthdays were exciting.

"It's the day after the sports meeting. I'll ask Maria to make a cake. How old will you be?"

He turned to her sternly.

"You will tell Maria nothing. No fuss. I'm past the age when birthdays are a cause for celebration."

"But we must do something. Mummy and Daddy will be away." An idea came to her. "What about a picnic? We could drive up into the Alps."

"Alright. But only if you win on Saturday."

"Creasy, that's not fair."

"It will give you an extra incentive. No win, no picnic."

She smiled. "OK. I'll win anyway."

"After all this effort," he growled, "you better!"

Her parents were in New York and Pinta was greatly disappointed. To be fair, Rika felt guilty, but she knew that Ettore needed her on this important trip. And there would be other sports days.

So when Creasy parked in the school courtyard, Pinta asked: "Will you come and watch, Creasy? Please."

He hesitated. There would be a lot of parents around, and he would be out of place, perhaps unwelcome.

'It will be alright," she pleaded. "Nobody will mind."

He looked at her anxious face and nodded and got out of the car.

It obviously was a social occasion. A big, striped marquee had been set up and parents were standing around, richly dressed and with drinks in their hands.

Pinta ran off to change and Creasy stood off to one side, feeling uncomfortable. He spotted Signora Deluca approaching and his discomfort increased.

"It's Mr. Creasy, isn't it?" she asked with a smile.

He nodded and explained about Pinta's parents being away. She was sympathetic.

"It's only natural that a child should want her parents along on a day like this."

She took his arm. "Never mind. Today you are a surrogate father. Come and have a drink. The hundred metres doesn't start for half an hour."

She took Creasy into the marquee and gave him a cold beer and introduced him to one or two parents. He still felt uncomfortable and was relieved when everyone moved off to watch the first events.

It was a warm spring day, and the girls, many of them maturing, were an attractive sight in their tiny running shorts. Creasy looked on approvingly. But when Pinta appeared for the start of the hundred metres, he didn't see her in the same light.

Many others did. She was the most beautiful and vivacious girl on the field, but to Creasy she was simply a child and a friend.

He watched critically as they prepared for the start, and felt a twinge of anxiety. He willed the girl to do well.

He need not have worried. The training had paid off. She left the blocks well ahead of the others and broke the tape five yards clear.

She continued running to where he stood and threw her arms around his neck.

"I won, Creasy! I won!"

He smiled down at her proudly.

"You did well. No one else was in it."

For Pinta, it rounded off a perfect day — it was the first time she had seen him smile.

"Happy birthday, Creasy."

He was laying the tartan blanket out on the grass and looked up in surprise.

She held out the small package.

"What's this?"

"A birthday present."

"I told you no fuss."

She plumped down on the blanket.

"It's just to say thank you for helping me win the race."

He put the package down and went to the car to get the picnic hamper. He was confused — not used to saying thank you. He remembered now that Pinta had gone shopping with her mother in Milan earlier in the week. She must have bought it then. He hoped it wasn't something expensive or silly. He didn't know how to pretend and say the right things.

The package lay untouched as Pinta opened the hamper. She was in tune and recognized his mood. Maria had taken trouble over the picnic lunch, and Pinta exclaimed in delight as she unwrapped it all. There was a cold roast chicken, eggs wrapped in veal and ham in the Florentine style, and small flat pizza called *gardenera*; crusty bread with pepper cheese, a selection of fruit, and finally two bottles of dry white wine, heavily wrapped in newspaper and still chilled.

They had picked a spot above Lake Maggiore. It was high summer grazing land studded with clumps of pines. Away to the north and west, snow-capped mountains rose ever higher toward

Switzerland. In front of them, to the south, the Po Valley swept away to the horizon.

Soon the blanket was scattered with plastic plates and tinfoil. Creasy poured wine into two beakers.

"A votre santé."

"What does it mean?"

"It's French. It means "Cheers."'

"*Yamsing*," she replied, and laughed at his look of surprise. "It's Chinese."

"I know, but how . . . ?" and then he remembered the book on Marco Polo. She absorbed everything.

They talked about different languages and he told her a joke.

A Texan went to Europe for the first time, travelling by sea on the steamship *France*. The first night out, the chief steward put him at a dinner table with a Frenchman who spoke no English. When the food arrived, the Frenchman said: "*Bon appétit*" and the Texan, assuming he was introducing himself, replied, "Harvey Granger."

The next morning at breakfast the Frenchman again said, "*Bon appétit*." The surprised Texan again replied, "Harvey Granger." This went on at every meal for the next five days.

On the last night out the Texan was having a drink in the bar before dinner and struck up a conversation with another American.

"Strange people, these French," remarked the Texan.

"How so?"

The Texan told how he'd met the Frenchman at least a dozen times and that he always introduced himself.

"What's his name?"

"*Bon appétit*."

The American laughed and explained that that wasn't the Frenchman's name. He was merely wishing him a good appetite.

The Texan was very embarrassed and, when he sat down for dinner that night, he smiled at the Frenchman and said, "*Bon appétit*."

The Frenchman beamed back and replied, "Harvey Granger."

The girl laughed and clapped her hands, and Creasy reached out, picked up the package, and unwrapped it. Inside was a small box, and as he opened it, Pinta's laughter stilled as she waited for his reaction.

It was a solid gold crucifix on a thin, finely wrought gold chain, and he knew why she had given it to him. They had talked once about religion. For him, it was a subject of massive contradiction. His parents had been Catholics, and he had been raised in that faith. His mother, like Guido's, had been fatalistic. God would provide — God hadn't. The grinding poverty had finally condemned his mother.

Ill with pneumonia, with no money to pay for adequate attention, she had died. A year later his father followed, in his case the passing eased by alcohol. Creasy, aged fourteen, had been taken in by neighbours and used in the fields as the cheapest form of labour. At sixteen he ran away and a year later had joined the Marines.

That early experience, followed by a lifetime of war, had not brought him to God. He could not fathom a Supreme Being so disinterested as to allow millions of innocents to die in all the wars he had seen.

A baby roasted in napalm could not have been punished for a sin. A young girl, endlessly raped, could call upon God and hear nothing. A sadist could torture a priest to death and live to a ripe age. Then to be consigned to hell? After spending a lifetime creating hell for others — for innocents? Creasy could not see the logic of it.

But he had seen the hierarchy of it, the panoply and wealth. He had been in the Philippines when the Pope visited. The biggest

Catholic country in Asia and perhaps the poorest. Beautiful churches set in a sea of poverty. The bishops of the area had convened in Manila to meet the Pope. Creasy had flown to Hong Kong a few days later, and a half a dozen bishops had travelled homewards on the same plane. They sat in first class and drank champagne. There was no logic to it.

But also there was no logic to the other side of the coin. He had seen missionaries, in the Congo and Vietnam, who had worked a lifetime for no material reward, who had never tasted champagne. He remembered driving with Guido to a mission hospital outside Leopoldville. They informed the four Belgian nuns that they must leave. The *simbas* were coming within twenty-four hours. They could not be protected. The nuns had refused. Their duty was to stay with their patients. Creasy pressed them hard, finally describing graphically what they could expect. They stayed. One of them had been young and attractive. As he sat in the Land Rover, reluctant to drive away, he beckoned her over. You will suffer the worst, he had told her. You will suffer long and then you will die. He had seen fear deep in her eyes, and also resolve. "Go with God," she had said, and smiled at him serenely.

Their unit had been forced to retreat, and it was a week before they had regrouped and fought their way back. He and Guido had been the first to reach the hospital. A generation of viewing barbarity had not prepared them for what they saw that day.

They had taken spades and dug a grave and tipped what was left into it. Later that day they caught up with the *simbas* and Creasy had killed more than his share, many more — long into the night. Guido had driven the Land Rover while Creasy manned the mounted machine gun. Perhaps he killed more than had raped and mutilated the young nun. Who knows? God's will? God's revenge?

Logic? Where was it? He had heard the argument that faith must be tested. But who was doing the testing? The bishops with champagne? Officials at the Vatican?

But some met the test. So could they all be fools? He had met enough to know that intellect and faith could go together, but he didn't understand how.

He had tried to tell Pinta some of this, how he saw the contradictions. She had surprised him.

You can never know, she had said. If you know for sure, you don't need faith.

Yes — the ultimate contradiction. The faith to be ignorant.

She had a very simple and uncomplicated view herself. She would believe until someone proved, beyond doubt, that it was all a load of rubbish. "And how will you know if it's proved?" he had asked. She had smiled at him impishly and answered: "It will be announced on television!"

"I bought it myself, with my own money," she said. "I saved it."

He didn't say anything, just looked at her.

"It can't hurt, can it?" she asked with a smile. "At least keep it until the announcement."

Now he smiled back, and lifted the chain and dropped it over his neck.

"Thank you." He reached out a hand to her shoulder and squeezed it and said, "I suddenly feel very holy."

She laughed and jumped up.

"If you ever meet the devil, Creasy, you must hold it up in front of you."

He smiled wryly. It would make a change from holding a machine gun.

A tinkling of bells intruded and a herd of cows came over the rise, being driven to the upper pastures. They moved toward the picnic spot and a dog bounded ahead to investigate.

Pinta offered a piece of ham in friendship, and it was gratefully accepted. She ran off with the dog to play while Creasy poured the herder a beaker of wine.

It was an afternoon to be remembered. The two men sat, talking casually, with the cows grazing around them and the girl and dog chasing each other among the herd.

"You have a fine girl," the herder remarked, and was puzzled at the look that crossed Creasy's face.

At sunset they packed the hamper and walked back to the car in the twilight.

The fresh air and exercise had made Pinta drowsy, and as the car wound down the hills toward Como she yawned and slipped lower in her seat. Finally she tucked up her legs and rested her head on Creasy's lap.

He drove home very slowly; occasionally glancing down at the girl's sleeping face. In the fading light his scarred features and brooding eyes were relaxed in rare contentment. He was at peace.

CHAPTER EIGHT

The day of the piano lesson.

It had become fashionable in Milanese society for parents to develop their children's musical talents — if they had any. Rika couldn't picture Pinta playing a trumpet or a flute. It had to be the piano.

An appointment was made with an eminent teacher and Creasy drove her to the all-important lesson. If the eminent teacher declared that Pinta had even a glimmer of talent, a piano would be purchased and regular lessons would start.

Pinta was not enthusiastic. Neither was Creasy. The thought of listening to the girl fumbling through her exercises was not pleasant.

Still, it was only a small cloud on the horizon. He had cut down his drinking to virtually nothing, merely taking a glass or two of wine at meals. He had started the morning exercises and had located a small gym in Como that stayed open late into the evening. The fence around the property was now repaired, and he would concentrate on getting fit.

His mood would have been less sanguine had he overheard a conversation between Rika and Ettore soon after their return from New York.

"He must go, Ettore, and quickly. I insist!"

"But why, *Cara*, after you were so pleased with him?"

There were two reasons, both genuine, but she could explain only one.

"She is getting too fond of him — to the exclusion of everything else."

"You don't think there's anything sinister to it?"

She shook her head. "Not in that way. It's mental — he looks on her as a friend." She paused for effect. "And she looks on him as a father."

"That's ridiculous."

"It's not. It's been developing, I just haven't noticed it before. Oh, I've known she's been fond of him, but since we got back this time it's become so obvious."

Ettore thought about it and said, "You exaggerate. Certainly she's fond of him. She's with him a lot, and perhaps we have been away too much — but as a father?"

Rika sighed. "Ettore, you have always been distant with her. Too distant. You never really talk to her. I wouldn't have believed it, but Creasy does, and she responds. She looks up to him, respects him. She begrudges every minute that she's not with him. God! She can't wait for dinner to end so she can run into the kitchen."

He had to admit the truth of it. He was made uncomfortable by the realization — found wanting.

"I've just been so busy, Rika, and when I get home I like to relax, not listen to a lot of childish chatter."

She sighed again. He really didn't know his daughter.

"I understand, darling, but you're going to have to make an effort, and if you listen to her you will find she's not so childish. She's very intelligent. Beyond her years."

Rika had started thinking about the problem when Pinta had bought the crucifix for Creasy's birthday. She had dragged her mother from shop to shop until she found just the one she wanted. It had seemed a strange present for such a man, and Rika had said so. Pinta had laughed.

"I know, Mama, it's exactly the opposite of what he might expect, but Creasy bear is a strange man. He will understand."

Rika had suddenly seen Creasy as a threat to Ettore. A double threat. One through Pinta and the other through herself. For that night with Creasy had lit a fuse. It had been several days before she caught herself remembering how she had felt, standing in the dawn light, looking down at him asleep. It hadn't only been the physical love, the deep satisfying. She had known that before, known it with Ettore and others. It had been the other effect, the losing herself. Losing the fine control. With Ettore and others, she had given and accepted pleasure. Measured it, even. With Creasy on that night she had given up more. Every day the memory had become more vivid. His body, his hands on her, the absorption of her will. The moment when she opened her eyes and the only thing in her vision had been the gun hanging over her and the only feeling his hardness spurting into her. Vision and feeling had been blended and confused. And more — the aftermath, when she lay in his arms and for so long a time her mind had been lost, while his hands moved on her, possessed her.

It had been on her mind in New York, and when they returned and she saw Creasy again, she knew that the danger was real. As she made love to Ettore that night she couldn't wrench her mind away from the man upstairs. The blunt fingers, the scars, and the blue black gun hanging by his head.

But she couldn't talk of that. Only of Pinta. She had never thought about her daughter's feelings for Ettore. There had been no one else before with whom to make a comparison. But seeing the girl with Creasy, she could recognize the depth of feeling in the child. If it wasn't channelled from Creasy to Ettore soon, it would be too late.

"So, *Caro*, he must go — immediately."

"Well," Ettore said reflectively, "the three-month trial ends in another week. I just won't confirm the position. That possibility was understood when I hired him."

She was strangely agitated.

"No, Ettore. Don't wait. Tell him tomorrow. Of course you must pay for the full time and also give him a good bonus. It's not his fault."

"Another week won't make any difference," he said reasonably. "And I don't want to create a bad feeling."

She started to insist, bringing her will to bear, even suggesting that, as an excuse, they could take Pinta to Rome for a few days, and then he could reasonably leave before the three months were fully up.

But Ettore had been firm. Another disruption at school would be bad for her.

They argued heatedly, Ettore reminding her that it was her original paranoia that had created the whole problem. Finally, for once, she had to give way. He would tell Creasy at the end of the week.

"It will be a hard break," he had commented.

Rika shrugged. "She's young — she'll get over it."

His reply was, for once, perceptive and also in character. "I wasn't thinking of Pinta."

Sublimely unaware, Creasy drove Pinta to her piano lesson. They talked of the coming Sunday. Creasy was going to Elio's again for lunch, and Pinta wanted to come along.

"Your parents are home. You should be with them."

"But I want to see Elio and Felicia again and the children."

He gently argued her out of it. There would be plenty of other opportunities. Her parents were away a lot.

He had difficulty locating the teacher's apartment, and she got out the map and guided him to the Corso Buenos Aires. It was a wide, tree lined avenue with the block of flats set well back beyond a lawn. He parked on the avenue and they walked across the grass to the entrance. The door had a security lock and intercom and Creasy announced her and the door buzzed open.

"I won't be long Creasy, just an hour."

"Play badly."

She grinned up at him. "I will."

He went back and sat in the car and picked up a newspaper. Faint tinklings reached him from an open upper window.

The hour passed and he looked up as the apartment door slammed shut on its spring. She waved at him and started toward the car. She was still forty metres away when the black car came round the corner behind him and mounted the curb onto the grass. He saw the four men and instantly realized what was happening. He came out of the car fast, reaching for his gun. Pinta had stopped in surprise.

"Run, Pinta, run!" he shouted.

The car skidded to a stop in front of her, blocking her path to Creasy. The back door opened and two men jumped out. But Pinta was quick. She ducked under a reaching arm and scampered round the back of the car toward her running bodyguard. The two men were fast behind her. They both held revolvers. Creasy tried to draw a line on them but the girl was between and he hesitated. Then one of them caught up and scooped an arm round her, lifting her off her feet and turning back to the car. The other faced Creasy and fired a shot — high. Creasy shot him in the chest twice.

The one holding Pinta was trying to force her into the back seat but she struggled wildly, screaming and kicking. Creasy was very close by the time he had finally flung her in and turned with his gun coming up. Creasy fired high aiming for the head, for fear of a bullet ricocheting into the car. The bullet hit the gunman below the nose, angling upward into the brain and slamming the body against the door — closing it. Then three shots rang out from the front seat and Creasy went down. Wheels spun and gripped and the car accelerated away. As it bounced back onto the road, the girl screamed out his name.

He could barely move, his nervous system stunned by the bullets. It was very quiet. He lay waiting for help. Through the pain and shock his one hope was not to die. He had heard Pinta scream his name. Not a cry for help — she had seen him fall — a cry of anguish.

CHAPTER NINE

A nurse sat by the bed, reading a book. Creasy was barely awake and heavily drugged. Above him two bottles were suspended upside down on a metal frame. Colourless liquid dripped rhythmically into transparent tubes. One snaked down to his left nostril. The other disappeared under a bandage around his right wrist.

The door opened and a uniformed policeman spoke to the nurse.

"A visitor. The doctor said just one minute."

Guido entered the room, crossed to the bed, and looked down.

"Can you hear me, Creasy?"

The nod was almost imperceptible.

"The worst is over. You're going to make it."

Again the faint nod.

"I'll stay in Milan. Come to see you later when you can talk." Guido turned to the nurse. "You will stay with him?"

"Somebody will always be with him," she said.

Guido thanked her and left the room.

Elio and Felicia waited in the corridor.

"He's awake, but it will be a day or two before he can talk. Let's go home, I'll come back tomorrow."

The doctor had told them that Creasy had been almost dead when they brought him in. They had operated immediately, patching and sewing rapidly. It was, the doctor explained, interim emergency surgery. If Creasy lived through the postoperative shock, they would build up his strength and operate again — more thoroughly. In the meantime — the doctor had shrugged eloquently. It was touch and go.

For two days Creasy had been on the edge, and then he had come through. He must have a will, the doctor had remarked to Guido. A great will to live.

The next day Creasy could talk.

His first question to Guido was, "Pinta?"

"They are negotiating," Guido replied. "Such matters can take time."

"My condition?"

Guido explained carefully and clinically. They were both experienced in such things.

"You were hit twice. In the stomach and the right lung. Fortunately the bullets were thirty-two calibre. Anything heavier and you would have had it. They've patched the lung, and it should be alright. The stomach wound is the problem. It needs more surgery, but the doctor is hopeful, and he's experienced. There have been many gunshot wounds in this hospital."

Creasy listened intently and asked:

"The two I shot are dead?"

Guido nodded. "You got one in the heart. Both bullets. The other through the brain. It was good shooting."

Creasy shook his head.

"I was slow — too damned slow!"

"They were professionals," said Guido flatly.

"I know, and they weren't expecting much opposition. They fired high at first, to frighten me off. If I'd been quicker I'd have gotten them all. They were too casual."

He was getting tired now, and Guido rose to go. "I'll go to Como and see Balletto. See if there's anything I can do."

Something caught his eye and he stood looking down, curiously. It was the crucifix. Creasy noted his gaze and said, "I'll tell you about it later."

The visit to Como was not a success. Guido took Elio with him. Vico Mansutti and his wife were at the house. He seemed to be taking charge of matters. Ettore was subdued, dazed by events. But Rika, when she entered the room, was in a fury. The facts had come out. She had learned that Creasy was hired for a pittance, just to appease her. Now she was aware of the flaw.

"A drunk!" she screamed at Guido. "A lousy drunk to protect my daughter." She looked at her husband scornfully. "A boy scout could have done better!"

Elio started to protest but Guido silenced him, and they picked up Creasy's things and left.

"She'll calm down when she gets her daughter back," Guido commented.

He didn't mention the meeting to Creasy, and a week later the doctors operated again — successfully.

Guido came into the room and pulled a chair up close to the bed. Creasy looked better, with more colour in his face. He noted Guido's troubled expression and his eyes asked the question.

"She's dead, Creasy."

The wounded man turned his head away and looked up at the ceiling, his face expressionless, the eyes empty.

Guido hesitated and then went on.

"It was unintentional. The ransom was paid two days ago. She was supposed to have been released that night. She didn't turn up, and in the morning the police found her in the trunk of a stolen car. There had been a big sweep for a Red Brigade gang.

It's thought that the kidnappers got nervous and went to ground for several hours. Her hands and mouth were taped and she had vomited — probably from petrol fumes. You know what can happen under those circumstances. There has been an autopsy. She choked to death."

His voice petered out and there was a long silence, then Creasy asked:

"Anything else?"

Guido stood up and walked to the window. He stood looking at the garden below. The voice cracked behind him.

"Well?"

He turned around and said softly, "She had been raped. Frequently. There were bruises on her shoulders and arms."

Another long silence. In the distance the bell of a church rang faintly.

Guido moved to the foot of the bed and looked down at Creasy.

The face was still set and expressionless. The eyes still looked up at the ceiling, but they were not empty — they glittered with hatred.

The overnight train from Milan to Naples clattered over the points outside Latina. It was the middle of June and the train was long, with many carriages carrying holidaymakers south to the sun. The last carriage, dark blue, was lettered with the insignia of the International Sleeping Car Company. In Compartment 3 Creasy sat on the lower bunk, reading from a notebook. He had wakened at Rome after four hours' sleep. In a while he would go down the corridor and have a shower, and if the steward was awake, get a coffee. He had slept well. He always did on trains.

The early light showed the face, thinner and pale. It had not seen much sun. He wore a pair of faded jeans and was bare from the waist up. The two recent scars were puckered, red weals.

He finished reading and picked up a ballpoint pen from the small corner table and made notes on the last blank page. At one point he smiled briefly. A memory triggered.

It was fully light when he finished. He tore out the page and slipped it into the pocket of his jacket, hanging behind the door.

He took a towel and his shaving gear and walked down the corridor. The steward was up and in the galley preparing breakfast trays. A small neat man, with a small neat moustache and, despite the early hour, a cheerful smile.

"Good morning — Naples in an hour."

Creasy smiled back.

"The coffee smells good. Are the showers vacant?"

The steward nodded.

"No one else up yet."

Creasy went through and took his shower and shaved leisurely. It beat travelling by car, or even by plane.

His recovery had been steady. He was a good patient, listening carefully to the doctor and following all instructions. A week after the second operation, he was able to get out of bed and into a wheelchair. A few days later he was walking.

He didn't push himself. He was experienced and knew that his body needed time. To move too fast would be counterproductive.

They let him into the garden and he walked a little each day, with his shirt off, and the sun warming his back between the bandages.

He was popular with the nurses and staff. Not bothering them unnecessarily and undergoing all the indignities of being an invalid quietly and without fuss. Also they had nursed him back from the very edge of death, and that made him special.

He had given one of the nurses some money and she brought him all the newspapers covering the period since the kidnapping.

Later she was able to borrow copies of newspapers going back many months. He asked her for a notebook and this gradually filled with his jottings.

He had had only one visitor and that was a surprise. Late one evening Signora Deluca was shown in, carrying a bag of fruit. She had stayed half an hour and talked of Pinta and had cried a little. He found himself comforting her. Of all her children, she had said, it had to be Pinta. She had dried her tears and looked at him with kindly eyes. She had heard the talk, that he was not a real bodyguard, had just been for show. But she knew of his affection for the girl. She asked him what he would do, and he had shrugged and told her he had no plans. But she had been puzzled. He seemed assured and at ease. Not what she had expected. Finally she had kissed his cheek and left.

He began to go to the physiotherapy room, gently exercising and swimming in the heated pool. They gave him small spring exercisers for his hands and, as he walked around the garden farther each day, he squeezed them constantly, feeling the strength returning to his fingers.

After a month the doctor told him his recovery was excellent — beyond expectation. He thought another week would be enough.

He spent most of that week in the physiotherapy department, using the full range of equipment.

When he left the hospital he was still weak and a long way from fit, but his body functioned in all aspects.

The doctor and matron and several nurses wished him goodbye and good luck and received his thanks. They stood at the steps and watched him walk down the drive, suitcase in hand.

"A strange man," the matron had commented.

The doctor agreed.

"He has much experience of hospitals."

The train pulled into the Naples central station and Creasy tipped the steward and followed the crowd out into the Piazza Garibaldi. He quickly found a taxi.

"Pensione Splendide" he told the driver, reaching forward to turn on the metre.

The driver cursed under his breath. He hadn't had a real tourist yet and it was June already.

The taxi arrived as Pietro pulled up in the van after his morning's visit to the market. He looked Creasy up and down, and they shook hands.

"How do you feel?"

"OK. Let me give you a hand with those baskets."

Guido was sitting at the kitchen table, drinking coffee, when they walked in.

"*Ça va*, Guido." He put a basket on the table.

"*Ça va*, Creasy." Guido studied him carefully and then stood up and they embraced.

"You don't look half bad. They patched you up well."

"Good mechanics up there," Creasy answered, and they both smiled at words often used before.

It was after dinner when the two men talked at length, sitting out on the terrace in the warm night. To Creasy it seemed a long age since he had last sat there.

He quietly explained to Guido what he intended to do. He did not invoke moral issues. It was not a question of justice — a crime to be punished.

Anyway, Guido knew him too well for that.

It was simply revenge. They had killed someone precious to him. He would kill in turn.

"An eye for an eye?" asked Guido quietly.

Creasy shook his head slowly and said with great emphasis, "More than that. More than an eye. Every bloody piece of them."

"You were really fond of the girl!" It was half question, half statement.

Creasy thought carefully before answering. He was searching for the words. It was so important that Guido understood. Really understood.

"Guido, you know what I am. Five months ago I sat here and saw nothing in front of me. I took the job only to keep myself from blowing my brains out."

He smiled wryly at Guido's look.

"It's true. I really thought about it. I felt things were over — pointless to go on. The girl changed that. I don't know how. She sort of crept up on me. Day by day she slipped into my life."

He shook himself at the memory. Guido remained silent, intrigued by the revelation.

"You know what I am." He repeated the phrase, trying to clarify exactly what had happened to him.

"Never had any truck with kids. Just a nuisance. Then this one comes along. She was so fresh. My life was over — all behind. Then I kept seeing things through her eyes. For her, nothing had existed before, as though the whole world suddenly appeared one morning, just for her."

The monologue stopped and he sat looking down over the lights and the dark sea. Then he said softly, "She loved me, Guido — me!" He looked up. "Not like that, you understand. Not physical. Better than that."

Guido said nothing, and Creasy went on.

"I cut right back on the drinking — didn't need it. In the mornings I'd bring the car around to the front and she'd run down the steps. Christ, man, she seemed to carry the sun on her shoulder. She had nothing bad in her. No malice, no greed, no hate."

His face showed the struggle of trying to explain. Using words alien to him. He suddenly asked, "You ever hear music by Dr. Hook?"

Guido shook his head.

"Well, he's Country and Western. He sings about a woman that's older. Tells her he can't touch the sun for her, can't reach the clouds, can't make her young again. But Guido, that's just what she did for me — touched the sun."

The words should have sounded incongruous, even ridiculous, coming from such a man. But to Guido they were real. Painful but real. And he understood. In a different way, the same thing had happened to him when Julia had entered his life.

He remembered something.

"The crucifix?"

"Yes, she gave it to me. A present — my birthday."

He smiled. "Told me if I met the devil to hold it up in front of me."

The smile faded, and his voice hardened.

"Then those bastards took her, and abused her and left her to choke to death in her own vomit! I keep seeing it. They would have kept her eyes taped. Tied to some dirty bed somewhere. Using her whenever they got bored — Filth!"

Anger and hatred radiated from him.

"Do you understand, Guido, why I'm going after them?"

Guido stood up and walked to the railing. He was very moved. He had seen the depth of Creasy's feelings. At last someone had turned the key, no matter that the lock had been rusty.

"Yes, Creasy, I understand. It happened to me. I loved Julia. Different, but the same. In a way I envy you. When she died I wanted to take revenge, but against who? The driver of the car was a kid. The accident unbalanced him." He shrugged. "It would have been empty. And she wouldn't have wanted it — but I know what you feel."

Creasy joined him at the railing.

"I need help, Guido."

Guido nodded and put his hand on Creasy's shoulder.

"You have it, Creasy. Anything I can do. But I won't kill again. I gave that up. Promised her. But anything else."

"I wouldn't ask you to, or want you to. I'll do the killing. But helping me could put you in some danger."

Guido smiled.

"It's possible, but that's no stranger."

He looked at Creasy quizzically.

"You know who did it?"

Creasy nodded.

"I'm certain. I got a good look at them and I've been doing some research. The man who shot me is called Sandri. The driver of the car is one Rabbia. They work for a man called Fossella."

He smiled grimly.

"They are so sure of themselves. They claimed they were in Turin at the time. Had a dozen witnesses."

"How do you know their names?"

"The police showed me a whole book of mug shots and I picked them out easily."

"You didn't tell the police?"

Creasy shook his head. "What would have happened to them? Tell me, Guido."

It was a rhetorical question, but Guido gave the answer.

"A few years in jail at the most. Comfortable years. Lots of perks. An early parole. You know the way it is."

"Exactly. Well, it won't be that way. Not this time."

Guido considered the project and said, "Shouldn't be difficult. They won't be expecting it. You'll be able to pick them off and get clear. They're probably not top-level men."

"It won't be like that, Guido." Creasy said it quietly but with emphasis, and Guido looked puzzled.

"How then?"

"Not just those two. I'm going after anyone who had a hand in it, or profited from it. Right to the top. The whole stinking, filthy nest."

Guido looked astonished and then laughed out loud. As the implication sank in, he laughed harder, not in disbelief, but at the sheer scope. Creasy smiled.

"So you see why I need your help."

"And how! You know what it means? You understand their setup?"

Creasy nodded. "Reasonably well. Not everything, but I know the basics. There are two main bosses in Milan. Fossella and Abrata. Fossella pulled this kidnap, so he's in line after Rabbia and Sandri. Conti in Rome would get a cut, so he gets it too, and finally the fat cat in Palermo — Cantarella. He gets a piece of everything. Now he gets a piece of the killing."

Guido laughed again, but quietly.

"Conti I know. I won't be at all sorry about him. I'll tell you why later. How did you get all this?"

Creasy shrugged.

"A lot of it's in the old newspapers. I had plenty of time to go through them. They are so damned arrogant that they practically advertise. I also read a book by a journalist called Andato — *The Other Country*. He really dug deep. It's a wonder he's still alive."

Guido shook his head.

"Not after the book was published. They only kill outside their own circle to protect a secret, and once the book was out there was no more secret."

He considered awhile.

"Anyway, I can help you. I still have a few old connections. I'll check the setup."

"Connections?"

Guido smiled.

"Yes. I never told you how I came to join the Legion. Now it's very ironical. But I'll tell you later. Meanwhile, how else can I help?"

The two of them went into the kitchen to get coffee, and they sat at the table and went into details.

Creasy had worked out a careful strategy. He mapped it out, and Guido was impressed. He made notes on a pad about requirements for transport and accommodations. Finally he sat back and took a sip of coffee and surveyed his friend over the cup.

"It's good, Creasy — very good. I can understand that you have to improvise after Milan, but by then you should have good information. But do you really know what you're up against?"

'Tell me."

Guido arranged his thoughts.

"They are even more powerful than most people believe, or want to believe. They defy the police and sometimes control them. They even subvert the courts. They bribe politicians at all levels, from village councillors to Cabinet ministers. In some areas, particularly the south and Sicily, they are literally the law, punishing and rewarding as they see fit. They practically run the prisons from within. Several times, over the years, the authorities have made an effort. They are making one now, in Calabria, There's a big trial in Reggio about corruption and forced purchase of land for the new steel complex, but . . ."

He waved his cup in an eloquent gesture and continued.

"The weapons the authorities have — the police, the *Carabinieri*, the courts and prisons — are often corrupt and infiltrated. There are a few good policemen and brave prosecutors and judges, but the system is too weak. Only Mussolini in the thirties had any success and only because he used Fascist methods. A lot of innocent people suffered along with the Mafia. After Mussolini, they came back stronger than ever. They can call on thousands of informers. Even contacts inside the police forces.

They have their own groups in every city and town of any size and, as you get south, in every village. A whole army of strong-arm men."

He poured more coffee and told Creasy of his early associations in Naples and particularly of Conti. Finally he sat back and waited for Creasy's reaction.

"It won't be easy," Creasy agreed. "But I have several points in my favour. First, like Mussolini, I can use tactics the police cannot use. Terror, for example. These people use it as a weapon but are not used to facing it themselves. Second, I'll get information as I move along — one to the next. Information the police can't get because they can't use my methods."

Guido took the point. Creasy would get them talking.

"Third," Creasy went on, "unlike the police, my aim is not to collect evidence and bring them to court. My aim is to kill them."

His voice went quieter.

"Fourth, I have more motivation than the police. Motivation that a policeman or a judge couldn't have.

They're doing a job. They have wives, families, careers to think about. I don't, and I'll come at them in a way they've never experienced."

Guido thought about it. They were distinct advantages, perhaps crucial.

"Weapons?" he asked.

Creasy reached into his jacket pocket.

"Is Leclerc still operating out of Marseilles?"

"I think so," Guido answered. "I can check with a phone call." He took the sheet of paper and read the list that Creasy had drawn up on the train. He whistled softly.

"Hell, Creasy, you really are going to war! Do you think Leclerc will have all this?"

"He can get it," said Creasy. "He was offering most of it to the Rhodesians a couple of years back. I was called in for advice.

He did good business. Do you think he'll play it straight? It's just peanuts to him."

"He should," answered Guido. "You pulled him out of that mess outside Bukavu. He should be suitably grateful."

"Maybe, but he's a sharp bastard, and he's made a lot of money since he's been selling arms instead of using them himself. Being rich can change people. You may have to lean on him."

"Any suggestions?"

"Tell him about a technicolour funeral."

Guido smiled at the memory. "That should do it." He waved the paper. "When will you need the stuff?"

"Not for two months. It will take me at least that long to get fully fit. I'll pick it up in Marseilles myself. I've worked out a way to get it in."

The question of fitness raised another point.

"I need to go somewhere quiet," he said. "Any suggestions?"

Guido thought for only a moment.

"Why not Malta? To Julia's family, on Gozo. They still have the farm and it's very quiet. You would be welcome. I know that. I go every year myself for a couple of weeks. I can phone them."

Creasy thought about it and then nodded. "Sounds good. Sure I won't be in the way?"

Guido smiled. "You can help Paul on the farm. It's hard work and will harden you up. You always liked working with your hands. You'll make a good farmer."

So that was settled. They went on to talk of money. Guido suggested he finance the weapons and various purchases in Italy. He still had an account in Brussels and it would be easier than for Creasy to transfer money around. He could pay Guido back when it was over.

"What if I don't make it?" asked Creasy seriously.

Guido grinned. "Remember me in your will!"

Creasy smiled back but didn't say anything, didn't need to.

They talked on into the night. It was decided that Creasy would leave in two days on the ferry to Palermo. He wanted a quiet look at Cantarella's base. From there he would take the train to Reggio di Calabria and pick up the ferry to Malta.

It was almost dawn when the two friends finished, but they hadn't noticed. It was the tonic of old times. When they finally rose from the table, Guido picked up his pad and flicked through the pages, checking that nothing had been forgotten. Then he looked up and said, "The main thing now is for you to get fit."

Creasy stretched and yawned and smiled grimly.

"Yes — fighting fit."

BOOK TWO

CHAPTER TEN

The *Melitaland* was not a beautiful example of marine architecture. It sat in the water squat and belligerent — disdainful of sleek lines or raked funnels. Its job was to transport cars, trucks, and people the two miles between Malta and Gozo.

Creasy stood on the top deck, suitcase at his feet. The Italian ferry from Reggio had been delayed twelve hours by a strike and so had arrived in Malta's Grand Harbour in the early morning. It had saved him from spending a night on the big island, and this had pleased him — he was eager to settle in and get started on his programme.

The ship passed the small island of Comino, with its old watchtower set high above the cliffs. The water below was a vivid blue above a sandy bottom — the Blue Lagoon. Creasy remembered swimming there, eight years before, with Guido and Julia.

Pollution had been minimized here by the tides and currents — the water was still clear and the shoreline uncluttered.

He looked ahead toward Gozo — steeper and greener than Malta, with villages crowning the hills. It was an island of intensive agriculture, and the fields were terraced right down to the water's edge.

He had liked Gozo on his previous visit. It was unique, in his experience, for having no class in its society. The poorest fisherman knew he was as good as the richest landowner. A man who thought himself better than others should avoid Gozo. He remembered the people as being noisy and cheerful and, once they knew you, friendly. The noise started now as they turned into the small harbour of Mgarr and the passengers bustled forward to be the first off.

He walked up the hill to a bar with the unlikely name of "Gleneagles." It was an old, oblong building and had a narrow balcony facing the water. Guido had told him to phone Julia's parents from there and they would pick him up. The interior was high-ceilinged and cool — a barn of a place, with paintings of local landscapes on the walls and an assortment of locals propping up the bar.

Creasy left his suitcase by the door. The sight of pint mugs of beer reminded him that he was thirsty, and he gestured at the draft pump. The bartender, a short, balding, round-faced man, asked, "Pint or half?"

"Pint, thanks." Creasy eased himself onto a stool and put a pound in front of him. The beer was cool and amber, and he drank deep. When the bartender brought back his change, Creasy asked, "Would you have the phone number of Paul Schembri?"

He received a blank look.

"Paul Schembri," he repeated. "He has a farm near Nadur, you must know him."

The bartender shrugged and said, "Schembri is a common name, and there are lots of farmers on Gozo." He went down the bar to serve someone else.

Creasy was not annoyed. In fact, he approved. The man had to know Paul Schembri. It was a very small island. But it was an island that protected its privacy. Even a mild invasion of tourists couldn't change that. They were friendly to strangers but didn't tell them anything until they knew who they were and what they wanted. A Gozitan would deny knowing his own brother until he knew who was doing the asking.

So Creasy drank his beer and bided his time. Then he called for another one, and when it arrived said, "Guido Arrellio sent me. I'm to stay with Paul Schembri."

Light dawned.

"Oh you mean that Paul Schembri? The farmer — near Nadur?"

Creasy nodded. "That's the one."

The bartender studied him and then smiled. He had one of those rare smiles that light a room. He held out a hand.

"I'm Tony. I remember you now. You were here when Guido married Julia." He gestured down the bar to a younger man. "My brother Sam," and then to a grease covered drinker, "That's 'Shreik,'" and to the two others, "Michele and Victor — when they're not drinking in here, they run the ferry."

Creasy remembered them supervising the loading of the cars and trucks and collecting the fares. He was no longer a stranger. Tony picked up the phone and dialled a number and spoke a few words in Maltese. Then the smile came again. "Joey will be down in a few minutes to pick you up."

Sam put another pint in front of Creasy and gestured towards the grease covered "Shreik." Creasy remembered the drinking prowess of the Gozitans, and how, once they started to buy each other rounds, a day and a half could go by. He felt good and relaxed. He could relate to these people. He wouldn't get a bunch of questions. No one would pry or try to slot him into a category or throw a spurious friendship at him. Everything would be face value. Be what you want to be. Do what you want to do. Just don't step on toes, and don't be mean when it's your round and, above all, don't be "proud." Being "proud" was the greatest possible sin in Gozo. It could be equated with being stuck-up. A man could be an arsonist or a sodomist and still be accepted, but if he was "proud" — forget it.

Creasy finished his beer and caught Tony's eye. Tony was one of those bartenders, the rare breed, that see everything, no matter how busy they are. He moved down the bar, filling drinks, and took more money from in front of Creasy.

"Yourself?" Creasy asked.

Tony shook his head. "Too early for me."

Ten minutes went by before the smile came again and he picked up another ten cents and said, "Why not," and pulled himself a beer.

Creasy was to learn that this was Tony's habit. He always turned down a drink and then spent anything from ten minutes to half an hour asking himself why. The cogitation always ended in a smile and the inevitable "Why not!"

Every Gozitan has a nickname, and it was no surprise to learn that this bartender was called "Why Not."

A battered Land Rover pulled up outside and a young man loped in — long-legged and open-faced, with black curly hair. He stuck out a work calloused hand.

"Hi, I'm Joey. Welcome to Gozo."

Creasy could vaguely remember Julia's young brother, but he would have been only ten at the time. Joey looked at Tony and panted exaggeratedly and was presented with a beer.

"You're not in a great rush, are you?" he asked with a smile. Creasy returned the smile and shook his head.

Joey downed half his beer. "That's good. I've been sacking onions all day and it's thirsty work."

A mild drinking session got under way with a lot of good humour. English is the second language of the Maltese Islands, and only occasionally the drinkers would lapse into Maltese to emphasize a point. The language contains a lot of Arabic and Italian, and has a curious singsong lilt to it. With his knowledge of both those languages, Creasy could pick up many words. Fishermen started to drift in, thirsty after a day in open boats under a hot sun, and then Victor and Michele went off to make the last ferry run.

Most of the drinkers had switched from beer to hard liquor when Joey looked at his watch.

"*Ghal Madonna*! Six o'clock — let's go, Creasy. Mother will be building up a head of steam."

They drove up the steep hill through the tiny village of Qala and then dipped down again before turning off the Nadur road.

The farmhouse was built around an inner courtyard in the old style — a sprawling stone building. One corner wing looked newer than the rest, and was reached by an outside staircase.

A tall, plump woman came out from the kitchen. She had a round, pleasant face, rich in character, and she smiled as Creasy climbed down, embraced him, and kissed his cheek.

"Welcome, Creasy. Long time." She glared at her son.

"Creasy was thirsty, Ma." This was said with a wink at Creasy and an impish smile.

She scolded him gently, told him to take the suitcase upstairs and led Creasy into the kitchen.

He remembered the huge, arched room. It was the centre of family activity — the dining room and lounge were used only on formal occasions.

It made him realize that he was within a family unit, and that could have made him uneasy, but Laura bustled around making a large pot of coffee and asking how Guido was and tending a trio of simmering pots on the big stove. He couldn't feel uneasy. His presence was quietly accepted, and this feeling was reinforced when Paul Schembri came in from the fields. He was smaller than his wife and at first appeared thin; but his arms were sinewy and corded, and Creasy got the impression of strength and compactness. He nodded at Creasy and asked, "Alright?"

It was the most commonly used word in Malta, in any language, and covered the spectrum of meaning from a question to a statement to a greeting or even a farewell. It equated the French "*Ça va*" and more.

"Alright," Creasy replied, and Paul sat down and accepted a cup of coffee from Laura.

His greeting was such that Creasy might have been gone just overnight instead of eight years, and it made the American relax even more.

Creasy had bought a small cassette player in Naples, and he slipped in one of the cassettes Guido had retrieved from the house at Como. Then he lay back on the bed, and as Dr. Hook sang a lament of love, he considered his situation and the people around him. Guido's suggestion that he use Gozo as a base had been a good one; he had known that Creasy would get a warm but undemonstrative welcome from the Schembris. He also knew that they had recently rented a series of fallow fields from the church, and that reterracing and preparing this land would be hard work. Creasy would enjoy and benefit from helping. Guido had spoken at length to Paul on the phone and explained Creasy's condition and recent events. He had not spoken of the future.

Creasy had been given a small suite of rooms to himself. It was the newer wing he had noticed, with its own entrance by the outside staircase. Over dinner, Paul had explained that it used to be storage rooms and a hay loft. Guido had sent money every year since his marriage to Julia, and this had continued after her death. At first, Paul had been angry — after all they were not poor people — and he had threatened to send it back. But Guido had been disarming, had told him that it was for tax reasons. "You know what he's like," Paul had commented to Creasy.

They had used part of the money to convert the old store-rooms, so that Guido would have a comfortable place and some privacy when he came to stay each year. There were two big rooms and a small bathroom, all arched and vaulted in the usual manner. The thick stones had been oiled, rather than painted, and they retained a soft ochre colour. The rooms were furnished simply. A big old bed and chest of drawers in the bedroom, with wooden pegs on the wall on which to hang clothes. In the other room, a grouping of low, comfortable chairs and a coffee table, and a well-stocked liquor cabinet. It would be home for at least two months and already, on his first night, Creasy felt comfortable and settled.

He thought about the Schembris. They were, to all appearances, simple farmers, but in Gozo the level of education is high, and while the people are conservative and close-knit, they take an interest in the outside world and are often well read. Because of overpopulation, many Gozitans have settled overseas, particularly in North America and Australia, and some of them, coming home to retire, buy houses in their original villages. So there is a rejuvenation of ideas, and a movement of people within the community.

Paul Schembri was a typical farmer, his values rooted in a life of hard work and the productive cycle. He kept his counsel and didn't parade his views for all to see. He had money in the bank and could look any man in the eye. He was a bit like the stone walls that surrounded his fields — dry and a bit dusty, but well made, each stone fitting against the other without cement or plaster and able to stand up to the Gregale winds that, in winter, come across the sea from Europe and scour the low hills.

Laura was more outgoing. A casual observer might have thought she dominated the marriage, but that was a surface impression. She was a big woman and confident of her intellect, and even if Paul had allowed it, she was wise enough not to take advantage of his seeming mildness. But her character had more facets than Paul's, she sparkled brighter, and her interests and curiosity ranged wider.

Joey mostly took after his mother, his inquiring guileless mind allied to overt goodwill. He would be attractive to women, Creasy decided. They would be drawn to his dark good looks, which would undoubtedly arouse maternal instincts.

He wondered about the girl, Nadia. She was working as a receptionist in a hotel on Malta but would be returning at the weekend, and staying to help her family on the farm.

Guido had told him that she had married an English naval officer and gone to England, but the marriage had failed a year before. Creasy remembered her vaguely at Guido's wedding. A teenager, with the same quiet good looks as Julia. He hoped she wouldn't present any complications. So far, the situation was good. In the morning he would start training. He didn't want complications.

He turned over the tape, and Dr. Hook sang of an old drunk in Brooklyn and a plea to be carried a little farther. Just a little farther.

He reached the long ridge overlooking the bay at Marsalforn and stopped for a breather. Sweat had darkened his track suit. The sun was still low — only an hour old, and the bay, sheltered by the surrounding hills, was shaded. He sat on a low stone wall and drew in air deeply. His body ached — all of it, muscles protesting in hurt astonishment at the sudden activity. He reminded himself not to overdo it. A pulled muscle now would set his program back days or weeks.

He had risen just before dawn and worked through a set of exercises, following the old Legion routine, but he had curtailed them, starting gently.

Then he had taken a cold shower and gone downstairs. He had been surprised to find Laura already in the kitchen, and said so.

"I go to early Mass at five o'clock," she had answered, smiling. "Someone has to pray for all the sinners in this family."

Creasy had smiled. "Pray for me too, Laura," he said lightly. "I've done my share of sinning."

She had nodded, suddenly serious, and looking at the small gold crucifix hanging from his neck.

"You are a Catholic?" she had asked, and Creasy had shrugged.

"I'm nothing very much."

She made him a big mug of black coffee and, as he sipped, Paul and Joey had come in, dressed for the fields.

"I'm going for a run," Creasy had said, "and then for a swim. Can I help you on the terracing later?"

The farmer had smiled and nodded and led the way outside, pointing down the hill to the sea.

"When you want to swim, follow that path. There's a small cove there and you can swim off the rocks. The water is deep, and it's private. It can only be reached through my land or by boat."

Laura had told him to come in for breakfast after his swim, and the thought of both the cool water and the food brought him back to his feet, and he retraced his steps at a slow trot.

The small cove was secluded and the water deep and clear. The limestone of the shore had been eroded from beneath, and a flat ledge jutted out over the sea. Creasy stripped off and plunged in. He swam about a hundred metres out into the north Comino channel. The small island looked beckoningly close, but he knew that it was almost a mile to its nearest point. Later, when he became fitter, he would swim over there; and later still, and fitter still, he would swim there and back.

At the farmhouse Laura cooked him a huge breakfast of ham and eggs, and fresh warm bread spread with the island's clear honey. She sat and drank coffee and watched with satisfaction as he silently cleared his plate.

She remembered him eight years before, when he had come with Guido — just as silent then. He looked older now and infinitely weary. Guido had told them on the phone how close he had been to death.

She had grown to love her son-in-law as a natural son, and when Julia had been killed, she had grieved for her daughter, and for Guido.

She remembered the night before the wedding. Guido had come alone to talk to her and Paul. He told them a little of his past and how the future would be different. How he loved their daughter and of their plans for the *pensione* in Naples. Finally he had told them that if anything happened to him, and if Julia needed any help, Creasy would provide it.

The next day she had watched the big, silent American as he tried to enter into the spirit and gaiety of a typical Gozitan wedding. She could sense his pleasure at his friend's happiness and had known instinctively that what Guido had told them the night before was true. Guido had given her Creasy's forwarding address in Brussels, and it had been Laura who sent the cable there when Julia had been killed, the cable that had brought Creasy from Africa to Naples to be with his friend. Now she was quietly determined to help this man build up his strength again. Exercise and hard work would play a big part, and she would fill him with plenty of fresh, good food.

After breakfast Creasy went out into the fields and located Paul and took off his shirt and worked alongside him. There is a skill to building a dry loose wall. The rocks have to be carefully selected and placed just right, one against the other. The old man was surprised at how quickly Creasy picked up the knack, but Creasy had a natural eye for that kind of construction.

Even so, after an hour, his back ached from the constant bending and his hands, long softened, were scratched and blistered from the stones. At noon Paul called a halt, and Creasy went down to the cove to bathe his hands in the seawater.

Lunch was a simple meal of cold meats and salad, and afterward everyone took a siesta during the hottest part of the day. The thick, stone walls and the high, arched ceilings kept the rooms very cool, and Creasy slept well even though his body ached. He rose at three o'clock, stiff and with his bruised hands painful. It would have been good to laze about and he was half tempted, but he switched his mind back to his purpose and went down to the terraces again with Paul. As his skill improved, the two men made good progress working silently side by side. After a couple of hours Laura came down with cold beers in a bucket of ice.

She scolded Creasy about his sunburned back and she looked with frank curiosity at the scars — old and new.

"You really got chopped up, Creasy," she commented. "You should take up farming full time."

Then she saw the state of his hands and turned to Paul, genuinely angry.

"How can you let him work with hands like that? Look at them!"

Paul shrugged. "You try telling him."

She took Creasy's hands in hers and examined them.

"It's alright," he told her. "I'll go for a swim later — the salt water is good treatment. In a few days, they'll harden." She turned the hands over and looked at the mottled scars and shook her head.

"Farming," she said firmly. "It's much safer."

The next three days were the hardest. Each night Creasy would fall into bed totally exhausted.

But he had established a routine and a pattern: an early morning run, followed by a swim, longer each day, then working in the fields, shirtless in the hot sun. Another swim in the evening, and early to bed after dinner. He exercised when he first got up and just before bed at night. Those first days were an agony, especially in the mornings, when he loosened stiff and unresponsive muscles. It would take about two weeks, he guessed, before he could get into full stride. But the pain acted as a stimulus. It reminded him constantly of his purpose, and it reminded him of the girl and what they had done to her, and his hatred more than matched the pain.

Paul and Joey saw it one evening as they sat on the outside patio after dinner, drinking coffee and brandy and looking out over the dark sea to the bulk of Comino and the lights of Malta beyond.

The lights reminded Creasy of his arrival in Naples, so many months before, and of the changes that had affected him. The growing friendship with Pinta, and those few last weeks, when he had been truly happy.

His mind went to the last day and then to Guido telling him in the hospital about her death.

Paul turned to say something, but when he saw Creasy's face, the words dried in his throat. He saw hatred rising from the man like mist from a cold sea.

Abruptly Creasy stood up and bade them good night and went to bed.

Joey looked at his father, his normally cheerful face troubled and somber.

"He's burning up inside. There's a fire in there. I've never seen anyone look so sad and so angry at the same time."

Paul nodded in agreement. "He's got it under control, but it's there. Someone will be burned by it."

Joey shook off the mood and grinned and stood up. "I've got a fire in me too, but for something else. I'm going to Barbarella's. Friday night, and the tourist girls will be lonely and grateful."

His father shook his head good-naturedly.

"Don't be too late or you'll be useless tomorrow, and there's still three fields of onions to pick."

The boy walked through the inner courtyard, avoiding his mother, who would lecture him about the morals of foreign girls. From the open window of Creasy's bedroom he could hear soft music and he stopped and listened. He recognized the song, it had been popular a couple of years before — "Blue Bayou." He was a little surprised. It added another dimension to the strange American. He climbed onto his Suzuki and kicked the starter and the music was drowned briefly as he gunned the motorbike up the track towards Xaghra.

On Saturday Nadia came home. She was sitting at the kitchen table when the three men came in for lunch.

"Creasy, you remember Nadia," Laura said, with a gesture at the girl.

"Only just," he replied, and to the girl, "You were in pigtails then."

She smiled, softening the severe lines of her attractive face, and then she got up and kissed him on the cheek.

She was tall and slim and she moved with a curious walk. Long legs, almost stiff — not unattractive, but different — her hips turning more than normal.

Over lunch he studied her covertly. She brought more conversation to the group, teasing Joey about his hangover and then supporting him when his mother scolded him for coming home at two a.m. and having to be dragged out of bed to go to work at dawn.

She had an intelligent face. Too severe for great beauty, but high cheekbones and a full mouth gave it interest. She had also a distinct eroticism — an aura. She looked up at Creasy and caught his eyes on her.

"How's Guido?" she asked. Her voice was deep, matching her looks. It had a resonance — a vibration.

"He's fine, and sends his love."

"Did he say when he's coming?"

Creasy shook his head and wondered if there was anything between Guido and this girl. She was very like Julia, a bit taller and slimmer, but the same grave eyes contradicted by a quick smile. It would have been natural for Guido to be attracted and it was five years since Julia's death. But then he remembered — she had been back in Malta less than a year, and anyway Guido would have told him. It was that kind of a situation.

After lunch, when the men had all gone to their rooms for a siesta, she stayed in the kitchen helping her mother wash the dishes.

They worked silently for a while and then she said suddenly. "I'd forgotten . . . I mean the way he is — sort of intimidating."

Laura said, "Yes. He's a hard case. Doesn't say much, but he's settled in and he's a big help to your father." She thought for a moment, then added: "I like him. I know what he is, and your father thinks he's getting fit for a special reason and will go off and commit a lot of violence. He's a violent man — but we all like him."

Nadia dried the dishes in silence, then asked, "How old is he?"

Laura thought about it. "He must be near fifty. He's a few years older than Guido. He's lucky to be alive. The scars on him are terrible."

Nadia stacked the dishes and put them into a cupboard.

"But he's a man," she mused, almost to herself, and then smiled at her mother's look of curiosity — curiosity tinged with sadness. "At least he's a man," she repeated. "There can't be any doubt about that."

It was not a strange comment for Nadia to make. She looked at all men in a special way — an instant first appraisal, informed by hard experience.

Her husband had been handsome, with a fine wit and intelligence. She had entered into marriage with joy and expectation. A fairy-tale, romantic courtship. Dances and parties and the excitement of going overseas and wide horizons, and then, slowly, the realisation that something was wrong and having to face a crushed dream.

He had homosexual tendencies — long suppressed. The marriage, for him, had been part of that suppression. He knew his inclinations and fought against them — had done so since puberty. But it had to be a losing war, and the last battle was his marriage to Nadia. That battle was lost in a series of delaying actions, self-accusations, and miserable and degrading lurches into a world that finally he couldn't deny.

They had talked it over — tried to fight it together. It was hard for her. She couldn't understand, felt her womanhood insulted. She might have been able to rationalize a threat from another woman; at least she would have the weapons of her own sex. But against such an enemy she felt helpless.

The end had come suddenly and sickeningly. A party at the naval base in Portsmouth. Everyone drinking too much. Not seeing him, and looking, and then finding him drunk and naked with a young midshipman, not caring anymore — accepting what he was.

She had left the next day and flown back to Malta.

It had been a terrible homecoming, but she had told Paul and Laura everything, and they had been mercifully strong and understanding. Sad both for her and for themselves — one daughter dead, the other with an emotional scar burned deep into her.

She had applied for an annulment, but such matters took forever. "The Cowboy" had married them, and he forwarded the papers to the Vatican and in his rough, blunt way tried to comfort her and explain why it all took so long, the many difficulties. Witnesses would be needed, depositions taken, and then anonymous, faceless judges would decide, and perhaps take years doing it. Why? Marriage is sacred. Do they not see the pain, and the people? "The Cowboy" saw and had a great sadness when she came to the confessional and asked forgiveness for the sins she had committed, the men she had slept with. First the young fisherman from Mgarr. "He is a man, Father, and I needed to know a man." And later, occasionally, the tourists whom she would meet at the hotel where she worked. In their way also faceless, like her judges. Staying for two weeks, acquiring a suntan and the rarity of a local girl.

She had not come to terms with it. She knew people talked, pitied her even, and she hated that. She wanted a normal life. She had been brought up in that way — a family, children, respect. Even if the judges in the Vatican gave her an annulment, decided that in the eyes of God her marriage had never taken place — what then? She was twenty-six years old. Would a local man marry her? After all the talk, in such a small community? So, to go abroad? The prospect didn't appeal. She needed her family — their steadiness and support. The house in which she had been born and grown up. The land itself. It didn't lie, or change, or dress itself in false clothing. That was the reason she had come home, even from Malta. Whatever she did, it would be done in this house where she felt secure.

In the late afternoon she took her swimsuit and walked down the path to the cove. She saw clothes lying on the flat, overhanging rock, and out in the channel Creasy swimming. She sat and watched as he swam out about two hundred metres and then turned and came back.

"I thought you were crossing to Comino," she said as he pulled himself out of the water.

"I will, next week when I'm fitter," he answered, sitting down beside her, and panting from the exertion.

She looked at the recent scars on his stomach and side, pink and lighter than the rest of his angry sunburn.

"Are you going to swim?" he asked.

"Yes, turn your back while I change."

A minute later, clad in a black, one-piece swimsuit, she plunged into the water in a neat dive.

She was a good swimmer and churned out of the little cove into the channel. She wondered if he really would swim over to Comino. The current could be strong. She could feel it even now, close to shore. She had been going to mention it, but stopped herself. He was the kind of man who might resent advice from a woman.

Later, back on the flat rock, they lay side by side in the late sun. She asked him about Guido and the pensione. She didn't mention the kidnapping and the shooting. She had read about it in the Italian newspapers. She would like to know more — but she would wait.

CHAPTER ELEVEN

Creasy drove the battered Land Rover fast down the winding road to Cirkewwa. He could see the *Melitaland* loading the last cars. If he missed it, he would have to spend the night in Malta. As he reached the approach road, the warps were being cast off and the ramp raised. He palmed the horn rapidly and was relieved to see Victor peer over the ramp and wave. The ramp was lowered and he drove gratefully on.

"You made it by one pubic hair," Victor said with a wide grin.

Creasy smiled back. "They told me you were always late." He looked at his watch. "In fact, you're two minutes early."

"Today's special," Victor answered. "There's a party tonight, and I want to get a few drinks in first. Sort of get in the mood."

Creasy knew that "a few drinks" meant a two-hour session in Gleneagles. Well, today he would join them. He felt he'd earned it. He was into his third week and the hardest part was over. His muscles had finally decided that the long holiday had ended, and they had begun to respond. He was still far from fit but it was only a matter of time; his toughness was returning. His coordination was good and would improve further.

He had also spent a satisfying afternoon at St. Elmo, the huge old fort guarding the entrance to Grand Harbour. This had come about because of a newspaper article Joey had been reading a couple of evenings before. It told of an aircraft hijack attempt in West Germany and described how a special antiterrorist squad had intervened. Paul had remarked that Malta had such a squad. His nephew, George Zammit, an inspector of police, was its commander.

This set Creasy thinking, and the next day he asked Paul if his nephew might allow him to train with the squad. Paul had made a phone call and it had been easily arranged.

It had been a useful afternoon. The squad used weapons donated by the departed British Army: Sterling submachine guns and a variety of handguns. They had a good animated range in the bowels of the fort, and Creasy had enjoyed getting the feel of weapons again. He was rusty and, by his own standards, clumsy; but that would improve over the coming weeks. After the firing range, the squad of fifteen plus Creasy had gone to the gym and worked out and practised unarmed combat. They were a good squad, recently formed; as yet inexperienced, but enthusiastic and hardworking. George Zammit, a big, friendly policeman, had been cordial, and then very thoughtful as he watched Creasy handle the weapons.

Now, as the *Melitaland* chugged across the channel to Gozo, George called his uncle on the phone.

"Paul, do you know what kind of man you have as a houseguest?"

"He's a friend of Guido's," Paul answered. "He didn't cause any trouble, did he?"

"Not at all. But Paul, he's a professional — an expert. Exactly what is he doing in Malta?"

Paul explained about the kidnapping and wounding, and how Creasy had come merely to get fit.

"He's not planning to work here, is he?" George asked.

"Definitely not. Of course, I know he's a mercenary."

"So was Guido. What kind of work would a man like that do here?"

George laughed.

"You're not planning a *coup d'etat*, then."

The laugh was returned. "Seems I have the man to do it. Is he that good?"

There was a pause and then George said, "The best I've seen, and I've been on training courses in England and Italy. He handled our weapons as though he'd carried them from his mother's womb — very, very practised."

There was another pause, and then George asked: "Invite me to dinner, will you, Paul? I didn't like to ask him any questions at this first meeting, it would have seemed rude. But I'd like to learn more about him. We're short of instructors, and maybe I could use him — very unofficially, of course."

Paul invited him to dinner for the coming Saturday and hung up, well pleased.

Creasy was the last off the ferry, and Victor climbed into the passenger seat for the short ride to Gleneagles. The bar was busy and noisy and the crowd opened to let them through. "Shreik" was getting a round in and passed a pint of beer to Creasy. It was the heavy drinking hour, work done for the day. Joey waved from across the room, and Creasy spotted Nadia sitting at one of the few tables with Victor's wife. She smiled at him and raised her glass, and he felt uncomfortable. There was a fatalistic ambience growing between them.

They swam together almost every day. She didn't intrude, was usually quiet — absorbed with her thoughts. But she was a presence, always on the periphery of his mind.

He had come to accept the fact that he was changed. Had been made more aware of people and their individuality — and she attracted him physically, with her stiff legged walk and long waist and serious face.

He glanced at her again and saw her watching him with a speculative look. He had grown used to that look. She seemed to be weighing him.

He turned away and signalled Tony to fill the glasses at the bar. "And have one yourself."

"Thanks, Creasy, but it's too early."

Creasy put money on the bar and waited patiently. Conversation swirled around him, and he had almost given up when Tony's big smile came.

"Why not!"

Just after dawn on Saturday morning Creasy set off to swim to Comino. He paced himself carefully, aiming for a point in front of the blue and white hotel. There was a slight breeze, barely ruffling the water, but it blew from the west down the channel and gave an added impetus to the current. Creasy had not checked the tide table, didn't think it necessary; but as he neared the midpoint between the islands, he could see more of the hotel and realized he was drifting to the east. He adjusted his angle of attack and quickened his stroke, but it soon became obvious that the current was winning. He thought he might make the second bay to the east of the hotel, but again that started to drift by and he silently cursed his stupidity. Beyond that bay, the shoreline rose in high, inhospitable cliffs, and so he turned back toward Gozo. He had begun to tire now and it was clear that he was going to be swept beyond both islands.

He stopped fighting the current, trying to conserve his strength for what would be a critical effort after he was in deep water and out of the grip of the tidal race. The southeast shore of Gozo opened up, and he could see the red sand of Ramla Beach. But it was a long way off; well over a mile. He started swimming again, slowly and tiring fast.

He was exhausted and treading water when he heard the chugging of the diesel engine and looked up to see the brightly coloured Luzzu fishing boat. He could make out two figures in the bows, scanning the water — Nadia and Joey. He tried to shout, and he waved an arm and sank under the water, sputtering for breath. Then they saw him and turned and came quickly alongside. He was too weak to pull himself up, and Joey dived in and put a shoulder under him and the two fishermen took an arm each and hauled him in.

He lay in the scuppers, gasping for breath, and then vomited out pints of seawater.

As they motored back to Mgarr, he sat silently in the stern, breathing deeply. Nadia covertly watched his angry face. She had stood at her bedroom window and seen him swim out into the channel in the early light, and guessed that he was trying for Comino. She had seen the current take him and his failed effort to get back to Gozo and had screamed for Joey. They had raced down to Mgarr in the Land Rover. Most of the fishermen were already far out to sea, but one boat was just getting ready. Fortunately the fishermen, two brothers called Mizzi, had drunk late the night before in Gleneagles, and hangovers had slowed them down. Nadia and Joey had leapt into the boat with urgent explanations.

"You were lucky, Creasy," she said. "We could have easily missed you."

"I know," he granted. "Damned stupid. I should have checked the tides."

She saw him look at Comino and then across to Gozo — his face malevolent. He hated that strip of water. She guessed he would try again, and soon.

Back in the harbour, Creasy asked Joey for five pounds and tried to press it on the fishermen. It was too late for them to go out now. They shook their heads, laughing.

"You're the biggest thing we've caught all summer," one brother said.

The other agreed. "I'm trying to decide whether to have you grilled or fried."

They all went in to Gleneagles and Creasy bought the drinks, standing at the bar in his swim suit.

It was an occasion, adding spice to routine. Tony prepared his patent remedy for near-drownings — a huge mug of hot, sweet tea laced with a great slug of brandy and a tot of rum for good measure. He was so proud of it he made one for himself. Then Victor and Michele came in from the first ferry run and, hearing the story, decided they would try it too.

"But you have to be either a bartender or half drowned," Tony explained.

"We qualify," Victor retorted. "We were half drowned in here last night — from the inside."

"Shreik" arrived for his pre-breakfast stiffener, and a celebration started.

"They are grateful to you, Creasy," Nadia said with mock disdain. "Anything for an excuse to get drunk before lunch."

"Shreik" nodded solemnly. "Pity you didn't get properly drowned, *Uomo*. We could have had a real party." He smiled. "In commiseration, you understand."

On the drive back to the house, Creasy asked, "What's this *Uomo* business?"

"Your nickname," Joey explained. "Everyone in Gozo has to have a nickname."

Creasy digested that in silence. *Uomo* meant "man" in Italian. It was a complimentary nickname. After the morning's effort, he mused, they ought to call him "jackass."

But it meant that he had been accepted. Outsiders don't merit nicknames.

Creasy and George sat on the outside patio alone. They had enjoyed a good dinner. Laura and Nadia had worked most of the afternoon preparing it: a *minestra*, and then *timpana*, Maltese style, followed by rabbit *stufato*, and rounded off with fruit and the local pepper cheese made from goat's milk. Creasy had spent a quiet day after his near mishap. In the afternoon he had driven into Rabat to the police station and picked up a set of tide tables.

He noted that Paul and Joey had deliberately gone off somewhere, leaving the two of them alone. Nadia brought out a tray with coffee and cognac and then went back into the kitchen.

George thoughtfully filled and tamped a large pipe, struck a match, and sucked flame down into the bowl. Creasy poured the coffee and cognac. He knew what was coming. Paul had felt it right to brief him.

Satisfied with the small furnace he had created, George leaned back and said, "You know I'm in charge of security for the islands?"

Creasy nodded and passed him a cup. "You want to know whether I'm a security risk?"

George waved his pipe deprecatingly. "No, Paul explained why you're here. In any event, I've already learned quite a lot about you." He was a little embarrassed. "I sent a telex this morning to Paris."

Creasy was puzzled. "Paris?"

"Yes — Interpol." His smile took away any potential offence. "Not what you think. It's just that for the past few years many countries have been keeping tabs on all known mercenaries — even since the fiasco in Angola. It's just convenient to have it centralized at Interpol. There is no criminal implication, you understand."

Creasy remained silent, and after a pause George continued.

"The fact is, I let you come and join our squad on Thursday because you're my uncle's friend; but if it's going to be a regular thing, it's my duty to check that there are no wrinkles."

"I understand that," Creasy said. "Are there any wrinkles?" George shook his head and reached into his jacket pocket and passed over a folded piece of paper.

"That's the telex reply I received this afternoon." He shrugged. "I really shouldn't show it to you."

Creasy read while George puffed at his pipe. There was a very long silence, then Creasy asked, "What does the bit at the end mean?"

George leaned over and translated the coded suffix: "Not politically motivated. No known criminal affiliations. No group affiliations. More details available on request."

Creasy folded the paper and handed it back and there was another pregnant silence.

"Is it basically correct?"

Creasy nodded and, for the first time, smiled. "Except that I'm no longer a bodyguard. What are the other details they refer to?"

"I sent a Grade Two inquiry," George explained. "It's cheaper, and we are not a rich department. So they sent brief details. A Grade One inquiry would have elicited every single thing they know about you."

Creasy was impressed. "How do they get their information?"

"Intelligence services, mainly," George answered. "We pool certain information. It's a sensitive world, and mercenaries can be a nuisance. For example, they've taken over the Comoro Islands in the Indian Ocean as a personal fief — there are some bums in your profession, Creasy."

"You're right," Creasy agreed, "and those bums sometimes make it tough for us bums." He looked at George appraisingly. "You're worried that it might happen here?"

George shook his head. "Not at all. But we're a neutral country. No more foreign bases. We can look after ourselves, although not everyone would agree. The fact is, Malta is in the middle of things. We don't want people basing themselves here who may be planning action elsewhere in the region."

It was deftly done. A question without form.

"I'm one man," Creasy said, with a faint smile. "As the report said, I've no group affiliations, and I've no plans which would embarrass you. I'm just here to get fit."

"That's fine," George said. "You're welcome to use our facilities — strictly unofficial, of course."

"I'm grateful."

George smiled. "There's one condition — nothing onerous." He tapped his pocket. "You are very experienced. I want to use that experience."

"How?"

George's pipe had gone out and he busied himself relighting it while he gathered his thoughts. Then he spoke at length.

"My squad was formed for brushfire incidents. Terrorist attacks — hijack attempts, and so forth. These days, almost every country has such a squad. But we lack actual experience. In the past, Malta has always been occupied by foreign powers who have provided security. We have a small military establishment, the AFM — Armed Forces of Malta. We are not a rich country, and we can't afford the luxury of a one purpose army, so the AFM is also involved in civil projects — road building and such. It's cost-effective, and I agree with it. The fact is, we can't afford to import skilled instructors for all facets of combat. The British helped before they left, and the Libyans have donated equipment — helicopters, naval patrol boats, and so on, and they help train our people to use them. But for specialist work we lack both actual experience or instructors. My squad, for example. I've been overseas for training and I'm passing on what I've learned, but I've never seen combat. We have to work with theory, based on set situations. In the world today — the world of terrorism — a lot of unforeseen things can happen."

He sat back in his chair, the pipe clenched between his teeth, and looked quizzically at Creasy, "You've been there, in all manner of situations — on both sides."

"Alright," Creasy agreed. "I'll do what I can. Apart from the stuff I saw on Thursday, what other equipment do you have?"

The two men went on to discuss technicalities, and it was after midnight when they finished. They had established a comfortable rapport. Both practical, undemonstrative men who had weighed each other and liked what they found.

This time he plunged off the flat rock fifteen minutes before the turn of the tide. Again there was a slight breeze blowing from the west, but the current was slack, and Creasy swam steadily towards his target. Nadia stood at the bedroom window and watched through her father's binoculars. She saw him reach the point of the small bay and continue swimming around to the hotel jetty. Then she went downstairs and phoned Joey. She had sent him down to Gleneagles every morning for the last three days to stand by — Creasy hadn't said anything about trying the swim again, but she knew him by now. Then she phoned her friend, the receptionist at the Comino Hotel.

Creasy was walking barefoot and wet past the front of the hotel when he heard his name called. The girl came down the steps carrying a plastic bag and a tall, frosted glass of beer,

"Compliments of Nadia," she said with a smile.

Creasy had to laugh. He turned and looked across the channel. He could pick out the farmhouse high on the hill and at an upper window a flash of light as the sun caught the binocular's lenses. He waved and held up the glass in a silent toast.

Inside the bag were a pair of jeans, a white T-shirt, and rubber sandals — all new; and a towel and a note.

"This is a very Catholic country," he read. "You can't walk around half naked!"

The girl pointed.

"There's a changing room around the side there, and that path leads to the Blue Lagoon." She glanced at her watch. "The ferry goes in forty minutes."

He thanked her and handed back the empty glass.

The jeans and the T-shirt fitted perfectly. An observant girl, he thought, as he pulled them on. The path rose to the brow of a low hill and then down again to the transparent water of the lagoon. The sun was well up now, and heat rose off the dry, barren ground. Up to his left, Creasy saw a man dressed in baggy trousers held up by a wide leather belt. The top of a bulging sack was tucked into the belt on one side, a plastic bag on the other. He wore a grey, long-sleeved shirt, buttoned at the wrists, and a flat cap on his head — the normal dress of a Gozitan farmer; but his actions were far from normal. He held a long, bushy branch in both hands and moved along the slope of the hill beating the ground with it, occasionally bending down to pick something up and put it in the plastic bag. Mystified, Creasy walked on down to the jetty. He could see the small, yellow ferry in the distance, just coming out of Mgarr harbour. He sat on a rock and watched the old man work his way steadily down the hill toward him.

He reached the jetty as the ferry pulled in and nodded to Creasy, who looked closely at the transparent bag at his waist. Grasshoppers! Live grasshoppers. He was still mystified as they climbed aboard, but as they chugged out of the bay, the old man reached into his voluminous sack and pulled out a fishing line. Bait — the grasshoppers must be for bait. But the line was attached to an old and battered rubber squid, which was quickly paid out into the boat's wake.

Curiosity won.

"What are the grasshoppers for?"

The old man took his eyes off the line. "I have a nightingale. They are to feed it."

Creasy was still puzzled.

"But there are plenty of grasshoppers on Gozo. I've seen them."

The old man smiled. "But the Comino grasshoppers are tastier."

That silenced Creasy for a while, and the two of them sat looking back toward the submerged rubber squid.

"You catch many fish?"

The old man shook his head. "Very infrequently."

Creasy thought that it might have something to do with the age and state of the bait, but then the infrequent happened. The water was so clear that he saw the flash of silver as the fish darted in from the side. Pandemonium erupted. Amid shouts and scrambling, the ferry was stopped and the three young crew members crowded to the stern, all offering unnecessary advice. The old man pulled in the line — evenly and unhurried.

It was a big fish, and as it neared the stern the excitement increased. The old man leaned forward to give it a final, boarding jerk and the fish was already in the air when it parted company with the hook. There came a slap as it hit the water and a final flash of silver, and it was gone.

There was a great wailing from the crew and numerous invocations to *Ghal Madonna*, but the old man remained calm and unruffled.

"We are all very sad," Creasy commiserated.

The old man shook his head. "Not all," he said. "The fish is not entirely unhappy."

"Why do grasshoppers on Comino taste better than grasshoppers on Gozo?" Creasy asked Paul at dinner. He got a blank look and told him about the philosophical fisherman.

"That's old Salvu." Paul laughed. "He has a small farm near Ramla. He only says that as an excuse to take the ferry every day and do some fishing."

"He's a character, that Salvu," Laura commented. "His wife died five years ago. Every Sunday he goes to the church in Nadur and confesses his sins to 'The Cowboy' — confesses to the worst imaginable things, just to get a rise out of him."

"I thought the confessional was secret," Creasy said.

"It is," said Laura. "'The Cowboy' wouldn't say anything, but Salvu brags about it — says it's just to help 'The Cowboy' understand a bit more about life: know what he's missing."

"Well," said Creasy, "he's invited me for dinner next time he catches a fish."

Paul was impressed. "That's unusual. He keeps to himself, old Salvu; but go. He makes the strongest wine on Gozo, and you'll get a good meal."

The conversation was interrupted by the phone. It was Guido calling from Naples. He and Creasy had a very oblique conversation. From it Creasy understood that contact had been made in Marseilles with Leclerc, who was being cooperative. All other preparations were going ahead smoothly. Creasy indicated that he would be ready to move in four to six weeks, and asked Guido to send him a letter when everything was complete.

That night Creasy lay in bed listening to Johnny Cash and reviewing his situation — physical and mental. He was satisfied with his progress. His body was responding well, the slackness going. In another month or so, it would be well tuned and responsive. He had been fortunate in finding George Zammit and in being allowed to train with his squad. By the time he left Malta, he would be fully prepared for the task ahead. Mentally also. He recognized the fundamental change in himself. He looked on life with greater clarity. With compassion, even. Before, in his life, the people around him had seemed incidental. He did not consider them on a personal or emotional basis. His interest had always been remote and clinical. Pinta had changed that. Everything she saw had affected her. He imagined her in Gozo — how delighted she would have been with old Salvu. How she would have reacted to the people he had met, seeing in them the angles and facets of life. He saw now through her eyes. A year ago Salvu would have been an uninteresting old man who kept a bird and chased grasshoppers for it and therefore was a bit simple in the head. But now Creasy looked forward to having dinner with him and talking to him and learning more about him. Pinta had done that, had made it possible that he could come to Gozo and be accepted by the introverted community. And also enjoy being accepted. He reflected on the unjust twist of fate that had ended her short life. No, not fate. Nothing was fated. Every incident, every event involving people, was the result of actions by themselves or others. Luck was not a random phenomenon. Destiny was predetermined by the destined.

His thoughts turned to Nadia. He knew what was happening, could feel the magnetic force. He would fight it. There were just too many complications — too little time — too much planned.

But then, surely, that was fate. A meeting at a different time and place could have resulted in a different ending. How often had that happened, he wondered. How many people had come together on the wrong occasion? But that too wasn't fate. That was a melding of separate experiences, the contact and recognition of similar hopes and expectations.

Well. His own expectations were clear and simple, his future, or lack of it, projected.

In another part of the house, in her own room, Nadia's thoughts ran parallel. Experience had made her cynical. Her future was also limited. Within her community, a woman, once married, was just that, no matter what the circumstances. Even if the Vatican eventually annulled her marriage, she could not expect to start again with fresh hopes. Mothers would not want their sons to marry a woman so scarred, and those sons would look at her only as a woman. Desirable, certainly, but not a potential wife.

This did not add to her cynicism. It left no extra bitterness. She would seek her own corner and put her back to it and face outward.

But there was something she wanted. She would not be denied everything. Others could have their husbands and their positions and their reputations and their communal security, but she at least would have something. People could talk and even criticize. She didn't care. Her own family would understand. That was important — vital. With that understanding, she would face out confidently from her corner.

There was little time. Four to six weeks, she had heard him say on the phone. It would have to be soon.

In the morning Paul and Joey were in the fields, and Creasy was swimming. Nadia could see the small dot of his head approaching Comino. Her mother was in Nadur at the market. She went downstairs and phoned Guido, She had always been close to her brother-in-law. She asked him about Creasy, about the future. What it held for Creasy. Where he was going and why.

Guido realized immediately what had happened. He felt a great sadness for her. Tried to explain that it was useless — had no future. But he would not answer her questions. She must ask Creasy.

By his tone and his sympathy and his refusal, he had, in effect, answered the question. But his conclusions had not been entirely accurate. She needed to know that Creasy's future was marginal. That confirmed the futile dimension, but it didn't alter her plans — only increased her determination.

In the early evening she walked down the fields to where her father and Creasy were finishing the last few metres of a terrace wall. She knew Creasy would go for a quick swim before he came back up to the house. She sat on the wall watching the two men, her father small and wiry and dwarfed by the huge American. She noted the change in Creasy, the deep brown tan, solid muscles, hands calloused from weeks of hard work.

"You have no work to do?" her father asked gruffly, but unable to keep the affection from his voice.

"I'm finished," she answered. "I'm going for a swim. I'll wait for Creasy."

Creasy lifted a large stone up onto the wall.

"Still worried I'll drown?" he asked mockingly.

She shook her head.

"No. I want to talk to you."

"What about?"

"I'll tell you after we swim."

"You go on, Creasy," Paul said. "Swim while it's still light. I'll finish the last bit in a few minutes."

They swam out a little way into the channel. Comino was bathed copper in the lowering sun. The water was flat calm, broken only by the occasional ripple of a fish. She turned and swam back, but he moved out farther, conscious of the tension in her. Disturbed by it.

When he returned to the cove she was lying on a towel, stretched out on the flat rock. He lay down wet beside her, letting the last of the sun dry him. Several minutes passed before she spoke.

"Creasy, I'm in love with you." She held up her hand.

"Please don't interrupt." She picked her words carefully.

'I know you also feel something, but don't want to get involved. I know that you're at least twenty years older than me.

I know you're leaving in about a month and probably won't come back."

She turned her head to look at him and said very quietly, "But for sure I love you, and while you are here I will be your woman."

He stared up at the sky, immobile, and then slowly shook his head.

"Nadia, you're crazy. All the things you said are true, especially that I'm not coming back. There's no future in it. As for being in love with me — that's a word too easily used."

"I know," she answered. "But I've only used it once before in my life and that turned out to be a joke — a sick joke." She told him about her marriage and her husband. He grimaced and got to his feet and looked down at her.

"So you should know better than to walk into hopeless situations."

She lay with her hands behind her head, olive skin against the black swimsuit, looking up at him impassively.

"Don't you like me?"

"You know I do. But it's not right. There's no future in it." He bent down to pick up his clothes. "You're very young. Compared to me, still a child. In spite of what's happened, you have a whole life in front of you. You'll find a good man to share it with."

He tried to sound matter-of-fact. Dismissing her declaration as an irrational outburst. She stood and picked up her towel.

"That's possible," she said evenly. "Who knows? But in the meantime I'll share it with you." Now her voice was matter-of-fact.

He became exasperated.

"Nadia, it's ridiculous. How can you just come out with it so calmly, as though you're inviting me to the cinema?"

A thought struck him. "Besides, what about your parents? I'm a guest in their house. It would be a great insult."

"They'll understand," she said. "I'll talk to them tonight."

He looked at her in astonishment.

"You will what!"

She smiled.

"Creasy, although my parents are old-fashioned Gozitan farmers, they are still my parents, and I understand them. I know exactly how to talk to them and explain. As long as we are not indiscreet, it will be alright."

She picked up her dress and slipped it on, while Creasy stood speechless. Then she started up the path.

"Wait a minute," Creasy called. "Just wait a minute!"

She turned and looked down at him, at his expression of puzzlement and rising consternation.

"What the hell is this? A damned cattle market?" He waved his clothes at her, trying to find the words. "Don't I have any say about it? You can forget the whole thing. I want no part of it. You understand!"

She smiled. A slow, enigmatic smile.

"But you said you liked me."

"Exactly," he said, as if discovering a sudden truth. "I said 'like you,' not 'love you.' It's not the same, you know."

"It's good enough for the moment," she replied over her shoulder and continued on up the path, leaving Creasy standing on the rock, disgruntled and disconcerted.

There was no lock on his door. He had considered wedging a chair under the knob, but that seemed silly. But she didn't come, and he lay in bed wondering whether she would really discuss such a thing with her parents. He considered leaving and finding some other place to finish his preparations, or talking to Paul himself, man to man. Explain the position and ask him to talk to Nadia. But how to tell a man that his daughter was throwing herself at him? He cursed the girl for a distracting nuisance and drifted into a troubled sleep.

In the morning, very early, he set off for a run. As he skirted below Nadur, he saw Laura coming down the path from early Mass. She waved at him and he waved back, running on. Probably a good sign, he thought. At least she didn't throw a rock at me. The clear light of morning diffused his problem. He saw it in perspective. Nadia had been flying a kite — testing his reaction. His obvious lack of enthusiasm would have turned her right off. As he jogged along he had to admit that he had been tempted. A young, desirable woman, offering herself like that. He was old enough to be her father. Still, getting fit must have added something. He slapped his flat stomach. Only one man in a hundred his age could be as fit, maybe one in a thousand. He preened himself gently.

He had worked his way down to Ramla Bay, and a voice interrupted his reverie, calling his nickname — *Uomo*. He looked up to see Salvu working in his fields and he stopped for a chat.

"I don't see you on Comino the last couple of days," said the old man.

"Tomorrow," Creasy answered. "I'll swim over tomorrow. No fish yet?"

Salvu shook his head.

"But soon, *Uomo*. I'm due for one — I'll leave word,"

Creasy went back to his running.

By the time he reached the cove, sweat glistened on his face. He pulled off his track suit and dived gratefully into the cool water.

Afterward, lying on the flat rock, he thought again about Nadia. She would probably be embarrassed when she saw him. He hoped the easy atmosphere in the house would not be changed. It would be a damned nuisance if he had to move at this stage. He would try to be relaxed with her. Treat the whole thing as a bit of a joke. That would make it easier. He knew she was sensitive. Who wouldn't be; after that mess of a marriage? Perhaps that's what made her irrational. If she tried it again he would be gentle, but firm. There was no place in his life for such a relationship.

He stood up, dried from the sun, and pulled on his track suit and walked up the rocky path to the house.

Nadia was nowhere to be seen, but Laura was in the kitchen.

He looked at her closely.

"Breakfast, Creasy?" she asked brightly. "You were up extra early this morning."

In spite of being mentally preconditioned, he felt relief. Laura was her normal self, nothing had been said the night before. He sat down, suddenly hungry, and Laura cracked four eggs into a skillet and slid a wedge of ham alongside them.

"Is it true that Americans eat pancakes for breakfast?" she asked over her shoulder.

He nodded. "With syrup. But I haven't eaten pancakes since I was a kid."

She put the plate in front of him and another piled high with warm bread. Then she poured him a big mug of black coffee and shovelled in three heaped spoonfuls of sugar. She poured herself a coffee and sat down opposite, watching with satisfaction as he ate hungrily. It made cooking worthwhile when a man could really eat. She was conscious of the change in him. Good food and exercise had done that.

She spoke conversationally:

"Nadia talked to Paul and me last night."

Creasy choked on the food.

"Don't be embarrassed," she said. "We are a very close family, and Nadia would not do anything behind our backs. She is an honest girl,"

"She's a silly girl!" Creasy burst out, angry in his discomfort. "The whole thing is crazy."

Laura smiled.

"Love is always crazy. Such a drama is made of it; but it's a natural thing, don't you think?"

"'Love!' he snorted. I'm told it's good when it's mutual. How can she talk of love? I never gave her any encouragement. I don't know why she talks of it."

Laura nodded solemnly.

"I know you didn't, so does Paul. That's why I brought up the subject. I want you to know that we don't blame you for anything."

Creasy spoke earnestly — persuasively.

"Look, Laura, I like Nadia very much. That's all. But even if I felt more for her, it would be useless. That's what she can't seem to understand. In a few weeks I'll be leaving. There's something I have to do. It's extremely unlikely that I'll ever return. Her hopes will be smashed again — it isn't logical."

Laura smiled at him again.

"Logical! Such words. When has love ever been logical?" She held up her hand. "Wait — listen. You know of her marriage. It affects her more than you think. Not what has happened. Not in her mind. It affects her status here in Gozo. She wants to stay here. She is determined. But we are not like other places. She cannot live here like other women. She cannot start again. But she is a warm girl. She wants to give of herself, not hiding it, or being ashamed. That's why she talked to us last night."

He shook his head.

"Laura, why me? There's too much against it. First, I'm so much older than she is, and second, I'm leaving — definitely leaving."

He thought of something.

"Maybe she thinks she can change my mind. Persuade me not to go." He looked hard at Laura, into her eyes, and said with great emphasis: "That's impossible. You must convince her. Then she may forget this nonsense."

Laura was thoughtful for a moment. This aspect did puzzle her, for Nadia was a practical girl. She was holding something back. Last night, when she confronted her parents, she had been simple and direct, and they had quickly pointed out that there was no future in it. Her father had been blunt. "He will go away and leave you," he had told her. "Nothing will stop him. I know that." But she had answered that she knew it too and accepted it. Meanwhile, she loved him. She was not a child. She was not looking for permanence. She knew that was impossible. But she was entitled to some happiness — even temporary happiness.

So now Laura shook her head and said, "I doubt it. I don't think she will try to persuade you to stay." She noted his expression. Puzzled and embarrassed and defiant. Her voice softened.

"Creasy, you are attractive to women. You must know that. And you can't live in isolation. You affect people. Everybody does, one way or another. You can't expect to go through life without having an influence on others. Without being influenced yourself. Take this house; in the case of Joey, he hero-worships you. That's natural. He's young, and you represent an exciting world he's never seen. In Nadia's case, it's love. That too may be natural. After the mess of her marriage perhaps she has swung the other way. Perhaps she sees, in you, everything her husband wasn't."

The thought amused her as she looked at Creasy: huge forearms resting on the table. Scarred hands and face.

"You're not exactly a delicate flower."

He didn't react. Didn't seem to hear her last words. Something she had said earlier had triggered a response in his mind. Had taken him back.

"You don't live in isolation." That was true. He had for so long. But that had changed.

He came back to the present and stood up and said, "Anyway, it takes two. Whatever's in her mind, she can forget it."

He turned to leave, and at the door he said, "Laura, I'm sorry this happened. I don't want to cause any problems. Perhaps I should go away?"

She shrugged.

"As far as we're concerned, there are no problems — and there won't be. We like having you here. And you have been a big help to Paul. He needed help this summer. But you have to work it out yourself with Nadia. I won't say anything more. I won't interfere with her — or with you." She smiled. "But you don't seem like a man who runs away — even from a woman."

He glared at her and saw the smile broaden and he went out banging the door behind him.

She came two nights later, just after midnight.

The door opened quietly and he heard the patter of bare feet on the stone floor. Moonlight through the small window showed her dimly at the bedroom door, standing still — watching him. She moved to the bed. A rustle of cloth on skin.

"Go back to your own room," he said.

She pulled back the single sheet and slipped in beside him.

"I don't want you here. Go back to your own room."

A soft arm crossed his waist and soft lips kissed his shoulder and moved up toward his neck.

He lay completely still — unresponsive.

"Nadia, understand. I don't want you."

She raised herself slightly. Small, soft breasts pressed down on his chest. Her mouth moved slowly from his neck to his chin and then to his lips. He tried to tell her again to leave; but it had become difficult.

CHAPTER TWELVE

He was short and thickset and clad in camouflage uniform. Grenades and a small transceiver hung from webbing on his chest, and he held a Sterling submachine gun. He leaned against the stone wall breathing deeply, steadying himself after the sprint across the open ground to the two storied building.

Ready now, he inched toward the corner. He knew that around it was a long windowless corridor, and at the end, a flight of stairs leading to the upper floor. He bunched and sprang forward in a low crouch, his finger tightening on the trigger. The staccato rattle of the Sterling echoed through the building.

Creasy stood at the foot of the stairs and watched him coming, eyes taking in every detail.

The man reached the stairs with a squeal of rubber soled boots and again flattened himself against the wall. An empty magazine clattered to the floor and a full one clicked into place. He lifted a hand to the transceiver. "Going up now," he said, and with a glance at Creasy, hurled himself up the stairs. Creasy followed, hearing more bursts of firing and, at the other end of the building, the crack of grenades.

They streamed out into the rocky garden, all fifteen of them, dressed in camouflage gear and talking excitedly. George brought up the rear, ushering them over to a low wall, telling them to sit.

The exercise had lasted five minutes, but the debriefing went on for an hour. George took them through all phases of attack, criticizing here, praising there. He stood in front of them, Creasy alongside. The squad was in high spirits; it was their first full-scale exercise and the noise and action had been stimulating.

George finished and turned to Creasy. "Any comments?"

Creasy stepped forward and the squad stilled expectantly.

"On the whole, good," he said, and there was a row of smiles.

"But in a real fight, half of you would be dead or wounded." The smiles faded.

He pointed at the short, squat one.

"Grazio, you came down that corridor hugging the wall — a stone wall. That just brings you closer to a ricochet. You've been told — always come down the centre. You feel more exposed, but it's safer. You came around the corner low, but straightened up almost immediately, and you were aiming waist high. Always aim low. An enemy can lie on the floor, but he can't fly in the air. In a stone or brick building like that, use the ricochet to your own advantage."

Grazio nodded, crestfallen, but Creasy didn't let up.

"If I'd been a terrorist, you'd be dead now. And another thing, your magazine change was slow — very slow. That's the critical time, when you're most vulnerable. You must practice until your fingers ache. Until it's reflexive." His eyes swept the line. "All of you — practice! It's the difference between being dead or alive. You don't have time to fumble."

He pointed to a taller man, with a heavy black moustache.

"Domi, you followed Charlie into Room Two. You should have stayed in the corridor, covering the doors of Rooms Three and Four. It didn't need both of you in there. It wasn't a bedroom. There were no girls waiting for you!"

The squad laughed. Domi was a noted Romeo.

Creasy went on to comment on the performance of almost every man in the squad. George was quietly astonished by the volume and scope of Creasy's observations. He noted again the change in Creasy's manner whenever he was instructing. Reticence gone — clear, incisive sentences. And he noticed how the men listened, absorbing everything. It was the voice of total experience and authority. They had seen Creasy change an empty Sterling magazine. A blur of motion, the thread of fire hardly broken. They had seen him fire handguns, SMGs, and carbines, and strip them down and reassemble them with the same assurance that they handled a knife and fork. And they had all practised unarmed combat with him and been amazed at his speed and reflexes. They were all fit, hard, young men in their twenties, and they knew that Creasy, so much older, could have beaten any of them in a serious fight. So they listened.

He ended by telling them that as a first exercise they had all done well. He praised their speed in the initial assault and their lack of hesitation once they were in the building.

"But don't hang around," he stressed. "Always keep moving. Moving and watching. You know yourselves how easy it is to hit a stationary target. So keep low, keep moving, and keep watching."

He stepped back and George spoke a few more words and dismissed the squad.

Creasy had been deliberately left out of the planning of the exercise. George had wanted an independent opinion. Now he took Creasy aside and asked him, "What about the overall tactics?"

Creasy stood looking at the building and considering. The scenario had been that four terrorists, without hostages, had been holed up, presumably on the top floor. Efforts to talk them out had failed, and the squad had been ordered to storm the building.

"It was out of balance," he said finally. "You had five men covering the outside and you sent in ten. Better the other way round.

First, because too many men in the assault force get in each other's way, and second, because once the assault started, the terrorists were likely to break out, and in different directions." He pointed to the upper-storey windows. "They could have jumped — it's not very high."

He softened his criticism: "The method and direction of entry were good. I liked the idea of driving the truck below the upper south windows; and the diversion from the front was well timed and realistic."

He put a hand on George's shoulder.

"It was imaginative planning, but I suggest less reliance on the transceivers. They're useful in a stakeout, but the assault force should ignore them unless they get bogged down. Reporting every move is inhibiting. They all know what to do, they're trained to react as individuals — let them." He smiled. "On the whole, George, good. Especially as a first effort."

George was pleased.

"Thanks," he said. "I have the building for a month. We'll have two more exercises with it and Air Malta will let us borrow one of their Boeings for a couple of hours next week for a simulated hijack assault."

The squad was grouped around the back of a police Land Rover, and cold bottles of beer were being passed out. Creasy and George walked over to join them. As they stood around drinking, George suddenly said with mock severity,

"By the way, I thought you weren't planning to work in Malta."

Creasy was puzzled for a moment, and then understood. He feigned innocence. "Christ, George, I'm only helping your uncle on the farm."

The fifteen young policemen were all listening and smiling. So was George. "That's not what I meant, Creasy, and you know it; but anyway, it was a good thing. It saved us some work and stopped an injustice."

He was referring to an incident that had occurred a few days before.

The lampuki season had started, lampuki being the favourite fish of the Maltese. Creasy had driven Nadia down to Mgarr one evening to buy the first of the catch direct from the fishermen. They could see the brightly painted boats coming up the Comino channel. He left her at the quay and went into Gleneagles for a drink.

There was a small group at the bar. Michele and Victor, Tony and Sam and "Shreik." The group opened to let him in and Sam poured him a beer, and they went back to their conversation. They were unusually serious, and Creasy listened with interest.

The problem centred on a Gozo "character" called Benny, nicknamed "Tattoo" — his huge arms were covered with them. Benny was very big, very strong, and in looks resembled a reject for Frankenstein. Although a Gozitan, he had spent many years on the big island. Creasy had heard some of the stories about him. One concerned the previous election. A politician had promised that, in return for help during the election, Benny would be given a plum job once the new government was installed. Benny, a trusting type, worked hard, and after the politician was duly elected turned up at his office for the promised job. He was kept waiting a couple of hours and then informed by a secretary that the politician had no recollection of any job offer and was too busy to see him. Benny, irritated, pushed past the secretary to the door of the office. The politician had foresight, and the door was locked. Benny became angry and smashed down the door. The politician disappeared through the window, blessing his luck that he had a ground floor office. It was a nice office, newly furnished and decorated. Benny vented his anger on it. When the police arrived they could still hear the sounds of splintering wood.

None of the policemen relished the idea of making an arrest — Benny had a reputation. They had two Alsatian dogs with them and they told Benny through a megaphone that if he didn't come out peacefully they would send the dogs in. There was a very brief silence, and then the sounds of destruction started again. They sent in the dogs. Within half a minute they came back — thrown out the window with broken necks.

Benny was lucky. The judge was neither an animal lover nor a supporter of that politician. Benny got only three months.

His latest brush with the law had occurred six months earlier. He had a temporary job as a "keeper of the peace" in a bar on Strait Street in Valletta. This street, known as "the gut," had been a favourite hangout of sailors for generations, but, with the closing of the British naval base, it had fallen on hard times. Only a few bars remained open, and some of these became the favourite drinking spots of various gangs of Malta's small but dedicated tough guy element. Benny had his enemies among this group and, in "keeping the peace" one night, sent two of them to the hospital for a long time.

The same judge had given him a year's sentence, suspended for six months. In order to keep out of the way of temptation, Benny had come home to Gozo to wait out the six months in relative seclusion.

He was often in Gleneagles and several times had drinks with Creasy. He was popular with the locals. Friendly and always ready to lend a helping hand — pulling up a boat or painting a house or threatening a difficult outsider.

Creasy liked him. On one occasion Benny had come in with a girl — a peroxide blonde tourist, a bit drunk and fascinated by his tough guy image. Twice she knocked Creasy's glass over, the second time while Benny was in the toilet. Creasy spoke to her sharply.

"It was an accident," she said indignantly. "Don't talk to me like that."

When Benny came back, she complained that Creasy had insulted her.

The room had gone quiet. Benny looked at Creasy inquiringly.

"She's trying to set us up," Creasy explained, and told him about the spilled drinks.

Benny nodded and gave Tony a look and two fresh drinks were put on the bar.

"Are you frightened of him, then?" the girl asked scornfully.

Benny shook his head. "No, and he's not frightened of me. Now shut up or get out."

So Creasy liked him and had listened sympathetically to the discussion of his problem.

It seemed that Benny's period of suspension would end in a few days. If he broke the peace before then, he would have to do the full year in jail. That thought appealed to some of his enemies on Malta. On the previous ferry run, Victor had seen two of those enemies at the Cirkewwa jetty. They were waiting in a line of cars to make the crossing and, by judicious spacing, Victor had ensured that they didn't get on. But they were first in line for the next trip. The group at the bar discussed what could be done. It was known that Benny was drinking that afternoon in Marsalforn but it was no good asking him to keep out of the way. His pride wouldn't permit that. It was also no use informing the police of the impending clash. It was obvious that Benny's two enemies were coming to provoke a fight, but they could bide their time, and Benny wouldn't need much provoking. They all cast about for a solution, but Creasy kept silent, holding a debate with himself. He didn't want to get involved; he never did, in other people's fights. It wasn't his business — but still, for six weeks he had lived in this community and been accepted by it. These people had been good to him. To some extent, their problems must be his problems. He liked Benny.

So when Victor looked at his watch and announced that he had to go, Creasy asked Tony to have someone drive Nadia home. "I'll make the trip with Victor — get some fresh air."

He stood with Victor in the wheelhouse as the *Melitaland* edged into the jetty at Cirkewwa.

'That's their car," Victor pointed. "At the front of the queue."

It was a big old Dodge, painted white and red and adorned with strips of chrome and a mascot of a rearing stallion.

"They all drive cars like that," Victor said. "Be careful, *Uomo*. They are not soft, those two."

Creasy nodded. "When do you leave?"

"In half an hour."

Creasy opened the wheelhouse door.

"If I'm not back I'll catch you on the next trip — don't wait."

The cars had started to roll down the ramp, and Victor leaned forward to watch as Creasy picked his moment and crossed in front of them and off the ferry. He walked casually to the line of waiting cars. As he passed the Dodge he suddenly stopped, and in one motion opened the rear door, got in, and closed it behind him.

The Dodge started to rock on its soft springs. From his position up in the wheelhouse, Victor couldn't see into the car. He ran to the wing of the bridge, but he still couldn't see anything. Then the rocking stopped. Victor heard the Dodge's engine start and, very slowly, it pulled out of the line, turned down the road away from the jetty, and a mile away disappeared round a bend.

Half an hour later all the cars were loaded. A crew member looked up to the bridge for the signal to raise the ramp. "Wait," Victor called down. He had seen the Dodge reappear.

It pulled up broadside to the ramp, and Creasy got out of the back seat and crossed onto the ferry. The Dodge headed back toward Valletta.

"What happened?" Victor asked eagerly when Creasy appeared at the wheelhouse door.

Creasy shrugged. "They decided not to visit Gozo this summer." His tone precluded any further questions, and they had crossed to Mgarr in silence.

"Do you know every single little thing that goes on in these islands?" Creasy asked.

George nodded. "Just about — what did you do to them?"

"We had a conversation." Creasy tried to change the subject. "When is the next exercise?"

George grinned. "Next week, same time. It must have been a hell of a conversation. Those two haven't shown a nose in three days."

"Reformed characters," Creasy grunted. He turned to one of the grinning men. "Grazio, you're ready to go?"

Paul's Land Rover was in for repair and Creasy had got a lift into Valletta in the morning. Grazio had offered to run him back to Cirkewwa.

As they drove along the winding coast road, Grazio tried to make conversation. He soon gave up. Creasy was obviously in a reflective mood. In fact, he was thinking of his impending departure. Two more weeks, he decided, and he'd be ready. The thought of leaving brought conflicting emotions. Now that he was reaching full fitness, he felt an impatience to get on with the job. The preparation had been long and hard, only endured because of the purpose. He was almost ready and his mind ranged forward, combing through his strategy, trying to foresee problems. His mind was ahead of his body — waiting for it to catch up. In two weeks they would come together.

Nadia — she was the other emotion. Nadia and his life on Gozo. Leaving would be final. He had a premonition of that. He loved her. Admitting that to himself had been a physical shock, releasing adrenalin into his blood.

After the first night, she had moved her clothes into his rooms. He had accepted it. A month, that was all. She had been warned — so be it. But it had taken only a few days. He woke early one morning. The sun lit her sleeping face. Serious and vulnerable; and he loved her.

She said she would be his woman and in those few short days had shown what it meant. Complete but not suffocating. She had the natural wisdom to make her presence a mere extension of himself. After that first day, she never spoke again of love. She was never clinging, never maudlin. She balanced passion with practicality.

She established a gentle routine.

At dawn she would slip out of bed and go down to the kitchen and prepare a pot of coffee. He was always up when she returned, doing his morning exercises. She would sit on the bed watching solemnly while he put his body on the rack. Then he would drink the coffee, sitting next to her on the bed. The early mornings were quiet. They didn't talk much. He would go on his run — up to five miles now, and when he finished, always at the cove, she would be waiting, with cold beer and towels. He would swim to Comino and back, and the tide didn't bother him. They would lie on the flat rock for half an hour or so, taking in the sun, and then walk up to the house. By an unspoken understanding, her mother had abdicated the job of making Creasy's breakfast. Nadia would fry the eggs and ham and serve him in a casual, comfortable way, as if from long habit. Later he would go to the fields and work through the day with Paul and Joey.

The evenings for Nadia were special. She would meet him again at the cove, and they would swim together and talk.

Nothing momentous: but the talk itself cementing the feelings — the communicating — the lack of stated commitment. The easy warmth of being together, and private. She would see him smile, sometimes joke. She discovered his dry sense of humour, tinged with cynicism. He discovered a woman, deeply intelligent and mysteriously erotic. A woman who could fill his life, but leave him unconstricted. After dinner they would often go out. At first, just to please her. He sensed she wanted it. Wanted people to see them together. She needed to establish, in the community, that she was his woman and not ashamed of it. They usually went first to Gleneagles for an early drink. Creasy would sit on the corner stool, part of the usual crowd, mostly just listening to the conversation and repartee flowing back and forth. Nadia would sit next to him, an arm round his waist — proclaiming possession by her attitude. Nobody commented. To "Shreik" and Benny and Tony and Sam, and all the rest, it was somehow right — the Schembri girl and *Uomo*. It was tidy.

Curiously, the only person to say anything at all had been Joey. The day after Nadia had moved her things into Creasy's rooms he had been helping Joey load sacks of onions into a trailer. Joey had been silent and preoccupied. Abruptly he said, "About Nadia." His tone was very serious. "I'm her brother . . . well, I know what's going on. I don't want you to misunderstand."

Creasy stood shirtless and huge beside him.

"Misunderstand what?" he asked softly.

Joey groped for words. "Well . . . normally, if a man seduced a fellow's sister under his own roof, he'd do something about it." He was both embarrassed and slightly defiant.

"I didn't seduce your sister," Creasy said shortly.

"I know." Joey heaved a sack onto the trailer, and turned and said, "It's just that I don't want you to think I'm not up to defending my sister's honour. If you had seduced her, or hurt her at all, I'd take you on. Tough as you are."

Creasy smiled. "I know you would. I won't hurt her . . . not intentionally. Not if I can help it."

They worked on in silence and then Joey smiled at a thought and said, "Anyway, if I'd tried to interfere, Nadia would have brained me with a frying pan."

After Gleneagles, they would occasionally go out for a meal: to Il-Katell in Marsalforn or to Ta Cenc, the small, deluxe, Italian owned hotel. Expensive food, but good.

Sometimes they would end the evening at Barbarella's, the discotheque on the hill above Marsalforn. It was a place Creasy enjoyed. An old, converted farmhouse — the dance floor being the central courtyard. It had a bar on the roof, cool and open to the stars. The bartender, Censu, was another favourite of his, shy and smiling, unruffled and all-knowing. Creasy would nurse a cognac and enjoy the disco music while Nadia chatted to her friends. She had been really surprised when, on the first visit, Creasy had said gruffly, "Let's dance." He just didn't seem the dancing type. But he was a natural dancer — his body gifted with coordination; and he moved perfectly with the music, his brooding eyes almost closed, letting the sounds wash over him.

"He shambles out like a bear," Joey had told his mother. "And then it's like he throws a switch and plugs right into the sound system."

They would always be home before midnight. She never asked him to stay out later. She knew the stress of his physical program.

In the big bed they would end the day making love. And that too was good. Complete and satisfying. Without artifice or pretence. They discovered each other's bodies and explored sensations. He was dominating, but gentle. She was submissive, but equal. Afterward, the brief time before she slept was the best time for her — the perfect time. The time when she lay, always lower than he in the bed, her head resting just under his chest, secure in the sweep of a muscled arm, her body against his, her feet twined in his feet. It was a time when she lost her memory. A time made perfect because she knew that, in the morning, the arm would still be there; she could sleep, peaceful as a child.

Laura had been right. Nadia never talked of his impending departure. By unspoken agreement the future was never mentioned.

He came out of his reverie as they bounced down the hill to Cirkewwa and onto the jetty. He got out and turned to the driver.

"Thanks, Grazio. See you next week — and practise that magazine change."

Grazio grinned. "I know. Until my fingers ache."

Creasy crossed over in the wheelhouse. Michele was on duty and told him that Salvu had, at last, caught his fish — a big silver bream.

"He's been waiting for you in Gleneagles all afternoon. If he doesn't leave there soon, he won't be able to find it, let alone cook it."

But Salvu was holding up well. His wide leather belt had sagged a bit and he had even unbuttoned his shirt sleeves. But he was standing. The bar was full and noisy, Tony and Sam working hard. Joey was in a corner with Nadia and waved at Creasy.

"We came to pick you up. The Land Rover's fixed."

Creasy moved through the throng of people, knowing suddenly that he would miss all this. "Shreik" was in deep conversation with Benny. They broke off with the standard greeting.

"Alright, *Uomo*?"

"Alright, Shreik?"

"Alright, Benny?"

"Alright!"

Salvu weaved over and passed him a beer. "Dinner tonight, *Uomo*. I got him at last."

"The same one, Salvu?"

The old man smiled. "The very same. The bastard that jumped off last month,"

"How do you know?" Creasy asked seriously.

The smile widened to a grin. "Because when I pulled him in, he took one look at me and said: 'Christ! Not you again.'"

"That's a blasphemous bream," Creasy said, keeping a straight face.

Salvu nodded. "Don't worry, I'll confess for him on Sunday. He'll do advanced penance tonight — in the hell fire of the oven." Salvu pointed with his chin at Nadia. "Bring your girl with you. Eight o'clock. You'll need her to carry you home."

It was a magic evening. They sat in the arched kitchen of old Salvu's old farmhouse, drinking his strong wine and watching as he prepared his fish. The farmhouse had been built in the sixteenth century and the black iron oven looked like an original fixture. The bream had been filleted in the early morning and marinated all day in wine and lemon juice. Salvu added herbs from a variety of unmarked jars, sniffing each one and humming to himself like an old sorcerer. Then everything went into the oven, and he joined them at the table and poured a mug of wine. "Forty minutes," he said, with a wink at Nadia. "Time for a quick sip."

A bird cage hung from a hook in the ceiling. The nightingale was somnolent and overawed by the rare company.

"That's a fat bird," Creasy said. "You feed him too many grasshoppers."

"You're right," Salvu agreed. "He needs exercise. Next time you go running, take him with you."

"Or on the swim to Comino," Nadia suggested. "He can catch his own grasshoppers."

Salvu shook his head sadly. "He'll think he's a duck, and demand fish every day."

The fish, when it came, was delicious. Soft and delicately flavoured and accompanied by vegetables from Salvu's own fields and crusty bread warmed in the oven.

Creasy and Nadia ate silently, while Salvu, mellowed by the wine, reminisced about the old days on Gozo. To Nadia's amusement and occasionally feigned shock, he told them some of the old scandals.

"You'd be surprised what goes on under the surface," he said to Creasy with a wink. "You take Nadia's grandfather, for example — on her father's side. He was a one."

"You dirty old man," Nadia said. "Don't you malign my grandfather. He's been dead twenty years!"

"That's true," agreed Salvu, "and many a female tear was shed on that day."

He went on to relate some of her grandfather's escapades. "Be careful," he warned Creasy. "She's got the same blood — she'll need watching."

They finished the meal with strong peppery cheese.

"It helps the drinking," Salvu said, emptying the jug of wine into Creasy's glass. He went out for a moment and when he returned the jug was brimming again.

They left well after midnight.

"There's a Chinese saying," Creasy told him at the door. "'Govern a country as you would cook a small fish.' You ought to be Prime Minister, Salvu."

"True — but I'd have no time for fishing." The old man smiled, propping himself up against the doorpost.

After the amount of wine he had drunk, it was a miracle he was standing at all.

Creasy felt it too, and although Nadia didn't exactly have to carry him home, she had to steady him occasionally as he stumbled on the rock-strewn path.

In the morning he was hung over, the first time in months. "No exercises today," she told him, putting the coffee tray on the bed.

He looked at her, bleary-eyed, and got up and went into the bathroom. She heard the shower running and a few minutes later he came out with a towel round his waist and started his exercises.

She sat on the bed, watching. Nothing is going to slow him down, she thought. I've cooked for him, and made love with him and last night I even put him to bed, but nothing I do can stop him.

He confirmed it a few minutes later, sitting with her on the bed, drinking the coffee.

"Nadia, in about ten days I'll be leaving." He spoke softly, not looking at her. "I'll be going to Marseilles. I'll check the sailings today."

"I'll do it," she said matter-of-factly. "I've a friend who works in a travel agency in Valletta. I'll call her. I think there's a ship once a week — the *Toletela*."

The next day Guido's letter arrived. Creasy took it up to his room and examined the envelope carefully. It had been opened and resealed. The flap had not been precisely realigned with the original gum. Creasy sat for a long time, thinking — the envelope in his hand. Then he opened it. Four pages covered by Guido's neat handwriting, and, clipped to the first page, a ticket stub for the baggage room at the Marseilles railway station.

That night he wrote two letters, one to Paris to a general in the French Army. At Dien Bien Phu the general had been a lowly subaltern, and badly wounded. After the surrender Creasy had carried him, on his back, for three weeks to the P.O.W. camp: and so saved his life.

Now Creasy needed a favour, a special piece of equipment. He asked the general to send it to Poste Restante, Marseilles.

The second letter was to a bar owner in Brussels, an ex-mercenary, who had become an official post office and repository. Again, a request for a parcel to be sent to Marseilles.

CHAPTER THIRTEEN

Time accelerated.

In two days he would sail for Marseilles, and tomorrow he would have his last practice with George's squad.

He worked late into the night. Through the open bedroom door he could see Nadia sleeping. Long black hair covering the white pillow.

He liked to pay his debts, and the work he did this night was for George. They had discussed pairings in the squad. Creasy had recommended it. He knew from his old days with Guido how two men, familiar with each other's thinking and actions, were more effective in fire fights than individuals, even in great numbers. So he evaluated each member of the squad and judged who would work well with whom.

Against each pairing, he made notes about specialised training, again making evaluations gleaned from the past weeks.

That done, he drew up a list of equipment that would be useful to the squad.

Finally he made notes on tactics, trying to envisage the type of situation George might face.

He had been working since nine o'clock, and when he finished it was well after midnight — the table covered with paper. He rose, stretched, flexed the cramped fingers of his right hand, and went into the bedroom.

He looked down at Nadia as he undressed. The night was warm, and only a sheet covered her to the waist. He found himself comparing her with Rika. The body slimmer but the same skin texture — velvet under glass. The face more severe, but the hair as black, as long, and as thick. A different kind of beauty, less conventional, more subtle. In his eyes, conditioned by love, Nadia's beauty was more personal and linked to her mind. A mirror to her character...

He slipped into the bed beside her, and she murmured in her sleep and reflexively slipped lower in the bed; moved her head against his chest, slid an arm across his waist, and resumed her deep, contented breathing.

The ultimate intimacy. To lie naked with a beautiful woman and not to make love. To draw pleasure only from the contact — to sleep together.

The improvement in the squad was obvious. It was their third exercise and they had learned, and they knew it. Afterward they faced George and Creasy confidently and received more praise than criticism.

Since it was Creasy's last session, they insisted he have a farewell drink. Creasy protested that he would miss the last ferry, but they had planned ahead. An AFM patrol boat would take him from the Customhouse steps to Mgarr.

"I've already phoned Nadia," George told him. "She'll meet you in Gleneagles at eight o'clock."

In the bar they presented him with a tie. It had a black eagle superimposed on red and white stripes — Malta's colours. It was the squad's own tie, and its presentation signified Creasy's unofficial membership. George made a brief speech, thanking him for his help and wishing him well in the future, and then the young policemen got into the heavy drinking.

After a while Creasy took George over to a corner table and gave him the notes he had drawn up the night before. He took him through the list of equipment, pointing out several items.

"These are made by Russia or its satellites — you might be able to get them from the Libyans."

George grinned. "I'll take their military attaché out for lunch tomorrow." He looked at Creasy reflectively and said, "You've been a great help. Is there anything I can do for you?"

Creasy's face had turned serious and his voice went flat as he said, "Yes, George. Tell me if you've been opening my mail."

George was an honest man and without guile, and the answer showed on his crestfallen face. Creasy relaxed and sat back and took a pull at his beer.

"You know what my job is, Creasy." George's voice was heavy with embarrassment. "I didn't want to pry . . . but . . . well, it's my job to pry. And you're not a regular type tourist."

"It's OK, George. I don't blame you. I just had to know that it wasn't done at the other end." Something occurred to him. "How many people in your outfit saw that letter?"

George shook his head. "Only me," he said emphatically, "and no copies were made. I even opened the envelope myself and resealed it."

Creasy smiled. 'You need practice."

George returned the smile, relieved that Creasy was taking the matter lightly, and then he became serious again. "Guido was very circumspect, but I could understand enough to guess what you're up to. Obviously you know the risks. I wish I could help, but you know I can't."

Creasy nodded. "But you head an intelligence organization. Will you feel obliged to report my plans to the Central Bureau at Interpol?"

George looked blank and asked, "What plans?" He glanced at his watch. "Drink up, the launch will be waiting, and if you're not in Gleneagles by eight o'clock, Nadia will be displeased with me. And that lady can be formidable."

The two men stood up, but before they rejoined the others, George added: "You've made friends here, Creasy, especially on Gozo. Whatever the outcome of your trip, don't forget that."

"I won't," said Creasy. "And thanks."

It was a night for farewells. Creasy was to take Nadia for dinner at Ta Cenc, but as he entered Gleneagles and saw the crowd, it was obvious he would have to spend at least an hour there first.

He had never made friends before, and it was a curious sensation for him to walk into the big, high-ceilinged room and be absorbed into the noise, and the circle of affection. They were all there: the fishermen and the farmers, "Shreik" and Benny, the Mizzi brothers; Paul, Laura and Joey. Victor passed him a drink and Nadia moved to his side and gave him a cable that had arrived in the morning. It was from the general in Paris. His request had been honoured.

The drink and the talk flowed easily, and Creasy felt a warmth and a sense of belonging. He did not feel sad and he did not question his decision to leave in the morning. Although, in this place, he had found happiness, he had lived long enough and hard enough to understand that to forget his purpose would mean the end of that happiness. He could not live on here with the thoughts of what he had turned away from.

And the will for revenge had never slackened. It had been like a closed drawer, and in the morning the drawer would be opened and in the coming weeks the emotion of revenge would dominate his mind — exclude everything else.

But on this last night, the drawer was still closed. There was no sadness. Even Nadia was vibrant and laughing. He would talk to her later, he decided. Try to explain to her. She was owed at least that much. Not once over the past weeks had she tried to persuade him to stay. Not once — no hint or gesture. It had surprised him a little, but he knew her determination and her composure. Once she had made up her mind, she would not change it.

Benny brought him over a fresh drink and said to Nadia, "I take him away for a minute."

They walked onto the quiet of the balcony, and the big, brawny Gozitan said solemnly, "*Uomo*. You ever need help, and you don't call me first — I get very mad."

Creasy smiled.

"I call you first — I promise."

Benny nodded, satisfied. "Just send a cable here to Gleneagles, Tony will find me — anytime."

They went back inside and this time Creasy took Paul aside. "I owe you money, Paul," he said.

The farmer looked surprised. "For what?"

"You know very well," Creasy answered, "I've lived in your house for over two months and eaten a mountain of food — it costs money."

Paul smiled. "OK," he said. "I'll charge you fifteen pounds a week — that's the same as a farm labourer gets here — that makes us even." He held up his hand to stop further argument. "Creasy, I could never have found a worker this summer who would have done as much as you — I'm serious. I won't talk of it."

He turned back to the crowd, and Creasy could do nothing but shrug and follow him.

A few minutes later he said his farewells and left with Nadia.

They were like young lovers on an early date. There was no sense of departure. No sadness. They had a table on the terrace and ordered fish. They agreed that though it was delicious, Salvu's was better. They drank a bottle of icy Soave wine, and then another. For Creasy, the occasion was made more poignant, because in the morning his mind would be occupied by plans and dispositions for death and destruction; and because Nadia, by her manner, comforted him. He had worried about what he would leave behind in Gozo, He didn't want to remember sadness, and she gave him no cause. Her attitude proclaimed her independence and her strength. It was a balm to his unadmitted conscience. And that was exactly what she intended.

After dinner they went to Barbarella's. Creasy wanted to say goodbye to Censu. He found he couldn't pay for the drinks. "It's on me," Censu said, with his gentle smile.

He asked Nadia if she wanted to dance and she shook her head. "It's almost a full moon — let's go for a last swim." So they finished their drinks, drove back to the farm, and walked down the rocky path to the cove.

They embraced in the cool water. Her skin was slippery — like wet glass.

On the flat rock they made love. Creasy lay on his back to take any discomfort from the rough stone; but as Nadia eased herself over him, he felt nothing except her warm softness. As always, they made love slowly, their passions rising up a gentle slope. He looked up at her small breasts, shining wetly in the moonlight, and her oval face and dark eyes, narrowed in pleasure. They reached the top of the slope and she moaned deep in her throat and her knees gripped him in a gentle vice.

Later he talked, and she sat, naked, with her arms clasping her knees and her eyes watching his intently.

He told her what he was going to do, and why. He described his mental and physical state when he had arrived in Naples. How Guido and Elio had arranged to get him the job. He told her of the first days and how he had deliberately shut Pinta off and then how, slowly but inexorably, they had grown together.

He had eloquence. For once in his life he was able to truly describe his feelings. It may have been the ambience in the night, or the recent lovemaking, or simply that he loved the woman who was listening so intently. He found the words to describe how he had felt and what had happened.

He told her of the day in the mountains when Pinta had given him the crucifix. Described it as the happiest, most natural day in his life. His words brought Pinta alive, and Nadia's head nodded in understanding as he talked of the girl's awareness, and curiosity, and simple joy of living.

And the final day. The kidnapping, and her shouting out his name as he lay on the grass. How he woke in the hospital, not sure if he would live, but willing it with every nerve in his body and always hearing that last shout and the anguish in her voice.

Then Guido telling him she was dead and how she had been abused.

He stopped talking and a silence engulfed the small cove. It was a long time before she spoke. She had lowered her head onto her knees and her wet, black hair fell almost to the rock. When she raised her head he saw the tears glistening in the pale light.

"I'm not crying because you're leaving, Creasy. I promised myself I wouldn't do that — not while you're here." Her low voice quivered. "I'm crying for Pinta. I knew her. You brought her alive when you talked, and I knew her, as though she were my own child, and when you talked of her death, I saw that too — I cry for her."

Her words comforted him. She could understand why, even though he loved her, he had to go.

He told her, "I love you."

Her head came up higher. "I know. I didn't expect you to tell me."

"I didn't intend to."

'Then why?"

'I'm not sure. Maybe it's talking about Pinta, and being honest, and wanting you to know before I leave — even though it's useless."

"It hasn't been useless, Creasy." She wanted to go on. To tell him everything. But like the tears, she had promised herself about that too. She stood up and looked out over the moonlit sea.

"What chance do you have of living through it?" she asked.

"A very slim chance," he answered flatly.

"But if you do, will you come back here to me?" She turned to face him, and he rose to his feet.

"Yes, but don't wait. I'm not going off to commit suicide. It's not suicide while there's even a one percent chance — but Nadia, that's about what the odds are." He moved and took her into his arms. "So don't wait."

"I just wanted to know," she said. She kissed him hard — fiercely. "Do it, Creasy!" Her voice was intense. "Do it. Kill them. All of them — they deserve it. I hate them as much as you hate them." She gripped him tightly, feeling his strength, moving her hands over the tight muscles of his back and shoulders. She spoke against his neck. "Don't worry about me. Don't think about me. Think only of them, and what they did." Her voice carried the hatred — he could feel it — feed off it.

"I'll go every morning with my mother to the church. I'll pray — pray that you kill them — I shall not confess. Just pray — when you are dead, or returned here — then I'll confess."

They picked up their clothes and walked up to the house. Her words and her mood had affected him deeply. There was something he didn't understand, a factor that eluded him. But her reaction and her emotion about his coming struggle, and her identifying with it, all combined to settle his mind and to clear it of everything but his purpose.

She didn't want to make love again. She didn't want to sleep. It was only a few hours to dawn. She lay with him in the bed, her head against his chest, listening to his steady breathing.

At first light, she quietly disengaged herself, got up and moved about the room collecting his clothes and packing his bag. On top she put the cassette player. The half dozen cassettes went into a side pocket. Then, with a faint smile, she took them out again, selected one and slotted it into the machine, ready to play.

Then she went down to the kitchen and cooked breakfast and brewed coffee and carried the tray up.

He was to catch the first ferry to Malta. Joey put his bag into the Land Rover and climbed into the driving seat. Laura put her arms around him, and kissed his cheek, and wished him luck. He held onto her and thanked her for helping him regain his strength.

Then he shook Paul's hand.

"Alright, Paul?"

"Alright, Creasy!"

Nadia decided not to go with him to the ferry. She came forward and reached up and kissed him on the mouth, and wished him luck, and then stood back with her parents while the Land Rover moved up the track. Her face was without expression.

Half an hour later, she went to the front of the house and watched the *Melitaland* as it pulled out of the harbour.

She knew he would be in the wheelhouse with Victor or Michele. As it cleared the entrance, she saw him come out onto the wing of the bridge and look up the hill toward her and wave. She waved back, and stood watching as the ferry turned to pass Comino, and he was hidden from view. She went into the kitchen to help her mother, who was mystified, for Gozitans are emotional, and her daughter's face showed no emotion.

In the evening she walked along the path to Ramla and stood on the brow of a hill and in the distance saw the white ship come out of Grand Harbour and steam northward.

Salvu, working his fields below, saw the girl standing looking out to sea, and was about to call to her but then followed her gaze and saw the ship and went silently back to his work.

It had gone over the horizon into the twilight before she turned and walked slowly back to the farmhouse. She went up to the rooms they had shared, and took off her clothes and climbed into the bed. She pulled his pillow down beside her, and hugged it to her belly.

Then she wept into the night.

BOOK THREE

CHAPTER FOURTEEN

The two Arabs drove a hard bargain. A package deal or nothing. Without the rocket launchers, they didn't want the fifty M.A.S. machine guns or the five hundred Armalites. It put Leclerc in a quandary. Like many arms dealers, he had semi-official backing — an outlet for his country's arms industry. His contact at the ministry had told him that these particular Arabs were not to be sold rocket launchers. Such is politics. Even though they had an end-user certificate from a small Persian Gulf state, the consignment was to be transhipped in Beirut, which could mean anything — left wing, right wing, Falangists, P.L.O. or Troop 4 of the Lebanese Boy Scouts.

He sighed; he would have to call his contact again.

"I might be able to get you a couple," he said to the older of the two, a smoothly dressed, hawk faced man, who shook his head.

"At least six, Monsieur Leclerc," he said, in excellent French. "Or we may be forced to take our order elsewhere — Monte Carlo, perhaps."

Leclerc sighed again and swore under his breath.

That damned American in Monte Carlo was trying to hog all the business. He'd sell them rocket launchers, alright — enough to start World War Three.

"I'll see what I can do." He stood up and moved around his desk. "Call me in the morning, at eleven."

They all shook hands, and Leclerc ushered them out of his office.

Creasy was sitting in the reception area, reading a magazine. "Go on through to my office," Leclerc said. "I'll be right with you."

Creasy was looking at the pictures of weapons adorning the walls when Leclerc returned. The Frenchman gestured at a chair and sat down behind his desk. The two men studied each other. Leclerc spoke first,

"You look very fit. A great difference from when I last saw you."

"I was a lush when you last saw me," Creasy said shortly.

There was antagonism in the air. Leclerc voiced it.

"There was no need to have Guido threaten me."

Creasy remained silent, brooding eyes studying the Frenchman — evaluating him. Leclerc was a tall, florid man, running slightly to fat. He wore a dark grey suit and was well barbered and manicured. He looked like a successful stockbroker, but Creasy had known him when he was a very hard and ruthless mercenary. Leclerc sighed, and shrugged his shoulders.

"Creasy, we've never been friends. That's not my fault. But I owe you. I owe you on two counts — you saved my life in Katanga, and that alone is enough." He smiled thinly. "I also owe you for Rhodesia, you helped me land a very good order — very profitable. So it's natural I would help you — without Guido talking about a technicolour funeral."

"You don't owe me for Rhodesia," Creasy said. "They paid me to give advice. It just happened you were offering what they needed."

"OK," Leclerc conceded, "but Katanga is different. Try to accept the fact that, apart from Guido, there are people who consider you a friend, whatever your own reaction."

There was a silence and then Leclerc received a great shock — Creasy smiled. An open, easy smile.

"Alright. Thanks," he said. "I accept that."

Leclerc recovered slowly, realizing that the man in front of him had truly changed. He was not just healthier — he had known him way back, when he was as fit as any man could be. He was changed mentally. He still gave off an aura of menace, but the smile had been genuine and unprecedented.

"Have you got all the stuff together?" Creasy asked.

Leclerc collected his thoughts and nodded.

"Yes. It was a diverse order, and I've got several alternatives. You can take your pick." He glanced at his watch. "Let's have lunch and go to the warehouse afterward. Meanwhile, I'll have my people put everything out."

Creasy nodded but didn't get up. He seemed to be considering something. He made up his mind.

"Leclerc, do you have connections to get false papers? — passport, driving licence — so on?"

"It's possible," the Frenchman said. "But of what country?"

"French, Belgian, Canadian, or American," Creasy answered. "It really doesn't matter — it's only a question of language. I speak French, and my English has a blurred North American accent. The problem is, I need them quickly — four to five days."

Leclerc steepled his fingers and thought about it. "French would be the easiest," he said finally, "but not if you plan to use them in this country."

"I don't — nor the weapons — you have my word on that."

Leclerc nodded. "I already have that assurance from Guido — photographs?"

Creasy reached into an inside pocket, drew out an envelope, and tossed it onto the desk,

"There's a dozen. I need papers that an ordinary Frenchman would carry on an overseas trip."

Leclerc opened a drawer and dropped in the envelope.

"OK, I'll get onto it this evening." He looked apologetic. "It will be expensive, Creasy. Not me, you understand — I won't charge any commission. But the time element adds to the price."

Creasy smiled again. "It's OK. Let's get that lunch."'

As they headed for the door, Leclerc was thinking that if Creasy smiled at him once more, he'd pass out.

The *Toletela* had arrived in Marseilles the night before. Creasy had taken a taxi straight to the railway station and picked up the black leather briefcase from the baggage room. At the station restaurant he found a quiet table, ordered a coffee and took out Guido's letter. He looked up the numbers and opened the combination lock. Inside was a large Manila envelope. It contained a key, a street map of Marseilles, and two sets of papers. One set was the passport and personal papers of one Luigi Racca — a vegetable importer from Amalfi. The other set were papers for a Toyota van. He opened the street map and noted the small inked circle and the instructions in the margin, then he put them all back into the briefcase and spun the lock. As he sipped the coffee, his eyes roamed around the restaurant and through the glass partition to the movement on the station concourse. But his mind was on Guido. Without his help the whole operation would have been infinitely harder. Creasy knew that Luigi Racca would be a genuine vegetable importer, quite unaware that his name was being borrowed. He knew that the passport and other papers would be the work of the best forger in Naples — a city justly proud of its forgers. When he arrived in Naples he knew that everything would be ready. Within a week the killing would begin.

He guessed that Pietro had delivered the van to Marseilles — driving overland. He must talk to Guido about his safety once the business started.

He finished his coffee and caught a taxi to the post office and picked up the parcels that had arrived from Paris and Brussels.

Then he checked into a small hotel, using the papers of Luigi Racca.

Their steps on the stone floor echoed up into the high steel girders. Long lines of packing cases were stacked on pallets under a maze of pipes and sprinklers. Creasy inhaled the familiar smell of an arsenal, the coppery odour of grease on metal. A section of the warehouse was partitioned off with heavy steel sheeting and a padlocked door. Leclerc unlocked it and threw a switch. A bank of overhead neon tubes flickered on, illuminating two long metal tables, one bare, the other covered with a variety of weapons and equipment.

Leclerc stood by the door while Creasy walked slowly past the laden table, examining the different groupings. Then he moved back and stopped at the first set — the pistols. Leclerc joined him.

"You wanted a forty-five and something smaller and lighter." He gestured. "Take your pick."

There were a dozen pistols on the table from a variety of countries, and several silencers. Creasy picked up a Colt 1911 and a British Webley .32. Leclerc looked a bit surprised at his second choice.

"I know," said Creasy. "It's old-fashioned, but it's reliable, and I'm used to it."

He turned and put the two guns on the table behind him, and then picked up two silencers and put them with the guns. "I'll take five hundred rounds for each."

Leclerc took out a small pad and a ballpoint pen and made a note. They moved to the next grouping — submachine guns. There were four types, the Israeli Uzi, the British Sterling, the Danish Madsen, and the one Creasy immediately picked up — the Ingram Model 10. The metal butt was folded, and the weapon measured only ten and a half inches. It looked more like a large pistol than a submachine gun, and it had a firing rate of eleven hundred rounds a minute.

"You've used one?" asked Leclerc, and Creasy nodded, hefting the gun in his hands.

"Yes. In Vietnam. Its biggest advantage is its size.

The rate of fire is too high if anything, but for my purposes it's perfect. Do you have a suppressor?"

"I can get one within a couple of days."

"Good." Creasy put the gun on the table behind him. "I'll take eight magazines and two thousand rounds."

Next were two sniper rifles, a modified M14 with the Weaver sight and the British L4A1 with the standard 32 sight. Creasy selected the M14.

"It's got twice the feed," he commented. "I'll have two spare magazines and a standard box of cartridges."

They moved to the rocket launchers.

"It's no contest," Creasy said. "For the size and weight, it's got to be the R.P.G.7."

Leclerc grinned and picked up the squat tube. "I could sell a million if I could get them." He held the tube at each end and twisted. It unscrewed in the middle. Creasy nodded with satisfaction. "The Stroke D," he said. "Better still. What's the standard packing for the missiles?"

"Cases of eight or twelve," Leclerc answered, screwing the launcher together and laying it next to the Ingram.

"A case of eight, then," Creasy said, passing on to the grenades. He picked out the British Fragmentation 36 and the Phosphorous 87.

"I'll need less than standard packing. Can your boys knock up a case for fifteen of each?"

"Can do," Leclerc replied.

Next Creasy picked up a double-barrelled shotgun, barrels and stock sawed off short. He flicked open the breach, held it up to the light, and examined it, then snapped it shut and put it down next to the grenades. It looked incongruous alongside the other weapons.

"A couple of boxes of S.S.G.," he said, and Leclerc made a note.

He went on to select a Trilux night sight, a commando knife in its sheath, and a variety of webbing.

Finally, at the end of the table, a number of small objects lay in a shallow metal tray. Creasy picked up several and examined them closely.

"They're the very latest," Leclerc said at his shoulder. "Perhaps you haven't seen them before?"

Creasy held a small circular tube in his hand. A narrow needle projected half an inch from one end.

"I've used this type of detonator," he said, "but not the timer."

Leclerc picked up another metal tube. It had two prongs, like an electric plug. He unscrewed the tube and showed Creasy the cadmium cell battery and the two graduated dials. Then he plugged the timer into the detonator. The combined mechanism was less than two inches long and three quarters of an inch in diameter.

Leclerc smiled. "Electronics make things so much easier. Guido specified a kilo of Plastique. I have it ready elsewhere."

"Good," Creasy said, looking back along the table. "That's everything I need."

Leclerc surveyed the assortment, his curiosity tinged with satisfaction. For him, fitting out Creasy was an exercise in professional pleasure. He wasn't sure what Creasy wanted the stuff for, and he wasn't about to ask, but he would be reading the Italian papers in the coming weeks. Knowing the American's background and experience, he could imagine the potential destruction that the weapons represented.

"Can you get me a good light shoulder holster for the Webley, and a belt holster for the Colt?"

Leclerc nodded. "Standard issue canvas for the Colt."

"That'll do fine." Creasy had taken out a tape measure and a notebook. "Do you have any scales?"

"Sure." Leclerc went out into the main warehouse and Creasy got busy with the tape measure.

"Where can I drop you?"

"Anywhere near the fishing harbour."

Creasy didn't mention the name of his hotel. He had decided that Leclerc could be trusted — but old habits die hard.

The Frenchman asked, "Anything else I can do for you in Marseilles? — Female company?"

Creasy smiled and shook his head. "I thought you were an arms dealer."

"You know what it's like," Leclerc answered. "When you're selling, you have to hang bells on the stuff. The Arabs are the worst — they get so little at home."

"Business must be good out that way," Creasy commented. "They've got enough little wars going on to keep half the arms factories in Europe on overtime."

"It's a fact," grunted Leclerc, "and it will get better — or worse, depending how you look at it. This Islamic resurgence means more wars — it's a violent religion." He glanced at Creasy. "Apart from arms dealers, there'll be a lot of work for men like you."

Creasy shrugged. "Could be."

They pulled up by the wharf, and Creasy opened the door.

"Ten o'clock then, Thursday night," he said.

Leclerc nodded. "I'll be waiting."

Creasy consulted the street map and told the taxi driver to leave him at the corner of Rue St. Honoré. He had changed at the hotel and now wore more simple work clothes — denim jeans and shirt. His eyes roamed the streets idly as they drove eastward through the city. He liked Marseilles. A man could sink into it and be anonymous. People minded their own business. It was an ideal city for drug smuggling, arms dealing, or just getting lost.

The taxi pulled up and Creasy paid the driver and walked for ten minutes until he reached the corner of Rue Catinat. He stood for several minutes, watching the street.

It was a working-class suburb. Tenement buildings, small workshops, and factories. Halfway down was a row of lockup garages. He located Number 11, and without looking around took out the key and unlocked it, then switched on the light and closed the door.

Most of the space was taken up by a Toyota Hiace van. It was painted a deep grey, with faded black lettering on the side: Luigi Racca — Vegetable Dealer.

The van looked old and suitably battered, but Creasy knew that the engine and suspension would be in perfect order. He opened the back doors. Immediately in front of him, on the van floor, was a coil of electrical cord attached to an electrical plug. He smiled briefly at Guido's forethought, picked up the plug, went over to the wall, and connected the plug to the socket. The bulb inside the van lit up the rest of the contents. There were lengths of timber, several sacks packed tight with cotton waste, a long roll of thick felt, a wooden bench with a vice attached, and a large toolbox. Creasy unloaded all this onto the floor behind the van, then moved to the front of the compartment and carefully examined the panelling that backed onto the driver's seat. He went to the toolbox, selected a screwdriver and, being careful not to mark the paint, eased out the dozen countersunk screws. The false panel fell gently back, revealing a space about a foot deep and as wide and high as the van's compartment. He grunted in satisfaction and carried the panel out and rested it gently against the garage wall. Next he took out a tape measure and a notebook and jotted down the exact dimensions of the secret compartment.

Referring to previous notes, he then drew a rough plan and stuck it on the garage door.

For the next two hours he worked steadily, measuring the timber and cutting it up with a small power saw.

He enjoyed the work, but eventually had to stop because the air in the closed garage had become stuffy. It was dark outside, and he walked for ten minutes in the cool night air to clear his head. Then he found a small bistro and went in to have dinner.

At eight the next morning he was back in the garage. He worked through till noon, then went for lunch to the same bistro. The food was simple and good, and with his rough clothes and colloquial French, he was not out of place among the other customers.

By mid-afternoon he had finished shaping the timber, and he fitted it into the compartment. First the heavy frame and then the cross pieces, each slotting exactly into its prepared joint. He stood back and surveyed his work. The compartment now resembled a giant, half-finished child's puzzle. On Thursday he would fit in the missing pieces.

Back at the hotel he looked in the yellow pages and rang a rental agency. In the name of Luigi Racca, he arranged to hire a Fiat van the next day, for twenty-four hours.

Leclerc waited with a watchman. There was no one else on the street. At five past ten, a dark blue van turned the corner and parked a hundred metres away. Its lights flickered twice and went out.

"Go down to the other corner and wait," Leclerc told the watchman. "Don't come back until that van has left." As the watchman disappeared into the dark, the van moved forward again.

"OK?" Creasy asked, jumping down from the cab.

"OK," Leclerc replied, and unlocked the warehouse door. Just inside were three wooden packing cases on a fork lift. They were lettered "A," "B," and "C." Leclerc pointed to each in turn. "Ammunition, weapons, other equipment." Within a couple of minutes the cases were loaded in the van and Creasy climbed back into the cab.

Leclerc looked up at him. "Come into my office tomorrow afternoon. Your papers will be ready."

Creasy nodded and drove away.

He drove around the city for forty minutes, varying his speed and making unpredictable turns. Then, satisfied that he wasn't being followed, he drove to Rue Catinat and parked fifty metres from the garage. He turned off the lights and engine and sat listening and watching for half an hour. Then he started the engine and backed up close to the garage door. He quickly wrestled the three cases from the van and into the garage. He locked up and drove back to his hotel — again constantly watching his mirror.

In the early morning he returned the rented van and by nine o'clock was back in the garage. He prized the lids off the three cases and, one by one, fitted the weapons, the boxes of ammunition, and the grenades into their allotted places. He took handfuls of cotton waste and packed it into all remaining gaps between equipment and frame. Then a curtain of felt was tacked across the entire framework. He fetched the false panel and, again being careful not to scratch the paint, he screwed it back into place. He banged the side of his fist against it in several places. It felt and sounded solid. Finally, he spread his legs and shifted his weight back and forth, rocking the van on its springs.

He nodded in satisfaction. His weapons carrier was ready and loaded.

Leclerc passed the envelope across the desk and Creasy shook out the passport and papers and examined them closely.

"They're good," he said. "Better than I expected — how much?"

Leclerc shrugged ruefully. "Eleven thousand francs."

"They're worth it," Creasy said, and took out a roll of money and counted out the notes. "You've arranged with Guido about payment for the other stuff."

Leclerc nodded. "He'll pay into my account in Brussels." He paused, and then said, "You're getting it for cost — I've added nothing."

"Thanks," Creasy said, and smiled slightly. "That evens us up."

Leclerc smiled and stood up. "Is my life worth so little? — I hope not."

Creasy held out his hand. "If a favour is returned, it's the act — not the size of it. Incidentally, I know you have to cooperate with the government in your business, and I know our transaction is very unofficial. If you get any pressure, tell them you thought I still acted for the Rhodesians. But don't mention the papers to anyone — not even Guido."

Leclerc smiled. "OK. I can look very innocent when necessary. Good luck."

At the door Creasy hesitated, and then made up his mind.

"You went to a lot of trouble," he said quietly. "I appreciate it. Ever I can do something for you, contact me through Guido."

Leclerc had been about to sit down, but as the door closed he remained half crouched over the chair, his mouth open in surprise. Then he sank slowly back, and crossed himself. Miracles do happen.

CHAPTER FIFTEEN

Guido stood on the terrace watching through binoculars as the blue and white ferry docked. He had confidence in the papers, but vehicles arriving from Marseilles were often thoroughly searched.

The ramp came down and a stream of private cars drove out and was directed into three lines. Several trucks and a container trailer followed. Then the grey van. He watched Creasy get out of the cab and lounge against the side of the van in an attitude of bored indifference. He was dressed in faded denim overalls and he carried a large Manila envelope which he slapped idly against his leg.

It was twenty minutes before the customs inspector reached him. In the meantime, Pietro had come out onto the terrace.

"He's arrived?"

"Yes," Guido grunted, without moving his gaze from the docks.

The official checked the papers carefully and then walked to the rear of the van. Creasy opened the doors and the customs man handed back the envelope and pulled himself up and in. It seemed an eternity before he reappeared, holding something. Guido stiffened and leaned forward, adjusting the binoculars for better vision. Finally he recognized the object and saw Creasy nodding, and his pent-up breath hissed out.

"What is it?" asked Pietro.

"A melon! — The bastard wants a melon."

Pietro laughed. "A small price to pay."

The grey van moved to the security gates; only a brief pause this time, and then it pulled out into the traffic. Guido lowered the binoculars and looked at his watch.

"He'll call within the hour. So I'll be out for lunch — can you handle it by yourself?"

"Sure," Pietro answered. "Tell him good luck for me."

"I will," Guido said seriously. "He's going to need it."

Guido entered the restaurant carrying a canvas bag. He paused at the door, letting his eyes adjust to the dim light. It was barely noon and apart from Creasy, sitting at a corner table, and a bored waiter, the place was deserted. Creasy rose as Guido approached and they embraced warmly. Guido stepped back and looked at his friend critically.

"Gozo agrees with you. You've shed ten years."

Creasy smiled. "They all send their love."

They sat down and ordered a light lunch of *calzoni* and salad.

"Everything OK in Marseilles?" Guido asked as soon as the waiter left.

"Perfect," answered Creasy. "Leclerc was very helpful but resented your threatening him."

Guido grinned. "Anyway, it didn't hurt — How's Nadia?"

The question threw Creasy for a moment.

"She's fine — You know about that?"

"I guessed."

Guido told him about the phone call and how he had tried to discourage her. "But I assume it didn't put her off."

Creasy shook his head. "It didn't."

"How did she take your leaving?"

Creasy shrugged — it puzzled him a bit.

"Very casual. No tears, no emotion — she's a strange girl."

The waiter approached with the food and a bottle of wine, and then left them alone.

"I sent Pietro to Marseilles," Guido said. "He's done most of the legwork, even in Rome and Milan."

"He's a good kid," Creasy remarked.

They ate in silence for a while. It was not necessary for Creasy to question Pietro's reliability, but still, something had to be said.

"He might be in danger."

Guido nodded. "I'm sending him to Gozo once it starts. He'll stay there until the whole thing is over. Anyway, he needs a holiday."

"He deserves it," Creasy agreed, and repeated, "He's a good kid — will you manage without him?"

Guido smiled. "I'm closing the pensione for the duration. I'll just do lunch and dinner for the regulars. The work load will be much lighter."

Creasy didn't utter platitudes about losing money. Nothing needed to be said.

Guido unzipped the canvas bag and took out five bunches of keys, two street maps and a folder. He passed the keys over. They all had tags attached. He said, "The apartment in Milan, the cottage at Vigentino, just outside the city, the Alfetta GT, the apartment in Rome, and the Renault 20 in Rome."

Creasy held the keys and smiled. "I feel like a property owner!"

"Renter." Guido smiled back. "They're all rented for three months, starting ten days ago."

"There's no way they can be traced to you?"

Guido shook his head. "No way — the apartments and cottage were rented by Remarque in Brussels, using a false name — and there's a cut-off in between. I rented the cars using the name of Luigi Racca. Incidentally, he's a widower, visiting his daughter in Australia — won't be back for months."

He opened the street maps and pointed out the circled locations of the apartment in Milan and the bungalow outside.

"It's very secluded and has a lockup garage — the Alfetta is inside." He pointed out the apartment in Rome, and the garage, two blocks away, which contained the Renault.

"The apartment and bungalow are provisioned with canned food and stuff." He tapped the folder. "Addresses in here."

"Good," Creasy said, well satisfied. "Did you remember the chargers?"

Guido grinned and reached into the bag and passed across two shiny cylinders. Creasy examined one of them carefully.

It was made of anodized aluminium — about three and a half inches long, three quarters of an inch in diameter, and bevelled at both ends. He held the ends and twisted gently and the cylinder opened on fine threading. He looked inside the two halves. The inner surface was as smooth as the outside.

"I had them made in a local machine shop," Guido said, taking the cylinders back and dropping them into the bag. "They are a bit bigger than normal — uncomfortable, I would think."

Creasy smiled thinly. "He can complain — I'll be very sympathetic."

Guido put away the keys and maps, leaving just the folder in front of him. "Do you remember Verrua?" he asked. "From the Legion?"

"Yes," Creasy replied. "Second R.E.P. He did two hitches and then left — he was getting old."

"Right," said Guido. "He lives here now, in Naples. For ten years, after he left the Legion, he worked for Cantarella in Sicily — strong-arm stuff. They put him out to grass a couple of years back, and he came to live here with his married daughter. He comes to eat at the pensione a lot. Likes to reminisce. I hardly remembered him — I was only in a few months before he left — but he remembers you. Often talks about you — about the early days in Vietnam."

Creasy nodded. "He talked too much even then. He doesn't know anything about this operation?"

Guido shook his head. "Nothing. But the point is, he's very disenchanted with Cantarella. Feels he wasn't looked after properly. Frankly, he's a complainer by nature. However, with a little nudging, he talked a lot about the Villa Colacci and the setup there." He passed over the folder. "It's in there, with other bits and pieces I've picked up."

Creasy looked through the folder. There was a sketch map of the villa and its grounds, and several pages of notes.

He looked up and said: "Guido, this is a real help — I appreciate it."

Guido shrugged and called out to the waiter to bring them coffee.

"I know you plan to get information as you go along," he said. "But that might save you some time."

"It will," Creasy agreed, looking down at the sketch map. "Villa Colacci is the tough one — and he rarely moves out of it."

Guido grinned. "He won't move at all when he knows he's a target. Any ideas on getting in?"

"Several," Creasy answered, "But I'll keep my options open till I know more."

In fact, he already knew exactly how he was going to get in. He had decided after his visit to Palermo three months before. He would have discussed it with Guido, but he had a reason for not doing so.

The coffee arrived, and Creasy took a sip and brought the subject up: "After Conti in Rome, I'll be entirely on my own. No contact and no fixed base. I'll have dumped both cars and the van by then — you understand why?"

Guido smiled briefly. “Sure. By then, both the police and Cantarella may have figured out who's doing the killings. It won't take them long to trace you back to me, and then they'll be asking me questions — I can't tell them what I don't know.”

Creasy nodded, his face serious.

“And if you don't know, it will become obvious. It always does — we've both had experience in asking such questions. If you genuinely don't know, you will be safer.”

“But you're making it difficult for yourself,” Guido commented. “And God knows it's going to be difficult enough.”

The American smiled. “I'll improvise — it won't be the first time. Meanwhile, how do I get in touch with you? I don't want to use the phone.”

Guido pointed at the folder. “Front page. There's a Post Restante number here in Naples — cable a phone number and a time, and I'll call you from outside.”

Creasy flicked open the folder and read the number.

“OK — if things go smoothly, I won't be in contact at all — until it's all over.”

There was a long silence.

“You are still as determined?”

“Yes — nothing's changed — I want them so bad, it's an ache.”

“I thought Nadia might have changed that — taken away some of the hate.”

Creasy was a long time answering — thinking about Guido's words. Then he shook his head and said softly, “I love her, Guido — and she loves me. But it hasn't changed anything. That child made it possible. That child allowed me — showed me how to let it happen.” His square face was somber, his voice thick with emotion, “I told Nadia everything and, in a strange way, she hates them as much as I do. I don't really understand, but it's as though she's with me — urging me on.”

He leaned back in his chair and drew in a deep breath, controlling his feelings.

"I know it's a contradiction — I try not to think of Nadia." He smiled faintly. "Would you believe it, Guido? Me! Fifty years old, and falling in love."

Guido shook his head. He felt very sad.

"When will you start?"

Creasy leaned forward again. His voice became matter-of-fact.

"I'll drive up to Milan today — I should arrive early tomorrow morning at the cottage. Rabbia and Sandri are the first targets, but I only need to talk to one of them — probably Rabbia. Apparently he's just muscle, and slow-witted — he'll crack faster than Sandri."

He shrugged. "A few days to watch him, then I'll pick him up."

Guido picked up the folder, dropped it into the bag, and zipped it up. The two men rose,

"You go first," Guido said.

"OK — Tell Pietro to have a good holiday — and tell him thanks."

"I will," said Guido. "He sends you luck."

They embraced and Creasy picked up the bag and left.

CHAPTER SIXTEEN

Giorgio Rabbia was at work. It was not strenuous. For the past two hours, he had moved in and out of a number of bars in the eastern part of Milan. It was Thursday night and, for his boss, that meant payday.

Rabbia was a huge, ponderous man with a vicious nature. When he became angry his movement quickened, and he liked to beat people. He was perfectly suited to his job, and he did it efficiently, if slowly — always following the same routine.

It was midnight, and he had finished the bars and was about to start the clubs. He wore a loose-fitting jacket which exaggerated further his great bulk. Beneath the jacket, under his left arm, he carried a Beretta pistol in a shoulder holster. Under his right arm hung a long, soft, chamois leather bag, closed with a drawstring. It was half full.

He pulled his Lancia into a No Parking zone in front of the Papagayo nightclub and eased his bulk out onto the pavement.

He was proud of the Lancia — it was painted metallic silver and fitted with a Braun stereo and a musical horn. On the ledge, behind the back seat, sat a toy dachshund; its head bobbed up and down with the car's motion. A present from a favourite girlfriend.

In spite of these expensive and sentimental attachments, Rabbia did not bother to lock the car or even take the key from the ignition. Every petty thief in Milan knew to whom it belonged, and the consequences of touching it.

He ambled into the club with mild anticipation for, according to his routine, he always took his first drink of the night here.

The owner saw him enter and snapped his fingers at the bartender. By the time Rabbia had reached the bar, a large Scotch was waiting. He drank appreciatively and surveyed the room.

Several couples danced to the soft music of a single pianist. The men were middle-aged, business types, the girls young hostesses. It was an expensive and successful club. He watched a girl walk from the powder room to a table — tall and blonde, with large breasts bulging out of a low-cut dress. He hadn't seen her before, so she must be new. He made a slow, mental note to have her sent over one afternoon.

He finished his drink and the club owner approached and gave him a sheaf of notes. Rabbia counted them carefully and then reached under his jacket, loosened the drawstring, and dropped them into the bag. He nodded at the smiling club owner and pointed with his chin.

"The new girl — the blonde. Send her over to my place, Monday afternoon at three."

"Of course, Signore Rabbia."

Back on the street, he inhaled the fresh air and moved to the Lancia. If there had been more light, and if he had been an observant man, he might have noticed that the dachshund's head was bobbing gently.

He got in, with a grunt of exertion, and was about to reach for the ignition when he felt the cold metal against the back of his neck and heard the cold voice: "Don't move at all."

His first reaction was astonishment. "Do you know who I am?"

"You are Giorgio Rabbia — if you speak again, it will be the last time."

A hand reached forward under his left arm and pulled his jacket open. He felt his gun being lifted out, and he kept very still;

for now he was frightened. The man behind knew his identity and so was not after the chamois bag. Robbery was not the motive. Perhaps trouble had started with the Abrata group.

The voice interrupted his nervous speculation.

"You will start the engine and follow my directions. You will drive slowly and not attract attention. Don't be clever, or you will die instantly."

Rabbia drove carefully, instinct telling him that the man in the back was not making idle threats.

He was directed out of the city to the south and as they cleared the outskirts his mind began to quicken. If a territory war had started, he would have been dead already, either outside the club or in the deserted warehouse district they had just passed. The voice puzzled him. It carried a slight Neapolitan accent, and something else he couldn't define. He decided that the man was not Italian and that made him think of something else. His boss Foseella had been in dispute, some months earlier, with a "Union Corse" group in Marseilles, over a drug shipment. Maybe their resentment had been stronger than anticipated; but why the Neapolitan accent?

Just before Vigentino he was instructed to turn down a side road and then again onto a dirt track. He would look for a chance when they got out of the car — the gun had to be taken away from his neck; and for all his bulk, Rabbia could move with deceptive speed.

A low bungalow appeared in the headlights. The kind of place rich Milanese build for weekends. The voice told him to drive around to the back. Gravel crunched under the tyres.

"Stop here. Put on the handbrake and turn off the ignition."

Rabbia leaned forward and the cold metal moved with him. He sat back slowly. Suddenly the pressure on his neck was gone. He tensed, and then his vision exploded.

He regained senses slowly — became aware of a throbbing pain at the back of his head. He tried to put a hand there, but it wouldn't move. His chin was slumped onto his chest, and as his vision cleared he saw his left wrist taped to the wooden arm of a chair. He painfully moved his head to the right. His right wrist was similarly taped. Memory returned with a jolt, and his mind sharpened. Lifting his head slowly, he first saw a wooden table. Spaced out on it were several objects: a hammer and two long steel spikes; beside them, a large heavy knife; and next to that, a metal rod about a foot long. From one end of the rod an electrical cord snaked over the edge of the table and out of sight. He raised his eyes higher and saw the man sitting across the table. The wide face — the scars, the narrowed eyes — somewhere — he had seen him somewhere before.

On the table beside the man lay an open notebook and a pen and a wide roll of adhesive tape.

"Can you hear me?"

Rabbia nodded painfully. "You will suffer for this, whoever you are."

The man ignored the words. He pointed to the items on the table.

"Look carefully at what is in front of you, and listen. I am going to ask you questions, many questions. If you don't answer fully and truthfully, I will untape your left hand, lay it on the table, and hammer a spike through it."

Rabbia's eyes shifted to the gleaming steel spikes. The cold, flat voice continued.

'Then I'll take that knife and cut your fingers off — one by one."

Rabbia's eyes moved to the knife.

"You won't bleed to death." The finger pointed to the metal rod. "That's an electric soldering iron. I'll use it to cauterize the stubs."

Sweat broke out on Rabbia's pallid face. The man looked at him impassively.

"After that, unless you're talking, I'll start on the right hand; and then your feet."

Rabbia, like many brutal men, was a coward. Looking into those eyes across the table, he had a cold, certain feeling that the man would do it; but why? Who was he? Where had he seen him?

He tried to generate anger — enough anger to restrain his fear.

"Go to hell!" he snarled. A string of obscenities followed, but died away as the man rose. He picked up the roll of tape, unwrapped a length, tore it off, and moved round the table.

Rabbia started to say something, but the tape came down quickly across his mouth, sealing off the words. He saw the blur of movement toward his stomach and doubled up from the blow. A second later his head rocked as he was struck behind the mastoid.

He remained barely conscious, his body paralyzed — the nerves stunned. He was vaguely aware that his left arm had been freed and pulled forward. Moments later his body arched in agony and he passed out.

When he came round the second time, he didn't notice the throbbing in his head. His left arm seemed to be on fire. His eyes opened and he found himself looking at his hand — flat down on the table. The head of the spike jutted up from its centre. Blood was seeping slowly onto the table between splayed fingers.

His brain tried to disbelieve his eyes, but a slight movement sent fresh waves of agony through his body. A low moan escaped from the taped mouth. His eyes showed the terror. It was not just the abrupt act of violence, but the unemotional way it had been carried out, as though the man had set about knocking up a bookshelf.

He looked again into those eyes. Not a flicker — the whole face expressionless. Then, as the man stood up and moved again around the table, Raffia stiffened and cringed into the chair and shook his head and moaned in his throat. The man grabbed a handful of hair and held his head still while he tore off the tape. He then walked back and sat down and watched calmly as Rabbia retched and shuddered in fear and pain.

It took many minutes for the huge, sweating man to bring himself under control. His eyes shifted constantly to his pinned left hand, and the knife and soldering iron beside it.

Slowly the spasms died away and he raised his eyes and in a broken, barely audible voice asked: "What do you want?"

The man pulled the notebook toward him and uncapped the pen.

"Let's start with the Balletto kidnapping."

And Rabbia remembered the face.

The questions went on for over an hour. Only once, when they began about Fossella, did Rabbia hesitate; but as his questioner laid down the pen and started to rise, the answers flowed again.

They began with the kidnap itself. Rabbia had driven the car and quickly pointed out that it was Sandri who had shot the bodyguard. The other men, the dead ones, were Dorigo and Cremasco.

He didn't know anything about the ransom money. They were simply ordered to pick the girl up at a specific time and place, and hold her at a house in Niguada.

The whole job had been a mess from the start. Fossella had explained that there would be a bodyguard who wouldn't present much of a problem. He told Dorigo to fire a couple of shots to scare him off. They had been careless.

"Who raped the girl?"

"Sandri," came the immediate answer. "He was very angry — Dorigo had been a good friend — and he likes very young girls, and this one had fought and scratched his face."

Rabbia nervously licked his dry lips.

"And you?" came the flat question. "Did you also rape her?"

There was a long silence and then, almost imperceptibly, Rabbia nodded, his voice quivering as he answered:

"Yes . . . well, after Sandri. I thought it didn't make any difference." He looked up across the table. The man was perfectly still; his mind seemed to be in another place. The questions started again.

"Anyone else?"

Rabbia shook his head. "We were alone with her. It was very boring — we thought it would be finished in a few days, but there was trouble with the ransom, and we were stuck in that house over two weeks."

"So you raped her many times?"

Rabbia's chin had sunk into his chest. His forehead glistened with sweat. His voice came out as a hoarse whisper.

"Yes . . . there was not much to do, and . . . she was very beautiful"

His voice trailed off, and he raised his eyes and across the table saw death looking back.

"Fossella? What did he think of it?"

"He was angry. The girl's death was a mistake. He was very angry — we were supposed to get ten million lire each, but Fossella gave us nothing."

The voice asked softly. "So for punishment he stopped your pay — that's all?"

Rabbia nodded, sweat dripping from his chin.

"We were lucky — Sandri is Fossella's nephew — his sister's son."

The man picked up the pen.

"Yes," he said softly. "You were lucky. Let's talk about Sandri."

He milked Rabbia of every detail: friends, movements, habits — everything. Then they turned to Fossella and went through the same sequence.

At one point Rabbia complained about the pain in his hand.

"It won't be long," the man said. "Tell me about Conti and Cantarella."

But Rabbia knew little of such eminences. Cantarella, he explained, hardly ever left the Villa Colacci. Rabbia had never even seen him.

"But Fossella goes there a lot," he said. "And to see Conti in Rome — at least once a month."

There were no more questions. The notebook was closed, the pen capped.

Rabbia's panic mounted. He started talking again, babbling about Sandri and Fossella, but the man across the table was no longer interested. He slowly stood up and reached under his jacket. Rabbia saw the gun and his flow of words stopped. He no longer felt any pain. He watched, mesmerized, as the silencer was screwed onto the muzzle and the man walked round the table. He kept his eyes on the gun, saw it raised — coming ever closer; felt the metal rest against his face just below his right eye. He heard the voice for the last time:

"You are going to hell, Rabbia — you will not be lonely."

Granelli's was busy, the atmosphere typical of a Friday lunch — relaxed customers noisily anticipating the weekend.

In the alcove table at the back, Mario Satta ate alone. He agreed with the old adage that the perfect number, when eating out, was two — himself and a damn good headwaiter.

Satta was a man set apart by good looks. Even now, as he ate the *cappon magro*, several elegant women at other tables cast covert glances in his direction. In a country which is a bastion of male fashion, he was dressed with unusual elegance — a beautifully cut, dark grey suit set off by a sky-blue shirt and a wide tie of maroon silk. Light gleamed on small, flat cuff links and a matching Patek Philippe watch.

He had a lean, tanned face and a slightly aquiline nose. Even men in the restaurant felt their eyes drawn and their curiosities stimulated.

He looked like a successful actor, a macho fashion designer, or the front flier of a very fast jet set.

In fact he was a policeman, although his mother, an aristocratic lady, would have winced at such a description. "A colonel in the *Carabinieri*," she would have corrected frostily. That was true, and at thirty-eight he was young to have reached such a rank. This could have been due to his mother's legendary connections or to his own ability, but even his enemies — and they were numerous — would admit that the latter was more likely.

But still he was a policeman, and his mother had never ceased to wonder why he chose such a profession when she could have opened, so easily, the broad doors of politics or commerce. Her elder son had surprised her by taking up medicine and becoming a respected surgeon — a profession she thought worthy, but infinitely dull. Far more acceptable, though, than being a policeman. Satta himself often wondered what had attracted him to the *Carabinieri*. It could be his cynicism — the dominant ingredient of his character. How better to observe the foibles, follies and conceits of a corrupt society?

In spite of this cynicism, or because of it, he was a good policeman. Honesty or abundant private wealth put him outside personal corruption, and a sharp analytical mind, allied to restless energy, had brought success.

His job was one of four passions that dominated his life. The others were good food, beautiful women, and backgammon.

For Mario Satta, a perfect day would begin with a satisfying piece of detective work, followed by lunch at one of Milan's top restaurants; an afternoon in his office, sifting and collating his extensive files; then cooking dinner himself in his elegant apartment for an equally elegant lady, who would have the intelligence to later offer some resistance on the backgammon board. Later still that resistance should melt away in his huge double bed, where she should apply herself to less mental pursuits.

The last four years of his career had been deeply satisfying. He had requested and received a transfer to that department which specialized in organized crime. The members of that fraternity fascinated him, and he spent long hours learning the intricacies and secrets of their weblike organization.

For three years it had been a mostly academic exercise: collecting information — comparing and evaluating, putting names and faces together. Cross-referencing between cities in the north and the south; between a prostitution ring in Milan and a wine adulterating group in Calabria or a drug smuggling syndicate in Naples.

After three years, he knew more about the Italian Mafia than anyone outside that secretive cabal, and many within it. His assistant, Bellu, had joked that if Satta ever changed sides, he could slip into his new job without a single day's delay.

For the past year Satta had been putting that knowledge to use. He had spearheaded the investigation into the great steel plant scandal in Reggio and had even seen Don Mommo himself go behind bars — albeit only for a two-year stretch. During the past few months he had concentrated on the two main Families in Milan, led by Abrata and Fossella, patiently accumulating evidence on prostitution, coercion, and drugs. He had set up an elaborate network, comprising telephone tapping, surveillance, and stool pigeons. He looked forward over the coming months to getting enough evidence to put away some of the big boys — perhaps even Abrata and Fossella themselves.

His work had been made easier during the past year by a ground swell of public opinion. People were finally getting fed up with the arrogance and apparent immunity of the organized criminal. Surprisingly, the rise in fortune of the Communist party had been a help. Their support of the government had brought about a stiffening of the laws. There was still far to go. Prison sentences were woefully inadequate and witnesses were always hard to find and harder still to protect. But matters were improving. Every time the Mafia committed a particularly outrageous and flagrant act, public opinion hardened further against them.

After lunch he was to visit a young actress. They had met at a reception the evening before. She was small and delicate and fragile and very beautiful — and she played backgammon. She had invited him to her apartment — to play backgammon. So at lunch this day he had ordered for dessert *gelato di tutti frutti.*

Satta had a sweet tooth and particularly liked the combination of candied fruit and ice cream. Conscious of his tightly cut suit, he permitted himself a dessert only at weekends. Strictly speaking, he was cheating, because today was only Friday. But he was feeling expansive, anticipating the afternoon. The head-waiter approached, but instead of carrying the dessert, he held a telephone.

"Your office, Colonel." He plugged the jack into a wall socket.

It was Bellu. Satta listened for a few minutes and said, "I'll be there in half an hour," and hung up. He summoned the head-waiter, and with a trace of grimace cancelled the *gelato di tutti frutti.* Then he phoned the young actress to cancel the rendezvous. She was desolate. He consoled her — he would cook dinner himself for her on Sunday night in his apartment.

As he paid his bill, he said to the headwaiter, "Tell the chef that the *cappon magro* had a trace too much rosemary."

Satta believed that a chef's skill derived from the sum total of complaints received.

The body of Giorgio Rabbia lay face up in a drainage ditch beside an access road to the Milan-Turin motorway. An ambulance and several police cars were grouped on the roadside. A large, black plastic bag lay folded on a stretcher. A police photographer was moving around between flashes.

Satta stood next to his assistant, Massimo Bellu, looking down at the body.

"So the collector was collected," he commented dryly.

"Sometime last night," said Bellu. "The body was found an hour ago."

"One bullet in the head?"

"That's right — very close range." He pointed to the face. "Burn marks around the point of entry."

"What happened to his hand?"

Bellu shook his head. "Pierced right through — by what, I don't know."

The photographer had finished, and a policeman approached. "Can we take him away now, colonel?"

"Yes," answered Satta. "I want the pathologist's report as soon as possible."

The ambulance attendants started easing the plastic bag over the corpse, and Satta turned away to his car. Bellu followed.

"You think a war has started?" he asked.

Satta leaned back against his car and his analytical mind slipped into gear. He thought aloud for Bellu's benefit.

"There are three alternatives: first, Abrata and Fossella have started a territory war. It's unlikely; they have the city neatly divided and they're getting on well together. Besides, Conti, and ultimately Cantarella, would have to sanction it, and for sure they don't want a war right now. Second, Rabbia was dipping his fingers into the till and got caught." He thought silently and then shook his head.

"It makes no sense. Rabbia has been a collector for fifteen years and he was loyal — stupid, but loyal — Third, it was done from outside."

Bellu interjected, "But who — and why?"

Satta shrugged and got into his car and said through the open window, "I want Rabbia's file and the transcripts of all telephone intercepts for the past seventy-two hours — all of them — understand?"

Bellu looked at his watch and sighed.

Satta said, "You can forget whatever plans you have for this evening." A look of irritation crossed his face. "I've already cancelled an interesting meeting myself."

He thought for a moment. "And increase the surveillance on all those on the red list."

He started the engine.

"I'll see you back at the office."

Bellu stood watching the car drive away. He had worked as Satta's assistant for three years. For the whole of the first year, he had tried to think up a plausible reason to ask for a transfer. It wasn't that he hadn't liked Satta — he had loathed him. There had been no single reason. Not his cynicism, or his sardonic humour, or his extravagant good looks; not even his aristocratic background and casual arrogance. It was just that Satta represented everything that Bellu considered was unsuitable for a senior *Carabinieri* officer — and perhaps he was jealous.

Two things had changed his mind. The first was that after working for a year he had begun to appreciate Satta's persevering but subtle mind — in fact, to understand him. The second concerned Bellu's younger sister. She had applied to enter Catanzaro University to study medicine. She was well qualified, but his family had no connections, and her application had been turned down. He may have mentioned it in the office, he couldn't remember, but a week later she received a letter from the university, reversing its decision. Only after starting the course did she discover that a certain Professor Satta, senior surgeon at Naples' Cardarelli Hospital, had intervened.

Bellu had confronted his boss, who had looked surprised.

"You work with me," he had said. "Of course I had to do something."

Bellu had no more thoughts of a transfer. It wasn't so much what Satta had done, but the way he had expressed it.

You work "with" me; not "for" me.

Over the past two years they had developed into a good team. Satta was still cynical, sardonic, and arrogant, and had certainly not become any uglier. But Bellu understood him and even began to absorb some of his characteristics: He took more interest in his food, paid more for his suits, and treated his women with a touch of arrogance — and they liked it. But he drew the line at backgammon.

Satta read the pathologist's report out loud.

"Time of death, between midnight and six a.m. on the thirteenth." He looked up at Bellu and said, "He left the Papagayo just after midnight, right?"

Bellu nodded. "That's what they tell us. And he never reached the Bluenote, which was next on his usual schedule."

Satta went back to the report.

"Cause of death, massive brain damage, presumably brought about by the passage of a projectile."

He looked up in disgust. "Presumably brought about by the passage of a projectile." He snorted. "Why can't the idiot simply state that he had his brains blown out by a bullet?"

Bellu smiled. "That would make him sound like everybody else."

Satta grunted and went back to the report.

"Scorch marks below subject's right eye around projectile entry point indicate that said projectile was fired at very close range."

Satta rolled his eyes but carried on. "Large exit hole, approximately fifteen centimetres diameter at back of cranium, indicates that said projectile was a large calibre, soft nosed bullet."

"Hooray!" He looked up triumphantly. "At last the projectile has become a bullet,"

But now, as he continued, his voice contained an edge of interest. "Subject had incision through left hand. Shape of said incision, and skin fragments within said incision, indicate that cause was from a sharp instrument driven through the back of the hand with exit through the palm. Fine wooden splinters embedded in the palm suggest that the hand was pinned to a wooden surface (exhibit: splinters sent to lab, for analysis).

Extent of blood clotting indicates that incision was inflicted within two hours before subject's death."

Satta sat back in his chair, a slight, sardonic smile on his lips. "Seems like friend Rabbia was half crucified."

Bellu smiled back. "But I doubt he'll be rising from the dead in three days."

His boss shook his head.

"Not after passage of said projectile through said brain." He went back to the report, and his voice sharpened again with interest: "Traces of an adhesive substance were found on subject's wrists and ankles and around subject's mouth."

Satta closed the folder and leaned back, thinking deeply. Bellu sat patiently, waiting for the pronouncement.

"Rabbia was picked up when he left the Papagayo," Satta said finally, "taken somewhere quiet, and taped to a chair. Then they asked him some questions." He smiled thinly. "Rabbia was probably reluctant, so they stuck a knife through his hand to encourage him. After learning all they wanted, they shot him through the head and dumped him."

He leaned forward, picked a file from his desk, and scanned it.

"Rabbia's car was found at two p.m. this afternoon in a side street near the Central Station — nothing in it of interest except" — the sardonic smile came again — "a plastic dachshund with a bobbing head!"

Next Satta studied the transcripts of the phone intercepts. He didn't expect to find much of interest because, although phone tapping is practically a national industry, the targets themselves are well aware of it.

As he skimmed through the pages, Bellu said, "Nothing much except a flurry of calls early this morning — trying to locate Rabbia."

Satta tossed the file back onto his desk.

"The 'Union Corse,'" he said firmly. "It's the only explanation — there's been bad blood since that final drug deal." He looked at Bellu speculatively. "If they're behind it, we can expect trouble, and it does follow a pattern. They pick up a small-time member of the group and pump him about the activities of the others — then they plan an all-out attack."

"It fits," Bellu agreed. "Surveillance shows that, since this morning, Fossella and his boys are taking extra precautions — more bodyguards, and not moving around too much."

Satta reached a decision.

"Get me Montpelier on the phone in Marseilles — he might know something."

The main strength of the "Union Corse," the French equivalent of the Mafia, was in Marseilles and Montpelier was Satta's opposite number in southern France. They had a good working relationship, having met several times at conferences.

But the Frenchman couldn't help. He had heard nothing. He thought that if the "Union Corse" were behind it, they might have drafted gunmen in from Corsica itself. He promised to keep an ear to the ground and let Satta know if anything developed.

Satta hung up and said positively, "It's got to be the 'Union Corse' — it's logical!"

In Palermo, Cantarella reached the same conclusion.

"It must be the 'Union Corse,'" he told the three men sitting round the table in his study.

One of them was Floriano Conti, visiting from Rome. The others were Gravelli and Dicandia — top advisers to Cantarella. Conti was irritated and slightly embarrassed — Milan came under his immediate control.

"Fossella has been making bad decisions lately," he said. "I told him it was stupid to short-change the French on that deal. He gets too clever sometimes. Because it was the last shipment, before he switched to Bangkok for supplies, he decided to make a little extra."

Dicandia voiced an opinion: "He seems to be losing his touch. That kidnapping was badly handled." He looked around. "You remember — the Balletto girl. She was abused and then died in the car. People don't like that — it looks bad and there was pressure for weeks afterward."

It was Gravelli's turn.

"That job, particularly, should have been done right. And the men responsible should have been severely punished. One of them was Fossella's nephew, and all Fossella did was confiscate their share of the take." He shook his head solemnly. "Discipline is important in a business — I think maybe Fossella is getting soft."

Conti nodded. "Rabbia was one of those involved, and frankly, he was a stupid man."

All having expressed an opinion, they looked to Cantarella for his reaction. The small man sat on his cushion and pondered awhile. Then he made his decision. His voice, as he turned to Gravelli, was soft and polite — it was always so when he issued orders.

"Cesare, it would please me if you would go to Marseilles and talk to Delorie. If they have started this, I want you to make things right with them. Explain that it is not our policy to do business the way that it was done by Fossella on that occasion. Tell him that Fossella will make good on the transaction." His voice sharpened slightly. "But do not be apologetic — make him understand that we do this, not because of weakness, but because we are honourable men and we deal fairly in our business."

"I'll leave tomorrow, via Rome," Granelli said, but his boss shook his head.

"Wait for two or three days. I don't want him to think we come running as soon as trouble starts."

He turned to Dicandia.

"Maurizio, please go to Milan and have a talk with Fossella. Indicate our displeasure and our wish that he exercise better control in the future — also, that he must make good on his deal with Delorie."

Cantarella's tone was conciliatory when he turned to speak to Conti.

"I know Fossella is your direct responsibility, but I think it better that this reprimand come from me."

Conti inclined his head slightly in acquiescence, and Cantarella turned back to Dicandia: "Do this thing privately and discreetly. I do not want Abrata to know that Fossella is very much out of favour. It might give him ideas and, overall, the situation in Milan is good."

He looked to Conti for agreement, and received it.

"They counterbalance each other well," said Conti. "It is wise not to disturb that."

Cantarella was pleased with the meeting. He stood up and walked to the cocktail cabinet — small and dapper in his dark blue suit.

The other followed, and he poured them all a measure of Chivas Regal with a dash of soda.

Conti would have preferred his usual Sambuca; but when Don Cantarella personally poured you a Scotch — you drank Scotch.

On Saturday morning in Naples, Guido sat on his terrace drinking coffee and relaxing before the lunchtime rush. He heard the door open behind him and turned to see Pietro carrying a newspaper. The boy laid the paper on the table and pointed to a small item on an inside page. It told of the death, by shooting, of one Giorgio Rabbia — believed to have connections with organized crime. It was just a few lines. Milan is a violent city, and a single death generates little excitement. Guido looked up.

"So it's started," he said. "Pack your things — tomorrow you leave for Gozo."

CHAPTER SEVENTEEN

Giacomo Sandri rolled off the bed, stood up, and stretched, flexing pleasantly tired muscles. He picked up his watch from the bedside table and glanced at the dial — just after ten. Naked, he padded over to the window, pulled aside the curtain, and looked down at the darkened street. His black Alfa Romeo was parked directly below, and he could just make out Violente's elbow sticking out from the driver's window. Satisfied, he dropped the curtain and turned back. The girl was watching him from the bed. He smiled at her.

"How are you, little one? Did I make you happy?"

The girl nodded, her eyes on his body.

"Do you have to leave now?" she asked in a sullen voice. "You only ever stay an hour, and I get bored."

Sandri was both pleased and irritated. Pleased that at his age he could still satisfy a fifteen-year-old girl; and irritated that this one was becoming possessive, and therefore a nuisance.

But as he pulled on his trousers he reflected that if a man liked his girls young, he had to put up with a little childish behaviour. He went to the bed, sat down, and reached to cup a breast; but she rolled away, and his irritation increased.

"That's the way it is," he said, standing up and reaching for his shirt. "You have a nice place here, and plenty of money to spend — you want to go back to Bettola?"

She didn't answer and he continued dressing, admiring himself in the full-length mirror. He decided that another change was due. He was uniquely placed to satisfy his desire for girls: he controlled the prostitution side of his uncle's business. As the young girls flocked to the big city, looking for excitement and money, Sandri and his assistants were on hand to channel them into the bars, clubs, and brothels controlled by the organization. When Sandri spotted a particularly young and attractive girl, he diverted her for his own use, and when he tired of her she was quickly replaced.

They never returned to Bettola, or anywhere else, except to a succession of brothels. Tomorrow, he decided, he would pass this one on to Pezzutto, who would quickly get her dependent on drugs and so dependent on the organization.

He felt pleased with himself. It was important to make decisions without emotion. He would look out for another girl — perhaps even younger. As he got older he liked them even younger. He remembered the girl they had kidnapped — how young she had been, her body just beginning to ripen. He felt himself stirring at the memory and for a moment considered getting back into bed; but he discarded the thought. Fossella had told him to stand by from eleven o'clock. Gravelli had arrived from Palermo, presumably to discuss Rabbia's death, and the implications if it had been done by the French.

He sat on the bed and thought about that, as he pulled on his shoes. It meant being extra careful for a while, which was a nuisance — especially having an extra man along all the time. Still, he was lucky; Violente was unobtrusive, and his assignment to Sandri was proof of his rising importance. He indulged in a little self-praise, deciding that his progress was the result of a quick brain. He was proud of his quick brain — so much faster than Rabbia's, who had been dull and stupid. He grimaced at the memory of having been cooped up with him for over two weeks, with only the girl to relieve boredom.

He stood up and pulled on his shoulder holster, slipped his gun into it, and put on his jacket. The girl had sat up in bed and was watching him.

"When will I see you again?" she asked petulantly.

He leaned over and kissed her lightly on the lips.

"Tomorrow," he answered with a smile. "I'll take you for lunch, as a special treat — and afterward I want you to meet a friend of mine."

He unlocked the door of the small apartment and stepped out onto the landing. A voice called, "Sandri," and he turned, reaching under his jacket.

He did have a quick brain. In an instant it registered that he was looking, very closely, down the black barrels of a shotgun. Then the black turned yellow white.

Satta became impatient. The actress was unusually lucky. Certainly she had a measure of skill and she understood some of the finer points of the game; but to beat him three times out of five meant she had to be lucky. He rattled the dice and tossed them out onto the green baize. A two and a one — damn! The actress gave him a smile of sympathy — she was a good actress. Then she reached for the doubling dice with an inquiring arch of a shapely eyebrow.

Satta nodded and gritted his teeth. There was no question of moving her into the bedroom until he had, at least, drawn level. Pride was at stake — after all, he was an expert. He glanced at his watch and cursed under his breath. Almost eleven.

The evening had started so well. She had arrived, dressed in a flame red dress cut low and loose. She had the fragile, delicate beauty that Satta so admired — and high, firm breasts. It was watching those breasts each time she leaned forward that lost him his concentration and the first games.

The meal had been a parade of his culinary skills. They had started with his own paté, washed down with champagne and followed by an artichoke antipasto prepared with parsley and marjoram in the Roman manner. She had stayed with the champagne while he had had a dry Colli Albani. The tour de force was his specialty, *abbacchio brodettato* — baby lamb with egg and lemon sauce. With this they drank a pale red Cecuba. They finished, naturally, with *gelato di tutti frutti*. The actress had been gratifyingly impressed, and Satta had looked forward to a brief, triumphant session at the backgammon board and a longer session in the bedroom.

His pulse quickened. She had made a bad throw and been forced to expose a counter on her bar point. If he threw a six he could hit it with a back runner and swing the game — in ten minutes they would be in bed. He tore his gaze from her cleavage, rattled the dice, and threw a double six — and the phone rang.

Bellu stood beside the Alfa Romeo. A police van with a generator was parked in front and floodlighted the scene. Satta climbed out of his car. He looked very irritated. In fact, he looked as he had sounded on the phone fifteen minutes before.

He greeted Bellu with a grunt and looked into the car.

"Violente," said Bellu. "Sandri's upstairs."

"He was found like that?" Satta asked.

"No," said Bellu. "He was propped up behind the wheel, with his elbow sticking out the window. The first policeman on the scene told him to get out and when he didn't, he opened the door. The body fell against him and he pushed it away — he got a shock, and blood all over him."

Satta looked again into the car. The body lay across the front seats with the head resting against the far door. There was blood everywhere — on the dashboard, on the seats, and in a pool on the floor. It still dripped rhythmically from the huge gash under Violente's chin.

Satta turned away with a sniff.

"Violent in name and in death," he commented. "Let's go upstairs."

Bellu gestured to the waiting fingerprint men to carry on and followed his boss.

Sandri lay on his back on the second floor landing. A once white towel covered his head and shoulders. The police photographer was packing away his camera.

The apartment door was open and Satta could see into the bedroom. A girl sat on the bed, loosely wrapped in a sheet. A young policeman sat next to her, writing in a notebook and trying not to look too obviously under the sheet.

Bellu pointed with his chin. "He was just leaving after a session with his girlfriend."

Satta looked down at the body and muttered, "He was luckier than me, then." He reached down and lifted a corner of the towel. "Perhaps not," he said quietly, and dropped the towel back into place. He looked distinctly pale under his tan.

"Shotgun," Bellu said. "At very close range."

Satta nodded, looking down at the blood-stained towel. His lips twitched in a slight smile.

"Yes, I can see the pathologist's report now: 'Massive brain damage, presumably brought about by passage of vast multitude of projectiles.'"

He looked through again into the apartment. "Give me what you know."

"This is Sandri's love nest," Bellu answered. "He keeps the place and changes the girls — regularly. He comes here almost every night. Lately, since Rabbia was hit, Violente has always waited for him outside. The killer cut Violente's throat from ear to ear and left him propped up in the seat. It's dark down there, and a casual passer by wouldn't notice anything. Meanwhile, the killer comes up here and waits. He probably wore a loose coat with the shotgun under it. When Sandri came out, he got both barrels full in the face."

"Did the girl see anything?" Satta asked.

"Nothing," Bellu replied. "She's very young but not entirely stupid. When she heard the blast, she stuck her head under the pillow and kept it there until the police arrived." He pointed up with his thumb. "The woman in the apartment upstairs heard the bang and came down the stairs a bit and took a peek. When she saw Sandri lying there with only half a head, she started screaming. She only stopped a few minutes ago. Someone's with her, trying to calm her down and get a statement."

"It's interesting," Satta commented.

"What is?"

"Earlier, you referred to the 'killer' in the singular — why only one?"

Bellu shrugged. "I don't know — it's just a feeling I have — Rabbia and these two were killed by a single man."

"Very logical," Satta sniffed, and walked through into the apartment. The young policeman saw him coming and walked over and read from his notebook:

"Amelia Zanbon, aged fifteen, from Bettola — probably a runaway. There's likely to be a missing person's call out for her, dated six weeks ago — that's how long she's been with Sandri."

Satta looked past him at the girl, sitting small and frightened on the bed.

"Tell her to get dressed and pack her things, and then take her down to headquarters. Find out all you can about her association with Sandri and then pass her on to Missing Persons. She's to have round-the-clock protection until she's out of Milan."

He turned and left the bedroom and the door closed behind him. He walked a few paces and then stopped, went back, and opened the door. "You can wait for her out here," he said dryly, and the disappointed policeman followed him out.

Bellu came over.

"It looks like a full-scale war is starting," he said. "That's three in three days."

Satta nodded, deep in thought. "It's the 'Union Corse,'" he said firmly. "They like to use knives and shotguns." His face showed his irritation.

"I don't like it — they're over reacting. Soon innocent people will get caught in the cross fire." He looked down at the body of Sandri. "Rabbia told them where he would be — I wonder what else he told them."

"Anything they asked, I suppose," Bellu said.

"Yes," agreed Satta. "But what did they ask?"

They stood watching as Sandri's body was eased into a plastic bag. Then Satta turned away, saying over his shoulder, "Follow me to the office — we've got a busy night — and a busy week."

Now the newspapers became interested. Three killings in three days was going some, even by Milan's standards. Crime reporters were hauled out of bars and beds and told to come up with plausible stories. Inevitably they reached the same conclusion as Satta and Cantarella. Headlines the next morning proclaimed a war with the "Union Corse." Editorials pontificated about international crime and naturally called for more law and order.

Satta began to feel the pressure from above. Something must be done, his boss, the general, told him. It's bad enough for Italian criminals to kill each other, but totally disgraceful that Frenchmen should be doing it.

In Gozo, "Shreik" walked into Gleneagles and tossed a copy of *Il Tempo* onto the bar. The regulars gathered around and discussed the story. Was it over? Had Creasy completed his mission?

Guido in Naples and Leclerc in Marseilles also read the story; they knew it had just begun.

Dino Fossella was worried and angry. Worried because his men were being killed and angry because of Cantarella's reprimand. He resented it — deeply. He had never liked Cantarella. For years the smug little "arbitrator" had sat in his villa outside Palermo, hardly ever going out, never getting his hands dirty, but getting a nice slice of all the action. Just like a son-of-a-bitch politician.

Fossella sat in his car and gritted his teeth as he recalled the message carried by Dicandia: "We are displeased with you."

Pompous little bastard! If it wasn't for Cantarella's alliance with Conti, he would tell him what to do with his displeasure. Still, the little weasel had alliances with every boss in Italy — a real politician.

It was Wednesday evening, and Fossella was on his way to the village of Bianco to have dinner with his mother. He was a good son and always had dinner with his mother on Wednesdays. If he failed to do so, he felt guilty and his mother became angry, and even Cantarella couldn't match his mother when she became angry.

He travelled with caution, his own car sandwiched between two others full of bodyguards.

Filthy "Union Corse"! Such a fuss over twenty million lire. Anyway, his own envoy would shortly arrive in Marseilles with the money, and he would be able to relax.

The convoy swept into Bianco and up the terraced street to his mother's house. Bodyguards leapt out, hands hovering near open jackets. Melodrama, thought Fossella; not even the animals of the "Union Corse" would involve family in business matters.

"Wait here," he instructed irritably. "I'll be two hours, no more."

He was short, balding, and running to fat, and he panted slightly as he climbed the stone stairway and walked into the small house.

His mother glared at him angrily. She didn't say anything because there was a strip of white tape across her mouth. Tape also bound her wrists and ankles to a chair. A very large man stood beside her, holding a shotgun. Its short barrels rested on the old woman's shoulders. The muzzles were against her left ear.

"One little sound," said the man quietly, "and you become an instant orphan."

Fossella was instructed to face the wall, place his hands against it and spread his feet. He didn't hear the man approaching and was trying to work out who he could be when the blow put an end to speculation.

The blow had been nicely calculated. As he regained senses, his knees and ankles were being pressed together and taped tight; his wrists were already bound and his mouth sealed. Then he was picked up and carried through to the back of the house. He cursed his stupidity and felt anger and humiliation. One man, picking him up like a child and carrying him off.

A grey van was parked on the cobbled street behind the house, its side door open. Fossella was quickly dumped inside and the door quietly eased shut. He felt the van move as it freewheeled down the gentle slope and he thought of his melodramatic bodyguards, no more than thirty metres away on the road below. He cursed again but his anger was being replaced by fear. He had not been blindfolded. He had seen the faded lettering on the side of the van: Luigi Racca — Vegetable Dealer. It didn't mean anything to him, but the fact that he had been allowed to see it indicated a one-way journey.

During the next two hours his limbs became stiff and sore and then numb. His mind remained active, but he had come up with no answers when the van finally pulled to a halt and the engine was switched off. The side door was opened and once again he was picked up with casual ease. It was dark, but he could see the outline of tall trees and a small whitewashed cottage. His abductor carried him to the door and pushed it open with a foot. Fossella was laid none too gently onto a stone floor and a light switched on. He kept still and heard the man moving around the room. After a few minutes the footsteps approached and he was rolled onto his back. From his position and foreshortened view, the man seemed to tower to the ceiling. Abruptly he knelt down and took off Fossella's shoes. Then he unwound the tape from his ankles and knees. Fossella flexed cramped muscles but didn't try anything violent. He knew that physically he had no chance at all. He lay back, his body arched over his bound hands, very frightened and then very puzzled as he felt his belt being loosened and his trousers unzipped. A hand moved under his back and he was lifted slightly as first his trousers and then his underpants were pulled off. Only when he was rolled over onto his belly and his legs pulled roughly open did puzzlement change to consternation and rising panic. He felt the hands on his buttocks, prizing them apart, and he screamed in his throat and struggled wildly. He was being sodomized!

The struggle was brief. The hands left his buttocks and a blow behind the ear put him into oblivion.

As he came to he felt no sharp pain, only discomfort, and his whole body ached.

In front of him was a rough wooden table. Slightly off centre, to the left, was a dark stain surrounding a small hole. He raised his eyes to the man sitting opposite. There was an open notebook in front of him and several other items, including an old-fashioned alarm clock. Its dial faced him. It showed 9:02,

"Can you hear me?"

Fossella nodded painfully. Although his wrists and ankles were bound to the chair, the tape had been removed from his mouth. But he didn't say anything — he was older and wiser than Rabbia.

The man reached forward and picked up one of the items — a metal cylinder, rounded at both ends. He unscrewed it in the middle and showed Fossella the two hollow halves.

"This is a 'charger.' It's used by convicts and others to conceal valuables — money — even drugs. It is hidden inside the body — in the rectum."

Fossella squirmed in the chair — remembering — feeling the discomfort. Opposite him the man picked up a lump of what looked like grey plasticine. The voice continued:

"This is Plastique — high explosive."

He moulded the lump into one end of the cylinder, tamping it tight with his thumb.

"This is a detonator."

He held up a small, round, metal object with a single prong jutting from one end. The prong was slipped into the Plastique.

"This is a timer."

Another round metal object, with two prongs. The two prongs were plugged into two sockets in the exposed end of the detonator, and the two halves of the cylinder were screwed together. The cylinder was held up between thumb and forefinger.

"So the charger becomes a bomb. Very small, but very powerful." The Voice became slightly conversational.

"It's modern science. Ten years ago a bomb of similar power would have weighed over a kilo."

The cold eyes bored into Fossella. The voice went very flat.

"You have an identical bomb up your ass. It's timed to explode at ten o'clock."

Fossella's eyes flicked to the alarm clock — 9:07.

The situation was explained. Fossella would answer some questions. If he did so, fully and honestly, and before ten o'clock, he would be allowed to remove the bomb.

Fossella demurred — he would be killed anyway.

It was explained that, unlike the others, Fossella was needed alive. Fossella didn't believe it. The man shrugged and remained silent, his face expressionless.

Minutes went by; the only sounds in the room the loud ticking of the clock and Fossella's short nervous breathing. Every feeling in his body was sublimated to the pressure in his bowels. It was 9:22 when he cracked. He had nothing to lose anyway.

"What do you want to know?"

The man picked up the pen and uncapped it.

"I want to know about Conti and Cantarella; but first I want to know why a man of your intelligence kidnapped a girl whose father had no money."

At 9:53, the questions ended. The man capped the pen, picked up the notebook and stood up. He looked at Fossella for a few moments and then walked to the door and went out. Fossella heard the sound of the van's engine. It faded away, leaving only the rhythmic ticking of the clock. He didn't shout or struggle. He just sat rigid, his eyes fixed on the dial. At 9:58, the alarm rang stridently, and Fossella's mind disintegrated. Two minutes later his body did the same — upward.

Satta looked down at the actress. Her curved, naked body was glossy with a sheen of sweat; her red, smudged mouth slack with desire.

He was waiting for her to say it.

For half an hour he had laboured with great skill to bring her to this peak of expectation. Every inch of her body had felt his lips and teasing fingers. He was only waiting for her to say it.

The evening had been a total success. Once again he had cooked a delicious meal and then gone on to win three quick, decisive games of backgammon. True, he had a suspicion she played deliberately badly; but no matter — it only remained for his tactile skills to be acknowledged.

She said it.

"Please, *caro*! — please!"

His heart sang. He slid a leg over slippery thighs, raised himself slightly, looked down into her imploring eyes and said masterfully: "Put it in."

A slim hand slithered between them, urgent fingers seeking and finding, drawing him against moist, silky hair. He groaned with the sensation and sank in an inch. God, she was tight! He leaned down, kissed the tip of her nose, flexed for the first consummating stroke — and the phone rang.

CHAPTER EIGHTEEN

"It's not the 'Union Corse.'"

Satta said it emphatically, looking down at the pathologist's report. Bellu sat opposite him, across the desk.

"What makes you so sure?"

Satta tapped the report. "They don't have that kind of imagination." He smiled. "Knives, yes, shotguns, yes, revolvers, yes. Bombs, yes; but not up the rectum."

He shook his head. "This is a different kind of mind."

It was two days after Fossella's death and Satta was under increasing pressure to come up with answers. The newspapers were full of the story and all its gory details.

Consultation with Montpelier in Marseilles had only convinced Satta that his deduction was correct. The "Union Corse" in that city had convinced both the Marseilles police and Gravelli that they were blameless, if not grief-stricken.

Among the bosses, suspicion was spreading like a brush fire. Cantarella was seething and worried. Someone was upsetting three decades of statesmanlike planning. But who?

It was to be expected that Satta, with his analytical mind, should be the first to work it out. For two days he hardly left his office. Anyway, his affair with the actress was over.

"There are limits," she had told him. Such interruptions could cause a girl to break out in a rash. Her career would never stand it.

So Satta was able to concentrate. He went endlessly through the different permutations: Rabbia, Violente, Sandri, and Fossella. It was only when he extracted Violente from the equation that he made the connection. He cursed himself for his stupidity — Violente's killing was incidental. He was protecting Sandri.

"The Balletto kidnapping!"

Bellu raised an eyebrow, "What about it?"

His boss's face showed increasing comprehension.

"That's the connection! Rabbia and Sandri worked together on it. Fossella organized it."

For the next hour the two policemen were very busy. They quickly decided that Balletto himself would not be directly involved, although he might be financing an act of revenge. They turned their attention to the bodyguard, although at first they were highly sceptical. They knew he had been only a "premium" bodyguard, and an alcoholic; but a phone call to the hospital quickened Satta's interest. He talked to the senior surgeon, who happened to be a friend of his brother, and he learned that the bodyguard had made an excellent recovery and had great determination to get fit. The next phone call was to the agency, and this supplied the information that the bodyguard had once been a mercenary. An urgent Grade One inquiry was telexed to Paris, and while they waited for the reply they traced the connection to one Guido Arrellio, owner of the Pensione Splendide in Naples.

In all these inquiries, Satta's rank, reputation, and connections brought rapid answers. He personally called the director of immigration in Rome and that department's computer quickly advised that the bodyguard had left Reggio di Calabria on the ferry for Malta six days after leaving the hospital. It had no information on his returning to Italy.

Next, Satta made an overseas call to his opposite number in Malta. He had met George Zammit at a training course the year before in Rome, and had liked him. When he hung up after the brief conversation, he looked at Bellu thoughtfully and said, "Interesting and curious."

"In what way?" asked Bellu.

"He confirmed the arrival time in Malta and told me that the subject had departed by sea for Marseilles three weeks ago."

"That's all?"

Satta nodded. "Yes, that's all."

"So what makes it curious and interesting?"

Satta smiled. "The Maltese police are efficient — it's a legacy from the British. But they're not that efficient, and their data is not computerized. Zammit had the information at his fingertips, which means he's taken a personal interest. Yet when I asked if he knew anything more about the man, he told me they have half a million visitors a year, and he's understaffed and overworked. He's holding something back — why?"

They were interrupted by the arrival of the telex reply from Paris. The machine clattered for a long time and the roll of paper that Satta eventually read was over three feet long. He read silently, and Bellu waited expectantly. Finally Satta rolled the paper into a tube, held it between his palms, and leaned back in his chair.

"The premium bodyguard," he said softly, "was, and maybe is again, a very lethal human being."

He stood up abruptly.

"Let's drive to Como and have a chat with Balletto and his exquisite wife."

In the house by the lake the Ballettos were at dinner sitting across from each other at the polished table. She was thinner but had retained her beauty. He appeared unchanged. She had lost something precious. He still had what was all-important.

The door opened and they turned expecting to see Maria with the dessert. The doorway was filled with the bulk of Creasy.

He stood still, his eyes moving from one to the other. They stared back, mesmerized.

Ettore recovered first. "What do you want?" he asked sharply.

Creasy moved forward, picked up a chair, reversed it and sat down, his arms resting on the back. He looked at Ettore. "I'm going to talk to your wife. If you move or say one word, I'm going to kill you."

He reached under his jacket and put a heavy pistol on the table before him.

"It's loaded," he said, with a trace of sarcasm.

Ettore looked at the gun and his body went slack and he sank down into his chair. Creasy turned to Rika. The hard lines of his face softened; his voice became gentle.

"I'm going to tell you a story."

He told her what he had learned from Fossella: that Pinta's kidnapping had been a setup — an insurance job. Ettore had taken out a policy with Lloyd's of London for two billion lire. The deal had been that Fossella would kick back half the ransom to Ettore. Vico Mansutti had been the go-between. He had connections with organized crime; he got a commission. As she listened, Rika's eyes never left Creasy's face. Only when he finished did she turn and look at her husband. The hatred that flowed across the table was incarnate — physical. Ettore slumped lower into his chair, his mouth opened and then closed, and his eyes slid away.

"The others? The ones that did it? You killed them?"

Creasy nodded. "I'm going to kill every one that profited. That includes the boss in Rome and the big one in Palermo."

Silence again in the large, elegant room, then Rika's voice, half talking to herself, musing.

"He comforted me. Told me we still had each other — life goes on."

She looked up at Creasy, her eyes no longer reflecting memories — hardening.

"You said all of them?"

He picked up the pistol from the table and nodded.

"I came here to kill him."

Ettore looked up, not at Creasy but at his wife. His handsome face had lost all its character; his eyes were windows into nothing.

Creasy put the pistol away and stood up.

"Perhaps I should leave him to you."

"Yes!" The word hissed out. "Leave him to me — please."

Creasy moved to the door, but Rika's voice stopped him.

"What about Mansutti?"

He turned and shook his head.

"Don't worry about Mansutti."

The door closed behind him.

As Satta and Bellu drove along the lakeshore road, a blue Alfetta passed them, going the other way.

In his penthouse apartment, Vico Mansutti received a phone call. Ettore was hysterical, almost incoherent. Vico could barely understand a word.

"Just wait," he said sharply. "I'll be there within an hour. Get a grip on yourself."

He quickly slipped on a jacket and told his inquiring wife that there was a slight crisis. He would be back late.

In the basement garage he climbed into his Mercedes, switched on the ignition — and half a kilo of Plastique.

Satta was profoundly impressed. He sat back in his chair and said, with great reverence:

"Never, I repeat never, have I tasted a better *fritto misto*."

Guido shrugged indifferently. "We are not all peasants in Naples."

"Obviously not," Satta agreed, wiping his mouth with a napkin. "But for an ex-criminal, ex-convict, ex-Legionnaire, ex-mercenary, you have some exotic talents. You don't play backgammon, by any chance?"

Guido looked puzzled. "I do, but what's that got to do with anything?"

Satta smiled. "It's prophetic. My stay here is going to be most enjoyable."

"I told you," Guido scowled. 'The pensione is closed — go to a hotel."

Satta poured the last of the chilled Lacrima Christi and sipped appreciatively. When he spoke, his voice had lost its bantering edge.

"You, of all people, understand the reality of the situation. It's certain that, by now, Cantarella knows who is running amok among his organization. His facilities are as good as mine — perhaps better. It won't be long before they trace him back to you, and then some of the boys will be around to ask you questions. They will be much less polite than me."

Guido shrugged again. "I can take care of myself."

But he took Satta's point. Only an hour ago Elio had phoned from Milan to advise that two well-dressed but covertly threatening men had called at his office to inquire about his recommendation of Creasy to the agency. Acting on Guido's instructions, he had told them simply that he had been doing his brother a favour. Very soon some of the locals would be knocking on the door of the pensione. It was true that, with the *Carabinieri* colonel in attendance, they would keep their distance.

"I'll make you up a room," he said shortly. "But don't expect breakfast in bed."

Satta waved a hand deprecatingly. "I'll be no trouble. And believe me, it's better — we have a lot to talk about."

Satta had arrived that evening, after driving all day from Milan. He preferred to drive; it gave him time to think, to review the events of the past week. To come to grips with the reality that one man had taken on the most powerful men in the country.

His mind had gone back to the interview with the Ballettos in the house by the lake. The extraordinary scene that had greeted them.

The normally urbane Balletto had been ashen and literally quivering, his wife all icy disdain, and beautiful. Satta remembered that beauty; fined down now and perhaps even enhanced by the emotional shocks of the past months.

At first Ettore had refused to talk, pending the arrival of his lawyer; but with the news of Mansutti's sudden death, he had broken completely and turned to Satta in desperation — a priest — a father figure — a protector. The story had poured from him; disjointed, rambling at times, and to Satta pathetic in its plea for understanding. He had hardly interrupted the flow, only occasionally breaking in to clarify a point, keeping his face and his voice sympathetic.

Bellu had taken notes frenetically while Rika had sat silent and cold, her eyes never leaving her husband's face, her attitude showing nothing more than disgust.

It was the revelation that Creasy was going on, going after Conti and Cantarella, that had astonished Satta. He had assumed that with the killing of Fossella revenge was satisfied; assumed that the bodyguard would now be running hard for the border — for a distant country.

He had left it to Bellu to start criminal proceedings against Balletto and gone to his apartment to think.

The situation created a deep division within him. On the one hand, Creasy's actions had struck right to the heart of the Mafia — to its pride. One man! If he should go on and get to Conti, the wound could be disastrous; and if the unthinkable happened, and he killed Cantarella, then the wound could be fatal.

The alliance between Cantarella and Conti was the linchpin of the organization. There would be chaos, and within that chaos he, Satta, would move against every boss left alive, and the organization would be set back by a decade or more. He had no illusions. His job as a policeman could only be one of containment. He couldn't destroy the monster forever, only stunt its growth. But what an opportunity!

On the other hand, his job was to apprehend killers, no matter whom they were killing, or why. It was not a crisis of conscience. Satta prided himself on having his conscience tidily locked away in a little steel lined box. One day, when he got bored with cynicism, he would open it and surprise himself.

It was a crisis of propriety. In his philosophy, laws could and should be bent; but there had to be laws, and only the enforcers should have the unspoken right to bend them. So Creasy presented a dilemma. He created a unique opportunity, but he affronted Satta's sense of propriety. He wrestled with his propriety late into the night and finally reached a dignified compromise. Early the next morning he reported to his boss, the general, and told him the whole story and explained the compromise. The general was sympathetic. He trusted Satta. Agreement was reached that Satta would be in full control of the case. The press would be told nothing, although inevitably they would sniff out the story within a few days.

So Bellu was left to tidy up in Milan and then proceed to Rome to be close to Conti, while Satta drove south to Naples. He saw Guido as the key, knew him to be Creasy's closest friend, and suspected his role in the preparations. Instructions were given to bug the telephone of the Pensione Splendide and intercept its mail. Meanwhile, Satta wanted to know everything about Creasy: his capability, his character, his philosophy. Reports could give him facts. Only Guido could give him substance.

On the same day that Satta drove to Naples, an officer in the records department of the Milan *Carabinieri* filed a copy of a confidential memo; filed it after reading it very carefully. That evening he took dinner with a friend and substantially increased his financial position. As Satta was enjoying his *fritto misto*, Conti in Rome was listening incredulously on the phone to Abrata, now the undisputed boss of Milan.

Abrata's information was complete, right down to the details of Creasy's past history. His voice on the phone was slightly solicitous. He, after all, was not on the death list.

Conti issued precise instructions and hung up and for several minutes sat deep in thought. Then he rang the special number in Palermo and spoke to Cantarella. The nub of this conversation dealt not so much with the identity of the killer but with the astonishing fact that the police and *Carabinieri* were taking little or no action. As far as Abrata knew, no general alert had been issued.

All inquiries were in the hands of Colonel Satta, who had left Milan that morning, destination unknown. Politics was obviously involved. Black deeds were being hatched!

After this conversation, Conti was even more thoughtful, for in Cantarella's voice he had detected a shred of fear. Instead of being forceful and deliberate with his instructions, the "arbitrator" had sounded uncertain, even asking for suggestions. Conti had reassured him. Even without the police, Creasy would soon be eliminated. Now that his identity was known, he would be found within hours. Instructions had already gone out through every tier of the organization.

But Conti wondered about Cantarella's reaction. Certainly the killer, with his background and motivation, was a dangerous threat, but so far he had operated with the benefit of secrecy and anonymity. Now he had lost that advantage. He would pay for his temerity.

But why Cantarella's unease? Conti concluded that it was the reaction of a politician. He himself had reached his present position due to the ruthless application of violence. He had seen death often.

Cantarella, on the other hand, had progressed through diplomacy. He had frequently ordered violence, but never taken part himself; never had to. Conti had been a soldier and a general. Cantarella always had been the statesman. Conversely, thinking back over the years, Conti decided that the "arbitrator" had never been directly threatened. At least, not physically. Perhaps that lack of experience now created the concern.

It interested Conti. It was something to think about. Finally, before going to bed, he issued instructions for his personal safety. He owned the ten story apartment building that housed the penthouse in which he lived. From its basement garage upward, security was to be tightened to such an extent that a mouse couldn't get in or out. The same applied to the building that housed his office, which he also owned.

He was not concerned about his movements between the two buildings. Some years earlier he had done a favour for a compatriot in New York. In return he had received, as a gift, a Cadillac. A very special Cadillac, with three-inch armour plating and bulletproof windows. Conti was very proud of the car. Twice over the years it had been fired on, once with heavy calibre pistols and once with submachine guns. On both occasions he had come through unscathed and unruffled. Even so, he ordered that until further notice a carload of bodyguards would follow the Cadillac at all times. He also decided that in the interim he would take all his meals at home. He was well aware that more bosses had died in restaurants than anywhere else, and not from food poisoning.

Cantarella was indeed frightened. It was a new sensation. The thought of a highly qualified killer making him a target sickened him. He went through stages of anger and indignation, but fear was the constant emotion.

Conti had been confident on the phone — only a matter of hours. But as Cantarella sat behind his desk in his panelled study, he had a very cold feeling. He crossed himself and pulled forward a pad of paper and turned his mind to the security of the Villa Colacci. It could and would be made impregnable.

Before he finished his notes, the phone rang. It was the boss in Naples to inform him that it was impossible to question the owner of the Pensione Splendide. It appeared that he and the forever-damned Colonel Satta of the *Carabinieri* were as thick as thieves. Cantarella's unease deepened.

Guido rolled a double four, took off his last three counters, and glanced at the doubling dice. Then he picked up a pen, made a quick calculation, and announced, "Eighty-five thousand lire."

Satta smiled. It was an effort.

"I should have taken your advice and stayed in a hotel."

It was the third day and he had eaten several excellent meals, even helping out in the kitchen on occasion, the regular customers having no idea that the salad had been tossed by a full colonel.

Apart from having lost over three hundred thousand lire at backgammon, he had enjoyed his stay. Even that loss had its compensations, for if a man could play with such skill and panache, he earned Satta's grudging respect.

But it was more than just respect. A positive friendship had developed. It may have been partly the attraction of opposites, for no two men could have been more different, at least on the outside: Guido, taciturn, stocky and broken-nosed; Satta, tall, elegant, talkative, and urbane. But Satta found much to admire in the Neapolitan. Once he began to relax and talk, he showed a deep vein of knowledge of his own society and the world. He also had a dry and perceptive sense of humour, which Satta much appreciated. Of course Satta knew a great deal about Guido's past. During one conversation he had asked whether Guido did not sometimes get bored with his present occupation. Wasn't it slightly mundane?

Guido had smiled and shaken his head and remarked that if he wanted excitement he could go back through the paths of his memory. No, he found the small, prosaic things in life made up a satisfying mosaic. He enjoyed running the pensione, the various quirks and foibles of the regulars who came to eat in the restaurant. He liked watching football on television on Sunday nights, and occasionally going out on the town, and perhaps finding a girl. He was content, especially when he had overeducated policemen to beat at backgammon.

On his part, Satta provided Guido with a puzzle. At first he had viewed the colonel as a misplaced social butterfly who had progressed through family connections. It was not long, however, before he saw through the sardonic exterior and recognized the dedicated and honest man beneath. On the second night, Satta's elder brother came for dinner and afterward the three of them sat late into the night on the terrace, talking and drinking.

There was a very deep affection between the two brothers, and they included Guido in their family conversation so naturally and easily that he felt a warmth of companionship, a warmth that before had come only in the presence of Creasy.

And they talked of Creasy at great length. Although Satta was convinced that Guido must have contact with him, he never pressed the matter. Several times a day he spoke to Bellu in Rome, and each time was told that there was nothing to report on the telephone or in mail intercepts.

"Only conversations between you and me," Bellu commented once. "And they are fascinating!"

But Satta was content to wait. Although the newspapers were, by now, very close to unravelling the full story, no mention had yet been made of Creasy. They were full of the scandal of the industrialist who had been charged with engineering his own daughter's kidnap, and of the prominent lawyer who had been blown to pieces, and the connection between the two; and with the Mafia killings of the past days. It wouldn't be long before they pieced it all together, and Satta tried to imagine the reaction of the public when the whole story came out — the on-going story.

He often thought about Creasy. He was able to build a picture in his mind as Guido talked of his friend. He understood clearly the motivation and felt a tangible sympathy and a bond for this man who moved alone to satiate a craving for revenge.

Guido would talk of the past, but never the present. He was emphatic. The last time he had seen Creasy was when he left the hospital. Satta didn't press, just shrugged and waited. He held all the aces. Let Conti and Cantarella worry.

But he wasn't playing cards, but backgammon — and he was losing.

"Enough," he said, as Guido laid out the counters again. "I'm a public servant and can't go on losing a week's salary every day."

They sat out on the terrace as the late afternoon sun edged toward the horizon. Soon Guido would start preparing dinner; but now was the quiet time, and they fell silent as they watched the changing colours around the bay. It was dusk when the phone rang. Milan calling Colonel Satta.

Guido had gone to the kitchen and was chopping vegetables when Satta came in after the long conversation.

"Balletto," he said. "He committed suicide."

"You're sure it was suicide?" Guido asked.

Satta nodded. "No question. He sat on the window ledge of his eighth floor office for half an hour before he made up his mind."

His hands moved in an expressive gesture.

"He was always a vacillating man."

Guido went back to the vegetables and Satta started to help around the kitchen. Then he stopped and asked, "You met his wife?"

"Once," answered Guido. "It was not a pleasant meeting."

He explained the circumstances and Satta nodded sympathetically.

"You picked a bad time. No doubt her opinion has changed. No doubt she herself has changed."

They worked in silence and then Satta said, "While Balletto was trying to make up his mind, the police phoned and asked her to come down and try to talk him out of it. You know what she said?"

"What?"

Satta shook his head.

"Nothing, nothing at all — she just laughed."

They worked on again, and then Satta said musingly, "A strange woman — and very beautiful."

Guido looked up at him quizzically, started to say something, but then shrugged and went back to work.

CHAPTER NINETEEN

In each of the capitals of Europe, there is an Australian Embassy, and on a side street close to each embassy, house trailers and mobile homes can be found, parked, during the daylight hours of summer. They are for sale, although why near the Australian Embassy, no one knows.

Rome was no exception, but because it was late summer, there was only one vehicle — a Mobex on a Bedford chassis. "Wally" Wightman and his girlfriend, "Paddy" Collins, sat on the high curb, waiting unexpectantly for a customer.

He was in his late twenties and short, his appearance made notable by hair. Hair flowed from his head to his shoulders and from his face and chin to his chest. Intelligent eyes peered through it all. He was dressed in denim overalls that could have qualified for a certificate of antiquity. She was in her early thirties and large all over. Not fat, simply oversized, from her toes to her nose. She was not unattractive, but her size contradicted femininity. She wore a peasant dress that looked incongruous.

They were Australians, and their story was at once typical and different. Typical in that they had both travelled to Europe to broaden their minds, and different in that they had met each other. Wally was a perennial student who had long ago found a temporary job teaching English to Italians in a night school in Turin. There he had met Paddy, who for twelve years had been an executive secretary in Brisbane. One day she had thrown it all up and taken off to "do" Europe. She also ended up teaching English in Turin. The result was that a whole generation of Italians spoke English with a strong Australian accent; and instead of "doing" Europe, she "did" Wally. In fact, she loved him. A love brought on by his total indifference to accepted standards of female beauty. Her size did not bother him. He liked her mind and her sense of humour, which was rough, and her ability to be dominating by day and totally submissive and quiescent by night. In bed he was the boss; outside it, she organized everything, including his creature comforts. It was an un-Australian arrangement, but it worked.

They'd had a good winter and early summer and had pooled their resources to buy the Mobex, the idea being to drive it as far east as possible, at least to Bombay, and then ship it down to Perth and drive across to Northern Queensland. There the government was giving land and grants to people who would develop remote areas and grow trees. The government needed trees, and Wally reasoned that they took a long time to grow, and they could live in the Mobex, and maybe grow children as well, and contribute to Australia's balance-of-payments problem and get paid for it. But things had not worked out. The changes in Iran meant that driving very Far East was a nonstarter, and then Paddy had got sick with jaundice and the hospital bills had piled up and at the end they had no choice but to sell the Mobex and travel home the cheapest way. So they sat on the curb and waited.

But they had been there three days, and the only inquiry had been from a Turk who had no money but an ingenious scheme for smuggling Pakistani immigrants into Britain. So they were not hopeful, and they hardly looked up when the big, scar faced man approached and did a circuit of the Mobex.

"It's for sale?" he asked, speaking in Italian.

Wally shook his head and answered in the same language.

"No, we just park here for the view."

The man didn't smile but went back to inspecting the vehicle. Paddy stood up, brushing dust from her ample backside.

"Are you really interested?"

The man turned and looked at her appraisingly and then nodded. Wally was ignored.

"Can I look at the motor?"

Wally followed them as she pointed out the advantages and then suggested that they go inside for a cool beer.

The Mobex was only two years old, with less than ten thousand miles on the clock, and Paddy argued fiercely over the price. Wally kept quiet, sipping his beer, admiring her determination.

They finally settled at ten million lire, and the man asked: "You have the transfer papers?"

Paddy nodded. "They have to be registered and stamped by the police."

They filled out the papers, the buyer's section reading: Patrice Duvalier. Nationality: French.

"I don't want delivery for three days," he said, pushing the papers across the small fold down table.

Paddy's face showed rank suspicion.

"You'll leave a deposit?"

Then they got a great shock. He reached into an inside pocket of his jacket and pulled out a great wad of hundred thousand lire notes. He counted out a hundred and pushed them across the table.

"But don't register the papers until then," he said. There was a long silence, ended by Wally making his first contribution to the conversation.

"You're bloody trusting, mate! What if we take the money and drive off?"

Creasy said softly, "I'm not trusting."

Wally looked into the narrow eyes. Then, to cover his sudden confusion, he reached behind to the refrigerator for more beers.

The air of tension eased and Paddy asked, 'You'll take delivery here?"

Creasy shook his head and pulled out a street map of Rome. He pointed to a small, inked x just outside the city, near the Eastern Autostrada.

"There's the Monte Antenne campside. I'll pick it up in the early afternoon, if that's OK."

Paddy nodded. "Meanwhile, we can leave our bags at the railway station."

"Where are you heading?" Creasy asked.

"Brindisi," she replied. "We get the ferry from there to Greece."

Creasy took a pull on his beer and looked thoughtfully around the small but comfortable interior. Then he silently studied the two Australians. Finally he said, "I'm going south myself. I could give you a lift — it would be a chance to point out the wrinkles, if there are any."

They discussed the idea, and it made sense. Creasy explained that he was in no hurry; in fact, he planned to take three or four days on the journey. So agreement was reached, and then Creasy suggested they wait until reaching Brindisi before registering the transfer.

To celebrate the deal, and since it was lunchtime, Paddy opened some cans and made a meal, and Wally opened more beers.

When Creasy left, Paddy commented, "He's not French, he's American."

"How do you know?" asked Wally.

"The way he eats. Only Americans eat like that."

Wally looked sceptical, but Paddy was adamant.

"It's true. They hold the knife and fork like everyone else, but when they've cut a piece of meat they lay down the knife and transfer the fork to the right hand. It's very inefficient, which is strange, being Americans; but they all do it."

"So?"

"So, nothing. But he's not French."

"You think he's alright? He didn't even leave an address or anything. Just walked off."

Paddy shrugged. "Anyway, we have his money." She paused thoughtfully. "He's not what he seems, but who is these days."

"He's a tough bastard," Wally said, and grinned. "Christ, he's even bigger than you!"

Paddy grinned back, but then was thoughtful again.

"I like him," she said. "Doesn't mince about. Doesn't talk for the sake of it. We'll see."

"The Cowboy" eased his buttocks on the hard bench. As a young priest, he had enjoyed the confessional — not something to admit to the bishop, but it did relieve the routine. Now, as he grew older, he found the whole thing increasingly tiresome. Perhaps in big cities there were more interesting sins, but here on Gozo, in the village of Nadur, he could predict just about every transgression of his parishioners. True, old Salvu, who had just left, did have an inventive mind; but he too was becoming predictable.

He heard the curtain rustle, and Laura Schembri's voice came through the grill.

"Forgive me, Father, for I have sinned."

"The Cowboy" leaned forward.

"What do you remember?"

There followed the list of usual minor infractions, and he duly admonished, set the minor penances, and leaned back to wait for the next parishioner.

But he didn't hear the rustle of her exit, only the shallow, uncertain breathing of a woman in doubt.

"You have something more?"

Doubt was resolved.

"Forgive her, Father. My daughter has sinned."

"Then it is she who must confess."

The routine had been broken.

The Schembri girl was an enigma to "the Cowboy." Every morning she came to early Mass, something she had not done before, but she never came into the confessional. Yet she prayed every day.

"You cannot confess for another."

The voice came back bluntly.

"I don't want to. I want advice."

Routine had been shattered.

In all his years as parish priest, Laura Schembri had never asked his advice, although she had quite frequently offered her own, especially in his younger days; she was not a woman to be overawed by the cloth. His interest was tinged with apprehension. Advice concerning Nadia might be difficult to formulate.

"She is with child."

Apprehension justified! "The Cowboy" sighed. That girl's journey through life was truly strewn with boulders.

"The American?"

"Who else? She is not given to indiscriminate fornication!"

He sensed that the combative tone was defensive, and he controlled his rising irritation. He asked gently, "So what advice do you seek?"

He felt the tension in her subside.

"She has not informed Creasy, and she has forbidden me or her father to do so. That is part of her sin. She conceived the child deliberately. She used him only as a provider of the seed."

"She does not love him?"

"I'm not sure — I don't know." Laura's voice indicated uncertainty.

"You are her mother, and you don't know?"

"I only know that in the beginning she went with him to get herself pregnant. I'm not sure now how she feels. She is different. She told me of the child, but that's all. She is not herself."

"So what advice do you seek?"

"Do I tell him or not?"

"The Cowboy" leaned back and collected his thoughts. He knew, like others in Gozo, that Creasy was engaged in dealing out violent death. The Schembri girl never did anything without its being complicated.

"You know what this American is doing?"

"Yes."

"It is a sinful thing."

"He has a reason."

"Vengeance belongs to God."

"God moves in strange ways."

"The Cowboy" sighed again. This woman would have made a good priest.

"Even if you wish to tell him, can you do so?"

"It's possible."

"Have you discussed it with your husband?"

"No — I know what his answer would be, and I don't wish to hear it:"

"The Cowboy" moved uneasily on the wooden bench. He was getting himself right into the middle of things. An uncomfortable position. But then he was a priest and had forsaken comfort. He considered all the aspects, knowing that if he gave advice it must not be couched in platitudes. His was a farming parish, his congregation hardnosed pragmatists, none more so than Laura Schembri.

He reached his decision: "A man should know."

"Thank you, Father."

Guido walked out onto the terrace and Satta sensed the change in him. He pulled up a chair and reached for the coffee-pot. His face showed the indecision. The phone call had come an hour earlier, and it was forty minutes since Guido had hung up. Satta was not impatient. Within an hour Bellu would let him know if the call had any significance.

Guido drank his coffee and then made up his mind.

"What would happen if Creasy gives himself up — to you personally?"

Satta's pulse quickened. The call had truly been significant. He made an expressive gesture.

"Of course he would go to prison. But in view of the type of people he's killed, and his motive, the sentence would probably be only around five years. Such things can be arranged, and with remission he could be out in three."

"Could he be kept alive in prison?"

Satta grimaced. "I know what you mean and the answer is, yes. We've just completed a new prison outside Rome for 'sensitive' prisoners. It's staffed and run by the *Carabinieri*. I guarantee his safety. Frankly, it's when he comes out that he will be in real danger."

Guido looked at the colonel thoughtfully, obviously assessing, weighing his decision. Satta kept quiet. It was not the time to ask questions.

"All right." Guido made up his mind. "We'll drive to Rome and I'll talk to him."

"But why? Tell me why?"

Guido stood up. "Come on. I'll tell you in the car — we may not have much time."

Satta held up a hand. "In that case, let me call Bellu. He's a good man and I trust him. He can pick Creasy up in ten minutes."

Guido shook his head. "If he killed your friend Bellu and half a dozen other policemen, how many years would he get?" Satta took the point. "You can't phone him?"

"He has no phone there — let's go."

As they reached Satta's car, a police motorcyclist drew up and handed him an envelope.

'Telex message for you, colonel."

Satta suggested that Guido drive and, as they threaded their way through the city toward the Autostrada, Guido explained: "He's going to be a father."

Satta's look of surprise was comical. For once he didn't have a quick or clever comment. Guido glanced at him and smiled wryly, then he told him about Gozo and Nadia. He told him in detail, because it was important that he understand everything.

"You think it will make a difference?" Satta asked. Guido nodded emphatically. "I do. It's absolutely the only thing that might stop him. It's hard to explain exactly why."

Satta thought it over, reviewing what he knew of the man. He was inclined to agree that it would make a difference. Abruptly he leaned forward and picked up the microphone of the radio transmitter. Guido looked at him sharply, but he held up a placating hand. Within two minutes he was patched through to Bellu in Rome, and was instructing him to collect the tape of the last phone intercept, and personally destroy it. The same with any transcript. He emphasized that nobody else was to handle them. To Bellu's puzzled query, he told him to wait at headquarters. They would be in Rome by lunchtime.

Guido expressed his thanks and Satta shrugged.

"You know what it's like. These people have their informers everywhere, but Bellu I trust implicitly." Suddenly he remembered the envelope. He ripped it open and read the long telex in silence, "Holy Mother of God."

Satta said it quietly.

"What is it?"

He waved the telex and explained that he had guessed that Creasy had gone to Marseilles for equipment. He had asked his counterpart there to apply pressure to find out who had supplied him, and with what. The telex contained the list.

"What's an R.P.G.7 Stroke D?" he asked.

"Antitank rocket launcher," Guido answered with a grim smile. "Mercenaries call it the 'Jewish Bazooka.'"

"It's an Israeli weapon?"

Guido shook his head. "Russian, but with the rocket loaded, it looks like a circumcised penis."

Satta didn't smile. "Creasy knows how to use it?" he asked.

Guido stayed with the analogy.

"He handles it with the same familiarity as you handle your pecker when you take a pee."

Now Satta smiled; but he was puzzled.

"The Mafia have most things, but they don't own tanks."

Guido explained, "It has other uses — demolishing buildings or blowing open steel gates. It will go through twelve inches of armour plate."

Satta digested that in silence. When he commented, his voice was wistful.

"Slightly more penetrative power than my pecker."

Guido smiled in agreement.

At that moment the R.P.G.7 Stroke D, together with two rockets, was being carried through the streets of Rome in a canvas bag. It was not a large bag. The rocket launcher was a simple tube, thirty-seven inches long, which unscrewed into two halves for easy handling. It weighed about fifteen pounds. The rockets weighed less than five pounds each.

Giuseppe and Theresa Benetti had just finished lunch when the knock came on the door. They were both in their late sixties and she had bad legs, so it was Giuseppe who went to answer it. The first thing he saw was the silenced pistol, and he became very frightened. Then he looked up at the man's face and his fright increased, freezing him like a statue. The man spoke softly, reassuringly.

"You are not in danger. I mean you no harm. I am not a thief."

He moved forward through the door, easing the old man back.

A few minutes later Giuseppe and Theresa were taped, immobile, to two of their chairs. The man had been very gentle, talking to them casually with his slight Neapolitan accent. He just wanted to borrow their home for a short time. They would not be harmed.

Their fear dissipated, and they watched with interest as he opened his bag and took out two fat tubes. He screwed them together and then slid an attachment into a grooved slot. In his youth, Giuseppe had served in the army and he guessed that the tube was a sophisticated weapon, the attachment a sight. His guess was confirmed when the man produced the squat, cone shaped missile. He depressed the fins and slipped it backward into the tube. The bulk of the missile projected outward, the point of the cone to the front.

The man pulled out a second missile and a pair of goggles and moved quietly out into the back yard. Giuseppe could see him peering cautiously over the low wall that separated the yard from the avenue.

In the penthouse of the building opposite, Conti had also just finished lunch.

At 2:30 precisely, the lift opened in the basement garage and he stepped out, followed by his personal bodyguard. The Cadillac was waiting, engine running. A black Lancia containing four bodyguards waited directly behind. Conti eased himself into the back seat and his bodyguard closed the door and got in beside the driver. The two cars moved up the ramp. At street level the bright sunlight made all three men narrow their eyes. But they still saw, across the wide avenue, the figure rise behind the low wall. His face was distorted by goggles, and a fat tube rested on his right shoulder. Before they could react, a great gout of flame erupted from the back of the tube and a black object detached itself, enlarging as it homed in. Conti screamed and the driver stood on the brakes. The heavy car dipped forward and then bounced up on reinforced springs. Its rise continued as the missile pierced the centre of the radiator, demolished the engine, and burned everything inside to a cinder. For a moment the Cadillac teetered upright on its rear fender and then the second missile arrived, striking just below the front axle and hurling the five ton car backward onto the Lancia behind.

Only one escaped instant death. As the Lancia crumpled, a rear door was popped open and a bodyguard ejected on all fours. He scrabbled away from the hissing, twisted mass of metal, rose to his feet and instinctively pulled out his gun. Again instinct started him up the ramp, but then he stopped and looked back. Instinct ended. Whatever was out there had caused this carnage.

Shock took over and he backed away until he came up against the garage wall. Slowly he sank to his haunches. The gun slipped from his fingers and clattered to the concrete. He was still crouched there when the first police car arrived.

Satta waited in the car, tense with anticipation; but, when Guido reappeared alone, his disappointment was tinged with slight relief.

"He's not there?"

Guido shook his head. "I guess we wait."

The wait was a short one. It was only three minutes before the radio came alive. Captain Bellu calling Colonel Satta — urgently.

Satta and Bellu stood at the top of the ramp looking down. Neither said anything. What they saw was beyond their experience. Finally Satta turned to look for Guido. He had his back to them, facing across the avenue. Satta followed his gaze and saw the circular, black burn mark on the side of the whitewashed house, "R.P.G.7 Stroke D?"

Guido turned and nodded.

"I told you — it has other uses."

Satta looked thoughtfully down the ramp. He couldn't help the sardonic smile as he said to Bellu, "Conti lost his no claims bonus."

BOOK FOUR

CHAPTER TWENTY

"Power grows from the barrel of a gun."

Cantarella knew the quotation and had witnessed its truth. But a gun must have a target. He felt like a weight lifter with nothing to lift — Michelangelo without a ceiling.

Frustration fertilized his fear. Conti had been a right arm, the physical instrument of diplomacy. His death struck to the core of Cantarella's fear. He tried to conceal it, but Dicandia and Gravelli were not misled. They sat across the desk and absorbed it from the atmosphere. It astonished them and created deep concern.

But he was their boss. Everything they had; their stature, their wealth, and their ambitions were linked to the power of Cantarella. They had no other route.

They listened to their orders for the strengthening of the security of the Villa Colacci. Two days ago they would have been astounded and would have advised restraint; but Conti's death and the manner of it had made a great impact on their minds. So had the thick dossier lying on the desk. It detailed the dimensions of a man who could practice violence on a scale that was alien — even to them.

So they listened in silence as Cantarella went on about floodlighting the outer walls and two hundred metres beyond. About the purchase and razing of all buildings within a radius of one kilometre. About twenty-four-hour patrolling of the entire area and the acquisition of guard dogs. A total of eighteen bodyguards were to be quartered in the villa. They would work in three shifts. A roadblock was to be set up half a kilometre from the villa's gates. No car was to pass that point without being searched, inside and out. No vehicle at all was to enter the grounds of the villa. No other boss or emissary was to enter the villa, except alone, and after being thoroughly searched. The state of Cantarella's mind was most clearly revealed when he gave orders to cut down over fifteen fruit trees that bordered the inside of the walls.

Twenty years ago, when Cantarella had first purchased the villa, he had personally supervised the planting of the orchard. It had become a great pride to him. His entourage would even joke about it; but only among themselves, and very quietly. Cantarella's wife had died childless thirty years before, and he had never remarried. They used to call the trees his children; and now to hear orders for even a small number to be destroyed illustrated vividly the depth of his fear.

Cantarella moved on to the general situation. Every point of entry into Sicily was to be watched. Every port down to the smallest fishing village; every airport, every airstrip, every train or car that crossed on the ferry from Reggio, His mouth twisted in irritation as he asked:

"The police? The *Carabinieri*? They still do nothing?"

"Very little," answered Dicandia. "They put up token road-blocks around Rome after Conti's death — several hours after; and they've put out a general alert for the American, and a description. But they haven't named him, and they haven't issued a photograph."

"Bastards!" snarled Cantarella. "Above all, that swine Satta. All this must give him such pleasure — bastard!"

"He arrived in Palermo this morning," Gravelli said.

"Together with his assistant Bellu and the Neapolitan." Cantarella's anger grew. "Bastards! They think this is one grand spectacle. You're sure there's no chance to get to this Neapolitan?" He tapped the dossier. "He must be in contact with this maniac."

Gravelli shook his head. "They are in a two bedroom suite in the Grand, and they never leave him alone for a moment. There's no chance unless we take out Satta and Bellu."

Dicandia interjected quickly, "That would cause more trouble than we've got now — there would be no end." Cantarella nodded reluctantly. "And Satta knows it. One day I'll settle the hash of that overbred vulture."

Gravelli shrugged. "Meanwhile, he causes problems. Even while he sits in Palermo, his people are cracking down all over. They even took Abrata in for questioning. He's feeling exposed and very nervous."

"Satta's using the situation," said Dicandia. "There's confusion in the north and in Rome. Satta is stirring it up like a sorcerer."

Cantarella leaned forward and opened the dossier. A blown-up passport photograph of Creasy was clipped to the inside cover. For several minutes Cantarella studied the face. His tongue moistened dry, thick lips, and he tapped the photograph.

"We'll have nothing but problems until he's dead." He looked up and said with great emphasis: "The man who kills him will want for nothing — nothing! You understand?"

Gravelli and Dicandia nodded silently, and then received another shock. Cantarella unclipped the photograph and tossed it across the desk.

"I want this photograph on the front page of every newspaper in the country tomorrow morning."

Dicandia recovered first:

"Don Cantarella! That will mean they have the whole story — is it wise?"

"They will have it anyway," his boss answered. "They know most of it now. It was only Satta clamping a silence on his department that's delayed things."

He explained his reasoning: "It's a distinctive face — look at the scars and the eyes. We have thousands of people looking for him. It would take days to distribute his picture. The papers will do it for us."

"You will make a hero of him," Gravelli warned.

"Then he'll be a dead hero," snapped Cantarella. "And the dead are soon forgotten."

Paddy stepped down from the Mobex and stretched her big frame. There were disadvantages to being tall, and feeling cramped when travelling was one of them. Wally followed her onto the pavement and turned back to ask: "You want anything?"

Creasy shook his head. "Have a good lunch. Sure you don't want me to pick you up?"

"No, the walk will do us good," Paddy said. "We'll wander round a bit. Don't worry, we'll find the site."

They had driven down the eastern coast from Pescara to Bari. Paddy thought that after three days Creasy would want a change from her admittedly basic cooking. She wanted a change herself, and also to buy a couple of sweaters — winter was chasing out autumn.

But Creasy had declined, preferring to drive on to the campsite south of the city. She noted that he hardly left the Mobex even when they were in a campsite. It increased her curiosity. She spoke a little French, and the first night she had tried it out on him. He had smiled and answered fluently. Then she spoke to him in English, and again he had smiled, and asked in English if she were probing. She had noticed the slight American drawl.

"No," she had answered. "It's just that you don't look like a Frenchman."

Wally had interrupted, telling her not to be so bloody nosy, but that hadn't dampened her curiosity.

Creasy had arrived on foot at the campsite in Rome carrying two very large leather suitcases and a canvas bag. Wally had helped him load them through the narrow door, and later commented to Paddy, that the bloke didn't exactly travel light.

He had not been very talkative, merely pointing at the map to a spot outside Avezzano and suggesting that they camp the night there. In fact, they had stayed two nights. The site, in a pleasantly wooded valley, had been almost deserted. He was tired, he had explained, and in no hurry.

"There's a boutique." Wally pointed across the busy street.

"And there's a restaurant," Paddy said, pointing farther ahead. "Let's eat first, I'm starving." She grinned. "Besides, after what I eat, I might need a bigger size,"

"They don't make a bigger size," Wally commented, ducking away, knowing that a playful swing from her huge arm could put him on the pavement.

But she didn't react. They were opposite a newsstand and she stood mesmerized. He followed her gaze.

From the front page of a dozen different newspapers, Creasy's face gazed back.

An hour later they were arguing fiercely. Wally was being stubborn.

"You've got the money and passports in your bag. We go straight to the bloody railway station and catch a bloody train. We buy what we need in Brindisi. Tomorrow morning we're on the bloody boat to Greece."

She shook her head. "I'm not going."

Wally sighed and pushed away his plate of half eaten food.

'Paddy, you're being sentimental. It doesn't suit you. He's a killer. We owe him nothing — he's got the Mobex. He's just been using us as cover."

Again she shook her head, and he picked up the paper and held it in front of her face.

"They're looking for him. Hundreds, maybe thousands — we're not going to be there when they find him."

"Then piss off, Wally Wightman."

The restaurant was busy and she said it quietly, but it rocked him back in his chair. She leaned forward, her angry face close to his.

"Yes, he's been using us. Why not! He's alone. He's doing it all alone. Hundreds, you say? Thousands? Also the police. He needs help. I'm going to help him. You can do what you bloody like."

"But why?" he asked desperately. "It's none of our business. Why get involved?"

She snorted. "When did an Aussie ever need a reason to get into a fight?" She tapped the paper. "They killed that girl. Those people raped her and killed her. Eleven years old! Now they're paying for it. He's making them pay. If he needs a little help, he'll get it from Paddy Collins. I'm not leaving him on his own."

Suddenly Wally grinned.

"Alright, you silly cow, calm down."

For a moment she was speechless, but only for a moment.

"You agree?"

"Yes, I agree."

"Why the sudden change?"

He shrugged. "It's not sudden. My instinct is to help, but it's dangerous. One thing for a bloke, but something else for a girl."

Paddy smiled at him and reached over and ruffled his hair.

"I like it when you're chivalrous — let's go."

Outside on the pavement, something occurred to him.

"How do you think he'll react when he finds out we know? He might get violent, might worry that we'll turn him in or something. Paddy, that's one tough bastard."

She shook her head and linked an arm in his.

"I doubt it. With his picture in the papers, he's going to need all the help he can get. He'll understand that. Anyway, tough as he is, I'm not frightened."

"You're not?"

She smiled down at him.

"Not with you to protect me, Wally."

Satta put down the phone and turned to face Guido and Bellu.

"It was almost certainly Cantarella," he said. "The papers all got the information at about the same time."

"But why?" asked Guido.

Bellu supplied the answer. "It's just another sign of his state of mind. It's the quickest way to generally identify Creasy." He looked at Satta quizzically and asked:

"What now, colonel?"

Satta gazed back at him enigmatically, and Guido felt the sudden air of tension.

Bellu spoke again. "Perhaps we should talk privately, colonel."

Satta sighed, glanced at Guido and shook his head.

"Not necessary."

He turned to the phone and called *Carabinieri* headquarters in Rome. For a long time he issued precise instructions, then hung up and turned to face Guido.

"You cynical bastard!"

Satta spread his hands in resignation. "It wouldn't have made any difference. If Cantarella couldn't find him until now, neither would our people."

He looked down at the newspapers spread over the low coffee table. "He has very little chance now. That face is easily recognized. Let's just hope we find him before they do."

Guido stood up and walked to the window and stood looking down at the busy street. A light rain was falling. Umbrellas obscured the moving people.

"Guido, believe me; there was very little chance. We'll do everything now. You heard me on the phone." Satta's voice was apologetic. Bellu had never heard him talk that way before.

Without turning, Guido asked bitterly, "Has he served his purpose now? Will they make you a general?"

Satta's voice lost its note of apology. "I didn't send him! I didn't arm him, or equip him with safe houses and transport and false papers; and I didn't encourage him. Aren't you being hypocritical?"

Guido turned and looked at him, his face, for once, showing emotion.

"Alright!" he snapped. "I helped him, and I'm not ashamed of it. Things changed. I confided in you. I thought you were a man with some honour. I was mistaken."

Now Bellu spoke up. "You're wrong, Guido, very wrong. The colonel has no personal responsibility for Creasy. But I know he has sympathy for him. He'll do everything he can now. Everything."

Guido's anger subsided. He asked sadly, "Well — has he been useful?"

Satta nodded. "Yes — very. I would never admit it to anyone else. His killing of Conti was the whole key. I never realized that Cantarella would react with such panic. Even if Creasy doesn't get to him, his power will be finished. Already the organization on the mainland is in a state of flux. He will never reimpose control. Only here, in Sicily, does he keep his power, and day by day that too will slip away."

He gestured sympathetically. "Come, Guido, sit down. The important thing now is to find Creasy. Only you know his mind. You must try and read it. How will he attack? How will he approach?"

Guido shrugged and walked over to join them.

"Let me see the plan again."

Bellu lifted the newspapers and pulled out the large-scale plan of the Villa Colacci and its surroundings. The three men leaned over it. Satta pointed.

"We learned this morning that Cantarella has cut down some trees between the orchard and the wall to form a lane. Also, the floodlighting has become operational. The outside of the wall and a radius stretching several hundred metres are as bright as day."

"And inside the walls?" asked Guido.

Satta shook his head. "No. Obviously Cantarella doesn't want to light up the villa itself. At night the grounds are dark — but not unprotected. Yesterday two guard dogs were delivered — Doberman pinschers. They're attack dogs — trained to kill."

Bellu interjected, "For one man, it looks impenetrable. The guards at the gate and outside the walls are armed with submachine guns, and there's a small army inside the villa itself. No car or vehicle of any kind is allowed even close to the walls."

Guido smiled grimly. "He'll be expecting all that. He knows exactly the layout of the grounds and the villa itself. He's a soldier, and Cantarella is a fool. He'd be safer moving around instead of closing himself in. The strongest fort ever built is a death trap once the walls are breached. Cantarella's little army won't save him if Creasy gets inside."

"But how will he get inside?" asked Satta.

"I don't know," answered Guido. "But for sure he has a plan, and for sure it won't be conventional."

"There's been an escalation," Bellu commented. "An escalation of method: Rabbia was killed with a pistol, Sandri with a shotgun, Fossella with a bomb, and Conti with an antitank missile." He spread his hands. "What's he going to use on Cantarella?"

There was a thoughtful silence, and then Satta smiled.

"I don't know, but I wouldn't be surprised if about now the boss of bosses is digging a fallout shelter!"

"There's another one!"

Paddy pointed at the Alfa Romeo that had just overtaken them. Across its rear window was a sticker printed with two words: "GO — CREASY!"

It was the fifth they had seen since leaving the outskirts of Brindisi. Wally shook his head in amazement and said: "We're transporting a bloody celebrity."

It was three days since they had stepped into the Mobex outside Bari and tossed the newspaper onto the table in front of Creasy. He had looked at the huge photograph and then slowly raised his eyes.

"It's in every newspaper," Wally had said. "And the full story — you show that ugly face anywhere in Italy and it will be recognized instantly. It's bound to be on TV as well."

He had spoken lightly, trying to keep the tension out of his voice.

Creasy hadn't said a word. Only his eyes moved between the two of them.

Paddy broke the tension.

"Bloody Frenchman! I knew you were a Yank."

"How?"

"The way you eat."

At that Creasy had smiled, and Wally's held breath had whooshed out in relief.

They had offered their help, and Creasy had shaken his head. It was a whole new situation. The danger was acute. He had told them to catch the train to Brindisi and be on their way. It wasn't their affair.

But logic had prevailed. Logic and stubbornness. They had argued for an hour. Driving the Mobex himself, it would be impossible not to be spotted. With them driving and him hidden in the back, they could take him anywhere in Italy. It made obvious sense, but he spent a long time trying to argue them out of it. Finally he had agreed. He needed only to get to Reggio, and not for three days. After that, they could keep the Mobex — he wouldn't be needing it.

Paddy had tried to force the money back on him; but then he too had been stubborn. They could use the money to ship the Mobex to Greece and then on to Australia. That was his condition.

They had stayed two days in the secluded campsite near Bari. Creasy never left the vehicle except at night to get exercise, and only then while Paddy and Wally kept watch. He hadn't told them how he would cross into Sicily, but he had a plan. He would explain in Reggio. Perhaps Wally could help him there before leaving.

"How does he look without all the hair?" he had asked Paddy. She had shaken her head.

"No idea — I've never seen him without it — I'd be frightened to look!"

"I'm bloody handsome," Wally had said. "I only grew this beard to keep hordes of lecherous females away. What's it all about?"

But Creasy had just smiled and said he'd tell him when they reached Reggio.

One evening Paddy had tried to talk him out of it. The newspapers had stressed the opposition. How little chance he had. She was about to say, "Don Quixote, tilting at windmills," but she had looked at his face and into his eyes; and stopped.

She remembered it now as they joined the Autostrada east of Taranto.

"Could you ever feel like that, Wally? Build up enough hatred to do what he's doing?"

Wally took his eyes off the road to glance at her. She was serious, and he thought about it.

"Many people could," he answered. "The difference is having both the hatred and the means. You read his story in the papers. How many men like that are walking around?"

"Do you think he'll do it? Get there and do it?"

He pursed his lips as he considered the question. "He might. He's come a long way, but he'll need luck — a lot of it. But then, he's had some already — he met us."

Paddy smiled at him, then was silent for a while.

"What are you thinking?"

She smiled again. "I was wondering how you'll look without that hair."

CHAPTER TWENTY-ONE

The walls had stood for centuries, but they had no answer to the bulldozer. It took only half an hour to reduce the small farmhouse to rubble.

Franco Masi stood next to the cart piled high with his belongings. His wife already sat on the cart. She faced away, unable to look, her eyes red from constant weeping.

But Franco looked, and beyond, to the walls of the Villa Colacci; hatred twisted his features. For generations his family had lived and farmed a few rocky acres on the hillside. The occupant of the villa had been a benefactor Franco had always lived under that protection. The produce of his farm, the cheeses his wife made, had always been given in homage.

He had not believed at first when they told him. It could not be. The benefactor would not do such a thing. He had begged for an audience, but they told him it was impossible. Don Cantarella would see no one. In twenty-four hours Franco must move. A house had been found for him in Palermo. They gave him the papers to sign.

The bulldozer finished its work, reversed on its tracks, and rumbled up toward the narrow lane.

From the core of his soul Franco uttered up a silent prayer: "Go with God, Creasy."

Wally argued fiercely. Seven thousand lire for a shave and a haircut was absurd. But the barber was unimpressed. He gestured eloquently at Wally's flowing locks. It was a major job, an hour's work. Take it or leave it.

Wally took it. He had a busy day in front of him and couldn't waste time comparison shopping. At least he didn't have to lose it all.

"A short, neat, conservative haircut," Creasy had explained. "And no beard."

Wally was still mystified. They had arrived at the campsite the night before, and over dinner Creasy had outlined in great detail what he wanted. He had not explained why. One step at a time, he had said; it's safer.

First Wally was to get the haircut and shave. Then he was to purchase a good quality leather suitcase and a briefcase; a sober business suit, a white shirt, a plain-coloured, muted tie, and lace up shoes. Dressed in this new attire, he was to check into the Excelsior Hotel; into their best suite, registering for three nights. He was then to go to the Avis office in the same building and hire a car for three days. The best model available. He was to take dinner in the hotel dining room and make a point of ordering a very expensive wine and, with his coffee, a very expensive cognac. Hennessy Extra, Creasy had suggested.

"You want him to appear to be a rich businessman?" Paddy had asked.

"Exactly," Creasy had answered.

Paddy had looked at Wally sceptically. "That would rival the frog turning into Prince Charming."

"Piss off," Wally had said with a grin. "You'll be surprised. I didn't always look like this."

After his expensive dinner, Wally was to go up to his suite and put in a phone call to Australia, an old friend — anyone — and talk for at least twenty minutes. He was to spend the night in the suite and meet them back at the campsite in the early morning.

While Wally ate stuffed *peperoni* in Reggio, Satta, Bellu, and Guido ate grilled lampuka in the Grand in Palermo.

"What's your opinion?" Satta asked his assistant.

"He'll come by boat," Bellu said. "Probably fishing boat — commandeered from somewhere in Calabria."

Satta shook his head impatiently and pointed at his plate. "I meant the fish."

Bellu smiled; on occasion he enjoyed irritating his boss. "Slightly overdone."

Satta nodded in agreement and turned to Guido. "It's possible, just possible, that one day the good captain will be promoted to colonel."

"That's a prerequisite?" Guido asked. "A colonel must have a discerning palate?"

"Essential," Satta answered. "We must have standards, or they'll start promoting people for being clever or dedicated. That would be a disaster."

"You mean you'd still be a corporal?"

Satta smiled and said to Bellu, "Have you noticed that Neapolitans have a vicious sense of humour? — Why do you think by fishing boat?"

Bellu shrugged. "How else? He can't use conventional transport. Every plane, ferry, and train is being watched. He's not a man that can be easily disguised."

"It's possible," Satta conceded. "What do you think, Guido?"

"I don't know," Guido said. 'It's idle speculation. I've given it enough thought, and I don't have an answer. One thing is sure, though; with his face so well-known, he can't afford to show it — anywhere."

Satta agreed. "It's probably the best known face in Italy today. What a reaction! I wouldn't have believed it." He shook his head in astonishment. "In Rome and the north, girls are wearing T-shirts printed with his photo and 'GO CREASY!' The public's right behind him, and the newspapers are having a field day. I'm not sure it's healthy."

"It's inevitable," Bellu said. "People are fed up with the power of the bosses, and their arrogance. The government fails to do anything, so they make a hero out of this one man — it's natural."

"For me," Satta said, "the great puzzle is, where does he stay? He must be isolated, totally unseen; but how?" He looked hard at Guido. "You're sure he had no safe house after Rome?"

"Not that I know of," Guido answered. "He never talked of his plans after Rome — you know why."

"It's a great pity," Satta said. "And no contact at your mail drop. We're monitoring it twenty-four hours a day."

"A pity?" Guido asked dryly. "You really want to find him now?"

Satta grimaced. "Guido, believe me. I don't want to see him die. He's done enough." He signalled the waiter, and they ordered desert. When the waiter had left, Satta reached out and put a hand on Guido's arm and said softly:

"It's true. I owe him. I feel I know him, would like to meet him. In fact, he fascinates me. If anyone had told me that one man could have done so much, I would have laughed. I still can't comprehend it, especially the way he killed Conti."

Guido smiled grimly. "Yes — a technicolour funeral."

The other two looked puzzled and Guido explained.

"It's sort of a catch phrase. Every closed fraternity has them. Mercenaries too. It came out in Laos many years ago. A bunch of us were standing around watching an Air America DC6 land at a remote strip. It was carrying ammunition, explosives, and gasoline. It lost its undercarriage and skidded a long way; a wing tip caught, and it cartwheeled." Guido paused as memory took him back.

"Well?" Bellu prompted. "What happened?"

"It blew up," said Guido. "Slowly, would you believe? First the gasoline, then the explosives, and finally the ammunition. We all knew the pilots — two Canadians, good men. When the noise died down, there was a long silence, then an Australian, Frank Miller, summed it up. He said, 'At least they had a technicolour funeral.'" Guido shrugged. "It became a catch phrase. If a mercenary wanted to threaten someone, he talked about a technicolour funeral.'"

"What makes a man become a mercenary?" Bellu asked.

Guido smiled at the question.

"A thousand reasons. No two are the same. There are all types: misfits, perverts, misguided do-gooders, plain fools." He shrugged. "Very often it's just an accident — not calculated."

The waiter brought the desserts — a local *zabaglione* — and, while they ate, there was silence.

But Bellu was curious. For him it was a different world, and his questions started again.

"But Creasy must be special — to achieve what he has. What makes him that good?"

"You've seen his dossier," Satta commented. "It's experience. Experience and training; and perhaps something more." He looked at Guido inquiringly.

"Yes, something more," Guido agreed. "It's like sex appeal — intangible. All the components can be there, but a soldier can lack it, no matter how good he is technically. Here and there, occasionally, you meet one that has it. He is set apart. Maybe it's a combination of luck and willpower. A platoon of trained and experienced soldiers can fail to take a position. One man, with that ingredient, will take it."

"Did you have it?" Satta asked softly.

"Yes," answered Guido. "But Creasy has it in abundance — that's what has carried him this far. And most likely will get him into the Villa Colacci."

"Will it get him out?" asked Satta.

"Who knows?" The question bothered Guido. He was sure that Creasy had figured out a way to get in, but he wasn't sure about the opposite.

Wally parked the hired Lancia alongside the Mobex. Paddy sat on the step and watched him get out. He closed the Lancia's door and stood looking at her silently. For a long while, she didn't move. Then she crossed her arms about herself and began rocking back and forth. Then the laughter started.

Creasy appeared behind her and studied Wally. He nodded and smiled. Paddy slipped off the step and rolled on the grass. Gusts of laughter swept round the deserted campsite.

"Bloody woman!" Wally said.

Creasy agreed. "No appreciation of real beauty."

Slowly Paddy got herself under control and sat up, her arms clasping her knees.

"Wally Wightman," she said, with a broad grin, "you look like a pooftah!"

Wally stood by the black Lancia in his dark blue, pinstripe suit, holding his black briefcase. He ignored her.

"Do I look alright?" he asked Creasy.

"Perfect," Creasy answered. He turned to Paddy. "You just don't appreciate class, and if he looks like a pooftah, why were you crying all last night?"

"Bullshit!" Paddy said, pushing herself up. "I wouldn't miss him for a year, let alone one bloody night!"

But she walked over and hugged Wally affectionately.

"Go easy, girl," he said with a grin. "You'll rumple my new suit."

They all went into the Mobex and squeezed around the small table. Wally related, in detail, how he had followed Creasy's instructions. "What now?" he asked expectantly.

Creasy reached behind for the map and pointed out the small airfield.

"This is the headquarters of the Aero Club of Reggio di Calabria. I want you to drive over there now and charter an aircraft to fly you to Trapani, on the west coast of Sicily."

Wally and Paddy exchanged glances.

"So that's it," Paddy said. "You're going to fly in."

"Not exactly," Creasy answered. He explained that originally he had planned to charter a night flight by telephone, and if necessary hijack the pilot and aircraft. Wally's offer of help had made it easier.

The previous day's charade had set the scene. Wally would explain that he was a businessman on a tight schedule. He had a series of meetings in Reggio and, as soon as they finished, he wanted to leave for Trapani. If the Aero Club or anyone else checked, they would discover that he was staying in the best suite in a luxury hotel. He spent unstintingly on the best food and drink, hired the best available car, and made expensive overseas phone calls. In short, he was plausible.

Creasy told him to explain that he was not sure exactly when he would want to leave. He would give six hours' notice. It would probably be late evening, and certainly within the next three days.

"Why can't you fix a time?" Wally asked.

"It depends on the weather."

"Then why within three days?"

"Because there's little or no moon."

Wally's curiosity was still not satisfied, but he held his questions while Creasy went on to explain that the Aero Club had four aircraft: two Cessna 172's; a Piper Comanche, and a Commander. It was essential he get one of the Cessnas. In the event of a query, Wally was to say that he had flown in that type before and was familiar with it. He was to pay for the charter in cash, in full, in advance.

"Why is the Cessna essential?" Wally asked.

"Because it's got high wing configuration."

"So?"

"So it's easier to jump out of."

Wally's curiosity was satisfied.

Gravelli and Dicandia did the rounds. They inspected everything, and in between they discussed the situation.

After conferring with the guards outside the main gates, they walked back through the gardens.

"Another week and it will be too late," Dicandia said.

"It may already be too late," responded Gravelli. "There's a war in Turin. In Rome, three Families are squaring up. Even in Calabria there's trouble. Don Mommo was promised tranquillity while he was in jail. Two days ago there was an attempt on his life. Cantarella does nothing. He squanders his respect sitting here like a mouse in its hole. Abrata is arriving tomorrow to confer with Cantarella. He won't believe it when he sees the state he's in."

Dicandia felt the words were a little strong. He had worked for Cantarella over twenty years — his loyalties were anchored deep. It would have to blow a little harder to shift them.

Suddenly Gravelli gripped his arm, and the two men froze on the gravel pathway.

The two black shadows came out of the darkness without a sound. They came very close, noses twitching, and then, as silently, disappeared.

Dicandia spoke fervently. "Those fucking dogs give me the creeps!"

"They're safe enough," Gravelli said with a short laugh. "As long as they smell what they know."

"They just better have good memories," Dicandia said, and continued on up the path.

They entered the villa through the kitchen door. It was a huge, stone flagged room and had been turned into a canteen for the extra bodyguards. Half a dozen of them sat around lounging and watching television in the corner. The remains of a meal were spread messily on the wooden table. Submachine guns and a couple of shotguns lay near to hand.

A passage led from the kitchen through the centre of the villa. In the first room, off this passage, wooden bunks had been installed, and more bodyguards were sleeping or resting before going on the midnight shift.

At the end of the passage a staircase led up to the first floor where Cantarella had his study and bedroom. Dicandia and Gravelli also had their rooms on the first floor.

They spoke a few words to the men in the kitchen and then went upstairs.

Cantarella's personal bodyguard sat on a chair outside the study, a submachine gun cradled in his arms. He stood up as they approached, tapped twice on the door, and opened it. They went in to report that all was secure.

After two days the gusty north wind abated. The forecast was for twenty-four hours of mild weather. There would be cloud patches and a light easterly wind over northern Sicily. Possibility of occasional showers.

Creasy prepared.

In the early evening he opened the big, wide suitcase and took out the parcel that the general had sent to Marseilles. Outside on the grass Paddy and Wally watched as he unwrapped it and pulled open the voluminous black folds of fabric.

"It doesn't look like a parachute," Wally commented.

"It's more like a wing," Creasy answered. "The old days of jumping out and trusting to luck are gone. This is a French 'Mistral.' A well-trained 'para' can fly one even upwind — and land within yards of his target."

They helped him lay out the cords and then stood back and watched as he expertly straightened and sorted them and folded the canopy.

"You don't have a spare?" Wally asked. He had seen pictures of parachutists with smaller packs strapped to their fronts.

Creasy shook his head. "I can't afford the weight." He went on to explain that a "para" would normally jump with an equipment bag dangling from a cord five metres below him. The heavy bag would impact first and so lighten the landing of the jumper: but precious seconds could be lost retrieving the bag and extracting weapons. Creasy would jump with his weapons ready. He would risk a heavy landing.

He finished packing the parachute and laid it against the side of the Mobex. He turned to Wally and said, "I'll be ready to leave in half an hour."

"Do you need any help?" Wally asked.

"No; I'll do it myself — please wait out here."

Inside the Mobex, Creasy took out the smaller parcel that had been sent from Brussels. As he unwrapped it, he smelled the slightly musty odour of clothing long unused. It was his old camouflage combat uniform. It still had the color-coded insignia of the 1st R.E.P.

He held it in his hands for a long time, his mind going back — going back over twelve years. Abruptly he tossed it onto the bunk and started undressing.

When he emerged from the Mobex it was almost dark. Paddy and Wally were leaning against the Lancia. Creasy stood by the door and Paddy started to cry softly.

They knew what he was, and what he was going to do; but it was only now, as he stood prepared, that they felt the real impact.

His normal bulk was expanded like an overinflated tyre. He wore mottled overalls tucked into black, high laced boots. Pockets bulged down the seam of each leg; webbing enclosed his upper body. Two rows of grenades were clipped to it on each side of his chest. Between them a flapped bulky pouch hung to his waist. A canvas snap down holster was on his belt to his right side. Beside it, to the front and rear, were several small canvas pouches. The Ingram submachine gun hung from a strap around his neck. His right forearm was looped through the strap, holding the stubby weapon flat against his side. From his left hand dangled a black, knitted skullcap.

He picked up the parachute and moved toward the Lancia and asked quietly, "You ready?"

Wally nodded and started to speak, but nothing came out. Numbly he opened the door of the car. Creasy tossed in the parachute and turned to Paddy.

"I don't have the words, Paddy; but you understand." She sniffed and shook her big head and said, "You're a stupid shit, Creasy — it's such a waste."

He smiled and reached out his hands to hold her by the shoulders.

"It'll be alright, I've done it before — it's almost routine."

She wiped a hand across her wet cheeks, and then hugged him. Hard metal pressed against her painfully, but she didn't care. Then she released him and walked to the Mobex and climbed inside and shut the door.

It was a twenty-minute drive to the airfield. Creasy lay across the back seat, out of sight. It was five minutes before Wally asked, "How will you get out?"

"The Cessna's door can be held open against the wind," Creasy said.

"I meant the Villa Colacci," Wally retorted. "I know you'll get in, but how will you get out?"

The answer was short, precluding further inquiry.

"If there's a way in, there's a way out."

They drove in silence for several minutes before Creasy asked, "You're clear on everything, Wally? The sequence?"

"Very clear," Wally answered. "There won't be any foul-ups."

"And about afterward?"

"Sure; we'll be on the road tonight."

"Don't delay a minute," Creasy said. "There'll be a lot of confusion, but you've got to be on that ferry in the morning."

Wally spoke firmly. "Creasy, don't worry, we'll be on it. Come visit us in Australia."

A soft laugh came from the back seat. "I will — look after her — you've got a good one there."

"I know it," Wally said. "Airfield coming up — only two cars outside. Looks OK."

Wally parked behind the hangar, reached for his suitcase, and opened the door. He didn't turn his head.

"Good luck, Creasy."

"Thanks, Wally. *Ciao!*"

Cesare Neri went through the start-up checks. He would be glad to get this charter over with. He was a conscientious pilot, trained by the Air Force, and he followed the rules. Being on six-hour standby for the past two days meant that he'd been unable to have a drink; and he liked to drink. He would stay over in Trapani and have a night out. He had good friends there.

He glanced at the Australian in the right-hand seat. He appeared to be a little nervous. Cesare was used to that. People would sit cheerfully in a great jet flying machine and think nothing of it; but put them in a small plane next to the pilot, and suddenly everything seemed fallible.

"We're ready to go."

The passenger nodded. "Fine."

The engine clattered to life. Cesare watched the oil pressure gauge. The passenger tapped him on the arm and spoke loudly above the noise of the engine.

"How long to Trapani?"

"Just under an hour," Cesare answered, his eyes moving over the dials.

"There's no toilet in here?"

Cesare shook his head, and the passenger said, "Do you mind? I'd better take a leak."

Cesare smiled slightly. This one really was nervous. He reached across and unlatched the right door.

"Go ahead. Stay clear of the prop."

The passenger undid his seat belt and climbed out. Cesare went back to the dials.

Two minutes went by and then a figure appeared at the door. Cesare's eyes flicked sideways and he went rigid. Slowly he turned his whole head, looked at the pistol and then at the man holding it.

"Just carry on," the man said, pulling himself, with difficulty, into the small cockpit. "You are not in danger. Just follow procedure."

He didn't attempt to strap himself in. He just leaned forward in the small seat, his right hand resting on the top of the instrument panel, his body turned sideways facing the pilot; the gun held low, close to Cesare's ribs.

"Complete your checks," he said. "Do everything by the book. I know how to fly one of these. I know the radio procedure; so don't get stupid."

Cesare sat absolutely still, his hands on his knees, his mind working. The new passenger didn't interrupt his thoughts, just sat waiting. Finally Cesare made up his mind. He didn't say anything; he simply went on with the take-off procedure.

Ten minutes later they were climbing through 4000 feet over the Strait of Messina, the lights of Sicily ahead.

"You can put away the gun. I know who you are."

Creasy considered for only a moment, then slipped the Colt into its canvas holster and snapped it down. He moved around, positioning the parachute pack more comfortably; then he reached between the seats and picked up Cesare's chart. The route to Trapani had been pencilled in. They would pass three miles to the south of Villa Colacci. He glanced at the pilot.

"After you cross the beacon at Termini Imerese, I want you to make a very slight detour."

Cesare smiled grimly.

"I should have charged more for this charter."

Creasy returned the smile.

"Less — your passenger isn't going all the way."

"Lucky I got paid in advance," Cesare said. "You'd better brief me."

Creasy leaned forward with the map and pointed,

"You can't miss it. It's five kilometres due south of Palermo and three kilometres due east of Monreale. It's lit up like a Christmas tree." He glanced at the instrument panel. They were climbing through 5000 feet.

"At what height would you normally level off?"

"Seven thousand feet."

"That's fine. Stay at that height until you cross the beacon. Then go up to twelve thousand feet."

Cesare glanced at him and Creasy said: "I'll do a 'Halo' drop." He noted the look of puzzlement and explained, "High altitude, low opening."

Cesare nodded. “We call it a delayed float. At what height will you open?”

“Not more than two thousand feet, depending on my free-fall drift. The wind is easterly at ten knots, so I’ll drop just short of the target.”

Cesare looked at the parachute pack.

“What is it?”

“A wing — a French ‘Mistral.’”

Now Cesare looked at the equipment festooning Creasy’s body.

“I know you’re an expert,” he said. “You’re going to need to be. You’ll come in fast and hard.” He thought for a moment, and then went on: “I know that area. You’re likely to meet a down draught off the side of the mountain. You won’t notice it on the free fall. It will start below two thousand feet. I would advise you to drop more to the south.”

Creasy hardly thought about it. The pilot’s voice was obviously sincere.

“Thanks, I will. Have you had experience?”

Cesare nodded.

“I had five years in the Air Force — on transports. I’ve dropped a lot of you people. Also amateurs — parachute clubs.”

“Alright,” Creasy said. “I’ll leave you to call it. I’m sorry. All this might cause you some trouble. I’m going to have to smash your radio.”

Cesare didn’t speak for a while. Just gazed out through the windshield. His voice, when it came, held a note of emotion.

“I’m glad it’s me. Many people — most people — are behind you. My family has lived for generations in Calabria. We know of the power of these people. We are all affected. We admire you. I’m glad it’s me. I’ll drop you exactly right.”

There was a silence, and then Creasy asked:

"Will you go on to Trapani?"

Cesare shook his head.

"I'll fly back to Reggio — it's safer. Who was the Australian?"

In the dull red light of the cockpit, Creasy's features softened slightly. He said simply, "A man like you."

In Palermo it was warm; and in the bar of the Grand Hotel the windows were open. Satta, Guido and Bellu stood at the bar drinking a pre-dinner cocktail. Satta was in an American mood, and his cocktail was a highball. The mood had been brought on by the presence of two American girls sitting at a corner table. They were late tourists, and one of them was a beautiful redhead. Satta was partial to redheads. The other was a blonde — passable. "Not a remora," Sata had commented, and to Bellu's query had explained, "Usually a beautiful girl has with her an ugly one. Both benefit. The beautiful girl is enhanced by the comparison, and the ugly one picks up the leftovers. A remora is a fish — a scavenger. By means of a sucker, it attaches itself to a shark and feeds off it." He looked at the blonde and smiled. "But she is not a remora; she can feed by herself. What do you think, Guido, is she your type?"

Guido looked across at the table. The blonde was attractive, and in the age-old language of glances, lowered eyelashes, and feigned indifference, had already indicated that Guido was to be favoured. Obviously the two girls had already divided the spoils. But Guido was not in the mood. For days a tension had been building within him. He couldn't tear his mind from Creasy.

A simple radio, designed by the human brain, can send signals around the world and millions of miles into space. It must be conceivable that the brain itself, infinitely more sophisticated, can also send signals, can communicate.

Guido did not think of that. But something told him that his friend was coming. Was near. He couldn't be drawn this night by a girl. So he shrugged and smiled and replied to Satta, "I defer to the *Carabinieri*, you all work so hard" — he glanced around the opulent bar — "and live so uncomfortably that we, the grateful public, should allow you an occasional bonus."

"Have you noticed," Satta asked Bellu, "that Neapolitans are invariably sarcastic?"

He raised an eyebrow at the bartender for more drinks.

"So be it," he said. "Captain Bellu, as further job training in your progress to promotion, the strategy of conquest is in your hands. Obviously we must start by inviting them to join us for dinner. How will you go about it?"

Bellu shrugged nonchalantly.

"I'll take them a bottle of champagne and tell them to join us for dinner."

"Tell them?" asked Satta, in mock surprise. "Not ask them?"

"Colonel," Bellu answered, "did you yourself not say that a woman should be treated like a headwaiter — politely but firmly?"

Satta beamed at Guido.

"Definitely promotion material."

But Guido didn't respond. He reached out and gripped Satta's arm.

"Listen!"

Very faintly through the open window came the drone of an aircraft.

"Creasy!"

Satta and Bellu looked at him blankly.

"Creasy! He comes."

Guido slammed down his drink and headed for the door.

"He's a "para,"" he called over his shoulder. "How else would he arrive? Come on!" Satta looked at Bellu and then across at the redhead.

"Come on," he snapped. "He hasn't improved his timing!"

The door had been pushed back. Creasy's face and shoulders were visible in the gap. His rubber soled boots rested on the undercarriage strut. The skullcap was pulled down tight; his lower face had been blackened. The eyes watched Cesare intently.

The pilot's face was set in concentration. He banked the plane gently, eyes flicking from left to right, picking up bearings, correlating them to the compass. His left foot moved on the rudder, flexing, ready to apply pressure when the weight was gone.

His right hand stabbed out.

"GO CREASY!"

He turned his head. The doorway was empty.

The windows were closed in the Villa Colacci. All of them. But Cantarella had opened the curtains slightly in his study and looked down at the garden. Darkness, relieved only by the faint glow of the floodlights beyond the walls. Over the last days his fear had been gradually overcome by emotions of frustration and anger. People subservient for generations were questioning his power. Even those around him. He could see it in their faces. Only a few minutes before, Abrata had been insolent in this very room. Soon this madman would be dead, and he would turn on the others and they would feel his power. They would understand. His smooth face hardened with the thought. The thick lips were compressed in determination. He drew the curtains tight and turned back to his desk.

Seconds later Creasy floated in over the wall like a great, black, pregnant bat.

CHAPTER TWENTY-TWO

He landed on grass, close beside the orchard. A good impact: legs cushioning, rolling easily, hitting the release, and dragging the canopy backward into the fruit trees.

The Colt came into his hand; the silencer, quickly pulled from a belt pouch, was screwed home. He crouched, his back against a tree, and from the chest pouch took out the Trilux night sight.

He scanned the grounds from left to right, picking them up as they rounded the side of the villa. Two low, black shapes, side by side, coming fast. The Trilux and the Colt were exactly aligned. He drew in air deeply and steadied himself. The Dobermans had been trained to attack silently and to kill silently.

They died silently. The first at ten metres with bullets in head and throat. The second had closed to five metres before the bullet took it in the heart. Momentum carried it on. It died, with a whimper, at Creasy's feet.

In the kitchen they were watching football. Juventus versus Naples. All eyes were on the TV screen. All eyes turned as the window shattered and the rounded, obscenely shaped grenade arced into the room.

Three died immediately; two were neutralized by shrapnel wounds. Two others, protected from the blast, were only stunned; but they hadn't begun to reach for weapons before the door was kicked in.

He stood with submachine gun gripped at chest height. Eyes evaluating, looking for life; finding it. The muzzle of the Ingram flickered white; and life left the room.

He appeared to move without haste but was quickly across to the open door leading to the passage. An empty magazine clattered to the stone floor. The snick of a full one, thrust home; ratchet click of the Ingram, being recocked; and he had his back to the wall close to the door; listening.

Shouts of inquiry from down the passage, and fainter from the top floor. Doors opening. Creasy slid down to a crouch, swung into the open door, Ingram held low: spewing bullets.

Three men in the passage. One managed to duck back into the room; the others were smashed back as though hit by a water cannon.

Again Creasy moved and again the Ingram was recharged in a flowing sequence. It had become a dance: rhythmic, stylized; movements to a perfect tempo. The music: screams blending with the stutter of gunfire, the tinkling of spent cartridges.

He glided past the makeshift dormitory and his right arm flicked and a grenade lobbed through the door. He turned at the explosion; saw the figure blown out into the passage, moaning and scrabbling, trying to raise the shotgun. A touch of the finger, a half second burst and then turning again, reaching the foot of the stairs; back to the wall, listening.

On the landing above, Cantarella stood at the door of his study holding a pistol in his right hand. His left hand gripped the sleeve of his personal bodyguard.

"Stay here!" he screamed, his face radiating panic. Dicandia, Gravelli, and Abrata stood at the top of the stairs, pistols pointing down. Dicandia was shirtless, his chest and back covered in a mat of black hair,

"Go down!"

They turned to look at Cantarella — hesitated. Cantarella's face worked in fury and fear.

"Go down!" He raised the pistol.

Dicandia moved, edging onto the first step. Only the top of his body was visible to Cantarella when the rippling clatter came. He saw Dicandia lift jerkily and, through the hair, the row of holes opening redly across his chest. Then he was gone, slumping and sliding down the steps.

Gravelli and Abrata backed away across the landing. They weren't going down. They looked to their right at Cantarella ten metres along the passage, shielded by the bodyguard. When they turned back, it was too late. The grenade exploded right between them. The corner of the landing protected Cantarella and the bodyguard.

Complete terror took over. Cantarella pushed the bodyguard forward and stumbled backward into his study. He slammed shut the door and rushed to the window, tearing aside the curtains. He didn't try to open it, just smashed the glass with his pistol and then screamed out:

"Where are you? Get up here! Get up here!"

Creasy reached the top of the steps, glanced at the smashed bodies, and eased close to the edge of the passage. He could hear Cantarella's hysterical shouts.

He held the Ingram in his right hand, and with his left he unclipped a grenade. He lowered it toward the Ingram and, with the little finger of his right hand, pulled out the pin. He released the spring; the clock in his head ticked twice, and his fingers opened. He swung his right boot and gently dropkicked the grenade round the corner.

At the blast Cantarella turned from the window. He saw the door splinter off its hinges and his bodyguard catapult backward into the room.

The boss of bosses stood rigid, looking at the mangled body on the carpet. His mouth opened but no sounds came out. His brain had stopped working.

Then, from below, he heard shouts. At last they were coming! Never taking his eyes from the door, he crouched down behind the heavy desk, pistol extended, breath coming in short gasps.

Creasy came through the door in a diving roll, clearing the dead bodyguard and rising to his knees in the centre of the room. Cantarella fired twice. Jerked shots — but one was lucky. He saw Creasy punched back and sideways, and he rose from behind his desk with a strangled cry of triumph and fired again twice — wildly. He was not experienced. Luck was not enough. Creasy's right shoulder was shattered; the arm useless. But the Ingram still hung from his neck, and his left hand gripped it and sent a swath of bullets across the room.

He stood up slowly; painfully. Keeping the Ingram steady, he moved carefully around the desk.

Cantarella lay on his back, his hands clutching the corpulence of his belly. Blood seeped through his fingers. He looked up into Creasy's face. His eyes showed a mixture of fear and hatred and pleading. Creasy stood over him, noted the wounds, knew they were fatal. He raised his right foot and with the shiny black toe cap lifted Cantarella's chin and slid the heavy boot onto his throat. He spoke very softly.

"Like her, Cantarella. Like her, you will choke to death." He moved his weight forward.

The two guards from the gate moved very cautiously, very reluctantly. They had passed through the kitchen and along the passage and up the stairs. Nothing they had seen prompted enthusiasm. The bodies of Gravelli and Abrata slowed them still further. They stood in the passageway looking through the doorway into the study. Looking at the dead bodyguard. They could hear only a low, gasping moan, and then it stopped.

Neither wanted to enter first, so they edged in together, submachine guns gripped tightly. They saw him behind the desk, looking down, and they fired simultaneously. They saw the body slam back against the wall, start to sink, and then steady. The Ingram came up; and bullets crisscrossed the room.

The car squealed to a halt outside the gates. Satta and Bellu leapt out. The gates were bolted from the inside. A small door was set into the right-hand gate. It was also locked. While Satta kicked at it impatiently, Bellu pulled the ornate bell handle.

Suddenly the horn sounded behind them and the engine revved. They jumped aside as the heavy police car shot forward.

Guido aimed at the side, near the heavy hinges. The impact was loud and effective. Although the gates remained standing, the upper hinge was torn loose from the wall, leaving a gap large enough to squeeze through.

In a moment Guido was through it and running up the gravel drive.

Satta looked in astonishment at the wrecked car, but Bellu was already scrambling through the gap and Satta shrugged and followed him.

They saw Guido pause at the main doors of the villa and then run across the grass to the corner of the building.

By the time they reached the kitchen he had disappeared. They stood at the door, looking in. Bellu was the first to react. He turned away and vomited. Satta waited silently for him to recover, and then they picked their way across the blood-soaked stone floor. They didn't speak as they skirted the bodies in the passage and glanced into the nearby room. At the foot of the stairs, Satta looked at the dead man spread-eagled over the bottom steps.

"Dicandia," he said to Bellu. "Right-hand man."

At the top of the steps they paused again.

"Not much left, but I think it's Gravelli and Abrata — that's tidy."

They moved on, stepping over more bodies and into the study. Guido was crouched over behind the desk. He turned at the sound of their entry.

"Quick!" he called. "Help me!"

They moved forward and Satta bent down and looked into Creasy's face. His eyes were open. They gazed back at Satta steadily. His teeth were clenched tight against the pain. Satta dropped his eyes and took in the blood and torn flesh. Guido had a hand under Creasy's armpit, gripping the arm.

"Your right hand!" he said urgently. "Put it here, next to mine."

Satta knelt down and reached forward. Guido positioned his hand.

"It's the artery. Press down with your thumb."

Satta followed the instructions and looked lower at the shattered wrist and the blood spurting out.

"Harder!" Guido demanded.

Satta pressed harder, his fingers digging deep into the muscled arm. Now the flow of blood abated, seeping slowly.

"What can I do?" Bellu asked behind them.

Satta turned his head, pointed with his chin at the desk.

"Get on the phone. They'll be coming, but make sure they're fully equipped. And I want a helicopter here — fast!"

Bellu talked urgently into the phone and Satta turned back and watched Guido wadding cloth against the wounds, stemming the blood that flowed onto and into the carpet. He looked to his left. At the body of Cantarella. At the face — bulging eyes — protruding tongue — purple hue. He turned back to Creasy. A flash of gold caught his eye. Crucifix amidst the blood. He looked up again at the face. The eyes were closed now.

Satta's fingers were getting tired, but he kept up the pressure. The life in front of him was literally in his hand. He was conscious of noise: wailing of sirens, and Guido sobbing with frustration as he worked.

CHAPTER TWENTY-THREE

The funeral was well attended. It was a cold day, hard into winter, and on the hill above Naples the wind bit deep. But there were many reporters. Since the day, a month before, that had been headlined "The Battle of Palermo," they had kept their interest, following closely the battle for life.

That battle had ebbed and flowed. At first, as Creasy lay in intensive care in Palermo, they had been told that he had little or no chance; but he clung to life, surprising the doctors. After two weeks, a special *Carabinieri* aircraft had flown him to Naples. It was at Satta's instigation. The Cardarelli Hospital in Naples was better equipped than the hospital in Palermo — and more secure.

Satta's brother had led the team of doctors in the fight for Creasy's life.

They fought hard and long, and at first had hope. But the damage had been too great, even for a man strong and determined to live.

So now the reporters looked on at the last act. Looked with curiosity at the small group around the open grave. Some they knew, some they didn't. Guido stood between his mother and Elio. She was old and stooped and dressed in black, her fingers constantly moving on her rosary. Next to them, Felicia stood with Pietro, her eyes red. Across the grave were Satta and Bellu, and between them, Rika. She too had been weeping. Now her eyes were fixed on the coffin as it lay suspended on straps over the gaping hole. An erect, elderly man stood next to Satta. He wore the full dress uniform of a French general. Medals and ribbons covered his chest.

The priest finished and stood back. Guido nodded at the attendants and slowly the coffin descended. The priest made the sign of the cross, and Guido bent down and picked up a lump of earth and tossed it into the grave. The general came to attention and saluted; and then the group broke up.

At the cars they all spoke a few words and then drifted away. Bellu and Guido were the last to leave. They watched as Satta handed Rika solicitously into his car, gave them a small wave, and drove off.

"When all is said and done," Guido muttered, with the trace of a smile, "he is still a cynical bastard."

EPILOGUE

It was in the New Year and after midnight. A cold *gregale* wind swept down from Europe and across the sea and scoured the bleak hills of Gozo.

The village of Mgarr was dark and very quiet, but not asleep.

On the balcony of Gleneagles a shadow moved and rested a heavily tattooed arm on the rail. Benny's eyes swept the bay and the steeply rising hills. The door opened behind him, and Tony moved out and passed him a brandy and stayed next to him; watching and waiting.

The *Melitaland* was lashed alongside the jetty, straining gently at each gust of wind. On the wing of the bridge, Victor and Michele were also watching, and also sipping brandy.

High up on the hill the Mizzi brothers sat on their patio with "Shreik." They were looking out beyond the harbour walls and were the first to see the tossing, slim, grey shape edging toward the entrance.

George Zammit braced himself in the small wheelhouse of the police launch as it rolled against the swell and then steadied as they entered the calm waters of the harbour. He issued an order, and two seamen carrying boathooks went out onto the wet deck.

In the shadows behind Gleneagles, a handbrake was released and a Land Rover freewheeled down the short road and out to the end of the jetty. It was dark there. The solitary light was not working.

The launch was held fast, and George stepped out onto the narrow deck. The Land Rover was parked ten metres away. He could just discern the two figures. The one nearest to him opened the door and got out and stood waiting. It was a woman, looking, even with the coat, bulky — heavy.

George gestured behind him and stood aside. The man came out of the wheelhouse and moved past him onto the jetty. He walked slowly to the woman. A big man with a curious walk, the outsides of his feet making first contact with the ground.

The woman moved forward and into his arms.

George signalled, and the engines throbbed and the launch pulled away. As it headed toward the entrance, he walked to the stern, looking back at the tableau of the embracing couple.

Then he looked up at the dark, silent, secret hills of Gozo.

Printed in Dunstable, United Kingdom

82209816R00198